The Black Cat

RICHARD JURY NOVELS

The Man with a Load of Mischief
The Old Fox Deceived
The Anodyne Necklace
The Dirty Duck
Jerusalem Inn
Help the Poor Struggler
The Deer Leap
I Am the Only Running Footman
The Five Bells and the Bladebone
The Old Silent
The Old Contemptibles
The Horse You Came In On
Rainbow's End
The Case Has Altered
The Stargazey
The Lamorna Wink
The Blue Last
The Grave Maurice
The Winds of Change
The Old Wine Shades
Dust

OTHER WORKS BY MARTHA GRIMES

The End of the Pier
Hotel Paradise
Biting the Moon
The Train Now Departing
Cold Flat Junction
Foul Matter
Belle Ruin
Dakota

POETRY

Send Bygraves

MARTHA GRIMES

The Black Cat

A RICHARD JURY MYSTERY

VIKING

VIKING
Published by the Penguin Group
Penguin Group (USA) Inc., 375 Hudson Street, New York, New York 10014, U.S.A. • Penguin Group (Canada), 90 Eglinton Avenue East, Suite 700, Toronto, Ontario, Canada M4P 2Y3 (a division of Pearson Penguin Canada Inc.) • Penguin Books Ltd, 80 Strand, London WC2R 0RL, England • Penguin Ireland, 25 St. Stephen's Green, Dublin 2, Ireland (a division of Penguin Books Ltd) • Penguin Books Australia Ltd, 250 Camberwell Road, Camberwell, Victoria 3124, Australia (a division of Pearson Australia Group Pty Ltd) • Penguin Books India Pvt Ltd, 11 Community Centre, Panchsheel Park, New Delhi – 110 017, India • Penguin Group (NZ), 67 Apollo Drive, Rosedale, North Shore 0632, New Zealand (a division of Pearson New Zealand Ltd) • Penguin Books (South Africa) (Pty) Ltd, 24 Sturdee Avenue, Rosebank, Johannesburg 2196, South Africa

Penguin Books Ltd, Registered Offices:
80 Strand, London WC2R 0RL, England

First published in 2010 by Viking Penguin,
a member of Penguin Group (USA) Inc.

10 9 8 7 6 5 4 3 2 1

Grateful acknowledgment is made for permission to reprint an excerpt from "Waving Adieu, Adieu, Adieu" from *The Collected Poems of Wallace Stevens*.
Copyright 1954 by Wallace Stevens and renewed 1982 by Holly Stevens. Used by permission of Alfred A. Knopf, a division of Random House, Inc.

Publisher's Note
This is a work of fiction. Names, characters, places, and incidents either are the product of the author's imagination or are used fictitiously, and any resemblance to actual persons, living or dead, business establishments, events, or locales is entirely coincidental.

Library of Congress Cataloging-in-Publication Data

Grimes, Martha.
   The black cat : a Richard Jury mystery / Martha Grimes.
      p. cm.
   ISBN 978-0-670-02160-4
1. Jury, Richard (Fictitious characters)—Fiction. 2. Police—England—Fiction. I. Title.
PS3557. R48998B586 2010
813'.54—dc22   2009030814

Printed in the United States of America
Set in Bembo with Baker Signet
Designed by Daniel Lagin

To my old cat, Blackie

November 1989–April 23, 2007

That would be waving and that would be crying,
Crying and shouting and meaning farewell

—WALLACE STEVENS

The Black Cat

Red Soles

I

It was already in the bloody London tabloids, the case not yet three days old and his own face plastered all over the paper when it was really Thames Valley police, and not the Met, not he, who owned the case.

Superintendent Richard Jury, high-ranking detective with the Metropolitan police, but without much feeling for rank, and who'd climbed the ladder without much feeling for the rungs, found himself at the moment in High Wycombe in Buckinghamshire, in a mortuary looking down at the body of an as yet unidentified woman.

What had made it so fascinating, he supposed, was not simply that the glamorous girl (woman, surely, only "Glam Girl" made much better copy) had been shot dead in the grounds of a pub not far away, in Chesham, but that forty-eight hours on, they hadn't discovered who she was.

Jury looked at her and wondered why the portrait of Chatterton came to mind; then he remembered Millais had also painted Ophelia, or his idea of her. And there was that larger concept that had looked so familiar—the Pre-Raphaelite period—that Romantic period of Rossetti, Holman Hunt, Millais, and rich fantasy, vibrant colors, and the death of youth. The Pre-Raphaelites were really into dying young.

Dr. Pindrop. Jury loved the name, although it didn't suit the doctor. Silence was not the doctor's milieu. He sputtered a lot, showing signs of being about to erupt but managing not to do so.

"Two shots," said Pindrop, "one missing the vital organs—" Here he pointed at the badly wounded shoulder in case Jury was blind. "It was the second one in the chest that did for her."

Jury nodded, said nothing, tried to memorize the woman's classically sculpted face.

"Superintendent?"

Jury looked up.

"You've had a right good look. Can I cover her up now?"

Jury assumed the irritation was for the usual reason: why was New Scotland Yard sending people round? "No. Leave it for a moment." Jury continued his "right good look." A .38 had done the job, according to forensic. No gun had been found, a couple of casings had.

The doctor had shown him the clothes she'd been wearing, designer dress, shoes, small handbag.

"Label's messed up. Looks like Lanvin. That's the French chap."

"No. Saint Laurent. The other one."

Pindrop smirked. "Oh. You know this French lot, do you?"

"I know a lot of things." Jury wanted to laugh.

The doctor gave a Dr.-Watson-as-played-by-Nigel-Bruce sort of grunt-laugh.

The dress was beautiful. It was sedate and yet not. The neckline consisted of layered ruffles. The sleeves were transparent as glass, reaching nearly to the elbow. The dress was the same color as her hair, a burnt orange. It was made of silk or air. He'd never seen a dress that looked so decorous and so sexy at the same time. The shoes were designed by Jimmy Choo. That name was writ large across the instep of a sandal of exquisitely crisscrossed, narrow leather ribbons of iridescent copper. The bag was Alexander McQueen. Jury didn't know him but imagined he ran with the others, along Upper Sloane Street. All of this getup would run to a couple thousand quid, he bet.

"Expensive," said the doctor. "Must've been well-fixed."

"Or someone was." He looked up. "Do you live in Chesham?"

"No. In Amersham. Old Amersham, not the one on the hill."

A proud distinction, apparently. "You can't say if she's a local, then?"

Dr. Pindrop ran his hand through thinning hair. Jury figured him to be at the back end of his sixties. "I'd swear I'd seen her before."

This surprised Jury, since the doctor brought this out with a bit of sympathy that he hadn't shown until now.

"She looks familiar to you." This at least was something.

"Yes, for some reason. Perhaps she is a local. If not Chesham, perhaps Amersham, Berkhamsted . . . well, you know."

"I'm not familiar with the area."

The doctor pulled up the sheet and dropped it over her face. "Then why did they want you?"

2

It was the same question Jury had posed and Detective Chief Superintendent Racer had answered, or rather half-answered. "Because they asked."

Oh, well, thought Jury. He waited for Racer to embellish. Racer didn't. "That's it? That's all? Who's 'they'? And why? Thames Valley is the best, certainly the biggest nonmetropolitan police force in the country, and they need us?"

Racer flapped his hand at Jury the imbecile. "No, no. Of course they're perfectly capable. Chief constable's a friend of mine. Discretion. You know how it is." He started shuffling the papers on his desk, which wasn't easy, as there were only three or four.

Again, Jury waited. The "why?" was still in abeyance, though he was the only one to realize this, apparently. He let it pass. "When did all of this happen?"

"You mean this woman's murder? On the Saturday night, as far as they can make out."

Jury looked at him. "Today is Monday."

"I've got a calendar, man; I know what day it is." Shuffle, shuffle.

And he also knew perfectly well how cold the trail was by now.

Racer glared. "I'm sorry we can't have a perfectly fresh body for you, lad. But there it is. Enough time's been wasted—"

As if Jury were the waster.

"So you'd better get your skates on. They're putting her on hold."

On hold. As if this poor woman had been making a phone call rather than being murdered.

"Chesham. Near Amersham in Bucks. I'll give police there a jingle, have somebody pick you up."

"That's all you can tell me, then, about this murdered woman? But if Thames Valley police don't know who she is, I fail to see the need to be discreet."

"You're no master of discretion yourself, man!" came the non sequitur.

3

Detective Sergeant David Cummins of the Thames Valley CID met Jury at the Chesham underground stop. The underground was a godsend for the residents here who worked in London. To be let off driving in London traffic was a miracle, in addition to the weary businessman's being able to lead a bucolic life out here in almost-country.

DS Cummins had kindly darted into the café by the station to purchase tea for Jury. Cummins was obviously impressed, not only to get a CID man from New Scotland Yard, but a detective superintendent, no less. They don't come much higher than that.

Jury didn't bother telling him that his boss was higher than that. He wondered when the last time was that Racer had actually worked a case.

"What can you tell me?"

Cummins took a deep breath, as if he were going to let loose a long and intricate story. "Not much, sir. Taxi picked her up at Chesham station, said she had him drop her at the Black Cat. Told her he'd get as close as he could; it's because the roadworks had burst pipes along the street and in front of the pub."

Cummins went on: "According to him she didn't say anything about a party or anything else. You'll want to talk to him, I expect.

The body was found by a woman who'd been walking this way with her dog, an Emily Devere."

"A local?"

"No. She lives in Amersham."

"But she was walking her dog in Chesham?"

"It's a public footpath that she especially likes. And the Black Cat's always been a favorite, she says."

Jury guessed the attraction was more pub than path.

"Did you get anything helpful from her?"

Cummins shook his head. "She was pretty rattled by the whole thing. She couldn't raise anyone in the pub, so she called police on her mobile."

"What way did she come onto the patio and tables?"

"She often came round from the footpath, walked behind the pub, and then up to the back and the patio through the trees. It's not really a wood, is it? Just the trees behind the pub. Said she saw a cat, a black cat, run off into the trees. Probably the pub cat." Cummins plowed on. "Now, as to the party idea: a well-to-do couple named Rexroth were throwing a pretty big one at their home, and it's near the pub. Deer Park House. According to them, they'd never seen the woman, didn't know anything about her. I'm pretty sure they were being truthful."

"Just how big a party?"

"Eighty or more, probably more. On that score they were a bit vague."

Jury smiled. "If I had eighty people around, I'd be more than vague; I'd be dead drunk."

Cummins liked the levity. "There was plenty of that, too, they said. Good-natured couple, the Rexroths."

"Then they'll be glad to see us."

The Black Cat was on the Lycrome Road, on the edge of Chesham. They were by then pulling into the small car park. The pub itself was pale yellow–washed, pleasant and unassuming. "Do Not Cross" tape cordoned off the back of it.

"Place has been closed off since," said Cummins, "but I expect that'll be taken down now. No reason to interfere with business any more than's necessary. Owners are on an extended holiday, and it's being looked after by a friend of theirs. Name's Sally Hawkins and she lives in Beaconsfield but helps out if they need it. Her niece, I think the child is, lives with her."

Jury turned from the small collection of trees to look at the pub. "Is Ms. Hawkins in?"

"Should be. I called to tell her you'd want a word with her. She wasn't happy."

"They never are. Show me where the Devere woman found the body."

They walked across the car park and a patch of grass, wet and in need of cutting, to a patio where several tables were set out for the use of the customers in fine weather. Each had an umbrella on it, furled now. On one of them lay a black cat, also furled, thought Jury, curled tightly and peacefully sleeping. Jury ran his hand along the cat's back. "Hello, cat," he said. To Cummins: "Pub cat?"

"I shouldn't wonder. Well, they'd have to have a black cat, now, wouldn't they?"

The place looked deserted, but any place would, thought Jury, with a streamer of police tape across its car park.

"It was this table here," said Cummins, moving to the table farthest from the car park. "She must've been sitting at it, we can't be sure, but she was found sprawled behind it. Body was lying mostly on the patio, shoulders and head on the grass. It was as if she'd fallen off the seat at the impact. Forensic say the shooter was probably standing, given the path of the bullet, the way it hit the victim." Cummins raised his hand, simulated a gun pointing downward.

"Drinks on the table?"

Cummins shook his head. "No. Nothing."

"It would seem, then, they weren't friends sharing a quiet drink together."

Cummins looked at him. "It would certainly seem they weren't friends."

Jury smiled; he liked the mild put-down. "Suppose we have a word with Ms. Hawkins."

They went through the door at the side, near the stone terrace, into a little hall and then into the bar. The room was long, narrow, not especially large, but certainly pleasant. Jury heard the tapping of high heels on stairs and a blond woman came into the room.

She wasn't bad-looking, only a bit hard. Her eyes were like slate, her blond hair brassy, weighed down with the extra color that came out of a bottle. "Saw you two messing about outside, so I thought I'd better come down."

DS Cummins told Sally Hawkins who Jury was. "He'd just like to put a few questions to you about the Saturday night."

She tossed a lock of yellow hair from her shoulder. "Well, I told you what I know, which is sod-all. I'm having a drink, me. You want something?" Without much interest in the answer, she went behind the bar, expertly flipped a glass down from a rack, and placed it under the optic that held one of the lesser-quality gins.

Jury wouldn't have expected her to be drinking Sambuca with coffee beans floating on top. He sat down on one of the bar stools. Cummins stood. "I'm sorry to be covering the same territory that you've already gone over, probably more than once," said Jury. "But things can always use a fresh perspective."

Her grunt said she didn't agree, but she drank her gin happily enough.

"You're here just temporarily?"

She nodded.

"You have a niece who lives with you?"

"Not a niece; she's by way of being a ward."

A vague designation, he thought, for a little girl's life. He waited, but she didn't enlarge upon "by way of being."

"Is she here now?"

"No. She's in Bletchley at her cousin's. She'll be here later tonight. I sent her off when that happened." Here, Sally Hawkins dipped her head toward the car park.

"Bletchley?" said Jury. "I'm going there with a friend. Bletchley Park. I expect you know it."

"Place where they messed about with codes during the war? Sounds bloody boring to me. What I want to know is, when are they taking down that tape out there? Don't I ever get the gawkers, though?"

Cummins said, "It should be down this evening, I expect. But you can understand the need for it; we don't want people trampling up the scene."

"Well, who's going to trample it, I'd like to know, what with that roadworks out there mucking about? Business is down over seventy-five percent because of that lot. No one could park until today. They've had it blocked off for nearly a week. I tell you."

She shook her head at a world bent on making her miserable; then, with nothing left to complain about, she sank further into discontent, pulling a cigarette out of a pack on the bar.

Jury asked, "Had you ever seen the woman before or had any idea who she was?"

"Course not. It's what I told the bloody police. I don't know what she was doing out there."

"There was a party Saturday night at . . ." Jury looked at DS Cummins.

"Rexroths'. Deer Park House, just up the road."

Jury went on: "Given the way the woman was dressed, the thought is she might have been there, or been going there."

"Funny old way to be going," said Sally, giving Jury a big helping of smoke right in his face. "In those shoes. I don't think so."

"You're right there. Jimmy Choo," said Cummins.

"Ha!" said Sally. "Would you listen to him." Her glass standing empty, she turned back to the optics.

Cummins's face flushed a little. "It's the wife. She's really into shoes. Loves them."

"Well, let's hope she loves you more, dearie," said Sally, back turned. "Those shoes cost the earth." She turned back to them, her glass holding two fingers of gin.

"She could have been at the Black Cat to meet someone. Was there anyone in the pub, any stranger, on the Saturday night?" But if the "stranger" was planning murder, he'd have avoided putting himself on display.

Sally tapped ash from her cigarette into the aluminum tray. "Ha! Any stranger? Not even the regulars were here except for Johnny Boy and his old dog and Mrs. Maltese."

When Jury looked at Cummins, the sergeant nodded. "Police have talked to them. No joy, no one saw a thing. No one was in the car park, no one sitting at the tables outside."

"Was there any other function around that might have called for dressing up?"

"Not bloody likely," said Sally.

The woman must have been bound for the Deer Park House party, then, going to or coming back. Despite the hosts' denying they knew her. It was quite possible they didn't, but it was also possible she was a guest, invited or not, perhaps the lady friend of someone who was invited. It made sense. You don't put on Yves Saint Laurent, Jimmy Choo, and Alexander McQueen, then take a train and a cab only to go to the Black Cat. *Look: meet me at the pub before you go to the party. Or after, or during. Just slip away. I can't go there, after all.* Why would the killer want to meet the victim in a public place? Because the victim would not have agreed to meet otherwise? The Black Cat was a good venue. Even on a Saturday night, it wouldn't have been crowded.

"Thank you, Sally," said Jury. "I might think of something else and be in contact with you."

"I'm sure you will; police always think of something else." But she said it in a good-natured way, and they left by the same door they'd entered.

They crunched across the gravel, Jury saying, "My guess is she wasn't involved; she hasn't enough passion for it."

"I dunno." David Cummins sighed. "People can fool you."

"Enough have." Jury moved to the table and patted the cat's head. "What about the Rexroths, then?"

"They own Deer Park House, as I said. There's a Deer Park Road, but the house isn't on it; it's across Lycrome Road and back a bit. If the woman was headed there, the Rexroths say they'd no knowledge of it."

"Let's have a talk with them."

Cummins got out his mobile.

The black cat looked up, its amber eyes staring intently into Jury's gray ones.

Did you see anything?

Jury tried to send the cat a message.

Tell me.

The black cat closed its eyes and told him nothing.

4

The Rexroths, Kit and Tip (and it was a challenge to remember which was he and which she), were an elderly British couple in tweeds and cashmere and sensible shoes. One could tell they were given to stout walks along public footpaths, their complexions telling they'd been up and out, meeting every dewy morning of their long lives.

"You wouldn't think, would you, I mean to look at us, that we're the hub of Chesham's social scene?" Kit Rexroth's eyes were glittery as sequins.

The Rexroths were old and reed thin. Flutes could have been made of their limbs. "I can imagine it. You seem to be as lively as people half your age." Jury hoped that didn't sound condescending; people fell into condescension so often with the old, but not always with the old and rich, as if it were quite remarkable to find them alive at all and they had to be dealt with gently.

He was struck by the way Tip and Kit seemed to operate in tandem, a couple of tap dancers: their feet in perfect step, hats tilted forward, canes gliding smoothly over fingers. Jury smiled; he'd never seen a couple so synchronized. If one of them thought murder a good idea, both would commit it.

"You're here," said Kit, raising her coffee cup as if to toast the fact, "about the murder."

"Yes, I am. Oh, no, thanks—" This was addressed to Tip, who was holding the coffeepot aloft. Cummins, though, accepted a cup.

"I know you've talked to Detective Sergeant Cummins, but I'd just like to get the picture clearer in my own mind. This woman was wearing a dress by Saint Laurent, an apricot color. Her hair was almost that same color, a darkish ginger. She was about five feet eight. Quite beautiful. The crime scene pictures don't really do her justice. Are you up for having a look?"

They nodded with a rather inappropriate enthusiasm.

Jury set out the least morbid of the photos.

Kit Rexroth looked at it, bending across the hands hugging her knees and bringing her face nearly level with the table. Jury wondered if she was shortsighted.

"You know, she does look a bit familiar. . . . Does she to you, Tip?" She pushed the photo toward him.

Tip grunted, looked again, pushing his glasses up the bridge of his nose. "Don't think so . . . still . . ." He turned the photo this way and that, looked hard at it. Then he shook his head. "No."

Jury picked up the photo and said, "Yours appeared to be the only party in town, at least of the formal sort."

"How enthralling," said Kit Rexroth. "You're thinking she was here." Kit was shaking her head. "A woman like that, well, I think someone would have paraded her, not stuck her out on the terrace with a gin and a promise."

Jury said, "How many people were here?"

"Oh, eighty? Something like that," said Kit. "Though we only invited half that crowd." She sounded extraordinarily pleased.

That comment only made it even more likely that the dead woman had been headed here, invited or not, for neither of the Rexroths seemed to be sure of who was at the party.

"We have the sort of brawl where people end up spilling out of windows."

They both laughed.

"That could get messy, Mr. Rexroth."

Now they looked startled, then saw Jury was joking and laughed again.

"What about the neighbors?" said Cummins. "Don't you get complaints?"

"We would do," said Kit, "except the neighbors were here!"

There was another peal of laughter. Jury wondered if the Rexroths were entertaining themselves to death.

"I wonder if I could have a copy of your guest list—"

Cummins broke in: "We've got that, sir. Sorry, I should have given it to you."

Kit waved her hand. "Oh, that's no problem. Here, I copied it for you." She handed over pages that had been on the coffee table.

It was a sheaf of paper, rather than a sheet, with names written in longhand.

"It's divided. Our friends and Tip's colleagues in the City. He works in Cannon Street. First, there are the people we actually extended invitations to; next, the guests our guests asked if they could bring; next, the guests who brought people they hadn't asked if they could bring; then, the people who dropped in that one or the other of us might have invited but couldn't remember, or meant to invite . . . well, you know what I mean—"

Jury didn't.

"—and then Tip's drinking friends at every pub in the City; then, the people we didn't know were coming but that we sighted in the course of the evening—" Here she put her hand over her eyes as if she were actually standing on a ship's bow, searching the horizon.

Jury leafed through the pages. Were there this many people in London? "If this woman was bound for your party, perhaps she was in the category of a date invited by one of your guests. Was anyone looking out for someone who never came?"

Kit and Tip both frowned in thought. "No, I don't recall . . . there was Neal, wasn't there?" said Kit, looking at her husband. "Wasn't he asking about some girl?"

"Um. Yes, I believe you're right."

Cummins said, "That'd be the Neal Carver you mentioned before."

The Rexroths looked at Cummins. "Did we?" said Kit. "Well, then I expect that's right. And Rudy . . . Rudy—what's his last name?"

Tip thought about it but came up empty. "Should be on the list."

Cummins said, "I believe you told me it was Lands, Rudy Lands."

"Oh?" said Tip, eyebrows raised, as if it were Cummins, not he, who had invited Rudy.

Jury smiled. The Rexroths were a bit too vague and suggestible for his tastes. He glanced at Cummins, nodded. They both rose. "Thanks very much. We'll be in touch."

In the car, Jury said, "What about this Neal Carver and Rudy Lands?"

"We talked to both. The Lands fellow said his girl turned out to have gotten sick; Carver was supposed to have collected his date at her flat in Chelsea. A Miss Helen Brown-Headly. A short brunette who forgot completely about the party, et cetera. She's not our girl.

"Also, I rang Emily Devere, the woman who actually found the body, and she's happy to see you."

"Is she enjoying this as much as the Rexroths seem to be?"

Cummins laughed. "Oh, yes."

It was getting on toward dinnertime, Emily Devere told him, but not to worry, that meant she could extend the cocktail hour, and would he like a drink? Her brown-and-white dog, like a box on legs, gave Jury a sour look that said he should refuse if he knew what was good for him.

Jury thanked her but declined. "Don't let me stop you, though," he added.

"As if you could." Emily Devere poured herself a whiskey, plunked in an ice cube, and sat down across from him. Miss Devere had pointed out that this house was not in Amersham-on-the-Hill but in Amersham Old Town.

"I'm a snob, but still it's a matter of history, you see. I prefer mine as old as possible. Like my whiskey." She smiled and raised her glass. "Sometimes I feel like the boy with his finger in the dike. The modern world will come crashing through more and more."

Emily Devere was closing in on her eighties, possessed a beautifully fine and roseate skin, and wore no-nonsense skirts and brown cardigans. Her graying hair was caught in a bun at the nape of her neck.

They sat in the front room of her small, cheery cottage off School Lane. The cottage was filled with flowery, chintz-covered chairs and sofa and hooked rugs and embroidered footrests. Her dog had folded himself on one of these and stared at Jury. The pulled-down face suggested he was part bulldog.

"One can't stop progress, of course, but I'd really like to stick out my foot and trip it. The abominable mobile phones! The world is my call box." One hand flew to her brow.

Jury smiled. Miss Devere was no stranger to drama.

But just as quickly she settled back into the matter-of-fact practical woman who'd recently found a dead body. "I've always been partial to that pub: I go there occasionally, though it's a bit out of the way. I can't say much for this woman who's taken it over while the owners are on holiday. Sally someone. Looks a bit dodgy to me." She drank her whiskey, pursed her lips. "But she's only temporary, thank heavens. Anyway, I like to get out and take Drummond for a walk along that footpath near the farm. Drummond's fond of it."

Drummond, Jury thought to look at him, wasn't about to be taken anywhere. Not against his will, anyway. "What did he do?"

"Pardon me?"

"Drummond. When he came upon this woman's body."

"Well . . . you know, I don't know; I mean, I was so shocked by the whole thing, I wasn't paying attention." She leaned forward in her chair. "Do you think he knows something?"

Jury wanted to laugh. She sounded serious. "You'd never seen her before, Miss Devere?"

"No, of course not. I'd have said." She cushioned her head on the small pillow that hung over the top of her chair and looked upward, puzzled, as if the ceiling were acting peculiarly.

"Is something bothering you?"

"Well, as I said, I don't think I'd ever seen her, but it's just that she looked familiar."

Jury thought of the doctor's comment "I'd swear I'd seen her before" and of Kit Rexroth's similar impression.

"That dress," she went on, "was crepe, a coppery color, with that swirly, leafy design. I bet it cost the earth. Quite beautiful."

"You're very observant, to take that in, in the circumstances."

"When I was younger, I was fascinated by Upper Sloane Street. Harvey Nicks, the shops. You know." A wry little smile.

"Police said you'd seen a black cat about. The pub's cat, was it?"

"I expect so. It streaked off when it saw Drummond. One black cat looks rather like any other."

Jury wondered. He got up. "Thank you, Miss Devere. I'll be in touch."

"I hope so. This is more fun than I've had in an age."

It was getting dark as they pulled up to the High Wycombe train station. David Cummins said, "You could kip here overnight. Crown's nice, or the King's Arms. If we had room, I'd say stay with us. We're on Lycrome Road, too, not far from the pub. You must meet Chris, my wife."

"Thanks, but I've a few things to do in London. A friend in hospital to visit. Tonight, tomorrow morning."

"Oh. Hope it's not serious."

"As serious as it gets. Thanks." Outside, Jury tapped the top of the car in a good-bye gesture.

Jury liked trains, even this small kind that reminded him of Tinker-toys with its narrow seats, three across and barely demarcated and no armrests, but tonight he had the three narrow seats to himself. It was thirty or forty minutes to Marylebone, and God knew it beat scrabbling around on the M25. During peak hours these commuter trains were probably crowded, but the motorways were hell.

What he liked was one's feeling of being in touch. They were all strangers, yes, but the looks—indifferent, sullen, distant, angry—at least they were the looks you chose, not the looks you were forced to trot out to negotiate social traffic. You could think your own thoughts and look what way you wanted, and all the rest could jolly well bugger off.

His mind should be on this young woman, richly gowned and shod, who'd come to meet someone, the wrong someone. He should have spoken to the driver of the cab at the station, but he could do that tomorrow. He thought she was a local, despite no one's having come forth to identify her. Three people had said she looked familiar. There had been this spark of recognition, but nothing burning brightly enough to claim "Yes, that's So-and-so. Known her all my life."

And then, weirdly, London's iconic black cabs came to him, for now there was the occasional cab painted silver or blue. Any color other than black was the wrong one for a London cab. Thinking about this, he was led to wonder, had the dead woman been painted the wrong color? In a couple thousand quids' worth of designer clothes?

He pulled out Kit Rexroth's guest list, ran his eye down the first, the second page. There were six, no, seven pages, written in her large but precise hand. The invited, the uninvited (pages four, five, six); the sighted, the unsighted—well, no, the unsighted would be . . . unsighted. *And Tip's drinking friends at every pub in the City.*

Jury thumbed back to the sixth page, thinking, surely, he must be wrong. No, he wasn't. The name was there: Harry Johnson. Oh, but there must be dozens of Harry Johnsons in London. Jury smiled. Surely there was only one.

It was too short a ride for a tea trolley, which he missed, and surprised himself in that. The little clatter of its approach down the aisle was somehow consoling. It spoke of ritual. People needed that, we need grounding, he thought. We're like tents that have to be pegged to keep from blowing off. Rituals, and the things that spoke of rituals. It wouldn't be long before they'd be phasing out the double-deckers; it would soon be good-bye to the cranky conductors with their ticket rolls. Black cabs. It was okay to see the odd silver or blue or patchwork one, but not the lot, please. Not the lot of them. Instead of the absent tea trolley, he should be thinking about Lu in hospital—

Don't go there.

He went.

5

St. Bart's Hospital was in the City, near Smithfield Market and next to the beautiful St. Bartholomew's Church. When he'd mentioned the hospital's proximity to Smithfield Market to his upstairs neighbor, Carole-anne Palutski, she'd told him to stop in and get some decent sausages for a fry-up. Good, he'd said, I'll back the truck in.

That made for about as much humor as he could muster.

The last time he'd seen Lu Aguilar, she'd told him that when she was released from hospital she was going back to Brazil. Her family, she said, were there, not here.

She said the same thing now she'd said then: "I don't think you can use a detective in a wheelchair."

Jury bent over the bed. "I'll take the detective any way I can get her." He was holding her hand, rubbing his thumb along the sheer bone that was left of her. Lu had lost weight she didn't need to lose. Because of the damage the accident had done, she wouldn't be walking again, not for a long time, and more likely never. It had been a simple traffic accident, two cars trying to make it through a yellow light, one straight on, one turning. The driver of the other car had died at the scene. In the short while since the crash on Upper Street—three weeks ago? four?—she must have lost twenty pounds, but none of her acerbity. To his compliment a moment ago, she said with a laugh, "Oh, no, you wouldn't."

Jury sat back. "Why? Do you think I'm so shallow?"

"Of course."

He knew she didn't think he was shallow; that was the easiest way of telling him he wasn't being truthful.

"You're wrong," he said. "Police work has been done before from a wheelchair. We don't prize you for your ability to hop in and out of zed-cars. It isn't a cross-country race you're doing; it's investigation."

"Oh, please."

She turned away, and Jury felt as if she'd slapped him. At that moment, he hated her. But the feeling washed over him and washed away, a wave receding in a moment.

But not her hatred of her condition. The air crackled with it. Along with the weight, Lu had lost the edge that had made her such a dominant force. So much of Lu was presentation. She was, certainly, not your classic introvert.

The neurosurgeon who'd done the procedure had unquestionably saved Lu's life. Phyllis Nancy had told him that. She herself had been the doctor at the scene of the accident. The imperturbable Phyllis Nancy. He wondered how she'd gotten through school with two first names. He could never think of Phyllis without smiling.

"What are you smiling about?"

Jury flinched. "What? Nothing." He felt ashamed.

"That wasn't a nothing smile and it wasn't about me."

"You've gotten a lot better at reading minds, Lu." He smiled again, a reprehensible, lying smile.

"Oh, I could always do that. Especially yours."

He felt her gaze.

"You're off the hook, Richard."

He wanted to feel that as another slap in the face, something he didn't deserve. It made him a little sick to think that he did.

She caught the look, not able to read it precisely but seeing uncertainty and ambivalence. "Come on," she said. "We didn't—we don't—love each other, for Christ's sake." She tried to sit up, and it looked to him as if her fragile spine exploded in pain. "Jesus! Doesn't anybody have a drink or at least a goddamned cigarette?"

Jury felt his walk down the white corridor must be almost as painful as hers, lying in that bed.

You're off the hook.

He did not want to explore that rush of feeling, distinctly like relief. He had been on the hook all right. He realized now that the hook had been sexual. If she'd intended to stay here, maybe even go back to her job with the Islington CID, he honestly didn't know what he'd have done. Marry her? Insist on taking care of her somehow? He couldn't imagine Lu Aguilar accepting either of those proposals. She'd know that they were offered out of guilt or pity or obligation.

The long white corridor seemed endless, the bank of elevators, the bright red "Exit" sign never getting any closer.

The way out never did.

6

He had left the flat the next morning for a mere twenty minutes, to get milk for his tea. Upon his return, when he went to put the milk in his refrigerator, he found a message affixed to the fridge door with a little magnet in the shape of a banana.

In his absence, Carole-anne had answered his phone. Probably on her way to work this morning she had heard the ring and had just popped in to answer it. Jury rarely locked his door.

The message was written in Carole-anne's inimitable style; if the angel Gabriel had delivered messages like Carole-anne, Christianity might never have gotten a toehold:

"S.W. c'd sed high w. ds rep. w'mn mss in Chess. Thought U should know."

Jury pondered. Maybe "S.W." had also called his mobile. He checked it to find the battery dead. He cursed himself for forgetting to charge it and pondered the message again. He left it to make his tea and look at the paper he had bought along with the milk.

The murder in Chesham should have been getting minor treatment at this point. But, no, the London paper even revved it up a little. Wasn't there enough going on in EC3 to make some murder in a Buckinghamshire village pale by comparison?

Apparently not. Jury supposed there was an element of fascination not only in the victim's being beautiful and Jimmy-Choo-Saint-

Laurent-clad, but also in being unidentified. His name in there, too; they were still milking it for all it was worth, once again going over the suspension because of the Hester Street affair a couple of months back, a boomerang effect, that had been. There had been a bit of a public outcry at this detective's being punished for saving the lives of the little girls. So Jury was being fashioned the Met police paladin, champion of the unfortunate.

Christ. Jury tossed the paper on his coffee table, took a pull on his mug of tea as if it were a pint, and regarded the message again. "S.W. c'd . . ." *Sergeant Wiggins* called. That must be it. Well, he would see this Sergeant Wiggins in a few minutes, if he was the caller.

Jury finished his tea, collected his coat and keys, and left the flat.

Sergeant Wiggins, stirring his own tea with a licorice root, raised his eyebrows in question when Jury walked into the office. "Did you get my message?"

"Ah, yes. I got a message, or what passes for one, from Carole-anne." He pulled it out and read, as phonetically as he could, " 'S.W. c'd sed high w. ds rep. w'mn mss in Chess. Thought U should know.' " He looked up to see Wiggins's deep frown. "I finally worked out that S.W. meant you."

"Yes, but what—" Light broke. "Of course. That 'w'mn mss in Chess': that's telling you a DS called from their High Wycombe HQ to let you know there's a woman been reported missing."

"Do they know who?"

"No. It was reported by an aunt who hasn't seen the niece for three days, nearly four if you count this morning—"

Jury frowned. "That's a bit of a wait."

"Thing is, the niece that's missing often goes into London for weekends, so the aunt thought that's where she was. Anyway, this niece of hers wasn't the victim. She's a local."

"And so might the victim be."

"Not in this case." Wiggins tapped the root against the tip of his mug. "The aunt—her name's Cox, Edna Cox—called police yesterday and said her niece should've been home by Sunday night, that she'd never miss work on Monday, that she hadn't rung. Then the Cox woman went to the morgue and said, no, it wasn't her, and anyway, her Mariah—Mariah Cox being the niece—Mariah would never wear clothes like that. Police are using her costume to help with the ID. I mean, how many women round that area would be wearing that dress and those narrow-toed shoes by . . ."

"Jimmy Choo. And when did Mariah Cox disappear?"

"Well, she first missed her on the Saturday—but remember, she thought Mariah was in London for the weekend. It was on Sundays that Mariah usually came back, but she didn't. Nor on the Monday—"

Jury was out of his chair. "I want to talk to the aunt."

"But she said it wasn't her niece, guv."

"I don't give a toss for that. One woman goes missing and a dead one turns up—what a bloody coincidence." He pulled on his coat.

"But surely the woman would know her own—" The phone rang and Wiggins snapped it up, gave his name, and listened. After five seconds of listening, he held up a finger to Jury. "It's DS Cummins again, guv, here—" He held out the phone.

Jury took it and sat on the edge of Wiggins's desk. He listened, said he'd be there inside of an hour, and handed the receiver back to Wiggins.

"Apparently, they got someone else to identify the body, the librarian the niece worked for. According to her, the dead woman's Mariah Cox."

7

He spent some time in High Wycombe gathering what forensic evidence was available and being treated with remarkable amiability by Thames Valley police, given he was hardly a necessary adjunct to their deliberations. He said as much to the DCI to whom David Cummins had introduced him.

DCI Stevens only laughed. "Oh, I don't know. We're not all Morse here."

Jury frowned, puzzled. "Morse?"

"My God, man, you don't know Morse? Thames Valley police? Oxford?"

"Oh, *that* Morse. The TV one. Well, you can take it to the bank that I'm not him either. But I would like to talk to the aunt, this Edna Cox."

"Sure. DS Cummins can take you. It's rather odd, but what made me wonder about the Cox woman's failure to identify the victim was that she was too *abrupt* in her denial. It was the way of someone who was refusing to face something unpleasant. Ordinarily, you'd register a huge relief, finding the body you're looking at *isn't* someone you love. That's why we got the librarian in, the one who runs the place, name of Mary"—he looked down at a paper—"Chivers. She identified her. Of course, she said too that it hardly looked like Mariah, and no wonder the aunt didn't recognize her: the ginger hair, the look of her, the clothes. D'you think Mariah was going off to London to work as a pro, weekends?"

"Could be. I want to talk to both of these women, if you don't mind."

"Mind? No. We're always happy to have someone from the Met come round."

Jury smiled. "No, you're not."

"Sorry," said David Cummins as they piled into the car. "I tried your cell but got no answer. Then I tried the Yard, got your sergeant."

"And he called my flat. The message was taken by a friend from upstairs. I've an answer machine that hasn't worked since the day I got it, so if she's passing and hears my phone, she goes in and answers." Jury saw a red light coming up and pulled out the scrap of paper. When Cummins braked, Jury handed it to him.

The DS read it, frowned, laughed. The light changed. "My God. How did you sort *that* out?"

Jury pocketed the message. "She spends most of her time reading runes and translating from Old English. Never quite got the hang of it myself." He looked out at the passing scenery. "You say the victim's with the local library. So how would a librarian's pay run to Yves Saint Laurent?"

"Wouldn't." Cummins laughed. "Nor the shoes." They were approaching a roundabout. "Not unless she got a pair from my wife."

"Your wife?"

"Chris has the lot: Jimmy Choo, Prada, Gucci, Tod's, Blahnik, you name it."

Jury couldn't. He was simply surprised, given he imagined a policeman's pay here might be only slightly higher than a librarian's.

"Chris knew straightaway whose shoes they were. From the photo—" Realizing he'd said too much, Cummins cut it off.

Jury looked over at him. "Police photos?"

"Look. I just showed her the one of the shoes. I know I'm not supposed to—"

"No, you're not."

"It's just . . . it's just Chris . . ." Negotiating the roundabout, he stopped talking again.

The DS's obvious embarrassment made Jury sympathetic. "So Chris has a shoe hang-up." He laughed.

Relieved now, Cummins laughed. "God, yes. You've got to meet her."

"I'd like to. She sounds fascinating. In the meantime, let's stop by the library."

Mary Chivers was one of those people who called all detectives "Inspector," no matter what their rank: constable, sergeant, superintendent. Detective Sergeant Cummins was anointed with the same inspectorhood as Superintendent Jury.

Mary Chivers had been holding a book, blowing dust off its spine, when they walked in. Jury liked the act of blowing dust from a book, he could not say why. Miss Chivers was a little bundle of a woman with whom one could tell books would be safe. Indeed, the whole little library felt like a safe house or sanctuary in its whispery silence. The whispers were supplied by three women at a reading table sharing news or secrets.

DS Cummins, who had been one of those to question her before, introduced Jury.

"I couldn't believe it at first," she said in answer to Jury's question. "I *could not believe* this dead woman was Mariah Cox. I don't mean I didn't recognize her, I did, despite that ginger hair—but I certainly had to look twice, let me tell you. It was the situation, where she was found, the way she'd been dressed, why it's perfectly understandable that Edna would have made that mistake. Poor Edna." Here Mary Chivers ran her hand over the cover of the book she still held, and her eyes over the high stacks of books, as if assuring herself they hadn't run away.

She went on. "Mariah was plain, but she had good bones. Yes, with the right makeup, and a bit of artistry, she could make herself another face. Yes, I can see that. . . ."

Jury said, "She got on well with your staff?"

"Of course."

"No one appeared to dislike her or be jealous of her or have any reason you know of to harm her?"

Mary Chivers shook her head slowly, decidedly. "Understand, Inspector, that Mariah Cox was as nice a person as could be—completely dependable, conscientious, kind. She was quiet, retiring, one of those women, you know, who would more or less fade into the background. Mariah was not one to stand out."

Not one to stand out. Mariah had scarcely disturbed the air around her and yet had morphed into a lovely, sophisticated, and—Jury was beginning to suspect—sex-for-sale woman. For Jury, it was not so much that she had done it, but why.

Edna Cox lived in the end one of a terraced row of houses, with lace curtains at the front window. The place was dispiriting enough on its own; with the additional blow of a death in the family, it was bleak as the North York moors.

Edna Cox still appeared to be denying the knowledge that the dead woman in the police photograph could possibly be her niece. "You know my Mariah, Mr. Cummins," she said, as if that took care of it.

DS Cummins said, "It wasn't like her, I agree, but . . ."

Edna Cox was having no buts about it. Given the way she was perched on an overstuffed chair edge, it wasn't like sitting at all. If she moved half an inch forward, she'd be on the hooked rug.

"I said it once and I'll say it again: Mariah does not own clothes like that. And her hair—it was never that color. Have you talked to Bobby? They got engaged hardly two weeks ago."

"No, I haven't," said Jury. "Bobby—?"

Edna Cox looked away, apparently done with answering.

"That'd be Bobby Devlin," said Cummins. "Bobby has the flower stall next the station. Nice fellow."

Edna Cox blurted out: "Mariah wouldn't be caught dead in those pointy-toed sandals."

Unfortunate choice of words, thought Jury.

"And she didn't have the money for them, neither. Shoes like that or that dress. That lot'd cost her half a year's wages."

Jury had picked up a framed photo of Mariah Cox and sat now looking at it. Here was a plain girl with straight dark hair to her shoulders, untidy bangs nearly eclipsing her eyes. But Mary Chivers was right: you could still see the bones, and they were very good. It was exactly the kind of face that someone trained in the art of makeup could do marvels with. Perhaps Mariah herself had the talent; perhaps there'd been a lot of practice in putting on another face. He set the photo on a glass-topped coffee table that didn't fit the rest of the furnishings and said, "She'd been gone before, hadn't she?"

"Well, yes, most weekends, and sometimes she'd stay over in London with this friend of hers she knew at school . . ." She looked down at the rug at her feet as her voice trailed away.

"Mrs. Cox, has it ever occurred to you your niece was leading a double life?" Jury was leaning forward, trying to make that sound the most natural thing in the world, a double life.

Her head came up smartly. "Whatever are you talking about?" Clearly unconvinced of her own judgment, she sounded like a person desperately wanting to avoid something.

"Maybe you simply didn't want this woman to be Mariah."

Her shoulders went back as if about to take Jury on. "So you're saying I lied."

"Not at all. I believe you made a mistake, that's all." He picked up the picture he'd set on the table. "Straight brown hair and a fringe almost covering her eyes. No makeup. The exact opposite of the young woman who was murdered. It's what I mean by a double life. They look like two different women. The doctor, who's a local, thought the dead woman looked familiar. So did another witness. You understand what I'm saying."

By now, Edna Cox had the handkerchief she'd pulled from her sleeve wadded against her mouth and shook her head. "I can't believe it."

But she did. She had. Jury sat back, giving the poor woman some space. He looked around, struck by the room's insipidity—its mush-room browns, its rainy-day grays. It fit the girl in the photo on the table. No, that was wrong: the girl was not insipid at all. And the room was more sad than insipid. The air around them seemed weighted with sadness. Or perhaps it was his. He was sorry he couldn't leave Edna Cox with her fantasy and her denial.

There were ample means to establish the two women were one: DNA, dental work, fingerprints.

"You mentioned the London friend. Do you know her name?"

"Oh, dear, I just can't get my mind round all this. Angela, I think . . . Adele—the last name, I think it's Astaire. It's like the dancer, I think. Yes, that's what she calls herself. Silly of her."

"Then that's not her real name?"

"No. Mariah said it was just her business name. Whatever that means."

Jury took out his small notebook, wrote down the name. "I don't imagine you have the address, do you?"

"I don't, no."

"Any idea what part of London it is?"

Mrs. Cox put her fingers to her temples, massaging them. "Par-sons Green, it could be. Or Fulham. Well, somewhere around that part of London. There might be something in Mariah's room, an address book or letters or something—"

"Yes, I'd appreciate it if you'd let police go over the room. Not now, of course, if you don't want us bumbling round the house. Detective Sergeant Cummins might do this later, when it won't be so disturbing for you."

Sadly, she nodded. "If you're right, then what was it she was doing dressed like that? Her face made over? Her hair that color?" She wad-ded the handkerchief in her hands. "She worked at the little library, you know. I always thought it was the perfect job for Mariah."

"Why's that?"

"She was such a quiet person, and she liked being around books. It's the kind of job that's not such a strain if you have to deal with the public. You don't have them complaining a lot or demanding too much. Checking out books, they're contented, somehow. Mariah didn't like dealing with the wide world. She kept herself to herself."

Like bandages coming off a patient's eyes, sighted or blind; or unwound from a burn victim's ruined face, Edna Cox's defensive covering unwound more and more. Jury felt very sorry for her.

"I know all of this must be a terrible mystery to you, but anything you can tell us would help. Things that might not have signified at the time." He paused, thinking. "Why did you report her missing, Mrs. Cox? I mean, she went off any number of times, yet those other times didn't appear to worry you."

She looked puzzled, as if this hadn't occurred to her before Jury said it. She sat thinking and worrying her handkerchief. "It was because she would have let me know, and she didn't." More pulling at the handkerchief, as if it were a knob of taffy. "I mean, Mariah would never just not come back on the Sunday without letting me know. And there was work, too. She worked on Monday at the library. You'd have to know her, how dependable, how considerate she is." She looked away. "Was."

"How long had she lived with you, Mrs. Cox?"

"Ten years, about. She came to me after her mother died—my sister. Mariah had been taking care of her; it was a long illness. Lungs. Emphysema. They lived up north in Tyne and Wear. Old Washington, where George was born. You probably don't know it. . . ."

Indeed he did; he knew it well.

"Her dad worked in Newcastle. You know, it's always been hard up there, jobs, I mean, and money tight. First her da died and then her mum. We didn't see each other often, well, hardly ever, really. Christmas and the long school holiday, that was about all."

"Did Mariah look then as she does in this photo?" He tapped the silver frame.

She frowned. "Not really. When she was younger, she was prettier. She seemed to just grow plainer, though usually it's the other way round, isn't it? I don't understand it; I don't understand any of it." She started crying in earnest now.

Jury moved over to the small sofa, put his arm round her shoulders, said, "I'm truly sorry for your loss, Edna."

He was beginning to feel sorry for his own, too.

8

"This Devlin, the fiancé. You know him?" Jury asked as they pulled away from the terraced house.

DS Cummins nodded. "A bit. Bobby's the flower guy."

"Sweet. But what does it mean?"

"He grows flowers and sells them. He's got a fabulous garden—a few acres outside of town."

Jury powered up his window; it was getting into evening and much cooler. "Any joy there? With Devlin?"

Cummins shook his head. "I'd guess not. I mean, if you're asking whether Bobby's a suspect. I know well enough he'd never have hurt Mariah. Never."

"Where can I find him?"

"Bobby? He'll be in Market Square. Tuesdays and Fridays he keeps a stall. I can take you there. Do you want me along?"

"No. That's okay. Just drop me there."

Cummins was pulling up by a curb outside of the square that had been marked off for pedestrian shopping. He told Jury where he'd find the flower stall, adding, "Listen, if you've nothing better going, come round to our place for a drink. Chris'd be glad for the company. Seriously."

Jury didn't feel like it, wanted to get back to London, but he hated turning David Cummins down for the second time. "That'd be nice, David. Can you pick me up back here in an hour?"

Looking pleased, Cummins nodded. "Right here, and if you're not, I'll wait. You can always call me on my mobile."

Jury inspected the sky. "Yes, well, let's just say an hour, okay?"

Cummins drove away.

Jury assumed it was Devlin, the intense, dark-haired young man with an armful of daisies and purple irises, talking to an elderly woman, apparently giving her advice about the care of a plant she was holding. She thanked him and left.

"Mr. Devlin?" said Jury.

He turned, still holding the shock of flowers.

"You're Robert Devlin?"

"Bobby. What can I do for you?" He submerged the flowers in a tub holding several inches of water.

"My name's Richard Jury. I'm with Scotland Yard CID." He held out his ID.

"Oh." The syllable was weighted with sadness.

He was pale and handsome and so wistful-looking, Jury wanted to clap him on the shoulder and tell him to buck up. Jury had never told anyone to buck up in his life.

Bobby Devlin looked down, up, down again. "It's Mariah, isn't it?" He pulled over an old crate and sat down, hard. His face was drawn, his body strained. "Sorry. There were two detectives just here. . . ." He shook his head.

"This must be hard for you. I understand you and Mariah Cox were engaged."

Bobby nodded. Then, becoming aware that Jury still stood while he sat, Bobby rose and pulled out one of the folding chairs leaning against the side of the stall. He opened it up, set it down for Jury, and sat back down again.

Jury thought it was an uncommonly thoughtful thing to do, in the circumstances. He sat down between daylilies and floribunda roses.

Bobby said, "We were going to get married in the fall, probably, and were going to live in my house. It's small, but fine for a couple. I bought it because of the gardens. There's over three acres. The old woman who lived there finally had to go into a nursing home. I felt really sorry for her because she loved the gardens. I told her—" He looked up. "Sorry. I'm talking to fill up space, I guess."

"Go on. I want to hear it."

Bobby sat back and relaxed a little. "I told her I loved flowers and plants and all that, that I did it for a living. She asked me if I knew anything about primulas, and I told her I know everything." He looked at Jury and smiled slightly. "Sounds conceited, but I do know an awful lot. When she took me out to the back, to the gardens, I was stunned by the variety of plants. Camellias dripping over old stone walls, a blue forest of hydrangeas and lavender and bluebells, even a rock garden. You don't see those much because they take such a lot of work. A huge spread of bright orange poppies. Even some mother-of-pearl poppies—a long sweep of them; it was lustrous.

"The thing was I'd visit her a couple of times a week for a few months, and she said it was such a relief knowing the house would be in my hands. I took flowers to her in the nursing home until she died. It was only a few months later that she died. I felt awful when she did. And I know I'm talking too much, but it keeps me from thinking." He stopped and regarded Jury.

"Where are you from, Bobby?"

"County Kerry. When my parents died I came to England. I worked at this and that, finally for a nursery, and then a series of nurseries. The last was in High Wycombe. I seem to have a natural bent for this kind of thing. I seem to speak the language of flowers, if that doesn't sound too sentimental."

Looking at all of these glowing colors and green leaves that seemed to want to burst beyond their crate and bucket boundaries, Jury believed it. "Did Mariah share your love of all this?" His gesture took in the stall.

"Yes, very much so. She knew a lot about flowers—" He stopped suddenly. The dead Mariah blotted out memory of the living one.

"You didn't know anything about a double life that Mariah might have been leading?"

"Double life?" He leaned down to reposition a large pot of hydrangeas and didn't look at Jury.

"Wouldn't you describe it that way? She was gone regularly to London and . . ."

Bobby put his hand on his forehead and pushed back his hair, as if he had a raging headache he couldn't get rid of. Probably he did. "The woman police found . . . she's just not like Mariah." He shook his head. "Mariah was so . . . retiring, that's the word I think of." He picked a few yellowing leaves from the stem of a lavender rose. "Funny about Edna. I would have known."

"Mrs. Cox? You mean you could have made the identification?"

He nodded. "I'd have known," he said again. "I know I just said she wasn't Mariah; I meant the idea of it. If I'd seen her, without hearing any of this, I'd have known her."

"Her aunt did know, on some level. It was a case of denial. I expect Mariah looked quite different, with that ginger hair, to allow anyone who didn't want to believe it, not to believe it."

Bobby nodded again. "Well, then, maybe I'd have done the same as Edna; I don't know. Nobody I know wanted to hurt Mariah, but the thing is, it might not be Mariah they wanted dead."

"What do you mean?"

"You spoke of a double life. It might've been the other one—that other self—the one you found. It could be the person who killed her didn't even know Mariah existed. Because I can't imagine anyone would want to hurt Mariah. That's it, plain and simple." He sat forward, elbows on knees, hands limply clasped, staring at the little bit of pavement not taken up by flower containers. He opened his mouth to say something but said nothing.

He looked helplessly at the big container of blue hydrangeas near his leg, as if their language had finally failed him.

9

Prada, Valentino, Fendi—Jury found himself in DS Cummins's house holding a whiskey and looking at a wall of shoes, cubbyhole after cubbyhole, designer after designer. In the corner beside this collection was a wooden coatrack holding a short red jacket (hers), a down-to-the-ground black wool coat (hers), and a rather worn-looking raincoat (either hers or his)—and all of them decidedly undesigner.

The shoes, though, would cover a painter's palette: rose red, blues that ran the gamut from cerulean to sapphire, silver straps of snakeskin, carmine straps of satin. There must have been a hundred pairs.

"It's an obsession, I expect you could say," said Chris Cummins with a good-natured laugh at herself.

David Cummins rolled his eyes. "It's her obsession all right."

But it can't be your money, thought Jury. If Mariah Cox's one pair of Jimmy Choos had been six or seven hundred, what must this collection be worth? DS Cummins couldn't afford this on his detective sergeant's salary; perhaps he was independently wealthy. Or she was. That was more likely.

Their modest cottage and its fittings were nowhere in line with Chris Cummins's shoes. The three-piece suite in front of the tile fireplace in the living room was covered with the rather clammy feel of microsuede. The curtains at the front windows were cotton splashed about with dahlias, gray blue on blue. Stuck about like matchstick displays were specimens of old reed chairs with turned or spindle legs that might have been antiques and possibly valuable.

That had been the front room—parlor (to the husband) or living room (to the wife). Jury detected the south of England in her speech, the north in his. Pretty far north, Newcastle north, possibly. He sounded much like Jury's cousin by marriage, Brendan. Someone here had money, he thought.

The shoes were in a small sitting room containing a large round table and four maple captain's chairs. It might have doubled as a dining room, with a wall of shoes in place of a wall of wine. Jury smiled.

"I knew it was Jimmy Choo," she said, "without seeing the label."

It was hard for Jury to fault Cummins's taking a police photograph out of the station, seeing that Chris would never wear any of these shoes to a policeman's hip-hop, or to tea at the Ritz, or on the Eurostar to Paris. Or skiing in the Alps. Chris was in a wheelchair. In the corner of the room, where those skis might have been leaning against the wall, were crutches instead.

She saw his look, looked herself at the crutches, and said, "I'm afraid I haven't mastered those. But I will." Her tone was exceptionally sad, but she quickly short-circuited this by wheeling over to the shoe collection. From her chair, she reached midway up the wall and took down a high-heeled shoe, a glittering nude-colored extravaganza, sequined and peep-toed. "Christian Louboutin. He's my favorite designer." It was actually quite beautiful, thought Jury.

"See the sole?" Her forefinger tapped it. She pulled down another, this one of black suede, its vamp consisting of a twist of material running like a lattice up and above the ankle. "Red, always red," she said. "I think that's clever. It's his signature—Louboutin's."

"They look pretty pricey."

"They're pricey all right." She shoved back the black-and-sequined numbers and dragged out another, a jeweled slingback. "Over a thousand pounds, this one."

Her husband winced. "Hell, Chris, the superintendent's going to think I've been on the take."

"What take? Is there anything around Chesham worth taking? There's nothing to take." As she pushed the red-soled shoe back, she sighed. "That murder is the most excitement we've had all the time we've been here."

"How long have you?"

David Cummins stretched out his long legs and then pulled them quickly back. It was as if he didn't want to call attention to his perfectly workable legs in front of his wife.

She hadn't noticed anyway, sitting in her wheelchair, drinking her tea.

"Just three years. I was with uniform before. South Ken. I expect I liked London a lot more than Chris—"

"I expect you did," said Chris with a small laugh. "It was never much good for a wheelchair."

There was no rancor in her voice, but there was still a message there.

And the expression on his face was oddly like that on Bobby Devlin's, as if David Cummins, too, missed a language that had meant a lot to him.

The cabbie who'd picked up Mariah Cox at the station told Jury no more than Cummins himself. Cummins had organized a meeting at the police station in Chesham.

"All dressed up like a dog's dinner, why, right off I thought she was headed to that swank party at Deer Park House. Took several fares there from other parts of town. So I was a mite s'prised when she said the Black Cat. Course, like I tol' 'er, I couldn't get to the pub's door. There's that roadworks out in front. Gone now, but it was a mess for a couple days, cars detourin' and business at the pub a shambles, and how she could walk in them high heels—" He shook his head, and that was all.

★ ★ ★

It was on the way to the train that Cummins told Jury about Chris. "It happened in London, Sloane Square. There are a lot of zebra crossings there, and drivers just bloody hate them. You can't assume they're going to stop. Chris doesn't assume, she insists. Pedestrians have the right of way, after all, so Chris just walks right on. Well, she did it this time, and the car didn't or maybe couldn't stop. It was going at a good clip. He hit Chris. But he did stop and call for an ambulance, so it wasn't a hit-and-run. He got nicked for it, huge fine and served some time. The thing is, Chris was pregnant and she had a miscarriage."

"God. How awful."

"Worse, we can't have kids now." He sighed and pulled up to the station. "Why can't drivers see that car crashes can be absolute bloody hell?"

Jury thought of Lu.

"We got a fairly hefty settlement out of it." Wanly, he smiled.

"Does that explain the shoe collection?"

"Oh, no. Or not wholly. Chris's family had money, quite a bit. She was always indulged, being the only child: nannies, good schools—that pricey one on the coast—and when she left there she could have gone to Oxford, Cambridge, you name it, but she chose not to. Instead, she married me." Bleakly, he smiled. "Some trade-off, right?"

"I'd say she got the best of the bargain, David."

That Jury's saying this pleased DS Cummins no end was very clear.

They sat in the car awhile, a no-parking zone in front of the station. Jury asked him if he'd lived all of his life in London. Was that why it seemed home to him?

"No. Northumberland's where I was born. We moved to the south, first to Portsmouth, then to Hastings. Mum loved the coast. Bit of a gypsy she was, liked moving. Hastings, Brighton, Bexhill-on-Sea, and back again. Drove poor Dad crazy." Cummins laughed, apparently in tune with the craziness.

"What kind of work did he do?"

"Greengrocer. Funny, isn't it? Back then I'd have done anything to get away from aubergines and apples. Now, I'm not so sure."

"You made the move from London because of Chris, then?"

Without answering directly, David said, "Well, you have to make small sacrifices, don't you? Like giving up my pack-a-day habit."

Jury gave a short laugh. "That's no small sacrifice. I know; I stopped three years ago myself."

David said after a pause, "I'm afraid I haven't done it yet. You know, the odd fag out behind the dustbins? Did you use any of the crutches—I mean, like those holders that let you down gradually? Or nicotine patches?"

"No. I always figured it was more than nicotine."

"Me, I'm waiting for a Stoli patch. Or a Guinness one. Something that'll really do me some good."

Jury laughed.

David went on, apparently fond of the subject. "It's hard for a woman, I mean, another person, a nonsmoker, to be around a guy who smokes. I guess a kiss doesn't taste right; it tastes of cigarettes."

Jury smiled. It sounded like a song by Cole Porter: *Your lips taste of cigarettes* . . . He said, "How romantic we once were about smoking. Remember *Now, Voyager*? Paul Henreid lighting up the two cigarettes? One for him, one for Bette Davis?" He looked at Cummins, assessing his age. "You probably weren't born yet."

"I'm no kid; I'm thirty-seven. But I've seen that film all right. It's great, except in the end. She could have had him; why didn't she take him?"

Jury thought but couldn't remember. "Well, as I remember it had a pretty grandiose moral tone. Most films did back then. Probably it had to do with honor."

"Bugger honor," said David with a grim smile.

10

Fifteen minutes later, Jury was on the Metropolitan Line train bound for London and talking on his mobile to Wiggins.

"Somebody's been spending a lot of money on Mariah Cox," said Jury. "There's got to be a well-heeled man in this mix somewhere." He hadn't meant the pun. "I've just been introduced to a world of shoes, Wiggins. By DS Cummins's wife, Chris."

"Shoes." Wiggins said it contemplatively rather than with curiosity. "You mean the Jimmy Choos?"

"His and others. I had no idea there were so many gorgeous women's shoes."

"Some are rather extreme."

Jury heard the sound of metal on metal. Spoon on kettle? No, Wiggins had gone off spoons. "Extreme? Which designer are you thinking of?"

Wiggins was silent for a few seconds. "Well, Jimmy Choo, for instance."

Slowly, Jury shook his head. "As I was saying, some man's been very generous with Mariah Cox." Too bad she hadn't just stuck to Bobby Devlin, he thought. "Or men."

"A bit sexist of you, guv." Before Jury could scathingly reply to that, Wiggins told him to hold on. "I'll be back in a second."

The train lurched for a moment, forcing the whey-faced child across the aisle back in her seat. She was probably eleven or twelve, and her empty brown eyes fastened on Jury like leeches. She should have been wearing a sign round her neck: "Nobody home." Jury stared back at her. He wasn't in the mood. "Wiggins? You there?"

No answer. The girl was chewing bubble gum and blew a big bubble right toward him, probably in lieu of sticking out her tongue.

The train shuddered to a stop at Rickmansworth. Wiggins came back from whatever expedition he'd been on. "I've liaised with all the divisional people. Talked to vice in case she's a pro—"

"Bit sexist of you, isn't it?" He smiled, and the smile accidentally took in the bubble-gum-blowing child, who stopped blowing and did stick out her tongue. "Anyway, I'm bound for London, going back to my flat. It's gone seven, Wiggins; why are you still at the Yard? Go home."

"Right, guv. I'm off. And you be sure and check your messages." There came a snuffling laugh.

Ha-ha, thought Jury as the train finally pulled away, heading into the City.

In the doorway of the small living room of Jury's Islington flat, Carole-anne Palutski, upstairs neighbor, stood rubbing her eyes as if he'd just dragged her down here from a deep sleep. The fact that she was dressed not in pj's and bathrobe but for a night on the tiles undercut the sleepy winsomeness. Her dress was a sapphire blue that matched her eyes; the neckline, low enough to sink a ship, was studded about with tiny bits of something flashy. In oilcloth and gum boots, Carole-anne would look sumptuous; the dress was gilding the lily. And in place of gum boots, she was wearing strappy sandals. They seemed to be the only thing on the streets these days.

Jury had called her in.

"Sit down, sweetheart. I want to read you something."

Daintily, she yawned and took her time arranging herself on his sofa. He thought of the gorgeous drift of hydrangeas in Bobby Devlin's flower stall. Gorgeousness, however, was not about to get her off. Jury unfolded the by now heavily creased scrap of paper and read phonetically: " 'S.W. c'd sed high w. ds rep. w'mn mss in Chess. Thought U should know.' "

Carole-anne just blinked at him. Then she said, " 'Thought you should know' what? The first part's gibberish. The way you read it, nobody'd know what it means."

"That's the way it's written."

"Don't be daft. Here, give it to me—" She reached out her hand. Her eyes, beneath eyebrows that fairly twinkled, scanned the scrap of paper. In a tone one might use for the recently comatose, she read, " 'Sergeant Wiggins called, said High Wycombe DS'—detective sergeant that means, I'd think you'd know that, at least—'reported woman missing in Chesham. Et cetera.' Perfectly clear."

"Of course it is to you. You wrote it. Let's begin with 'S.W.' Now how am I supposed to know who that is?"

Adjusting a couple of pearly bangles round her arm, she said with more than a little impatience, "Well, how many S.W.'s do you know, anyway?"

Hopeless, but Jury soldiered on: "The odd thing is you took the trouble to spell out 'Thought U should know,' but what I ought to know is written in code."

She rooted in her blue satin clutch and came out with a nail file. "The idea was this—"

No, it wasn't; there'd been no idea until she'd had these few moments to come up with one. "If by some chance a person—an unauthorized person—"

(That was good.)

"—were to get in here looking for classified information—"

"Like Jason Bourne, you mean."

"Him I don't know, but, okay, there's an example. If Jason were to get in here, he'd make straight for your personal phone book and message pad. He'd know all your business."

She seemed satisfied with that explanation, so he said, "Why did you leave it on the fridge door?"

There was a pause as she filed away at a troublesome bit of nail. "Well, I took the added precaution of taking it *off* the message pad;

see, no one would think, with the other stuff on the fridge, that there's an important message they'd want to read."

"Brilliant." He sat there looking at her looking smug. Then he said smoothly, "You forgot something."

That raised her eyebrows. "Such as what?"

"The impression." Pleased with her confusion, he got up and went to the phone table, returning with the message pad. "See this?" He tapped the blank page on which there was a faint image of penciled words. "Right there. Spies always do that; they look at the imprint left on the page underneath."

"They do?" The news did not bother her.

"Absolutely. Jason would have this sussed out in five seconds."

Carole-anne sighed, dropped her nail file into her bag, clicked the bag shut, and rose. "And you said no one could understand it." Then, in a swirl of sapphire and scent, she sashayed out of the room.

Jury listened to her strappy sandals tapping down the steps, got up, and, accompanied by his sturdy six-year-old self, stomped to his door and yelled down the stairs: "I'm not bloody Jason Bourne, am I?"

I I

The little girl standing uninvited by his table in the window was the untidiest Melrose had ever seen. More of a scrap than a girl, as if she were among the leavings of material cut away from a gown, a ragged piece, mere oddment. Her doe-colored eyes, large and clouded with tears either past or to come, were fastened on him as if he were expected to do something.

What could he do? He was only a middle-aged man—granted a rich one, he reminded himself, in case she wanted a house of her own in the Highlands or Belgravia so she could get away from this pub and her parents (of whom he'd seen no sign). So in what way could he serve this child who got left behind when Charles Dickens shut the book? She got tossed out of his pages, left to wander the narrow streets of Chesham, to pop in and out of pubs with a sign on her back: "Waif."

He had, amid these reflections, gone on reading—or pretending to—while the little Dickens revenant eyed him. Well, he should at least be nice enough to say, "Hi there," or, "And you're staring at me because . . . ?" No, that didn't set the right tone. How about, "My name is Melrose Plant, and you are . . . ?" But he was saved from coming up with something when she said:

"My cat was murdered."

That dropped his *Times* down! Surely it was not the child who had spoken. Surely it was the old woman at the corner table with the racing form, whose hand crept toward her half-pint. Or the old, rough-looking fellow with his equally rough-looking dog at one of the side tables.

"She got murdered or kidnapped."

He was forced to acknowledge her. "Well, that's rum, isn't it? You mean your cat died, is that it?"

A shake of her mousy brown head. "Murdered."

"That's really bad. How did it happen?"

She was full of the details, and having scored a listener, she said, "Maybe Sally took her to the cat hospital and they—" Here, she made a gesture of a hand with a needle plunging into flesh. The small finger came down hard on Melrose's jacket sleeve. "That's what." She stepped back.

The Black Cat, in Chesham, was short on customers save for he himself and the horse-betting woman and the surly man and dog, but then it had just gone eleven a.m. He had been finding this lack of custom supremely restful—this lack of complication—until the little girl dropped her cat on the table.

"Well, but that's not really murder," Melrose said loftily.

"If it happened to you, you'd say it was."

He frowned, looking for reason where there likely was none. "Was the cat sick?"

"Yes. I'm sick, too. You're probably sick. Everything's sick. Everybody is sick, but we don't get murdered for it."

That was on a lofty philosophical level Melrose didn't choose to ascend to. "The thing is—"

"She didn't want to die. She looked and looked at me and her eyes said it. She didn't want to."

This was getting to be a bit tangled. "So it *did* happen at the cat hospital."

Again she shook her head. "No. That was another time. Whoever killed her should go to jail and so should Sally."

"For how long?" *That* was an intelligent question.

"Forever. That's how long Morris will be gone. I have her picture.

Here—" From a pocket of her too-long skirt she pulled out a snap-shot, much creased, and handed it over.

The cat was bunched up on a table outside in the garden. The eyes, caught in the glare, were like white flames in the black face. The cat was all black. Of course, he thought, the pub cat, the Black Cat.

"Anyway, that's not the only way it could've been done. And don't forget the 'kidnapped' part, either."

There was no end to the cat's dreadful fate.

"Why would someone kidnap your cat?"

"Kidnapped or *murdered*." Her eyes looked feverish with this knowledge of thievery and murder.

Melrose hoped his smile wasn't too superior. "As for the murder, what you really mean is your cat was in an accident. Car ran into him or something?"

Again the pained eye squinch, the head shake. "*No*, I mean *murdered*." She was holding a soft stuffed animal, an unidentified primate of some sort, and now squashed it as if to demonstrate what mischief a pair of strangling hands might get up to. "Just like that lady they found." Her head tilted back. "Out there."

Ah! That explained it. She was extrapolating, extending the murder horizon to take in her cat. Just what a child might do. "But why would someone intentionally murder your cat?"

"Maybe because Morris saw what happened. I want a policeman." She stopped kneading her stuffed animal and dropped her sad eyes. "He got away."

Melrose was having difficulty following her constant shift of gears. "But then the cat must be alive somewhere." No letup of the staring eyes. "When did this happen?"

"Last night. Morris must've seen what happened on Saturday night and the murderer took her."

"Morris is a female?" He frowned.

The cat's gender was clearly not the point here. More was expected of this grown man. When she looked at him, Melrose knew just how one must have felt trying to get by the Sphinx without knowing the answer to that damned riddle.

Looking not a little Sphinx-like herself, she walked off to the bar and then behind it. Melrose watched her, or, rather, the top of her head, as she was too short to be seen on the other side. She rummaged, moved along, and rummaged some more until she found what she wanted; whereupon she marched back and solemnly handed over a chunky, cheap mobile phone. "I can't get anybody else to do it. Call the police."

Just then a band of sunlight struck the door now opening, as if God had tossed down this spear of light to make sure men would listen to the little girl, God's minister for Truth and Justice.

Melrose smiled and put down the phone. To the child he said, "It seems you've come to the right place."

12

Fate rarely returns from holiday. Coincidence seldom lives up to its name, but today, they did. Richard Jury walked in.

"Over here," Melrose called, as if the pub were teeming with customers and he were looking over a sea of faces.

"Sorry I'm late," said Jury. Then to the girl, "Hello." He stood there, very tall, looking down at her, very small, and closed the gap between them. "I like that monkey. I used to have one, but mine was blue." He removed his coat and sat down. "My name's Richard."

With hardly a blink, she took in the blue monkey, as if all monkeys were blue, save for hers, which earned it a doubtful look. "My name's Dora. Do you have a cat?" She moved closer.

"No, but there's one where I work."

Melrose was a bit miffed. She hadn't asked him if *he* had a cat. He did have a goat. "I have quite a good goat. Her name's Aghast."

They both looked at Melrose. What was he doing here?

Then away. Jury said, "I'll bet you have a cat. I saw one go by when I came in. A black cat in a huge hurry."

"That's not Morris. Sally wants me to think it is, but it's not."

"Did something happen to Morris?"

"Yes. I need a policeman."

"I'm a policeman."

Her mouth dropped open. She suddenly looked alight, as if a bulb inside her had switched on.

"So sit down here"—Jury pulled out a chair—"and tell me about it."

Dora was only too pleased to wrench herself up beside him, holding tight to the monkey.

It was a long story, longer than the one she had told Melrose, to whom she'd told only the salient facts. Salient fact, actually: Morris was either kidnapped or murdered.

With Jury, she was not so stingy. Children seldom were. Melrose checked his watch occasionally, in case the Ancient Mariner wanted to know the time.

She got round to Morris's replacement. "Anyone could tell that one's not Morris. Morris loves to lie and nap. The other one just runs around all the time."

At that moment, the outside door opened and several customers walked in. Then the blond woman, Sally Hawkins, whom Jury had talked to on the Monday night, emerged from an arched opening and went behind the bar. The customers all looked at each other as if they were wondering what beer was, while Dora continued to talk about her missing cat, Morris, and insisting the black cat who'd just crisscrossed the pub was not the real Morris.

"It's a fake."

"Oh, I don't know," said Melrose, "seems like a perfectly serviceable black cat."

Both Jury and Dora stared at him.

"Can you find him?" Her small face was a study in worry.

Jury appeared to be considering this. He said, "I think so." Then, seeing Melrose tapping his watch, said, "I'd like a beer."

"I'll get it," Dora chimed. "What kind?"

Jury inclined his head toward Melrose's pint. "Whatever he's drinking."

"Guinness," said Melrose.

Dora flew to the bar.

The black cat, Morris Two, who'd come back in from the nowhere he seemed to inhabit, flew after her.

"Are we still going to Bletchley Park?" asked Melrose. This had been the reason for their meeting here.

"I don't see why not. It's only a half hour away. We can take the A5." It was Sir Oswald Maples that had got Jury interested in the code-breaking machines. "We can leave when we're done here."

Sally Hawkins, having served the group at the bar, listened to Dora's order and drew the beer. She stood hands on hips, waiting for the top on the Guinness to settle, then knifed the surface and carried the pint to the table.

Dora's disappointment at not being allowed to serve Jury was evident. She set about getting crisps.

The blonde was still pretty in middle age and would have been prettier still had she a more pleasant temperament.

"Has Dora been telling you that story about her cat?" She set down the pints.

"Yes. What happened?"

She lowered her voice. Perhaps she could feel Dora behind her. "Nothing happened. She's got it in her mind that Morris isn't Morris. I honestly don't know what to do about her."

And why, wondered Jury, are you bothering to tell us this?

Dora, several feet behind her, clamped her lips shut and, looking at Jury and Plant, slowly shook her head back and forth, back and forth. When the blond woman turned and saw her, Dora smiled and held up the crisps. "It's salt-and-vinegar ones." She distributed the crisps and left again on another mission.

"Anything else, gentlemen?" asked Sally Hawkins. They shook their heads, and with her tray under her arm, Sally left.

"Is she the owner?"

Jury shook his head. "Sally Hawkins. She's taking care of the place while her friends are on holiday. Her relationship to Dora is somewhat vague."

Now Dora returned and placed before Jury a different dog-eared little snapshot of the black cat curled asleep atop one of the tables in the garden. "This is Morris."

They both looked at the picture.

"That's Morris's favorite spot—on that table outside. She likes to sun herself. Sometimes she even likes it out there at night."

Jury smiled. "I believe I must've run into Morris the other evening."

Dora was wide-eyed. "You did? How—" But she was interrupted just then by the other black cat (if it was indeed the "other") hurrying by. "That cat's a lot thinner than Morris. You can tell from the picture, Morris is fatter."

"How can we?" said Melrose. "The cat's bunched up like a doughnut."

After telling them both he'd be back in a second, Jury went to the bar where Sally Hawkins was talking to a thin reed of a man. "If I could just have a word, Miss Hawkins." To the man he said, "Sorry to interrupt."

"Go on, Reg," said Sally.

Reg was quick to move off to a table on the other side of the room.

Jury said, "I don't know if you've heard about the identity of the dead woman—"

"We was just talking about it," she whispered. "Mariah Cox, is what police said. I never knew her, except she works in the library."

"You saw her at the library."

"Only just."

"Meaning?"

"Well, Dora and me, we checked out some books, right? And it was her, at least I think it was, only she had dark hair and was kind of plain, then."

"You saw her just that once?"

Sally was obviously hard put to answer. "Maybe another time, yeah; I went with Dora a couple times, I guess."

"Nothing wrong with that. And you didn't recognize the dead woman as Mariah Cox?"

"God, no! I'd've said, wouldn't I?"

"I'm sorry. We ask questions again and again in the hopes of a witness recalling some detail. I know it's tiresome."

She was prepared to be generous. "I expect you're just doing your job."

Jury leaned toward her, put his hand on her arm. "Look, Sally—keep your eyes and ears open, will you? The way you're positioned here, I mean in the pub, you might hear something. You know the way people talk after they've had a few." He took a card from his pocket and placed it in front of her. "Anytime, don't hesitate to call."

This increase in intimacy was not lost on Sally Hawkins. She ran her hand over her hair and smiled at him.

Jury returned the smile, patted her arm, and went back to the table where Melrose was talking to Dora, or rather arguing with her, given the frown on her face. She looked relieved when he sat down.

"You'll find her, won't you?" said Dora, her two fingers pleating the arm of Jury's jacket.

"Morris? We'll do our best."

That didn't sound like top-notch investigation to Dora, who reluctantly left their sides at Sally's insistence.

Melrose said, "I can tell you right now what happened: A woman's been murdered right on Dora's doorstep, so to speak, and young Dora, unable to accept this awful event, substitutes her cat as the victim. She can handle the thing that way; she sublimates the actual killing because it's too frightening to be believed. It's called displacement. You take something out of its usual context and put it down in another context. In this case: Morris. Morris takes on all of the dread that would have been felt for the murdered woman." Melrose was rather proud of this theory. "So what do you think?"

"About Morris? Morris was either kidnapped or murdered." Jury drank his beer.

13

They took both cars, and Melrose insisted that Jury follow him.

"Why?"

"In case my car breaks down."

"Your car is a Rolls-Royce. My car is a Vauxhall of questionable provenance with a million miles clocked. Now, which car is more likely to break down?"

"Mine." Melrose turned on the engine. It thrummed like Yo-Yo Ma's cello.

"Oh, my, yes. The rattle and clang's enough to deafen you."

"I'll wait for you," called Melrose to Jury's departing back. And again: "Don't forget we're stopping if we see a Little Chef."

Twenty miles on, well past Leighton Buzzard, they came to one, and Melrose pulled off the road and into the car park.

The Little Chef was crisp and bright as if the whole place had just been polished. It looked pleased with its black-checkered self.

Melrose studied the menu.

Jury didn't bother. "I can tell you what's on it; I've seen it often enough."

"I like looking."

"While you're doing that, let me tell you about the Rexroths' party, where, I'm pretty sure, the murdered woman was going." Jury did so, including the guest list.

"You're kidding. Harry Johnson was at that party?"

"He was on the list. Whether he was actually there is in question."

"The house isn't far from the Black Cat?"

"I'm not jumping to the conclusion that he knew her."

"No, you're merely jumping to the conclusion that he murdered her."

"Don't be daft."

"Daft? You're absolutely delighted you have some reason to go after Harry Johnson again. Ah, here's our waitress."

The waitress, whose name tag said "Sonia," came over on squeaky rubber soles and with a huge, not-meaning-it smile. "Ready, are we?"

"No."

"Yes." Jury pointed to the paint-bright picture of the plate he wanted.

Melrose said, "I'll have pancakes with sausages." The waitress left and he said, "As you are now confronted with a murder and a vanished, perhaps murdered, cat, why are we going to Bletchley Park?"

"Because of Sir Oswald Maples."

"He asked you to go?"

"No. Because the mysterious workings of code breaking in World War Two interest me, and he's an expert on the subject, and I'd just like to be able to talk about it."

Jury watched a family of at least a dozen people enter and secure three tables pushed together. They were all fat. "If you didn't want to see Bletchley Park, why did you come?"

"Simple. Because it's near Milton Keynes, and that's only fifty miles from home, and I thought we'd be spending most of the day at Ardry End swilling my single malt whiskey, after which we'd go to the Jack and Hammer and swill some more."

"Sorry, but I can't take you up on that invitation. I've got to get back to London."

Melrose was disappointed. "It's a long time since you've been to my place."

"Yes, a whole month."

Sonia was back setting down their plates.

Jury started in on his eggs.

"Um, um," murmured Melrose, mouth full of syrupy pancakes. He ate a few bites and said, "I'm intrigued by your murder victim's clothes."

"So am I." Jury picked up a triangle of buttered toast and wondered which point to start on. Sonia, he noticed, was watching them as if they'd both walked in with tire irons and nasty intentions.

"Well, if our unidentified victim could afford that dress and those shoes . . . ," Melrose began.

"Jimmy Choo. How can women wear heels four inches high? These shoes, according to Detective Sergeant Cummins, would have cost around six or seven hundred quid."

"And that's a sandal?"

"All straps." Jury smiled. "Strappy, you say."

"I don't say it. How does Detective Sergeant Cummins come by such arcane knowledge?"

"It's hardly arcane. Jimmy's popular. It's Mrs. Cummins, our sergeant's wife, who knows this stuff; she's a woman who's really into designer shoes. The dress cost—get this—around three thousand quid. That's Yves Saint Laurent. The handbag by Alexander McQueen cost another thousand. It's mind-boggling."

"Astonishing. What item of clothing could possibly be worth it?"

Jury looked at him. "What did that jacket you're wearing set you back?"

Melrose looked down as if surprised to see he wasn't wearing sackcloth and ashes. "This rag?" He shrugged.

"Bespoke. Your old tailor. Don't tell me it didn't cost as much as her dress."

"Don't be ridiculous. The point is: is prostitution so well paid a woman can buy that stuff?"

"Who says she's that?" Jury bit down on his toast, nearly cold and slightly burnt.

"Come on. Woman leading a 'second life' in London, goes from Chesham librarian to London Saint Laurent?"

Jury reached across the table and speared one of Melrose's sausages.

"Hey! Get your own! You should have a look in this woman's cupboard to see the rest of her wardrobe. Is she filthy rich? Even so, what does it say about her that she'd spend that kind of money on shoes? Self-indulgent, spoiled, egocentric . . ."

Jury chewed slowly and looked at him.

"What? . . . What?"

"Well, there you go, working up a stereotype."

"I'm not stereotyping; I'm . . . profiling."

"Then you're one sorry profiler. Typical of the male ego, he would find such extravagance joined either to prostitution or to a spoiled, shallow, self-indulgent woman, when there are certainly other viable interpretations, the least of which would explain this behavior. We're making too much of the lady's extravagance. After all, some women spend money like they're minting it. If they didn't, the entire fashion industry would go down."

"Then you don't think these Jimmy Choo shoes are important?"

"Of course I do. The shoes and the dress are very important. But I wouldn't think twice if I saw them at the Albert Hall. It's finding them in the grounds of the Black Cat that's interesting."

"And everything points to her having been killed where she was found? I mean, that she wasn't transported there?"

"Everything: beginning with lividity, to the arterial blood-splatter, to the onset of rigor mortis, to an examination of the ground beneath the body to determine the amount of blood that soaked into it—everything."

"Oh, you're just guessing."

In Bletchley Park, they stood looking down at this machine that was no bigger than a typewriter, the genius machine that had broken the German Navy's Enigma code.

"Imagine," said Jury, "billions of possibilities—"

"I'd rather not, I'm having a hard enough time imagining dinner. So this could encipher messages?"

★ ★ ★

Jury nodded. "Scramble plaintext into ciphertext." He bent his head closer to it. "This machine had been commercial, you know, I mean used for other purposes. It was just that the Germans realized its potential for encrypting messages."

"So this was what Oswald Maples worked on."

"This or those." Jury turned to look at the other machines housed here in what used to be the huts occupied by experts in codes and ciphers. "That's what this arm of the War Ministry was called: GC&CS, Government Code and Cypher School. Cribs were largely guesses, guessing a word would appear in a message because past messages had used it so much. Say you sent a lot of messages to Agatha where the word 'idiot' popped up all the time."

"I'm with you so far."

"Anyone then reading a new message from you to Agatha would figure that the word 'idiot' would appear in the message. Thereby making it easy to decipher the message."

"It sounds extremely complex."

"It is. The Enigma machine had the capacity to make billions of combinations."

"You're really into this code and cipher stuff; you and Sir Oswald must get along like a house on fire."

"We do." Jury was by the large machine called the bombe, bending down to read the explanatory material. "This is interesting; this one didn't prove a particular Enigma setting; it disproved every incorrect one."

Hands behind him, Melrose leaned back on his heels and thought about it. "But wouldn't it amount to the same thing? Wouldn't you be doing that anyway?"

"What?"

"Proving. To prove a thing is, you'd be disproving what it's not."

"No. If that were the case, this bombe wouldn't be disproving other possibilities."

"Hold it." Melrose pushed out his hand like a traffic cop. "You're begging the question. You're saying the bombe disproves because it disproves. That's no argument."

"It isn't the way you're putting it."

"Okay, forget that. I don't see how you can disprove something without assuming a proof. Take the black cat, for instance—"

"Which one?"

"Ah! That's my point. Right now, to our knowledge there are two black cats."

"Oh, I believe that, but—"

"Let me finish."

Jury folded his arms across his chest. "Are you going to wipe out two years of Alan Turing's work here?"

"The cats are Morris One, Dora's cat; Morris Two, the pretender cat. To our knowledge, there are two because we've been told there are. Anything else is deduction. In order to prove Morris One is Dora's cat, we have to disprove number two is not."

"Can we continue this argument later? I've got to get back to London."

Melrose threw up his hands. "A detective superintendent and you don't get it!"

They were walking toward the door. "I don't get a lot of things. I particularly don't get how it is you know more than Alan Turing."

"It's a cross I bear. So, in your greater wisdom, was Morris murdered or kidnapped?"

"Kidnapped."

"Just how do you work that out?"

"How would I have worked my way up to detective superintendent if I couldn't?"

14

Mungo, sitting several feet from a kitchen door in a house in Belgravia, listened to the voice of Mrs. Tobias coming from the kitchen. *Yelling* from the kitchen was more like it.

"Look what you've done, my lad! Ruined my good cake! Haven't I told you—"

Here, "my lad" came running from the kitchen, giggling, chocolate cake still in his hand and on his mouth.

This was the ignominious Jasper, who was the most loathsome child Mungo had ever known. He was twelve, and if Mungo had anything to do with it, he'd never see thirteen. Jasper had been visiting for a week while his mum and new stepfather were on their honeymoon—a romantic getaway to Blackpool—and now it was to be another week relaxing at home in Bayswater before collecting Jasper. So the boy was destined to stay here another week, but a new destiny could always be arranged, thought Mungo darkly.

The kitchen door swung open again, and Mrs. Tobias came into the dining room, one of his little Matchbox cars in her hand. "And get these things out of my kitchen!" She stood in the dining room, calling into empty air, "One more of your tricks and you'll be out of here, my lad, honeymoon or no honeymoon!" The silver car, like a gauntlet, was thrown down. "Why, if Mr. Harry ever slid on one of these, you'd be out of this house quick as a wink."

Jasper had a dozen of these Corgi cars. They were always underfoot, and Mrs. Tobias, walking upstairs, had stepped on one and nearly landed downstairs on her head but just managed to grab at the banister in time. Jasper liked to roll them at Mungo and the cat Schrödinger when they slept. Mungo was sick of cars hitting him on the nose.

Jasper Seines. The name was like a sneeze or a hiss. Yes, he was going to have to do something about Jasper Seines.

He sloped off to have a dekko at Schrödinger's kittens, still sleeping in the bottom drawer of the bureau in the music room. They were all sprawled out, including Elf, who was Mungo's favorite, but now almost too big to be carried around by the skin of his neck, although Schrödinger managed to do it.

It was time Jasper Seines went. What surprised Mungo was that Harry hadn't bumped him off. He had seen Harry cast truly malevolent looks at the boy, but Harry was taking the gentlemanly approach (and Harry was always *that*) by merely suggesting to Mrs. Tobias, his housekeeper and sometime cook, that Jasper Seines must be missing school. Hint, hint, nod, nod, wink, wink. But Mrs. Tobias wasn't one to pick up a hint and a nod, so Harry might hand her a broader message by kicking Jasper Seines down the cellar stairs.

Mungo looked over the kittens as if they were licorice allsorts. He saw one was even smaller than Elf and was about to pick it up when Schrödinger padded over to scotch *that* particular bit of fun. Schrödinger was as black as squid's ink and with almost as many appendages, or so it seemed, when she started routing Mungo.

He sent her the message Don't be daft. I'm not doing anything. She stared at him round-eyed, refusing to return a message, probably feeling it beneath her.

So into this voiceless habitation came Jasper Seines. "Well, well, well, wot's all this, then?" doing his imitation of some beat copper. Then suddenly, like a magician grabbing an object out of the air, he yanked up one of the kittens by its tail. The little thing screeched, and this earned Jasper Seines an attack from both sides: Schrödinger clawing his leg and Mungo sinking his teeth into the boy's ankle.

"You little fuckers! Get offa me!" ·

The kitten dropped back into the drawer, and Jasper Seines yelled and, unable to shake off Mungo, yelled some more. Finally released, he ran crying to Mrs. Tobias; tears went flying from his doughy face as if even they wanted to get as far away from Master Seines as they could.

Neither Schrödinger nor Mungo subscribed to that old saw about my enemy's enemy. Nonetheless, Mungo thought, if they worked together (for once), they might be able to get rid of Jasper Seines.

Schrödinger jumped into the drawer to see that no other devilment befell her brood; Mungo left the music room and went clicking across the gorgeously polished hardwood floor to sit near the kitchen and take in what was going on.

Tearily, Jasper Seines was denying any action on his part. "No, I never done nuttin'. . . ."

"My patience is wearing thin, my lad."

Mungo sighed. Mrs. Tobias was nobody's fool.

"Aw right, I'd as soon go home! I don't like it here!"

What a nasty nephew. But what a promising bit of conversation. Now all Mungo had to do was give this beastly child a little nudge out the front door.

Afternoon was drawing in and Mungo had his eye on his favorite spot, underneath a small wrought-iron bench in the rear garden. There was a doghouse, too, but he wouldn't bother himself.

Trotting toward the bench, he could already feel the cool grass against his stomach, the feathery shade made by the thin and delicate fronds of a willow, moving in the breeze.

That's why he was brought up smartly by finding his spot occupied by a black cat calmly snoozing there, not bothered by the traffic blaring its way along Upper Sloane Street. The cat lay with its front paws hooked around its chest, in that deft way of cats. It looked like a loaf of pumpernickel.

Carefully, Mungo crept closer to the bench and sat down far enough away that the cat would miss him if he woke suddenly and took a swipe at Mungo. The cat slept on, sensing nothing. For one crazy moment, he thought it might be Schrödinger. It was just as black, certainly, and looked just like her, except for the bright blue collar round the stranger's neck.

Mungo pulled a pebble from beneath a tree and aimed it toward the cat. The pebble rolled against a paw, but the cat only twitched its nose before it resettled itself even more deeply into pumpernickel posture. This was irritating. If someone hit *him*, Mungo, with a pebble, he'd be off the ground and flailing. He jumped onto the bench, from which position he could watch the cat through the wrought-iron interstices of the seat. There were large openings in the fussy scrollwork through which he could reach his paw, but he couldn't reach the cat.

He could bark to wake the cat up, but he didn't like to bark; barking was a last-ditch effort. Mungo hopped down from the bench and moved around to where he was before. He lay down, his head on his paws, his gaze level with the cat's closed eyes. When the cat woke, he would be startled; it would be fun.

The cat's eyes opened so slowly, they seemed not to move. Mungo raised himself to a sitting position, leaned on one paw, then the other, back and forth as if getting ready to make a dash.

The cat yawned.

That annoyed him. Mungo was, after all, a dog. He pricked up his ears: the cat was sending him a message:

I hope I'm not dead and you're not heaven.

Mungo took a startled step back. He wasn't at all sure that message was complimentary. He sent a message back: No, it's not heaven; it's Belgravia, though some here would argue there's a difference. Who are you?

Morris.

The cat shoveled its rear end back and assumed one of those sloping Zen-like stretches that cats were so good at. Even Schrödinger looked agile in that butt-to-sky pose.

Do you live around here? asked Mungo. I mean in one of these other houses? Because this is my garden.

Morris lay back down in the paws-to-chest position that Mungo envied.

No, I live off somewhere.

That's not going to get you far. You don't even know the name of the place?

Never thought I'd have to know. I never thought I'd be kid-napped before. The slow-blinking eyes blinked again.

Kidnapped! Wow! That was supposed to have happened to Mungo once, but it hadn't. That story was Harry's invention. If there was one thing Harry was good at, it was making up stories and otherwise lying.

You mean honest-to-God kidnapping? Or do you know Harry?

Harry who?

Never mind. (Less said the better.) You don't know where you were kidnapped from? Or to?

It'll come back to me. I know it's a pub. One minute I was on my table in the pub gardens, having a kip. There I lay until someone jerked me up and started roughing me around. Then I was in a car. Then I don't remember.

What pub is it?

I think it's called the Black Cat. Once in a while a customer would remark on me being the pub's cat and wasn't that clever? Clever. I ask you. Anyway, I'm not. My owner's name is Dora.

Go on.

Well, I'm wandering about outside looking for field mice, and I come across a person lying on the patio where the tables are.

Mungo sat straight up, big-eyed.

It didn't move, this person. I sniffed all around and smelled some-thing like blood, I think.

Blood! Mungo could feel the small stiff hairs rise along his spine. He would like to be a bloodhound.

It must've been a dead body.

I expect so. Then I saw an old woman coming along with a fat dog and ran back inside the pub. Do you have anything to eat? I'm really hungry. A nice piece of fish would go down a treat. Of course, I'd take anything.

Mungo was thinking furiously. *I'm going in for a bit.*

Back to the house? Will you come back?

Yes. I'll bring some food. You stay here. I won't be long.

The rear door was open, as it often was off the latch in good weather. Mungo hated the dog door because he was afraid of getting stuck in it. All he needed to do here was get a paw in between door and doorjamb and pull.

Mrs. Tobias was busy arranging thin cucumber slices on a cold salmon. "Mungo! Where have you been?"

Mrs. Tobias always sounded surprised to see Mungo was still living here. "This is for your master's dinner. Doesn't it look nice?"

My what? Was she kidding?

"He does like his bit of salmon."

I'd like my bit, too.

Mrs. Tobias went twittering on about cooking this and that and sounded settled in forever with the cucumber decoration. She was opening a jar of pimiento when the telephone rang from somewhere deep in the house.

The blessed telephone! That should keep her busy, she was such a talker.

He raced out to the dining room, knowing exactly where that Corgi car had fallen when Mrs. Tobias had flung it. He picked it up in his teeth and made his way back to the kitchen. From the hallway came the sound of Mrs. Tobias on the phone: talk, talk, talk, talk.

Back to the kitchen he went. He was up to the chair, then to the stool, and then to the kitchen counter. Mrs. Tobias's cold salmon lay on a long china plate on the counter. Its eye was a circle of black olive; its scales, the overlapped cucumber slices.

He deposited the little silver car with its nose to the pepper grinder, then knocked over the grinder for good measure. Delicately, he put his teeth around the lower part of the salmon with its cucumber garnish. Carefully, he slid down to the floor and carefully held his head high so as to keep the salmon intact. Then, just as carefully, he was out the back door.

He dropped the salmon and a cucumber slice in front of Morris.

They were in a little clearing within the bushes defined by a box hedge. Morris had been eyeing two wrens having a clamorous talk. When Morris saw the fish, she nearly fell on it, eating as if she were inhaling it. Including the cucumber.

Mrs. Tobias had, of course, returned to the kitchen and half a salmon and was yelling for Jasper, calling out, "This is it, my lad! You go in the morning!"

Who's Jasper? asked Morris between bites.

A thing of the past, answered Mungo. He was mightily pleased. Hello, Morris. Good-bye, Jasper.

When she'd finished the salmon, Morris thanked Mungo with great enthusiasm and began washing her face. He wanted to hear the rest of the story, which was the best he'd heard since Harry tried to convince the Spotter—Oh, but that was for another time.

Now, tell me the rest. You stopped when this old woman came along. Mungo settled in to listen. He tried to fold his paws into his chest and couldn't. So he just stretched his legs out.

Morris lay down, easily curving her paws. Well, she didn't scream, exactly, but she made some kind of noise. Her dog was yapping; it was enough to wake the dead. Then she put a leaf against her ear and—

A leaf? What do you mean?

Everybody has them. You've seen people with leaves; they're always talking to them. People just can't let leaves alone. Sometimes I'd be on my window seat, napping, when customers would sit down and right away pull out a leaf and talk, talk, talk—

I get the idea.

—talk, talk, talk. Do you think there's anybody on the other end?

I think maybe it doesn't make any difference to them. Mungo stretched out, feeling quite philosophical. Back to the pub: what did the old woman say to the leaf?

She said for someone to come quick. There was a body.

Was she talking to the Spotters? You know, the ones who go nosing around whenever there's a dead body. Some of them are Uniforms and some of them are something else. I call them Spotters.

I guess that's who came, finally. There was a big commotion

around the body. They took a lot of pictures. Why anyone would want pictures of a dead body, I don't know.

Then what happened?

Nothing until the cars came. People messed about.

How did you get here, then?

In a car, I guess, but that was days later. I think I was gassed.

Mungo would have said it was the strangest tale he'd ever heard, except for what had happened to him, or at least what was supposed to have.

Now, the only person who really notices Schrödinger is Mrs. Tobias. Harry is too bogged down in his own mind to pay any attention. So there's no reason why you couldn't live here and pretend you're Shoe. After all, one black cat looks pretty much like another.

Morris wasn't sure she liked that. But what if we appear together at the same time? And I have this collar, too. Does your cat wear one?

No. We'll be on the lookout, won't we? Anyway, Mrs. Tobias is old and she'd just think she was seeing double. You can make anyone think they're bonkers except for the ones who really are.

Morris sat up, paws placed neatly on the grass. Mungo sat up too and tried to get his paws that way, but he couldn't. Come on.

But Morris didn't move except to pick up a paw and set it down, pick up the other one and set it down, in the way Mungo himself had done if he didn't know what to do.

I want to go home, said Morris.

Mungo felt sad, as homesickness seemed to fill the place that hunger had just left.

Really, said Morris.

Mungo didn't know how to send a message back, with that.

15

Wasn't it possible, Jury wondered, looking down at his telephone message pad on this late Thursday morning for Carole-anne Palutski to write in the King's English? And hadn't they pretty much exhausted this subject? Apparently not, for here was another one:

"S.W. c'ld t' tell you the b.c. w'mn was i.d. by o'nr of ag'cy c'd ♥."

A heart. Was something called "Heart"? No. Was Valentine's Day coming up? No. It was May. "Sergeant Wiggins called to tell you—" That much was clear. Of course, what wasn't clear was the point of what S.W. called to tell you, right?

Hell. Jury picked up the receiver and punched in his office number. No answer. He mashed the receiver into the cradle (he had a telephone left over from the Pleistocene age), collected his keys, and left the flat.

"'Heart.' That's funny, guv." Wiggins gave a spluttery laugh.

Jury stitched his lips shut to keep from yelling. "Then do you think you could enlighten me as to what 'heart' means here?"

"Sorry. What that refers to is Valentine. Valentine's Escorts. Mariah wasn't exactly soliciting the curb crawlers in Shepherd Market, see. She was with an escort service. A little more respectable, maybe, but still pros. Valentine's has offices in Tottenham Court Road."

At last. "Good for you, Wiggins. I forgive you the message."

"Nothing wrong with the message. It's the one who took it you should have a word with." Wiggins said this self-righteously.

"I have had a word. A word does not penetrate. How did you work it out about this escort agency?"

"Well, I didn't, did I? It was her flatmate called us—"

"Adele—I think Edna Cox said."

"Yeah, that's right." Wiggins whipped out his notepad. "Adele Astaire. There's a name for you. Adele said she'd only just now seen the paper and that she was sure it must be Stacy."

Jury waited. But Wiggins didn't continue. "Stacy? Is there a surname to go with that?"

"What? Oh. Stacy Storm. There's another name, right? That's Mariah Cox, when she's at home. I mean, literally. 'When she's at home.'"

Wiggins thought this extremely funny. Jury didn't. "Look, can you just stick to it?"

"Sorry. I bet Adele Astaire's not *her* real name, either. Maybe working for an escort service, they don't want to give out their names."

Jury didn't comment. "Where's Adele live? Mariah's aunt said Parsons Green or Fulham."

"Fulham. You want to go and see her?"

"Of course." Jury extended his hand. "Give me that." When Wiggins handed over the paper on which he'd written the address, Jury said, "You get onto this Valentine's place. Take that list of names the Rexroths gave me with you. The person who runs Valentine's—"

"That's a Blanche Vann. But she's going to scream client privilege and make me get a warrant."

"Probably. Nevertheless, what you'll want to do is match up names, the names of the men at the Rexroths' party who came without women on their arms, against any such names on Valentine's list."

"Her clients would likely change their names, wouldn't they?"

"Some would, yes. Assuming that Ms. Vann is helpful at all, if the full names don't ring a bell, then try just the first names. A person might change the last name but leave the first in place."

Wiggins had the list out and studied the names. He said, "Here's a Simon; Simon's a common name. She's bound to have a few of those."

"Depends how many clients she has. But if a surname is being disguised, it could be the person comes up with an absurdly common substitute, like 'Jones.' So 'John Jones' would be a red flag." Jury was up and getting into his raincoat, which he liked. He liked rain, too. "Adele . . . ," he said in a musing way. "Doesn't she know that was Fred's sister?"

Wiggins was dropping a teabag in his mug as the electric kettle hissed and burbled. His lunch waited beside his tea mug. It was something peculiar-looking wrapped in what appeared to be a cabbage leaf and purchased at Good Earth, a tiny healthy-eats place nearby that Jury had never patronized and never would. "Guv?" He frowned.

"Fred Astaire. His sister was his dancing partner for years."

Wiggins poured steaming water into his mug. "We used to do the same thing." He was sitting down, reflecting, stirring his tea like the old Wiggins.

"What?" What was he talking about?

"My sister. Me and my sister, B.J.—Brenda Jean's her name. We used to dance a lot."

Jury stood in the doorway, trying to get his mind around that. Or trying not to. "Wiggins, this is Fred *Astaire* we're talking about."

"Right. The tap dancer," said Wiggins.

Jury chewed his lip to keep from talking. Then he was out the door.

16

"Adele Astaire?"

Over the key chain, she nodded. Or the half of her face he could see did. The half looked rather young to be employed by an escort service. "I'm Richard Jury, Scotland Yard CID." He held out his ID.

She slid back the chain and opened the door and took the ID as if it were a calling card. She studied it, frowning, as though trying to memorize the fact of it before she handed it back.

Jury found the close scrutiny amusing. Rarely did people do more than glance at it.

"Well, you better come on in, then." Her tone was more friendly than resentful of this detective on her doorstep.

Now he could see all of Adele Astaire—not her real name, as she was quick to tell him, apparently embarrassed by her made-up one—and she still looked a lot younger than she must be. She wore her brown hair in bunches, with an uneven fringe that she scraped this way and that on her forehead. Her cotton dress was pinaforelike, pink and white stripes that made it a little hard to discern the figure beneath it. He hadn't seen anything like it in years; she must buy her clothes at some retro shop. On her feet were furry slippers.

Her flat was neat and furnished with worn chairs and a small cream-colored sofa. On the shelves of a built-in arched bookcase were some Beatrix Potter figurines—he recognized Benjamin Bunny, for he had had one as a child. On a small table by a chair stood a Paddington Bear lamp.

"It's really Rose, Rose Moss," she said. "People call me Rosie, mostly."

Jury smiled, thinking of one of the little girls they'd rescued from the Hester Street operation. And then he stopped smiling, remembering the cupboard full of little clothes, miniature versions of the costumes he imagined this Rosie might have in her own cupboard. Hester Street had been a pederast ring. That tiny girl's name had been Rosie, too.

Rosie said, "Blanche Vann—she runs the place where I work—says we're to have phony names to make us untraceable. Like we couldn't have clients coming round or ringing us in the middle of the night, could we?"

Untraceable. No matter how clear the prints of the Jimmy Choo shoes, they might not lead to the killer.

Rosie was giving him a great deal of unasked-for information. He'd said nothing about where she worked. Now she continued.

"I just thought, you know, Rosie was kind of unsophisticated. You know, childish."

Which fit her perfectly, for it was the way she looked, childlike, and the way she coiled an errant lock of dark hair round her finger. No makeup. Skin as pale and smooth as sand left by receding waves. Startled brown eyes; small, neat nose.

"Thing is," she went on to say after they were seated on the sofa, and as if she'd read his mind, "I'm popular with the clients who've got these little-girl fantasies, you know what I mean."

Yes. They're a step away from pederasty. Again, he thought of Hester Street.

"I can dress up—I've got like schoolgirl costumes—"

Jury thought she would have been a knockout as a child. He felt himself flush at such a thought. And he wondered if pederasts saw the woman in the child, the child holding the woman at bay. A strange inversion of woman and child.

"But of course, I can be an adult, too, if required." She lit a cigarette.

What a bleak statement. But he had to smile at the way she was processing her cigarette, blowing smoke out in little puffs, off to the side so as not to blow it his way. She did this in the way Bette Davis did it. No one smoked the way Bette Davis had smoked. *All About Eve.* "*I ran all the way.*" Phyllis Nancy, rain-soaked, in his doorway, saying that. Lu Aguilar. The crashed car. Jury tried to shut it all out.

". . . nervous. You know."

He'd missed her first few words. "Nervous?"

"You being Scotland Yard. Being here."

"Please don't be. It's only routine. We just need your help with information about Stacy—the name she was using, Stacy Storm." What sadly affected made-up names. "Mariah Cox was her real name."

"I know. But I can't see how I'll be much help."

"Your friendship with her could be important. You'd be surprised at how sparse the information has been on her."

Rosie picked up her glass, whiskey or tea, rattled the ice cubes in it. "I don't know as I'd call it friendship, exactly; I mean, she never talked, well, hardly ever talked about her other life."

"Well, mates, then."

Her accent was a little rough around the edges, a little nasal, a far cry from Chelsea or Knightsbridge, more Brixton, perhaps. She could relate to "mates."

"Yeah, mebbe. You could say. We worked together, I mean for the same firm."

"This is Valentine's?"

She shrugged. "Yeah. Nothing to tell except that I think they treated the girls fair. I been working there years."

"You don't look old enough."

"Now, how old do you think I am?" She stubbed out her cigarette.

Jury shrugged, generously guessing, "Twenty?"

That went further than two dozen roses would have. "Listen to you. I'm thirty-one years old."

She was, too. The eyes always give it away. In hers was a kind of flatness, inexpressiveness, weariness. "My Lord, Rosie. Where's the fountain of youth? I could use a glassful of that stuff."

Now, she'd be on his side. "Oh, I don't know. You look okay to me." Fetchingly she said this, as she let one leg slide off the sofa.

Before a full-blown flirtation could get under way, he said, "How did Stacy feel about her job? Did she ever mention any of the men she dated?"

Rosie leaned forward and shook another cigarette out of a pack, lit it, then minded her manners and pushed the pack toward Jury.

"No thanks." Jury thought everyone in Britain must smoke except him, Dora, and Harry's dog, Mungo. And he wouldn't take bets on Mungo.

Pulling over a tin ashtray that advertised a pub named "Batty's" or maybe it was a beer, she said, "Thing is, she never told me their names."

"Whose names?"

"There was this one bloke she really liked; she dated him awhile—I mean, off the clock. Well, we're not supposed to, you know."

"Was she serious about him?"

Rosie looked away and out the window behind them. "Not really. I think she just liked him better than the others."

"Did she describe him? Do you have any idea what he looks like?"

She shook her head. "Only he was handsome, is all. He bought her things. 'Like a prince,' he was, she once said."

Was it the Cinderella story in Jimmy Choo shoes? Or Snow White's story, the men always charming, handsome, rich? The women always in jeopardy? He didn't imagine any of Valentine's clients would have qualified as Prince Charming. In any event, Prince Charming wouldn't have needed Valentine's.

"Funny thing, though. He wanted her to dress a certain way and change her hair."

"What do you mean?"

"Stacy said it must be someone in his past. He wanted her to color her hair red. So she did. I mean, I did."

"You did?"

"See, I used to be a stylist. I was in that real chic shop in Bayswater. I was good at color. Good at makeup, too."

Jury asked, "You mean every weekend she'd have you color her hair?"

She nodded. "With this semipermanent color I use, it's not so hard on the hair. But her real hair was darkish brown, and it's tricky turning that coppery color back to brown. You have to use an ash brown to get it that shade. Her clothes, though, he must've paid for most of them. Those shoes alone cost seven, eight hundred quid." Rosie stretched out one leg and moved the furry slipper up and down. "Me, I got myself a pair of Christian Louboutin for a tiny price at one of those consignment stores. It's called Go Around Twice."

Jury had a feeling it was hard enough for Rosie to go around once. "How does it work? How do you meet up with the clients?"

"Blanche calls us—that's Blanche Vann, did I say?—and tells us who and where to meet the bloke. He'd already have paid. So any money changes hands between me and him, that's a tip."

"And what about you? Ever met anybody who's like that? The man Stacy met?"

"Ha! Not bloody likely." Again, she looped a strand of hair round her finger, curled it and uncurled it.

"Still, it's possible."

But as he was the police and fairly out of bounds as a client, she said only, "Yeah."

Jury said, "Her aunt didn't know about Stacy Storm, either. Mariah kept the two identities separate."

"You know, I always did think—"

Jury sensed hindsight coming down the road.

"—she was worried about something, something was bothering

her, and I asked, but she never would say. I don't think it was him, though, causing whatever the trouble was. Not him—he was ever so generous." She sighed. "Stacy, she was always a bit of a mystery, wasn't she?"

He wasn't expected to answer that. He said, "Did he buy her the Saint Laurent she was wearing when she died?"

"He must've bought it all."

Yves Saint Laurent was on Upper Sloane Street; so was Jimmy Choo. He rose. "Thank you so much, Rosie. You've really been a big help. I may want to talk to you again."

"All right," she said. Saddened by the death of her friend or by his leaving or both, as if he'd brought Stacy with him and was now taking her away, Rosie got up and walked with him to the door.

In the hallway, he gave her his card and told her to get in touch if she remembered anything else. He looked down at her.

Rosie Moss, in her candy-cane-striped dress, her furry slippers, and her hair in bunches, and felt as if he'd weep, and turned away.

17

The door buzzed as Jury entered; a salesperson in a knockout draped black dress came toward him. The dress would look stunning on Phyllis, but then again, what wouldn't?

"Sir?" Her smile was wide, but it faded when he showed her his ID. She looked stricken, as if he'd slapped her.

Then Jury smiled and all was well again, the waters calm. "I just need to ask you a few questions, Miss . . . ?"

"Ondine—"

Did she work for Valentine's, too, with a name like that?

"—Overalls."

No. "Miss Overalls—" He bit his lip to keep from smiling.

"Just Ondine."

"Ondine. Thank you. Is this the main Yves Saint Laurent in London?"

"Of course. We're not a chain." She whipped out a "just kidding" smile.

"Ah. I'm interested in a dress purchased by this woman—" Jury hated showing morgue shots, but the only others would have been of a very different-looking Mariah Cox. The photographer had managed to polish this one so that she didn't look, well, too dead.

Ondine picked up narrow glasses with metal frames and put them on. Her head bent over the photo, she nodded. "I remember.

I thought she was a model; I mean, the way she moved. She looked wonderful in our gowns."

She gestured toward the mannequins stationed side by side in one area, as at the rail of a luxury ocean liner, watching, blind-eyed as they were, the coast of some country fall away.

Ondine looked like a model herself, makeup perfectly applied in little dots of cream-something, gray dust whisked across her eyelids with a supple brush, lipstick drawn on.

"You mean she's—dead?"

"I'm afraid so. She was shot to death."

Ondine looked a little wildly around the shop and at the mannequins, as if some guilt might attach to them. Then, sensibly, she placed her hand on her breast and took a deep breath, then another. She said, "Yes, that's one of ours. Poor thing, she'll never wear it again."

Jury smiled a little at this summing-up of the good life.

"When was she here?"

"It was . . . Tuesday week. I remember it very well. She tried on several dresses and looked, I must say, delicious in each. That"—she looked again at the picture as she spoke—"was the best of them. Well, given the price"—she looked round the room, blameless and empty except for the mannequins—"it should have been: three thousand seven hundred pounds."

Jury gave a low, appreciative whistle. "Was she alone?"

"Oh, yes, quite alone. But she did make a call. I didn't hear what she said."

"Did she use a mobile phone?"

"Yes. The battery was down in hers, so I let her use mine."

"You did? Do you have it here?"

Ondine moved over to a counter, reached behind it, and came back and handed the mobile phone to Jury. He brought up a list of phone calls; there were probably a good fifty of them. "Have you erased any outgoing calls here?"

"Not lately. I forget to do it, anyway."

Jury handed back the mobile, saying, "Take a look at these and see if there are any numbers you don't recognize."

Ondine ran her eyes down the list and was about to say something when the door chimed and a couple walked in, probably in their seventies, clearly rich and rather fragile. They moved with their torsos slightly inclined, not bent, just forward, as if trying to get somewhere ahead of themselves. They both wore light gray capes, his part of his coat, hers a coat in itself. They made Jury think of shorebirds.

"Excuse me just a moment," Ondine whispered before she went to the couple to offer assistance. Jury couldn't hear what she said; he thought it rather pleasant that nothing got above a murmur in this elegant, graceful room. As moneyed as these people seemed to be and as expensive as the clothes that were sold, the atmosphere still wasn't steeped in materialism.

Ondine was back. "Let me look at this—" She took the mobile and pointed out a number. "I think it was this one: I don't know it, and it was placed just about when she was here."

Jury pulled out his notebook, wrote it down, a London number.

At this juncture, the gray-haired couple, who appeared to act always in concert, raised their hands to beckon Ondine over.

"Sorry," she whispered again. "There's just me here today. Charlotte's sick again." She sighed. As if Jury knew Charlotte and her sham illnesses.

Jury watched her glide over to them. Murmurs again.

Honestly, the place would do for a meditation center; he smiled at the idea of several monks sitting around the room on the silk and satin cushions. He watched Ondine go to the counter, where she seemed to be checking something, possibly the price of the gray gown the two of them—the man and the woman—were holding between them. Folds of gray chiffon and silk. The man seemed perfectly at ease in this room sacred to women.

Wiggins walked through the glass door at that moment. "Guv. Blanche—"

Wiggins got on a first-name basis very quickly with witnesses.

"—was pretty cooperative, and it may be you were right about the names: there were no matches with the Rexroths, but Blanche did turn up two Simons—a Simon St. Cyr and a Simon Smith." He was looking at his notebook and thumbed up a page. "According to the Valentine's records, Simon Smith was down with Stacy Storm five times. I've got the dates. Five isn't much for a hot romance, but he was down in the book those five times, and something tells me that's not every time that he saw her."

Jury nodded. "According to Rose Moss, she was seeing some fellow off the books. I don't suppose Blanche Vann could describe him."

Wiggins shook his head. "Their clients don't call round; they ring and set up times according to Valentine's schedule. The office isn't much, just a room. But it's nicely fitted out: big, airy, fresh flowers and fruit. The girls come round every so often. 'My girls,' she calls them. Bit of a mother hen, you ask me. I got the impression she was genuinely fond of Stacy. Pretty broken up about her death. And very surprised about this double life Stacy and Mariah led."

"How'd she find out? Papers?"

"No, from your Adele Astaire. Blanche said she rang up and told her. Blanche doesn't read the papers a lot."

"Okay, get onto Thames Valley, to DS Cummins, and get this Simon Smith's address, or, rather, get him to find out if the Rexroths have any idea who the 'Smith' might actually be."

Wiggins nodded, turned away while punching in the number on his mobile phone.

Finding Ondine free of the gray-winged couple, Jury walked over to the counter. "Ondine."

She looked up with a slightly mischievous smile.

"How did Stacy Storm pay for the dress?"

Ondine pulled over a large black ledger, opened it, and ran a red-coated fingernail up and down columns. "Barclaycard."

"That must have been quite a credit line she had."

"I don't know, except it was approved."

"All right. I won't take up any more of your time. You've been a world of help, Ondine." He handed her his card. "If you remember anything at all—"

"Including my name." Big smile. "Believe me, I will."

What a flirt.

"I have a friend who'd look terrific in that black gown in the window."

Again, Ondine whispered, "Tell her to pop round. I might be able to give her a very nice price."

"I'll do that," Jury whispered back.

The doorman or security guard or greeter at the door told them in chilly tones that the shop was just closing.

"No, it isn't," said Jury, holding up his ID and pushing past him into the light, bright air of Jimmy Choo.

Whereupon the man immediately went to get someone else, a lithesome-looking woman who had a way of standing with her feet crossed and her hands crossed inside out before her. He thought this difficult pose came naturally to her, and he wondered if she had been a model. Models seemed able to accomplish the most unusual and uncomfortable-looking postures.

In this clear and uncluttered interior, Jury thought he might be reassessing the common attitudes toward wealth and materialism. In the cathedral-like quiet, in their little niches, the artfully arranged jewel-toned shoes covered the walls like stained-glass windows.

These shoes looked both impossibly rich and flyaway at the same time. They were displayed, in their lit-up little alcoves, as works of art. And rightly so, Jury thought as he took in that metallic silver sandal with the jewels running all the way up the instep, or that silver snakeskin with its four-inch heel and straps twining up the ankle, or that glittery leather with its narrow straps impossibly entwined. The architectural detail of these sandals was remarkable. Wiggins was nearly inhaling them, he was so close to the wall. He was getting down with the shoes.

Jury made a guess and asked the saleswoman if she recalled a woman purchasing the shoes in the photo he held out, perhaps a week ago? He thought after buying the dress, Mariah might have walked across the street to Jimmy Choo's.

He was right. The purchase had been made, but there was no phone call that she remembered. Yes, she'd paid with a Barclaycard.

He walked over to Wiggins. "You thinking of buying a pair for that cousin in Manchester?"

"Not bloody likely; do you see what these things cost? That'd be—" Wiggins's mobile sounded, and he flipped it open, spoke his name, and listened. Then he thanked the caller. "That was Cummins. Simon Smith is probably Simon Santos. He knows Timothy Rexroth from his work in the City. Simon's in mergers and acquisitions. And we're in luck; he lives right around the corner." Wiggins inclined his head in that direction. "Pont Street. I've the number; should I call?"

Jury looked at his watch. It was nearly six, a good time for drinks before dinner. From whatever he did in the City, Simon Santos might just be relaxing over one. "No. Let's surprise him."

18

He answered the door with a drink in his hand, whiskey by the look of it, and in a cut-glass tumbler that cost a hundred pounds by the look of *it*. It was, after all, Pont Street, just steps away from Beauchamp Place and Harrods, high in the Knightsbridge heavens.

Simon Santos had his French cuffs rolled up, his silk jacket casually tossed over a rosewood banister, and his Italian leather shoes polished to mirror brightness.

Jury and Wiggins pulled out their IDs simultaneously, and Simon Santos regarded them, apparently unsurprised.

And, Jury noticed, apparently unresentful.

Holding the door open wider, Santos said, "I just got in."

Not from work, surely, Jury thought. Nothing he could thus far see in this house looked as if it had done a day's work in its life.

Santos invited them to sit down in a room that could serve as a template for any voguish magazine spread. A massive fireplace with all sorts of baronial brass fittings, above which hung a portrait of a truly beautiful woman dressed in green velvet with white skin against which her dark red hair burned. On the hearth lay two chocolate Labradors, their heads raised, and so alike that they could have been a pair of andirons. Well-mannered, too. After a brief scrutiny of the interlopers, they yawned and lowered their heads to their paws and resumed their snooze. Jury reached out his hand and ran it over the silky head of one, which made the dog sigh.

There was a lot of butter leather interspersed with damask furniture and a ton of dark green velvet dripping down the long windows and puddling on the floor. Jury and Wiggins sat in club chairs from which Jury wondered if they would ever rise. There was something to be said for money.

It was one of those rooms one could only describe in accents of taste: luscious, delectable, ambrosial, scrumptious. The room's rich brown walls and creamy moldings made Jury feel as if he were sunk in a chocolate mousse.

"What can I do for you? Care for a drink?"

"No, thank you, Mr. Santos. We're looking into the death of a young woman named Mariah Cox."

Jury saw a muscle tighten in Santos's handsome face, then relax when he heard the name, which Jury supposed meant nothing to him.

"I don't know anyone of that name."

"No, but you do—or did—know Stacy Storm. That was Mariah's professional name, so to speak."

Tightness returned and went to every muscle, not just the one in his face. He killed a little time by rising to get himself a fresh drink: a cube of ice plinked; a siphon hissed. He returned to the sofa.

Jury wondered if he'd be stupid enough to deny all knowledge of Stacy Storm.

No. Santos took a couple of swallows of his whiskey, then he returned to the sofa and said, "That was terrible. Awful. I was . . ." He had been leaning forward, glass dangerously loose in his fingers (considering the plummage-swept rug beneath it), and now he sat back to consider what he was: "Devastated."

Jury studied the man's expression and what it told of devastation, but he couldn't read it.

It was Wiggins who asked, "How well did you know her, sir?"

Santos's smile was tight as he looked from Wiggins to Jury and back again. "I expect you know, or you wouldn't be here."

"No, actually, we don't, other than that you, ah, engaged her on several occasions as a Valentine's escort."

"I did, yes." The tone was bitter, and he looked away.

"What we're interested in, though, is whether you saw her at other times; that is, as Ms. Storm's flatmate put it: 'off the books.' Not as a Valentine's escort."

"Well, I expect she won't get in trouble now with Valentine's."

"No, Stacy's in as much trouble as she'll ever be in again."

Santos regarded him. "You say that, Superintendent, as if you sympathize."

Jury said nothing, just went on looking at him.

"So, yes. We saw each other any number of times 'off the books,' as you say."

Wiggins said, "What's 'any number'?"

"Every week in the last three months. She was only in London on weekends. Now I know why. I mean, if she was also, or really, another woman. Mariah?"

"Mariah Cox. So, getting down to it, Mr. Santos, you went to a party given by a couple named Rexroth last Saturday night, is that true?"

He nodded. "And you're wondering, of course, how that's connected to Stacy. She was to meet me there. I wanted to pick her up—wherever she was. You see, I didn't know where the devil she was during the week. She'd never tell me—"

"You didn't know she lived in Chesham?"

"No. She told me nothing."

"When she was found, when Stacy Storm was found, she was wearing a dress bought at the Yves Saint Laurent shop on Sloane Street. And Jimmy Choo shoes, also Sloane Street. Did you buy her gifts like that?"

"Not gifts like that, but those very ones. That costume, those shoes. It was actually my idea. I wanted her to feel no woman in the room could touch her. Stacy was rather . . . I don't know . . ."

Jury waited, but Santos still didn't know.

"She was to meet you at the Rexroths', was she? How did she come to be at the Black Cat?"

"Christ!" The dogs both looked up, disturbed, first glancing at Santos, then at the two strangers, as if they, the dogs, were making up their minds about them. They resettled themselves when Simon Santos spoke in a quieter tone. "Do you think I haven't asked myself that a hundred times? I've no idea."

"No idea?"

He shook his head. "The Black Cat must've been part of her other life . . ." He shrugged. Then he sat forward, rolling the whiskey glass in his hands, forearms on knees. "I could never quite take her measure. There was something I didn't get about her. What I thought was that there was somebody else, some other man. Which she denied."

"What time did you leave the Rexroths' party?"

"About ten, I think. When she didn't come and still didn't, I had no reason to stick around."

"You came back to London? To here?"

Santos looked a mite surprised Jury would even wonder about this. "Yes, of course."

"I only meant you might have stopped off someplace, to have a drink, get a bite to eat, somewhere along the way."

Santos shook his head, looked at the dogs, sleeping soundly, looked up at Jury, puzzled. "I'm being stupid, aren't I?"

Wiggins half-smiled. "Are you, sir? About what?"

"Well, for God's sake, I'm a bloody suspect!"

Dogs awake again, looking worried.

Looking at the anxious dogs, he sat back and lowered his voice a little. "A suspect without an alibi. To answer your question: No, I didn't stop off to eat or for any other reason. I came directly home, had a nightcap, and went upstairs to bed. No telephone calls, nothing. Just me alone."

The way he said it, without self-pity, held an awful poignance.

Jury said, "Is it correct to assume Stacy meant a lot to you? Your meetings . . . well, they were more than a casual arrangement."

Santos glanced up at the portrait, then looked away. He nodded. "Much more. At least on my part. Stacy—as I said, Stacy was difficult to read. She was extremely kind, and I might have misinterpreted the kindness as love." He paused, then said, "Mariah Cox, Stacy's other self, what was she like?"

Jury told Simon Santos about Mariah's rather circumscribed life, lacking glamour, lacking Saint Laurent, lacking those bejeweled shoes that lined the walls of Jimmy Choo. But he left out Bobby Devlin.

Then he rose, nodded to Wiggins. "We'll be in touch, Mr. Santos. We'd appreciate it if you'd stay in London for a time."

Simon Santos had risen too as Jury said this and stood, hands in pockets, looking uncertain and rather bereft. He was directly beneath the portrait over the fireplace, and Jury could see the resemblance.

Santos followed his glance and turned to look back at the portrait. "My mother, Isabelle. Beautiful, wasn't she?"

That needed no confirmation. "I see the resemblance between you," said Jury. But one not nearly so strong as the resemblance between the woman in the portrait and Mariah Cox.

This must have been Simon Santos's obsession.

Jury thought of Lu Aguilar; he knew about obsession.

"What do you think, sir? Here's what I can't understand: a man like that, got everything going for him and a ton of money besides. Must have women lined up on his doorstep. So why does a man like that go and hire an escort, a tart? Doesn't make sense."

She wasn't a tart, Jury wanted to say yet knew he had no business saying. "You saw the photo of Stacy."

"Yes—"

"You don't see the resemblance to Isabelle Santos? Stacy Storm was solace."

They were standing by the car in Pont Street. "You want me to drop you in Islington? Then I'll take the car in."

Jury shook his head. "I'm taking a cab. I want to go to the City."

"It's near seven. What for?"

"The Old Wine Shades." Jury pulled the Rexroths' guest list out of his pocket, smiling.

Wiggins snuffled up a laugh. "Harry Johnson."

"Right. I can hardly wait to hear him on this." Jury held up the list.

"Do you think you'll ever get him in the frame?"

"Oh, I'll get him, never you worry. In the frame and in the end."

Wiggins had the car door open. "Let's hope it's not."

"What?"

"The end."

They said good night, and Jury hailed a cab.

19

Dickens, as history had it, drank here. But more important (at least to Jury right now), so did Harry Johnson; this was his favorite place. He was sitting in his usual bar chair, drinking some bloodred vintage and talking to Trevor, barman of the Old Wine Shades.

"Hello, Harry," said Jury, sliding into the chair beside him. "How've you been keeping?" As if he cared.

"Well, for Lord's sake, it's the Filth. I haven't seen you in a whole couple of weeks." Harry had drawn out his silver cigarette case and was now lighting up.

What Jury had drawn out was the Rexroth guest list. He assumed a patently insincere smile and tapped the folded pages against Harry's arm.

"Ah! You finally got a warrant, did you? High time, as it saves you looting my house illegally. But go ahead and search away." Harry's smile put in its own claim for a patent on insincerity.

That Jury had never been able to get a warrant because there was no probable cause—nada, nil, nothing, zip—really stuck in his craw. Harry had done that murder in Surrey, and Jury meant to prove it.

But at the moment he had this list of names. "Where were you last Saturday night, Harry?"

"In Chesham. At a party. As you know or you wouldn't be asking.

It's your case, isn't it?" Harry tried on the smile again, then a woeful look, just as insincere: "I'm sorry about the wretched girl—"

No, he wasn't. He couldn't care less.

"—lying in the cold outside of the Black Cat in nothing but Yves Saint Laurent."

"How do you know *that*, Harry? That detail wasn't in the paper."

Harry looked at Jury with the sort of indulgence one reserved for little children. "Are you dim just one night a week and is this the night? The Rexroths, of course. The Rexroths were in a frenzy of excitement. They would have steeped themselves in the details. Not much happens in Chesham. I called them when I read about it."

"How do you know the Rexroths?"

Harry sighed. "Is this what tonight's conversation will be? A lot of 'how do you know' questions? I know Timothy, or Tip, as he's called, because he comes in here for lunch."

"Where did you go after you left the party?"

"Home. Would you care for a glass of wine? It's a Côte de Nuits." He pointed to the bottle that Trevor had rested in a wine bucket and that Harry now pulled out in invitation.

"How long were you at the Rexroths'?"

Harry thought. "Got there around nine, left around ten. I didn't stay long because I had to allow enough time for meeting up with and murdering your victim."

Jury managed to suppress his desire to throw Harry off his bar chair. It wasn't easy.

Harry blew a perfect smoke ring. "It's getting tiresome. Any woman murdered within thirty miles of London you think is down to me."

Jury pulled over the bottle of Burgundy, looked hard at the label (as if he'd know). "Are there any witnesses to place you at any stop on your journey back to Belgravia?"

"No stops. I got home before eleven. That's it."

"You didn't stop in at the Black Cat?"

Harry frowned. "In Chesham? No, of course not."

"You've never been there?"

Harry sighed. "To save you the trouble of taking my picture so as to show it around—or stealing one from my house—I have been to the Black Cat. Back in . . . March, or early April. I'll say this—" His smile was gleeful. "The motive is going to be bloody hard to pin down—I don't mean my motive, as I didn't kill her, and consequently had no motive. No, you've got not one, but two victims, haven't you? The glamour girl escort and the plain Jane librarian."

"How do you know about the librarian?"

"Well, it just so happens I can read." Neatly, Harry folded the tabloid at his elbow and slid it in front of Jury.

Who, irritated again, ignored it. Instead, he spoke to Trevor, who had come down the bar from the crowded far end. "Couple of fingers of something incredibly strong, Trev."

"Right." Trevor moved away.

Harry said, "This young woman—and this is all according to the *Daily News*, whose rigorous journalistic practices leave no doubt as to the truth of their reporting—"

"Shut up, Harry. Thanks," he said to Trevor, who placed a glass of tar-dark whiskey before Jury.

Harry did not shut up; he smiled at the idea of it. "The paper showed pictures of her—beautiful woman, wouldn't you say? And then today, of a picture of that lovely girl looking much plainer. But she was clearly not working as a librarian in that dress she was wearing."

"You didn't know her, then?"

"I didn't know either of them."

"Then who was your date?"

Harry looked puzzled. "My 'date'? I didn't have one."

"I believe the Rexroths think you did," Jury lied.

Harry studied the very devil out of his cigarette. "Am I to be responsible for everybody's errant thinking? If they thought it, they were wrong." He paused and blew another smoke ring.

Their perfection annoyed Jury no end.

Then Harry said, "We always think of disguise as elaboration, for some reason."

"I don't follow you."

"No. I suppose you don't, as you've been hopeless sorting my own case."

"I can't imagine why, given you're a pathological liar. It's hard to put two and two together when in your case they make three."

"Trevor . . ." Harry raised his voice but kept it under a shout. "Give me a bottle of the Musigny. You know the one."

"I've a nice half-bottle of that," said Trevor, coming nearer.

"Not a whole one?"

"Well, yes, I could dust one off if you want to spend the extra hundred quid."

Harry swiped ash from his cigarette off the counter. "Nothing is too good for my friend here. So bring it on."

Harry was heavily invested in wine.

"Don't do it for me," said Jury, raising his glass of whiskey, of which only a shadow remained.

Harry was busy with another smoke ring. "It's all about you, isn't it?"

"You bet."

"So, tell me. Have you sorted it?"

"What?"

"My *God*, but you have the attention span of a flea. Mungo would have worked it out by now."

Jury looked around. "I know. Where is Mungo?"

"Home, being extremely busy about something. He gets like that."

"Tell me, do you keep Mungo around because he's so independent? Or is he independent because he's stuck with you?"

"Both."

"Do you have to hedge every bet? Can't you just pick one or the other?"

"And you a detective superintendent. You can't go much higher. What's above you?"

"Chief superintendent."

"What's above him?"

"Divisional commander. London's divided into areas. But you know that."

"I don't know nuffin', mate. I do know the City of London has its own police force."

"A friend of mine, Mickey Haggerty—" Jury stopped. He had no idea why he'd brought Mickey up. Jury had returned to that dock many times in dreams. In dreams he and Mickey would walk back from the dock, toward the lights of the City, arms flung around each other's shoulders.

"Something wrong?"

"Sad end of a friendship. One of us died."

"You sure it wasn't both of you?"

Jury flinched. Harry could be nerve-racking at times in his prescience. He wondered if it was true, that part of him had really died on that dock on the Thames.

Trevor was back with the wine and the glasses. He poured a mite into Harry's glass, and Harry raised, sniffed, and tasted. "It's worth every penny, Trevor." Trevor filled both glasses.

"Now, let's get back to it. You've got a story—"

Everything was a story to Harry. It wasn't a case Jury was dealing with, but a story.

"—about a young woman found murdered in the grounds of the Black Cat in Chesham, dressed in a gown by Yves Saint Laurent and shoes by Jimmy Choo—"

"And the shoe designer was not in the paper, either. There was a picture of the dress and the shoes, but Mr. Choo was not mentioned."

Harry's sigh was dramatically Harry's. "I live on the fringes of Upper Sloane Street. I've often walked by Jimmy Choo and stared at his shoes enough to think I'd recognize them. Like you, I found the way she was dressed fascinating. All I had to do was go online—it's called the Internet—and there were the shoes. Six, seven hundred quid, I think. Okay, now, we've got the resplendently dressed young woman, who is also the quite unsplendid little librarian. That's the backstory—"

"I'm aware of the backstory." Jury signaled Trevor.

"Good. The question, your question: why would a plain little librarian keep going off to London to work for an escort service, trick herself out in expensive finery, and go to a lot of trouble to keep her London life a secret?"

Jury twisted the stem of his glass around in the accumulated condensation on the bar. "I'm waiting for you to tell me."

"Well, I don't know, do I? The thing is, you're not looking at this problem the other way round."

"What other way?"

"It's as I said before: we always seem to look at disguise as elaboration—the fright wig, the chalk white face, the painted face. Makeup. Remember what Hamlet said to Ophelia?"

"I'm trying my level best."

"'God gave you one face and you paint yourself another.' We speak of making ourselves *up*, not down—simple librarian turns into gorgeous call girl. How do you know it wasn't the other way round? That it wasn't the librarian hiding herself in the hooker, but the hooker hiding herself in the librarian? The librarian was the disguise."

Jury looked at him. "If that's the case—"

"The librarian wasn't keeping the escort secret; the escort was keeping *the librarian* a secret. The face that was kept plain and unadorned—that was the life to be kept secret." He turned in his chair and looked at Jury. "So you'd better get your skates on, pal. You could have a long way to go."

20

A t ten-thirty the next morning, Jury was standing in the door of his flat, waiting for the clump clump clump of Carole-anne's Tod's. Tod's, she had told him (as if he wanted to know), were really hot at the moment and sturdy enough for work. Her job at the Starrdust in Covent Garden hardly needed "sturdiness," but he let that pass.

Clump clump clump. Here she came.

"Super! You waiting for me?"

In that sunrise misty yellow getup with one sleeve off the shoulder, anyone would be waiting for her. The Tod's were ankle boots with a pointed toe. Jury said nothing; he merely held up her unreadable telephone message with the heart.

She took it. Her pearly pink lips moved as she mimed the words. She handed it back, her aquamarine eyes (sunrise over the sea, this morning), said, "Better get Jason."

Then down the stairs, clippity-clippity clop, quick as could be before Jury's mouth could close around, "Get back here!"

Again in his flat, he tossed the bit of paper in the trash and sat on the sofa. Before him on the coffee table, in addition to his mug of tea, he'd laid out the photo of Mariah Cox, the snapshot of Morris that Dora had pressed on him, the Rexroths' guest list, and the rough map he'd made of the area of the Lycrome Road between the Black

Cat and Deer Park House. An easy walk, he'd make it inside of ten minutes.

Jury picked up the guest list again, noted the other names of men who'd gone unaccompanied by women, wondering if any of them had had experience with the Valentine's escort service. Even though Simon Santos had already agreed that he himself was to meet Stacy Storm, still . . .

Still, nothing. He picked up the phone and rang Wiggins.

"Meet me at Valentine's Escorts in half an hour, will you? The other men on the list, the single men Cummins said he'd spoken to. They'd been at the party all night from nine to midnight."

"Why are you interested in them? She was there to meet Simon Santos." Wiggins's voice was frowning.

"I know."

"He's really the prime suspect, sir."

"If he killed her, he was being pretty stupid about it, about not covering his tracks and not seeing he had an alibi somehow. Pretty stupid."

"Most murderers are pretty stupid."

"Right. Meet me there."

Maybe they were, as Wiggins said, pretty stupid. He dropped the receiver into its cradle; he refused to trade the old black phone for one—as Carole-anne suggested—"you can take with you round the flat."

"I'm not going anywhere; I don't want to take a phone round the flat. I want to sit and talk or at least stand in one place. I don't want to be in the kitchen frying up sausages whilst I'm talking about a serial killer."

He was grumpy even in fantasy. He pulled his jacket from the back of a chair, picked up his keys, and left.

Mrs. Blanche Vann was gracious. Jury doubted many of the owners of escort services would be offering them bananas and cups of coffee, coffee made, for heaven's sake, in a *cafetière*. Jury was never sure how long to wait before you pushed down the plunger. He didn't much like these devices; he wanted to see coffee run from the little tongue of a pot.

"Thank you, Mrs. Vann. You're very kind." He left his banana on the small table she had pulled over between Wiggins and him. Wiggins had started in on his own banana.

Jury said, "I talked to Rose Moss—or Adele Astaire, as she calls herself—"

"Silly name," said Blanche Vann. "I told her she might just do well to think up another."

"Fred Astaire's sister, that was," said Wiggins. "Married the son of the Duke of Devonshire." He peeled his banana down another inch.

Jury fixed him with an icy smile.

Said Mrs. Vann: "No? I didn't know that!"

Neither did Wiggins, yesterday. Jury said, "I'll call her Rose. She said Stacy had been living in her flat with her most weekends for the last six months."

"That's right, as far as I know." Mrs. Vann stirred cream into her coffee with a tiny spoon.

"Rose has been with the agency how long?" he asked.

"Quite a few years. Six, eight. She looks younger than she is. One or two clients like a girl on the young side." She sipped her coffee, showing no embarrassment at all at the implications of that statement.

"Were Rose and Stacy good friends?"

"Were they? Well, I'd think so, sharing a flat and all that."

"But only on weekends. Did you know that Stacy lived in Chesham?"

Her mouth tight shut as if to emphasize her point, she shook her head, then said, "I did not. The address she gave was in Fulham, same as Rose's. Well, I'd have no reason to doubt that, would I?"

"You would have had to reach her at times she wasn't there, though, to set up appointments."

"That's right. Usually the girls called in. But if I needed to ring her, it was all done on her mobile; indeed, all the girls worked that way, since they're so often not at home."

"That makes sense." Jury looked around the room again, at the dark moldings, the restful pale gray walls, the comfortable furniture, surprised the room could be so pleasant here in this nondescript office block in the Tottenham Court Road.

She said, looking thoughtfully at her cup, "Adele once said she thought Stacy a bit of a mystery."

"I'd say that Adele is right." Jury smiled at her and got up. "Thank you, Mrs. Vann. We'll be talking to you."

Walking to the car, Jury said, "You hungry, Wiggins?"

"Yes. That banana didn't really fill me up."

As if it were supposed to.

"It's nearly two. I have to make my weekly check on Danny Wu."

Wiggins broke out in a big smile as he opened the car door. "I'm with you; but it'll be bloody crowded now."

"Ruiya's always crowded."

"Right, boss."

Jury rolled his eyes. So now it was "boss."

21

The queue even at this late hour stretched out the door, nearly to the corner. Jury and Wiggins didn't bother with it but went straightaway to the front.

When the old waiter saw them at the door, he held up his hand, fingers crooked, bidding them come back to where he was. The waiting lunch crowd, those who saw this, acted as if it were some sort of guerrilla takeover and objected strenuously until Jury whipped out his ID and said, "Police business." That struck some of them as a poor excuse, and their reproaches followed the two detectives on the way to their table. Jury was used to it; it happened nearly every time he'd been here.

Theirs was the only table in the room with a "Reserved" sign. Ruiya didn't take reservations; hence the crowd beyond the door.

"You'd think they'd learn, wouldn't you?" said Wiggins, looking disdainfully at the line.

"Learn what? What choice have they unless they want to get here at five a.m.? Like a Springsteen concert, this is."

The old waiter, who might or might not have understood these words, smiled and swept the plastic sign from the table, motioning for them to be seated. He bowed and went away. Jury and Wiggins sat down. Wiggins began immediately looking at the long, thin menu as he always did before he would order the crispy fish as he always did.

A little elderly woman replaced the old waiter now, probably kin. She came with tea and to take their orders.

Jury said he'd have the shrimp tempura.

Wiggins was still concentrating on the menu, brows knit together in rapt thought.

"And he'll have the crispy fish."

Annoyed eyes regarded Jury over the menu's edge. "You might allow me to order my own lunch."

"Might, but won't. You always eat the crispy fish."

The little woman looked amused, which was reward enough for the bulletlike glances still zinging their way, the long queue looking as if it hadn't shortened at all. No one had moved a foot forward.

"I wasn't planning on ordering that this time."

"Sure you were." Jury sipped tea from the thimble of a cup.

Wiggins was silent, put down the menu with a martyred sigh. "I'll have the crispy fish, I think."

The woman's nod was closer to a bow. She padded off.

It was a little like their own private cabaret, for the next person to show up was Danny Wu, the owner. Today he was wearing Hugo Boss, more constructed than Armani, another designer Danny favored. He was as good as any model. With his dove gray suit he wore a shirt the shade of a blue iris, a tie several shades darker. The only person Jury knew of with such sartorial elegance was Marshall Trueblood. Trueblood, though, sometimes tipped the scales into flamboyance, which Danny didn't. Both of them made Jury think that perhaps he should revisit his own wardrobe, until he thought, What wardrobe?

"Are you here professionally?"

"No, we're here amateurishly. We seem to have caved completely in discovering who left the dead man on your doorstep." That investigation had been going on for months now, booted over to the drug squad, then back to CID, given the Met's conviction that Danny was a serious contender for London's drug king—a conviction Jury had found dubious at least and ridiculous at best. Danny was too smart for that crown (which would rest extremely uneasily on one's head);

he was also too fastidious to shoot a man in his own restaurant. Jury went on: "No one's sussed it, Danny, why he was killed here."

"This is Soho, remember? You'll find bodies on a lot of doorsteps. Soho is no stranger to murder."

"Thanks for that lesson in social dynamics. I hadn't heard."

Danny sported a smile.

Jury started to say something, then stopped when he saw Phyllis Nancy shoving past the queue and coming toward them. "Phyllis!"

She looked worn. It would take a lot of wearing to make her look that way.

"Ah, the beautiful medical examiner," said Danny, who immediately pulled a chair round from another table.

Phyllis thanked him, and Danny bowed out gracefully. It would have been clear to him that Phyllis had something to report.

"I thought you'd be here," she said. "I've just come from hospital. I'm sorry, Richard, but Lu Aguilar has sunk into a coma. It happened this morning."

Jury looked at Phyllis, shocked, but the shock was not only for Lu's condition; some was for his own response to it. In that brutally honest moment when one first hears of someone's misfortune and before one can throw up defenses against one's own selfishness and insensitivity—feelings that constitute a person's image of himself as a good and caring person—in that single swift moment, what he felt was relief. That moment had to be drowned, sunk from consciousness. He was on his feet.

Phyllis clamped her hand around his wrist. "There's nothing you can do; she won't know you're there."

No, he thought in a cold assessment of this new picture of himself, *but I'll know.*

Then the old Jury slipped back in place; he reconstructed his old self, his self of ten seconds ago, a caring man who deeply wanted Lu Aguilar to recover and take up her old life, or at least manage the new life in another country.

He left Ruiya and the car to Wiggins and flagged down a taxi.

★ ★ ★

At the nurses' station, the doctor had told him that the prospects of Lu's coming out of the coma were not especially good. "Still, don't lose hope; people do come out. Usually within two or three weeks. If not by then, well, it's a safe bet they won't at all. It can be less or more devastating."

Less or more. For God's sake, that about covered it, didn't it?

And the doctor told him something else: *"She did not want heroic measures taken."*

"What do you mean?" Jury knew exactly what the doctor meant. But he wanted to distance himself from the meaning. He literally stepped back.

The doctor was kind-eyed and rather young. He had slid a paper from a folder and passed it to Jury. *"She doesn't want to be kept alive by machines."*

Everything in him rebelled against this. "Heroic measures." What a stunning euphemism.

White. That was all he could see, as if he had stumbled into some polar country: the corridors, the walls, the sheets, her face.

The silence in her room was all there was. Except for the steady ping or hiccup of the monitors and machines, there was nothing.

He took her hand and found it marble cold. He thought for a panicky moment she must be dead and leaned close to her face and felt her frail breath. Cordelia. The broken Lear and Cordelia. "Come on, Lu. Come out of it. Come on." He shook her hand in a way he remembered someone doing to him when he was a kid; some adult, seeing his attention wavering, shook it back again.

Jury sat for a few minutes watching her before he rose and walked round the room, back and forth, stopping to look at her. An effigy was what she reminded him of. The incomparable, commanding, relentless detective inspector Lu Aguilar, still as stone and helpless. What he felt now was that he would never be able to understand his feelings for her, what they had been. Or hers for him. That part of his mind would be still as stone and helpless, too.

Jury turned to look out the window, seeing shadowed grass in the distance, thinking, It should be covered with snow; there should be the blankness of snow to render shapes null and void, the way the sheet did her own shape, the way it was drawn up to her shoulders.

Nurses in white entered from time to time to adjust tubes and check fluid levels and look at the machine. They smiled and left. One—but they might all have been the same one—said something about visiting hours. Jury nodded, although he hadn't really heard her, and stayed. He didn't know how long.

Finally, he got up from a chair, bent, and kissed her forehead. He was surprised to find it was not marble cold, but warm.

"Wake up, Lu."

He meant it, too.

22

He left St. Bart's, near Smithfield, and after that didn't look up, walking down one narrow street then another, all snaking into some center and making him feel pleasantly claustrophobic. He felt as if he'd wound himself into the center of a ball of string. Tired, he'd been walking for hours. It was dark now.

When "Three Blind Mice" started up, he yanked out the bloody mobile (what Orpheus should have had instead of string). "What?"

"I'm in Bidwell Street. Near St. Bride. There's been a woman shot."

Jury frowned. "St. Bride. That's not us, Wiggins; that's City police. Right near Snow Hill station, isn't it?"

"I know. They're here."

Jury could hear the background noise. "All right. But why are you there?"

"I was trawling for information about the Mariah Cox murder. I've a friend at Snow Hill, and I was there when he caught this one and came along. Thing is—this woman, put her in her early thirties, very good-looking, and dressed to kill, you might say—well, I'm probably wrong, but it seems similar to the Chesham murder."

"Okay. I'm in . . ." Where? He looked up to see the very familiar area in Clerkenwell in which he and Lu Aguilar had spent so much time. He could see the Zetter hotel down there at St. John's Square.

Why was he here? As if he didn't know. "Clerkenwell. I'll find a cab and be there in five minutes."

There were a couple of cabs moving along the Clerkenwell Road directly in front of him. He flagged one down, shoved the mobile back in his pocket, and opened the door. "You know Bidwell Street? It's near—"

The driver smiled. "I know it."

Jury pulled the door shut and fell back against the seat. Or gravity pushed him back. Yes, they knew all of them, these drivers, every last inch of street, road, alley, courtyard—all of it. Plus every shortcut.

"It's amazing. What you drivers know."

The driver laughed. "It's called the Knowledge. You know."

Jury nodded. "There ought to be a pub by that name. The Knowledge."

"Maybe there is."

Even if the driver hadn't got "the Knowledge," it wouldn't be hard finding Bidwell Street. Not given all of the activity—lights and vehicles, CID, uniform, fire brigade, ambulance, photographers, forensic, medical. It was astonishing what one murder in the streets of a city could call out.

The doctor was a man Jury didn't know, maybe pulled over from Bart's, which was nearby. He was kneeling beside the body.

Wiggins said, nodding in that direction, "Pathologist got here ten minutes ago. His name's Bellsin."

Dr. Bellsin rose at Jury's approach. He was a small, sad-eyed man who looked as if he were permanently stationed in the outskirts of regret. The first words out of his mouth were "I'm sorry." He shook Jury's hand as if the loss had been personal. To one or the other or both.

Jury looked down at the body and then knelt. The doctor did so, too.

The woman was young—in her thirties, as Wiggins had said, which surely must still qualify as young. And she was pretty—

beautiful, when there'd been life in her. Her hair was dark and wavy, her eyes now shut.

"The shot that killed her caught her just under the right breast, made a messy exit out the back. A twenty-two, probably. Second or probably the first shot to the stomach. Well, let's get her in and I'll nip round to the morgue." He paused. "Looks like she might have been partying."

Jury looked around at what he could see of the street. No pubs, no restaurants, but a few shops. "Doesn't look much like a partying street, though it's not far from a lot of partying places. She's dressed up, certainly." The dress was a midnight blue of some crepey material. More strappy sandals, these a dark satin. He rose, motioned to Wiggins. "Has she been ID'd?"

Wiggins shook his head. One of the uniforms handed Jury a bagged purse. "Sir."

Jury thanked him and asked for gloves. Through the plastic, he saw a small black bag, an evening bag with a silver clasp. He snapped on the plastic gloves given to him, removed the bag, and opened the little silver catch. Inside were lipstick, comb, pack of fags, and bills: 750 pounds.

"I know," said Wiggins, reacting to Jury's look. "That's a lot of money to be carting around dark and silent streets. I mean, in that small bag, at night. It's suggestive."

The notes were held in a silver money clip. He closed the purse, handed it to Wiggins, who had been joined by someone Jury didn't know.

"This is Detective Inspector Jenkins, sir."

Jenkins smiled and put out his hand. The smile was sardonic, but Jury didn't think its mood was aimed at him.

"Dennis Jenkins," the detective said, setting things on a first-name basis.

There was something about Jenkins that made one relax. And, Jury imagined, that went for suspects, too. Probably foolish of them. Jenkins's manner was too laid-back not to be dangerous.

"And you're," Jenkins went on, saving Jury the trouble, "Super-intendent Jury. I've heard about you."

"Not, I hope, from the tabloids."

Jenkins smiled his sardonic smile. "That, too. But I meant from Mickey."

That "Mickey" was Mickey Haggerty was crystal clear. Jury would rather not have to keep up one end of that conversation. He said nothing.

"I'm sorry," said DI Jenkins, actually looking it.

Jury nodded. "And I'm sorry to be stepping into your patch. Hope it's okay."

"Walk all over it, if you like. Your sergeant here told me there's the possibility that this is connected to a shooting in Chesham."

"That's right."

"What's the connection?"

Jury hesitated, then said, "Age, appearance, possible occupa-tion, and clothes." He looked down at the victim's feet. "Shoes, for example."

Jenkins turned to look, too, then turned back. He said nothing. He waited.

"Christian Louboutin. It's the red soles. They're his trademark."

Jenkins looked again. "Right. I know sod-all about women's footwear. Was the one in Chesham wearing the same kind?"

"No. Those were Jimmy Choo." Jury added, "Both of them dressed for something: party, big date, or client. The victim in Chesham worked for an escort agency."

Jenkins frowned. "Tell me more."

Jury hesitated again. He knew he could be completely wrong about any connection. "The Chesham murder: we had a hard time ID'ing the victim, eventually discovered she was indeed a local named Mariah Cox, but was working under the name Stacy Storm, working for an escort service. She was to meet a man at a party in Chesham named Simon Santos, but she didn't show up. There was a difficulty in identifying her; not even the aunt she'd been living with recog-nized her. The clothes, the hair, the cut, the color." Jury didn't know why he went on to tell Jenkins about Santos and his mother, Isabelle, and the portrait.

"I think that's why Santos was so adamant that Stacy be his escort. Santos had asked her to change her hair color so that she looked even more like the woman in the portrait—"

"*Vertigo,*" said Jenkins.

"What?"

"Kim Novak. You remember *Vertigo,* don't you?"

"Oh. You mean the Hitchcock film?"

Jenkins nodded. "Look, I know you probably agree the connection is kind of wobbly—" He rocked his hand to demonstrate. "But I will say this: she was carting around a hell of a lot of cash for just cab fare. Seven hundred quid"—he nodded toward the black clutch—"in that little bag. It's the kind of money a high-class pro might get, and just to look at her, I'd say very high class. She was dressed for something, certainly. A party? Coming or going? Early to be coming back from one; it's not gone ten yet. Where might she have been going? This is hardly party land or the sparkling center of the West, is it?"

Bidwell appeared to be a street of small enterprises, shut down for the night: a leather goods store selling mostly luggage that probably wasn't leather; a launderette on the corner; a jeweler, probably not doing much trade in diamonds; an electronics shop; a small grocery. That and the launderette were the only businesses open now. Inside, Jury could see a customer, a woman, staring out the window at the general tumult, the cars and lights and uniforms.

Jenkins scanned the areas over the shops. "I've told my men to visit the flats over these shops. If there's a grocer and a launderette, there are residents. Those two places wouldn't be depending on the shops themselves for business. And she'll need talking to." He indicated the woman in the launderette.

"I think I'd like a talk with that shopkeeper at the end of the street, the grocer."

"Go ahead. I'm about finished here."

"Could I get one of your photos for an ID?"

"Sure." Jenkins went up to one of the crime scene technicians and asked him if he'd got a picture. He handed it to Jury. "Keep me posted. I'll do the same."

The grocer was Indian, a tall, thin man with brilliant brown and anxious eyes. Ordinarily, this part of London was not an immigrant enclave. That was more the makeup of outlying areas, East Ham, Mile End, Watford.

His name was Banerjee. Jury asked Mr. Banerjee if he'd seen anything at all, heard anything.

The grocer shook his head, hard. "No. Never."

"Does this woman look familiar to you?"

Mr. Banerjee didn't dismiss the photo out of hand but studied it carefully. Nor did he flinch from the face of the dead.

Jury expected an immediate no, but he got a thoughtful "I believe so. I think I see her here in the shop. More than once." He looked off through the black window, as if something in the dark had caught his attention. But it was only the dark.

"You've seen her? Did she live here in Bidwell Street?"

"I would think so, though I do get customers from other streets, mainly. But more likely, yes, she lives in this street. Lived." He looked sadly at the photo. "A pretty woman. Maybe that's why I remember. She bought cigarettes. Yes, and food—milk, eggs, bread—basic things." He handed back the photo. "I'm sorry I do not know her name. I can't help you more."

"You've been an enormous help already, Mr. Banerjee. Thanks. If you remember anything at all later . . ." Jury handed over one of his cards.

"I will call you, certainly."

As Jury left the shop it started to rain, but gently. He saw up ahead fewer cars angled along the street. SOCO had packed up; the body had been transported. Wiggins was there with DI Wilkes, another detective, and several uniforms.

"Nothing so far. We've been to two houses, figure four or five flats. We can't be sure if the lack of a name card means a flat is empty or just that the resident's out. There was one old lady who clearly didn't want to know anything about anything. No joy there." He flicked his notebook shut.

"Never mind. We have more to go on now. The grocer's seen our lady more than once, so she lived either in this street or close by. Keep at it. One of the flats might well have been hers."

"Will do."

"I'm going home. I'm tired."

Wiggins nodded toward the small clutch of officers. "One of them can give you a lift."

"No. I feel like walking. Clear my mind. When I'm tired of that, I'll grab a taxi. 'Night."

"Sir!"

Jury turned. "What?"

"It might do to show that photo around. To the streets."

"You could do, but I'm pretty certain the victim wasn't on the streets. Not the way she looked. And not with that much money."

"You think maybe . . . ?"

Jury nodded. "Escort service."

Wiggins's smile was grim. "We should be so lucky."

"I wouldn't call it luck."

Old Dog
in a Doorway

23

The old dog in the doorway was making a valiant attempt to keep his legs upright and steady, but the effort was too much and they buckled and he had to lie down.

The doorway belonged to a leather goods shop in the Farringdon Road, which Jury was passing as he walked through Clerkenwell. The metal gate was pulled across the store's front. In the window was a host of hard-sided and expensive suitcases. There was a whole suite of cases in a dark red. Who would need all of those bags for a trip?

Jury knelt beside the dog. "Hey, boy." Tentatively, he reached out his hand and ran it over the dog's side. He could have counted the ribs. The dog's coat, black and white with brownish markings, was dry, the hairs coming off into Jury's hand. Perhaps the dog had mange; certainly he needed looking after.

He looked up and down the street, a busy street, for the nearest source of food and saw the McDonald's he and Wiggins had stopped in not many weeks before. That at least would be quick.

Inside, he ordered three burgers and bottled water and asked the girl, eyes like dry ice, if they had any sort of bowl he could use for the water. She went on chewing her gum and looking at him as if she didn't know what bowls were for. When he suggested soup, a little life came into her eyes and she scouted for one. He paid, took the sack, and left.

The dog still lay in the same place, shadows pooling around him.

Jury started with the water. He poured some in the bowl and put it directly under the dog's nose. When he began drinking and then slurping the water, Jury set the bowl on the stoop. The dog kept on drinking. Jury broke the meat up into small pieces and put it on a napkin. The dog sniffed but wouldn't eat.

This lack of interest in the food worried Jury. The dog needed a vet and probably fast. He took out his mobile, hoping the battery hadn't run down completely, which it had. Damn. Then he thought of the cabdriver who'd taken him to Bidwell Street. The Knowledge. He picked up the dog, the bowl, and the bottle of water, stuck the beef rolled in a couple of napkins into his raincoat pocket.

The dog weighed very little and was easy to carry. On Clerkenwell Road, Jury found a stopped cab and asked the driver about an animal hospital or vet that might be open this time of night.

"Your dog taken sick, has he?"

"Yes. Very sick." Indeed, the dog seemed not to notice, and certainly not to reckon with, the forced ride in a black cab.

"Not to worry, mate. We'll find one. Right off, I know there's one in Islington along the North Road."

That one turned out to be closed, but the driver knew of another he was sure was open all hours.

Jury certainly hoped so.

And thank God for "the Knowledge."

It was the All-Hours Animal Hospital, and its lights were on, blazing in the darkness.

Jury thanked the cabbie, gave him a huge tip, and complimented him on his knowledge.

"Well, we'd be a sorry lot without it. Night, mate."

Jury watched him speed off, not knowing, probably, how many people he had helped and would help, driving around with the knowledge of all of London in his head.

To the receptionist behind the counter, too young to look so sour, Jury said the dog needed attention right away. There were several people in the waiting room, and this girl wasn't helping.

"Just take a seat." She didn't look up from her crossword puzzle.

"The dog's in a very bad way; I—"

Now she looked up. "Why'd you wait so long to bring it in, then?"

"Because I had to comb all of the doorways in Clerkenwell before I found one with a sick dog in it." Jury didn't try to mute his voice. He heard a giggle behind him.

The girl was not used to back talk from a patient's handler, considering she held sway over the appointment book, and gave him a frosty look. Then she backed off and went through a door.

Jury sat down with the dog by an elderly woman in a crisp black suit who was still keeping up appearances as if there were hope. After a moment or two, she laid a hand on the dog's head and its eyes fluttered open. "Poor thing. Did you really find him in a doorway?"

Jury smiled, finding the source of the giggle. "I did. In Clerkenwell."

"One can find just about anything there."

He laughed. "I know what you mean."

"And you're right; he really does need attention. But he looks like a beautiful dog, really. A breed I'm unfamiliar with."

The receptionist was now standing in the doorway to the back rooms and calling, "Mrs. Bromley!" as if wanting to squash any friendly interaction with this man. "The doctor can see Silky now."

"My cat," she whispered to Jury. But instead of rising, Mrs. Bromley called back, "This gentleman can have my spot. His dog needs a doctor more than Silky does."

"But Dr. Kavitz—"

The lady rose. "Maureen—" She was no more than five one or two, but Maureen didn't want to mess with her, that was clear. She had about her some granite quality Maureen would break her hand on if she tried.

"All right, all right," said Maureen. Then she nodded to Jury, "Come on, then."

Jury's smile was genuinely brighter when he thanked Mrs. Bromley.

"I just hope your dog will be all right," she said.

Dr. Kavitz's temperament was considerably sunnier than Maureen's as he set about his examination, palpating here, listening there, prodding, reflecting, sometimes squint-eyed, as if to see the outlines of an abstract painting or to hear a note of some fading music. There was artistry involved.

More probing, more puzzlement, turning to look at the blank wall. Dr. Kavitz nodded and stood right where he'd been leaning over the dog. "He's quite sound, really. Terribly dehydrated—"

"I gave him water; he drank a lot."

"Good. But he'll need to take some intravenously. And he needs food."

"He wouldn't eat." Jury pulled the minced beef out of his pocket. "Maybe this wasn't the best thing."

Kavitz smiled. "Not surprising he wouldn't eat it; he'd have lost his appetite." He was scratching the dog's neck. The dog had his eyes wide open now. "What we'll do is keep him overnight, get him hydrated and eating. We'll see how he does. It was his brilliant luck, you finding him. I'm afraid he'd have been dead by the morning."

It made Jury's blood run cold, that it was so close. "He didn't look like he'd last very long."

"No. Well, you can be thinking of what to do with him. There's the RSPCA, of course, or one of the animal refuge places. If you can't keep him yourself, that might be the solution." Dr. Kavitz regarded the dog. "You know, I've a person who's been looking for one of these. I can get on to her about him."

Jury was puzzled. "One of these?"

"He's an Appenzell, you know, one of the mountain dogs. A cattle dog. But this one—the Appenzell—is the hardest of the lot to find."

"You mean, he's purebred?"

"Oh, yes. And as I said, they're not common."

"What would such a dog be doing in a doorway? And with no tags or anything?"

Dr. Kavitz shrugged. "Got lost, maybe. And he did at one time have identification. A collar." The doctor indicated a line round the neck where the coat looked worn. "Somehow, he lost it. Or someone took it off. It's possible his owner took off the collar and dumped him." Dr. Kavitz shook his head sadly. "A dog like this."

Anything's likely, thought Jury. He knew what people were capable of. "But more likely he could have got away, as you said. I think I should put an ad in the paper, shouldn't I?"

"Good idea."

Jury patted the dog, said, "All right, then. I'll be back tomorrow morning to pick him up." He thanked Dr. Kavitz, turned to leave. Behind him, he heard a woof.

Dr. Kavitz laughed. "Appenzells bark like hell. Our friend here's just warming up. Good night."

"Good night, Doctor. Thanks."

Jury left the building, stood on the dark street for a while, feeling a little better.

There were times when you just had to save something.

24

"A dog?" said Carole-anne, and then said it again. "A dog?" Her gaze slid around the room as if one would jump out and verify Jury's announcement. When one didn't, she said, "We've got a dog."

" 'We' do not." Jury pointed to the ceiling and the flat over his head. "Stone is Stan Keeler's dog. We do not have a dog."

Carole-anne was filing her nails with a huge four-grain file. Jury had suggested she bake it in a cake in case he landed in the nick.

"But we don't need another dog. Especially not one that's washed up from God knows where."

Jury had been drinking his morning cup of tea prior to going to Dr. Kavitz's. Carole-anne was not one to accept change, any change, in the dynamic of their four-flat terraced house: four flats, four tenants. Five, if one included the dog, Stone. That was it, and thus it would remain. Forever.

"I'm surprised," said Jury, "that you're not more sympathetic to the plight of homeless animals." No, he wasn't. Carole-anne had to see homelessness in situ. An actual dog in trouble would arouse her sympathy. She was no good at dealing with abstractions, such as "homelessness."

"You're gone all day. What's the poor dog to do?"

"Go on walks with you and Stone."

She flounced on the sofa. Only Carole-anne could come up with a real flounce—sending up little tufts of dust, bobbing her ginger hair into waves and curls, derigging cushion arrangements. Jury enjoyed the flouncing.

"Don't forget, will you, that I have a job, too," she said.

"Yes, but it's more haphazard than mine." Could any work be more haphazard than his?

"Haphazard? That's what you're calling it? Andrew has us on a very tight schedule."

Andrew was Andrew Starr, owner of Starrdust, the little shop in Covent Garden where she worked. "Andrew," said Jury, "has the moon, sun, stars, and peripheral planets on a tight schedule, but not his employees." Andrew was an astrologist, a very popular one. Possibly because he really was an astrologist, a meter-out of good and bad fortunes, but mostly good. "All I mean is, your schedule is more flexible than mine."

Jury wondered why he was winding her up. He had just that morning put ads in the papers. The dog would probably never see this house or his flat. He would be taking it straightaway to the shelter that Dr. Kavitz had mentioned. He must be telling Carole-anne about the dog just in case. In case of what?

"Anyway, I've got to pick him up at the vet's this morning." He had his raincoat on and his keys in hand. Was she going to leave? Apparently not.

She sat there filing away. "Ta, then."

"Don't bother getting up. I'll see myself out."

Jury was surprised at the change in the dog: the coat was softer, with even a hint of shine to it. And the dog's face, his whole head, was structurally beautiful. Jury didn't know why he hadn't seen that.

"Astonishing powers of recovery," said Dr. Kavitz. "Incredible resilience. These dogs are extremely tough and hardy. But the thing is, they're not meant to be an urban dog. They need a farm, something like that."

Jury said, "I put an ad in the *Times* and *Telegraph*. I was wondering, if somebody answers the ad, how will I know they're really the owners? You know the way dogs get stolen and sold for research. And I couldn't put a price on him because I'm looking for his owner." He felt absurd. A detective superintendent and he couldn't sort bogus claims of identity from the real thing? Good Lord.

"Good question. In the ad you placed, how did you describe him?" The doctor was checking the dog's teeth.

"Well, I said midsized, black, white, copper coat, collar missing. Found in the Farringdon Road."

"You didn't say he was an Appenzell mountain dog."

"No."

"That should do it, then. Anyone calls, ask them the breed. It's rare, so if they're guessing, they'll never get it. And if they say they're speaking for the real owner and don't know the breed, well, you know where you can stick that one, I'm sure."

Jury smiled. "I do."

The doctor had placed the dog in a large dog carrier, holes cut into it for seeing out as well as for breathing.

Jury took it from him and thanked him again for all the trouble he'd taken.

"If I can't take a little trouble, I shouldn't be in this business, should I? Emergencies are common; I imagine you face the same thing—one emergency after another. Here's the address of the place in Battersea, True Friends shelter. I'll call them up and tell them you're coming; that is, if you like."

"Yes. That would be fine."

"Okay, good luck, then." He reached his finger in to let the dog give him one last lick. "Swear to God, if I didn't live in a tiny little mews house, I'd take him, myself. But they need space. That might be what happened: dog got bored, couldn't stand it, ran off, then couldn't get back."

Jury thought Dr. Kavitz seemed not to want to let go.

* * *

The girl in the reception area of True Friends was a great improvement over the one in Dr. Kavitz's. Her pleasant, almost sunny disposition was more in keeping with animal rescue, thought Jury.

She was telling him Dr. Kavitz had rung and told her about the dog. "Hello," she said to him, opening the carrier and running her hand over his back. "You found him in a doorway, he said." She had the dog out, and his eyes—they were a beautiful walnut color—almost sparkled. She picked him up and put him over her shoulder while she filled out some kind of form. On the counter beside the forms was a little stack of white caps with "True Friends" written along the side in dark blue.

"Did he tell you he's an Appenzell mountain dog? And we think he might have just run off, looking for something interesting to do."

She laughed. "Mountain dogs aren't best kept in the city, or even the suburbs."

"No. The thing is, given he's pretty valuable, I'd think he had an owner somewhere looking for him, so I put ads in the papers."

She nodded, raised her face a bit, and looked round at the dog. "He's quite beautiful, isn't he? Well, you did the right thing. This dog"—which was still across her shoulder—"will have no trouble at all in getting adopted. And also, he likes you." She put another word down on her form.

"Me? Likes me? That's not my shoulder he's sprawled on. If it's the dog's happiness that concerns you, then you'll have to come along, too."

She blushed. Then she cocked her head and looked at Jury. "I know you can't take on the dog permanently, but we've a foster program here where a person gives the animal—the dog or cat—shelter for a short time while we find a home for it."

"The trouble is, I have a very irregular schedule and I'm out most of the time—"

She looked so pained, and so in extremis, he'd have felt like a heel not to fall in with this plan. "Yes, okay, I could do that."

Beaming as if the sun had risen, she said, "That's really nice of you, sir. I'll just make arrangements."

She was about to go off when Jury stopped her. "I can't take him with me right this minute. I'm leaving town. It might be a couple of days until I can get back."

The sun sank. "Oh."

Again, he felt like a heel. But he hadn't been lying. Somehow he felt this girl was always being lied to. He could imagine someone bringing in a great strapping animal who looked as though his last meal had been taken five minutes ago, claiming he'd "just found him in the streets" and dumping him.

Yes, she must have been through this time and time again. *I'll be back,* but never coming back. He took out his ID. "The thing is, I'm a policeman and I have a case that takes me out of London."

Her eyes widened as she looked at the ID.

"That's all right, then, Mr.—Inspector . . ."

"Jury. Superintendent Jury. I really will come back."

"Well, we'd be pleased to keep him until you do." She had her arms around the dog now, lifting him off the counter. "He needs a name. I guess you haven't named him yet. What can we call him?"

"I don't know. What's your name?"

She giggled. "Joely. But I'm a girl."

"I can see that. What a gorgeous name. Well, how about Joey?"

Joely looked into the dog's eyes, as if measuring him for this name. "Joey." She nodded in approval. "He's got his rabies tag now, but he needs a collar."

"With his name on it, yes."

She looked at Jury for a long moment, frowning and thinking. Then her face cleared and she said, "I know! Wait here." She carried the dog off with her. In a moment she was back with a cigar box, which she plopped on the counter, together with the dog. "When we find dogs, sometimes they have collars that we take off and save—here!" She turned an old leather collar with a small metal plate on it so that Jury could see it.

"Joe, it says. Now, wait." Here she took a small, sharp tool and scraped away on the end of the name, adding a "y." "I use this for different things on metal. Well, it doesn't look very professional, but—" She held it up for Jury (and Joey) to see.

Jury smiled. It was indeed not very professional, but the "y" was certainly workmanlike. "That's brilliant." The dog didn't resist at all as Jury put the collar round his neck.

They both admired her handiwork. She asked, "Did Dr. Kavitz tell you about mountain dogs?"

"A little. He said this particular kind—Appenzell?—is rare."

"It is in London, that's for sure. Here—" She pushed the filled-in form toward him. "Would you just sign here? And date it?" As Jury did this, she said: "They're herding dogs. You know, cattle, sheep, goats, and so forth. They're very active. I can see if you live in a flat, you'd probably be better off with another kind of dog."

She appeared to have forgotten what had landed him this one. He hadn't been looking for a dog at all. When he finished, she took back the form, impulsively snatched up one of the white caps, handed it to him, and said, laughing, "I don't suppose you know anyone with a lot of land and some sheep or goats, do you?"

Jury put on the cap, thought for a moment, and smiled. "Funny you should ask that."

His mobile was trilling as he was letting himself into his flat.

"Jury."

"It's me, guv. We did the door-to-door, found three tenants home, but no one who knows who she is. I wonder if maybe this grocer made a mistake."

"No. He was quite deliberate about her. She bought not just cigarettes but bread and milk and so forth. Not purchases you'd make if you were going to another part of the city. I could be wrong in assuming she must live in Bidwell Street, though. She could live several streets away." He thought for a moment. "Or quite possibly she visits a friend who lives there."

"That's a distinct possibility. Or perhaps she takes care of someone. Anyway, I'll keep checking. 'Bye."

25

"You were right, guv; she worked as an escort."

Jury had just walked into his office and was taking off his coat. "Tell me it's the same agency."

"No. Chelsea. King's Road Companions, it's called. Kind of sedate name for an escort place, isn't it? Her name's Kate Banks, and according to the manager, 'Kate's the best we had on offer.'"

Like a plate of cockles, thought Jury. "More or less what Blanche Vann said about Stacy Storm."

Wiggins nodded. "This Kate was the most popular, always busy, could get five, six hundred an hour if she wanted. In one week, Kate brought in five thousand quid."

"Do I hear a 'poor Kate' in there anywhere from this person? Did she spare a thought for Kate herself?" Jury creaked back in his chair and watched Wiggins stirring his tea. For once he was using a spoon, not a twig or a stick.

"No, Una was thinking more along the lines of 'poor Una.' That's the owner, Una Upshur."

"A name nobody was born with." He thought of Joey. Wiggins snorted.

"Did you squeeze anything else out of her besides Kate's earning power?"

"Not an awful lot. Kate's from Slough. There's reason enough to go on the game." Wiggins laughed into his tea.

"Why have people got it in for Slough? I like Slough. It's a good place."

Wiggins rolled his eyes. "Kate's been in London since she was in her early twenties, according to Una. Well-educated, she was. Started at King's Road a few years later." He thumbed up pages in his notebook, looked at it. "Una says she's been with her for about three years. But it's not her regular job; she's a steno typist days."

"Who was last night's client?"

"According to Una, there was no one on the books for Kate."

"That must have been unusual, given she was the agency's star. So she either wasn't with a client or was doing a bit on the side. Given the clothes and given the money, I'd certainly subscribe to the second idea. Like Stacy. And I'll bet Ms. Upshur wasn't giving out any names, either."

Wiggins stirred his tea. "'Clients have my assurance of absolute confidentiality.'"

"Until such future time as Una might want to try a spot of blackmail. Get a warrant, Wiggins."

"That might not be all that easy; there's not much probable cause."

"The hell there's not. She was with one of the agency's clients. Even if Kate was seeing this guy on the sly, he would still have been on the King's Road whatever books."

"Companions. Incidentally, Una made it clear that her setup wasn't about sex."

Jury made a blubbery noise of amused disbelief. "Then what, may I venture to ask, is it about?"

"Like it says: companionship."

"Sure."

"It's just possible; I mean, it could be some blokes want just that, boss."

Boss. Wiggins had started this more edgy mode of address. He was also rendering more opinions than was usual. He frowned more. He contemplated more. "I hope you're not losing your common touch, Wiggins."

There it was. Wiggins frowned. "What do you mean?"

"That you're sounding more coplike. More *Prime Suspect*."

"She's a woman. Helen Mirren."

"I'm aware Helen Mirren is a woman. Her team still calls her 'guv' and 'boss.'"

"But that's what we do, guv. There something wrong with that?"

"No. Not at all. Except you're sounding more like you're on our side."

Wiggins's frown deepened. "But . . . whose side would I be on if not ours?"

"The other side. The poor bloody public's that's got to put up with us. As I said, you could be losing the common touch."

Now Wiggins was contemplating. "Losing the common touch? You've lost me." He shook his head as if a child had been speaking. "I'm not sure what you mean."

Jury smiled. "I know. That's why you have it. Come on." He was up and unhitching his coat from the wooden rack. "We'll go and see what else we can drag out of the good Una."

King's Road Companions was housed in a sedate terraced house just off the King's Road in Chelsea. The reception area was equally sedate and well-appointed—Italian leather, silk-and-damask curtains, the walls lined with fairly stunning photographs of, presumably, the agency's girls.

"It's a terrible thing, a great tragedy," said Una Upshur, leaning forward over her desk. The wood was so fine that it looked warm, almost soft, as if it would have some give to it if you pressed down with your fingers. More give, thought Jury, than Mrs. Upshur had. She looked hard as rock, as if her frontage were not a well-spun gray wool but armor plate.

She kept flicking looks at Sergeant Wiggins, who was out of his assigned chair and moving about the room, taking in the wall of photos.

"You told my sergeant, Ms. Upshur, that Kate Banks wasn't with one of the agency's clients last night."

"That's quite right. Here, you can see for yourself—" She turned an appointment book, open to the day—or night—toward Jury.

Who glanced and glanced away, since Wiggins had already covered this territory. "You're selling sex."

As if this assessment astounded her, she fell back in her cushy leather chair. "We most certainly are not! These young women act as escorts to different events in London. It might be a society party, or an art gallery, or the opening of a play, or simply as a dinner companion or to go with a gentleman to a club."

"What you told Sergeant Wiggins was that Kate Banks could bring in upwards of five hundred quid an hour. That's one hell of a lot to pay for an arm to lean on as you wander through the Van Goghs and Sargents."

Her small mouth grew smaller, tightening. Then she rethought her situation and said: "There are many wealthy, lonely men out there for whom five hundred pounds is, well, nothing."

"Chump change." Jury smiled. "Come on, Ms. Upshur. No man's going to pay out that kind of money for simple presence."

"You'd have to have known Kate."

"I wish I had. But that's not in the cards, is it?"

Wiggins was back and sitting down, apparently having made his selection.

Not caring for where Jury was going, she switched to Wiggins. "Charming, aren't they? The most beautiful in London, I'd say."

"I don't see Kate Banks"—he hitched his thumb over his shoulder—"back there."

"Oh. That's because she'd had a new photograph taken and it's not up yet." Una Upshur was not meeting anybody's eyes.

Jury said, "Then why take down the old one?" No answer, so he said, "She quit, didn't she?"

"Certainly not!"

"She thought the kickback was excessive, especially given her remarkable earning power."

"That's absolutely untrue."

Wiggins deflected the anger. "She lived in Crouch End, didn't she?"

"Yes, she did."

"That's a long way from the West."

"It is. But it suited her, I expect. She'd lived there years."

"Did she also have a place in EC1 in the City? Near St. Bart's Hospital?"

Una shook her head, frowning. "No. At least not that I know of." She looked at both of them. "That's where she was found, wasn't it?"

Jury nodded. "Getting back to your clients. Could it be that one of them was displeased with Kate? I mean, could any of the men she went with have reason to do this?"

"Oh, my, no. I never heard a bit of a complaint. No, I can't imagine any of them wanting to hurt Kate." At this point, a tissue was produced from a drawer. It went with a tearless series of sniffs. That was apparently the best Una Upshur could do in the grieving department.

"What about your other girls? Escorts?"

"They were all fond of Kate."

"I seriously doubt that. Considering she was the high roller."

Una Upshur said nothing, looking glum.

Wiggins said, "Well, maybe you avoided trouble because there's not much occasion for the girls to meet, is there? They don't work out of this office, do they? I mean, they don't have to physically come in here." His tone was nice and conversational, Wigginsy.

Her smile wasn't sunny, but it was more smile than Jury had gotten. "Yes, you're quite right. They do come in here, but not on a regular basis. I just call them with the information."

Jury rose. They were getting sod-all from this woman. "We'll need a photo of Kate Banks, if you don't mind."

"Very well. I keep pictures on file." She turned and went through to another room.

He heard metal drawers opening and closing, then she was back and holding out a five-by-seven photo. "This is one she had taken a year ago."

She was beautiful, for certain. She didn't look hard, used, or unhappy. He pocketed the photo. "Thanks. We'll be in touch."

Wiggins rose and they left.

"A little impatient, weren't you, guv? A bit dyspeptic, maybe."

"More than a little." When he found Wiggins looking at him speculatively, evaluating, no doubt, the state of Jury's liver, he said, "No, I don't want one of your bloody homeopathic medications, shoots, roots, vines, biscuits, powders, or gums from the sacred bolla-wolla tree." Jury gestured toward the car. "Drop me off at the Snow Hill station, will you?"

26

"Two shots, one to the stomach and one to the chest." Dennis Jenkins held up two casings in a plastic sleeve. "Recovered from the victim. A twenty-two snubnose. Tiny little gun, would fit in a rolled-down sock or a tiny little purse." He held up the clutch that had been lying by the body of Kate Banks. "It doesn't have much power, but at close range aimed at soft tissue, it'll certainly do the job. As we saw."

Jury frowned. "You think it was Kate Banks's?"

Jenkins shook his head. "We haven't traced it yet. But if she was on the game, it wouldn't be surprising that she'd carry a weapon for defense. Which is how one of these snubbies is ordinarily used. The thing is, it's very easy to conceal."

Jury thought about this, shook his head. "Not in Kate Banks's purse. Not with that wad of money in it."

Jenkins nodded.

"Mariah Cox was shot with a thirty-eight. But I still think it's the same shooter." Jury smiled briefly.

"The escort-cum-librarian. That fascinates me."

At first Jury thought Jenkins was being sarcastic. But he looked at Jenkins's small smile and decided, no, he really was fascinated.

Jenkins continued: "A double life. Was that it? Was that the rush? Not the sex, not the money?"

"I don't know. I certainly get a different picture from her boy-friend, I mean the one back in Chesham. He was pretty much blindsided by this. Not just her death, her life. Lives."

Jenkins creaked back in his chair. "Remember Kim Novak? *Vertigo?*"

"You brought that up last night. You think Kate Banks was thrown off a bell tower?"

Jenkins frowned but not at Jury. "There was something really sick about that film."

"You mean the Jimmy Stewart character?"

"The whole film. Her, too. She fell in with it." Jenkins was rolling a pencil over his knuckles, back and forth. "You ever study obsession?"

"Aside from my own? No."

"Yeah. Cops tend to be. It doesn't have much to do with love or any other feeling. It has to do with the idea of it. Obsession has to do with itself."

"You've lost me."

Jenkins sighed. "Yeah. Me, too." He tossed up the pencil and caught it like a baton twirler. "No . . . wait. I did have a thought there." He paused. "Hitchcock was way off base with *Vertigo*. That character just wasn't set up right. Now, take Norman Bates. Norman was completely mad—"

"*Psycho?*"

Jenkins nodded. "But the guy in *Strangers on a Train*, Bruno. Now, there was a characterization. Bruno was only half-mad. Both of those characters were more believable than the James Stewart character."

A WPC rapped on the door frame—the door itself was open—came in, and handed Jenkins a folder. On her way out, she smiled at Jury.

Jenkins slapped the folder open. "Okay." He muttered a few hmm's.

"Is that Kate's?" Jury thought he was picking up Wiggins's habit of speaking of victims on a first-name basis.

Jenkins nodded. "No surprises. No cartridges found at the scene. Two recovered from the victim. There's not really much to link these shootings other than the escort service angle."

"And that nothing happened."

Jenkins frowned, puzzled. "What?"

"Nothing happened aside from the two women being shot: there was no rape and, what was more curious, considering the seven hundred and fifty pounds—no robbery. They were both dressed up, as if for a party."

"Yet where they happened, those places are completely different. It wasn't as if they'd both occurred in a certain part of London. One in London, one outside of it. That's what distances them. That would make you think this isn't a serial killer; it makes you think the two killings aren't related."

"But you don't think that?" said Jury.

"No. I think they're related." Jenkins sat brooding on something. Obsession, Jury guessed, and asked, "What did you mean when you said obsession 'has to do with itself'?"

Jenkins chewed at the corner of his mouth. "Look at Iago."

Jury liked that trip from Hitchcock to Shakespeare.

"There's nothing to explain Iago. The reasons given are absurd. No, it's like Hamlet: nothing in the plays explains their actions. Iago didn't act out of jealousy or rage or revenge. He was just being Iago— you know what I mean."

Jury smiled. "This is good, but can we get back to our own little drama? Can we talk about our two dead women?"

Jenkins looked genuinely puzzled. "I thought we were."

"Meaning, you think our killer was obsessed with sex, or prostitutes, or . . . ?"

But Jenkins was shaking his head. "I don't think he knew what his reasons were."

Jury gave a brief laugh. "This is getting away from me." He glanced at his watch. "It's lunchtime. I'm off to a pub to have a word with my own Iago. 'Bye, Dennis."

27

"Where were you last night, Harry?"

In the Old Wine Shades, Harry Johnson was languidly smoking a small, thin cigar. Jury hadn't bothered with a greeting, at least not for Harry Johnson. He did say hello to Mungo.

"Where did you want me to be, and at what time?" Harry blew a smoke ring. "There's been another murder, I take it."

"Just a hop, skip, and a jump from here."

"A hop, skip, and a jump from here lies the part of inner London with the highest crime rate in the city. Could that perhaps explain your murder? Or do you have it in mind to tie the one in the City together with the one in Chesham?"

Mungo lurched up and froze like a pointer, as if Chesham had fallen somewhere out there in the fields.

"Something wrong?" asked Jury.

"Yes," said Harry. "Stop trying to—"

"I'm talking to Mungo."

"Mungo's nerves seem to be in a state. God knows why."

Mungo had defrosted but still sat up alert, all ears.

As if something spooked him, thought Jury. "You still haven't answered me. Where were you last night?"

Harry sighed. "I was here." He tipped his head in the direction of Trevor, who was serving a couple at the end of the bar. "Ask Trev."

"I will. Were you here all night?"

"Did I doss down here? No."

"You know what I mean. You came when and left when?"

"Came at nine; left at ten or eleven. Does that fit the killer's schedule?"

"Close." Jury smiled. "That ten or eleven's a bit vague."

Harry shrugged. "I can always change it. Have some wine. It's a great Bordeaux." Trevor had come along and placed a glass before Jury.

"You're pretty cavalier about a double murder."

"I can afford to be, given I didn't do them." Harry tapped ash from his cigar with his little finger, looked at the cigar, scrubbed it out.

"You were in Chesham. You've been to the Black Cat—"

Again, Mungo stood up between the two bar chairs and froze like a pointer.

Harry looked down. Ineffectively he gave a command: "Sit, Mungo."

As if.

"You're giving Mungo commands?"

"I like to see if it has any effect."

"It doesn't."

"No."

"The Black Cat, Harry?"

Mungo quivered.

"It's interesting to me that there's a black cat gone missing from the pub. I'm wondering if there's a relationship."

"Wonder away," said Harry.

Mungo started turning in circles.

"Is Mungo trying to say something?" He reached down to the dog. "What's up, boy?"

What's up, boy? Mungo cringed.

Jury looked at him and then went on. "The little girl who lives at the pub thinks the cat was either murdered or kidnapped. Like the woman found outside. She claims that the black cat there now isn't her cat, that it's been put in the real cat's place—" Jury frowned at Mungo, who was clawing at his leg, something he never did. Jury reached down to pet his head, and Mungo flopped onto the floor.

Harry looked at Mungo, shook his head, and set another cigar on fire. A tiny flame leapt up when he put his gold lighter to it. "You've read E. A. Poe, I expect. Have you read 'The Black Cat'?" He didn't wait for an answer. "Interesting tale, and a very sick one, but it's Poe, after all. Narrator has a black cat. They're inseparable. Cat follows him around all the time. The fellow starts drinking and is soon deep into an alcoholic mind-set. He does something horrible to the cat and eventually hangs the animal. The story's pretty ghoulish."

"Why does he do it?"

"The narrator's idea is that one does things just because they're perverse. No motive other than that."

What came to Jury's mind was the conversation he'd just had with Jenkins. *Vertigo.*

Harry continued, "I think it has more to do with the man's psychological state, not his spiritual one. Perversion for the sake of perversion. Interesting. The black cat, of course, comes back to haunt him in particularly nasty ways. The only thing I don't like about Poe is the payback. There's always a payback, a punishment. I find that unconvincing." He mused. "This little girl at the pub you mentioned, she could be making it up about the kidnapped cat."

Mungo was off the floor and turning in circles again.

"It's just too strange a story," Harry went on. "Why would someone kidnap a cat? It's ludicrous. Like the other one."

Jury turned full face to stare at him. "Oh, you mean the one you told me about Mungo disappearing and magically coming back? That story you stuffed into me over drinks and dinners, and me, idiot that I am, believing it? That story?"

Harry blew another smoke ring and said, "Get over it, will you? It's going on your tombstone, 'The dog came back.'"

On the floor, Mungo seemed literally to have his paw over his eyes.

With an energetic shake of his head, Jury said, "No, it's going on *your* tombstone, Harry. I'll carve it out myself."

Harry sighed. "You just won't let that go, will you? Did it ever occur to you that your memory might be equally faulty? Like that child's memory? That incredible story might never have happened."

Jury looked at Harry Johnson, holding his glass of wine in the path of light cast by the pendant above their heads. "You've got so many versions of stories, it's hard to tell which one you're referring to, which story, and which of its dozen lives. If you're talking about the Tilda version, surely you're not resorting to that old cliché: the witness's memory is faulty."

Harry turned the glass as if it were prismatic, a diamond. "Why not? Proust did."

"Oh, please. First Poe, now Proust?" Jury took a long drink of his wine.

Harry set down his glass and turned to him with a faint, ironic smile. "You've read him, have you?"

"Of course, the same as most people have. *Swann's Way.* I stopped around page thirty, where he's dipping the cake in the tea."

"It was a bit of a madeleine in a spoon that was dipped in tea. And from that taste, an entire world blossomed in his mind. That's all you read, is it? Too bad. At least you ought to read *Time Regained.* You can hardly grasp his purpose on the basis of thirty pages. And all along the way, there are episodes similar to the madeleine bit. In one of these, he's in a salon at a piano recital and he hears a phrase—only that, two notes—and he has a similar experience. The 'little phrase,' he calls it. Then in *Time Regained* he's about to enter the home of the Guermantes when his toe hits one of the stones in the walk, and that calls up a memory. When he's seated inside, waiting, a starched napkin is the next trigger. It's fascinating."

"But that's the exact opposite of what you're saying—that memory can be faulty. Proust is talking about lost memory, not fabricated memory."

"My word, Richard, you got a hell of a lot out of your thirty pages! But that's only part of it, you see. There must be some action that precipitates memory—the madeleine, the little phrase of music, the napkin—the buried memory—"

Jury interrupted. "This isn't buried memory, damn it, you're talking about faulty memory. And on the basis of this you're deconstructing the girl Tilda's entire account of that afternoon!" He was going to hit him in a moment. Sourly, Jury contemplated his glass.

"Then look at this other little girl's story—what's her name? So I can keep them straight?"

"Dora. Keep them straight? That's all it is to you, a story, two stories."

Harry ignored that. "Look at Tilda's story from another point of view." He was again moving his glass around until light sparked it. "On this one afternoon, a child is playing in the grounds of a large, untenanted country house, playing with dolls or stuffed animals, and she looks up and across this desolate and untended garden—"

"Oh, stop editorializing. You weren't—" Jury stopped. He wanted to cut out his tongue.

Harry laughed. "You nearly said 'weren't there.' That's good. Especially since it should be obvious that the so-called editorializing would show that I was there."

"You were." Jury tried not to break his wineglass over Harry's head. "Don't try and pull this again, Harry. Don't try dazzling me with your agile arguments. I'm not falling for it a second time."

"I wasn't. Let me finish, will you? The little girl looks over these silent gardens toward the terrace, where she sees a man—no, there were two children. I forgot the boy—"

"Timmy."

"Yes. Two of them. This is beginning to sound like *The Turn of the Screw*. With me as the sinister Peter Quint."

"You'd make a poor Quint. He hadn't your personality. And he was dead." Jury finished off his wine.

Harry laughed and signaled to Trevor. "Then the girl claims that this man chased the two of them, caught them, and kidnapped them. Now, does this Jamesian spin really sound like an accounting of events free of fantasy?"

"You're leaving out the blindfolding and keeping them captive in his cellar."

"Oh, yes! How could I have forgotten? That lends such a note of realism to the story."

Trevor had come down the bar with a bottle. He winked at Jury. "Mr. Johnson telling you another tall tale, Mr. Jury?"

"That's just what I'm doing," said Harry. "Only it's not my tale. It's someone else's." He turned from Trevor to Jury. "That's all you have: the testimony of a couple of kids who can't even describe their captor."

"They do have names: Timmy and Tilda."

"Hansel and Gretel, more likely." Harry shrugged. "Well, I wouldn't know, would I?" He smiled. "Never having met them."

28

Joey launched himself out of the car the moment Jury opened the door. He made off across the wide green grass of Ardry End and ran round the corner of the house, with Jury following.

What was he heading for? Nothing and anything. The stable? The hermitage? There was no sign of Mr. Blodgett, resident hermit. But Jury (and presumably Joey) did see Aggrieved, Melrose Plant's horse, and his goat, Aghast, out there beyond the stable, their heads down, grazing.

Jury had by this time reached the rear of the house and the wide kitchen garden and an unfamiliar man standing before the kitchen door. Had the man been a professional clown or a music hall hold-over, Jury would have said he was dressed in motley. He wore a faded purple velvet jacket, probably once a smoking jacket, a bright scarf round his neck, and a satin waistcoat. Checkered trousers completed this outfit. In his pocket was what looked like a half-pint of Cinzano.

Joey was running a circle round the horse and goat, barking. It sounded like a measured, tempered bark, as if it had a specific purpose.

The tall man inclined his head by way of acknowledging Jury. Jury returned the gesture, and at that point the door was opened by

Ruthven, Melrose Plant's manservant. Ruthven was taken aback by this duo at the kitchen door, seeming to have come here together.

"Superintendent Jury! Why—please come in."

Ruthven did not appear surprised at the sight of the other visitor, who must have been here before. "And Mr. Jarvis, come in."

On his way through the door, Jury said, "You might want to see to the dog out there harassing the other animals." When Jarvis was out of earshot, Jury said, "Must be his, don't you think?"

"I don't know. Lord Ardry's expecting you; he's in the drawing room. If you'll just follow—"

"Oh, don't bother, Ruthven, I know where it is. Go and see to your visitor."

Ruthven bowed and went off toward the kitchen.

In the handsome drawing room, Melrose was situated at one of the floor-to-ceiling windows and talking to someone on the outside of it—Mr. Blodgett, probably. Blodgett came up to the windows regularly, either to make wild faces at Melrose's aunt Agatha or to make a request or to keep Melrose abreast of estate happenings. Today's happening (as Jury well knew) was the presence of a dog.

"My word," said Melrose, mostly to the sky and earth, as he was leaning out the window. "Damned if you're not right, Blodgett. D'you think it's rabid, or what?"

"Don't be ridiculous," said Jury, joining them at the window. "It's just an old dog. Must belong to the man in the kitchen. Jarvis? That his name? I told Ruthven about it."

"I didn't hear the front door. How long have you been here that you know more than I do?"

"That's not hard." Jury was leaning out the window now, elbowing Melrose aside. He could see Joey running herd on Aghast while Aggrieved looked on with seeming indifference. Jury couldn't see the horse's expression, but indifference figured in the tilt of his large brown head. Aggrieved would watch for a moment, then go back to chomping grass.

"The dog's just enjoying himself. Hello, Mr. Blodgett."

"'Lo, Mr. Jury. Nice t'see ya ag'in. Well, I best be goin', fer I got things to do. Just thought mabbe you'd want to know 'bout the dog." Blodgett, who wasn't going off at all, went on, " 'E looks a bit like one o' them sheepdogs."

Ruthven came in then, and Melrose motioned him over to the window. "There's a dog out there, Ruthven. Know anything about him?"

Ruthven seemed to sail when he moved, gliding smoothly over the Turkish carpet. "I expect he belongs to the man in the kitchen, Jarvis."

"Oh, I see. First I've got a dog in the garden, and now I've got a man in the kitchen. Good Lord, the place could be taken over by an army of elves and I'd be the last to know—there he goes!"

The three of them—or four, if one included Mr. Blodgett on the outside—moved to another window on the other side of the fireplace that gave them a better view of the stables. Joey was still attempting to round up the goat, Aghast. Aggrieved watched.

"Look at him! He's barking at Aghast. Who in hell does he think he is?"

"A dog," said Jury. "Looks like he's herding." Melrose looked at him. "Herding?"

"Well, as Blodgett said, he looks like a sheepdog. Aggrieved and Aghast don't seem to mind him."

"If he's a border collie," said Ruthven, "he'll probably carry on—" Then, mindful that it was not his place to be standing here giving his opinion, Ruthven swanned off.

"Wait. Who's in the kitchen?"

Ruthven turned. "It's Jarvis, sir. You remember."

"Oh, him. So it's his dog?"

"I'd say so. Martha's fixed him a meal."

"Well, bring us a bottle of that Médoc and tell Jarvis to collect his dog before he leaves."

Joey and Aghast were lying down now. Aggrieved stood, still munching quietly. The grass he nibbled at was such an evenly bright green, it looked enameled; the maples and willows shone in the brilliant light of early afternoon.

Melrose still leaned against the wall, peering out the window. "I can't tell if he's wearing a collar."

Ruthven was back almost immediately with wine and glasses on a tray. "Mr. Jarvis says he knows nothing about the dog. But if you like, he could take the dog with him, get him off your hands."

"Oh, I don't think you'd want to do that," said Jury rather quickly. "Probably he belongs to some tourist who was passing through and the dog got away from them."

Ruthven had uncorked the bottle and was pouring the wine. "I agree with Mr. Jury, m'lord."

"When's the last time you ever saw a tourist pass through? Long Piddleton is not exactly a destination village. But you're probably right." They both accepted a glass of wine from the tray Ruthven passed.

Melrose thanked Ruthven and told him to see the dog got his dinner along with the goat and the horse.

"And use the good silver," said Jury.

Ruthven allowed himself a brief snicker and sailed off.

Melrose plopped himself down in his wing chair. From the corners of the ceiling molding, unconcerned cupids observed. "I should put an ad in the paper, shouldn't I?"

"That's what I'd do," said Jury. "He's got tags, at least a rabies tag." Dr. Kavitz had seen to that. But how would Jury know it? "I saw him up close when I was waiting. And he's got a name tag, too. His name's Joey." Jury smiled.

A little later, done with wine and talk about the dog and Jarvis—a homeless soul who stopped by from time to time (which struck Jury as even more unlikely than a tourist)—they walked down the drive and crossed the Northampton road after a party of cyclists, all in black leather, gunned on by.

Jury thought he was caught up in a dream. Motorcyclists were even more unlikely than homeless men.

Melrose watched them out of sight, looking thoughtful, then said, "You know, I read a poem by some American poet. He's describing the coming on of night, comparing it with an onslaught of cyclists on a blacktop road. I used to hate motorcycles, but after reading that, I've never looked at them the same way. Now they have a kind of exotic beauty. Now they look as if they're ushering in something we should know about."

"The next big thing. That's what poetry should do: usher in the next big thing."

They were passing Lavinia Vine's cottage and stopped to admire the garden, a late May idyll.

"Look at those apricot roses," said Melrose. "And those tulips." With a riot of colors from pale blue to a red so strong they looked dipped in blood, a large square of tulips shouted down the flowers around them. Jury wished he'd stop thinking about death. The next big thing.

A couple of drunken butterflies were sorting through the yellow blossoms of some shrubby plant. Against the low wall on the left was a border of peonies and clouds of white hydrangeas.

"The fragrance is sleep-inducing," Jury said. "That must be what put the cat down." He was referring to a big cat sleeping atop one of the stone pillars set by the walk.

"Desperado's a nasty piece of work. I've seen him take down dogs."

They walked on.

"Speaking of dogs, the new one should have a name," Melrose said, ignoring Jury's earlier comment. "We'll have to have a naming competition."

"I told you, his name's Joey," said Jury. He was getting irritable. They were near Long Piddleton's center, if it could be said to have one. It did have a pleasant green, where a shallow little lake served as home to an extended family of ducks, a few of which were, like the butterflies, drunkenly floating around. Why, Jury wondered, lifting his face toward the sky, couldn't humans get drunk on air?

"You know, you haven't mentioned your friend Detective Inspector Aguilar. I assume she's still in hospital?"

"Yes. Not good. She's in a coma."

Melrose stopped. "Good Lord. That's terrible. I'm so sorry."

Jury nodded.

They resumed their walk. Through the window of the local library, Miss Tooley, the librarian, waved at them. Melrose raised his hand in a dispirited way to return the wave. "What's the chance she'll come out of it?"

"Just that—a chance. But if she doesn't, she's signed a paper saying she doesn't want what they call 'heroic measures' instituted. The doctor says a person usually comes back from a coma in a couple of weeks, or not at all."

Melrose shook his head. "I'm really sorry."

Across the village green sat Vivian Rivington's house. "That place is beautiful," said Jury. "I wouldn't mind a house like that."

"Then marry her. I bet she'd be delighted."

How dense can you be? thought Jury. "I bet she wouldn't. I proposed once and got turned down."

Melrose stopped again. "You didn't!"

"She was engaged, if you remember, to Simon Matchett. Didn't love him, though, that was clear."

"I've never understood her."

"I know. That's because you're as thick as two planks."

29

Melrose tapped on the leaded window of the Jack and Hammer, and the group sitting at the table in the bay window peered out and waved. Except for Marshall Trueblood, apparently not finished with his morning calisthenics, who stood and threw his arms about in meaningless gestures.

Inside, Melrose asked, "What in God's name was all of that semaphore about?"

"To warn you off," said Trueblood. "Theo Wrenn hyphen Brown saw the two of you and is now leaving his shop and coming here. Hell."

Jury said hello to the four—no, five, for here was Dick Scroggs the publican, bringing fresh drinks; no, six, for here was Mrs. Withersby, Dick's char, who was slapping her slippered feet toward them. She had a cigarette behind her ear and was hoping for another, along with her free favorite pint.

"Wrenn hyphen Brown? What's that about?"

"He thinks a double-barreled last name has more cachet."

Said Melrose, "I have the care of a new dog. A homeless man came to the door and I'm sure he had the dog with him, but he denied it, so we don't know where the dog came from. He's lost or something. Maybe got free of his owner."

"What kind of dog?" asked Diane Demorney.

"Sheepdog."

"Mountain dog," said Jury, who had remained standing.

Melrose looked at him. "You know the difference?"

Nonchalantly, Jury shrugged. "You can just tell about this dog."

Melrose frowned, then said, "For heaven's sakes, sit down, will you? You're making us nervous."

Jury laughed, looking at the group slouched comfortably round the table. "Yes, I can see all of you are a bundle of nerves."

Diane Demorney, taking precious time from her martini, asked, "Does the dog have a name?"

"No," said Melrose.

"Joey," said Jury at the same time.

They stared at Jury; they wanted evidence.

"It's on his collar."

"When did you ever see his collar?" said Melrose.

"I told you. When he went by, I got up close to him."

Vivian Rivington frowned. "He stopped for you?"

"Well, no, not exactly."

They were all frowning at Jury now. He knew why, too. They wanted to have a name contest and he could be throwing a spanner into the works with his "Joey."

Right, Trueblood apparently decided. He said, "We'll have to name him."

Theo Wrenn-Brown had come and pulled a chair round as if he were welcome. He shoved it in between Trueblood and Diane. He called over to Dick Scroggs, who was reading the Sidbury paper, leaning over it on the bar. Theo called for a gimlet. He could have called for his fiddlers three with more success.

He then settled in to get attention paid him. "Superintendent! Solved any cases lately?" "Hee-haw" was precisely and phonetically what Theo's laugh sounded like. Hee-haw. "Where's my drink? Dick!"

Dick blew his nose with a big handkerchief and went back to his paper.

"Oh, for God's—" Theo shoved back his chair and stomped over to the bar.

"Should we do the naming the same way we did for Aghast?" said Joanna Lewes, who wrote books that were a commercial success.

"Nobody won that," said Diane. "Melrose rejected all of our suggestions and went with his own name."

"Well, it was my goat. Anyway, it was really Agatha who came up with it, by accident, of course. She was 'aghast' that I had a goat."

"All right, all right." Trueblood leaned over the table next door and plucked up a few small paper napkins. These he dealt out like a card shark.

Jury sighed. "I don't have time to stay through another one of your contests. I've got to get to Chesham."

"You mean Amersham?" asked Trueblood.

"No. I mean Chesham. Thanks." The thanks was for Dick Scroggs, who had just handed Jury a pint of Adnams. "Besides, the dog's already got a name: Joey."

Diane said, "Yes, but you don't know if it's really his name." On the edge of her glass, she tapped the toothpick that had lately speared the olive in her martini.

Jury knew better than to use reason with this crowd, but his line of work condemned him always to try. "Then is 'Aggrieved' real? Is 'Aghast' the goat's *real* name?"

"Well, of course. We named him."

That made sense. Jury drank half his pint and set it down. "I've got to get going. I'm meeting my sergeant in Chesham."

"Yes, old scout. You didn't tell us what was going on in Chesham."

"A killer-naming contest. See you later."

They stared after him openmouthed, clearly wondering, and he let them.

30

Mungo had paced for so long, he felt he'd worn his paws to nubbins.

Morris was lying on the carpet in the music room, watching him. She yawned and slowly closed her eyes; all that pacing tired her. Most things did.

Mungo stopped. Why is it all down to me? This is your fate we're talking about. I'm not the one who wants to get back to Amerslum.

Amer-sham. Anyway, it's Chesham. I told you, more than once.

More than once. More than once. He lay down and tried to curl his legs into his chest. Do you have more joints than me?

I don't know. Morris yawned again: How are you going to get me back to Chesham?

Mungo didn't answer. He went over to the walnut bureau and its bottom drawer, looking at the pile of kittens, looking for Elf. He needed to relax. The kittens were piled on top of one another. Was there nothing but black cats in this whole wide world? No wonder Mrs. Tobias thought Morris was Schrödinger. It was amazing that the two cats could coexist in this house without anyone's knowing.

Mungo rolled two kittens away from the pile. They spat at him. Then he unearthed Elf.

What are you doing with that kitten? Morris asked.

Nothing. Mungo had Elf in his mouth, looking around for a

hiding place. This activity relaxed him a bit; he could do it and think about a problem at the same time. He looked over the music room. Not the grand piano; he'd done that, along with the coal scuttle, the umbrella urn, the planters.

Put that kitten down, said Morris.

Boss, boss, boss, boss. Mungo didn't care; he wasn't all that interested in hiding Elf, so he dropped him.

Elf made his way fuzzily back to the drawer, trying to think nasty thoughts about his tormentor, but he couldn't, as he was too little and his mind was formless and without messages.

The Spotter had been talking about Chesham and a case. Then he'd gone on about the "two kids"—oh, what an adventure that had been! But if there was a "case" in Chesham, was it possible it was Morris related? Mungo stopped his pacing and stared at Morris (who was taking a nap, no help there). Morris had been witness, if not to the murder, then certainly to the dead body.

Mungo hitched up one paw, set it down, picked up the other paw, set it down, the other up, down, up, down. Nervous excitement. He paced again, head down as if he meant to ram through a— Wait! Morris might not have known what she was seeing. How could you see a murder and not know?

He trotted over to Morris and gave her a shove where she lay.

Wake up!

Morris shifted and recurled herself.

Wake up! Listen— Think! Did you see a murder? Did you see anything at all that might have been a murder?

Morris narrowed her eyes. Of course not. I saw this person lying there, and then the woman and dog came along.

Mungo paced again and wished he smoked cigars. He could stand reflectively by the bay window, tapping ash. All right, maybe she hadn't seen anything. What if she had? What would they do with the knowledge? Go to the local station and fill out a report?

Pacing. Stopping. But . . . what if the Spotter were to see Morris?

Well, maybe . . .

What did they have to lose?

Nothing at all.

Mungo went over and plopped himself down beside Morris. Listen: Here's what we'll do. There's this pub called the Old Wine Shades Harry's always going to. The Shades, for short.

I'd rather go to my own pub.

Don't go all weepy on me. Life's hard enough.

It is for Dora.

Oh, God, thought Mungo, I'll run away and be a hobo dog. But he knew he wouldn't. The food was tasty here, and the beds were good. And there was Elf and the rest.

He said, The Shades.

31

Was Sally Hawkins so hopelessly blind that she really thought she could pass this thug off as the real Morris? Either she did or she didn't care.

Waiting in the Black Cat for Wiggins, Jury drank his beer and thought about Joey. Joey would sort out Morris Two in an eyeblink. In his mind's eye he saw his friends in the Jack and Hammer, casting their votes for a name that would no doubt be absurd.

His mobile trilled its tune. He nearly stubbed his finger racing to turn it off.

It was Wiggins. "I'm in a cab on my way to the pub. I did find out something from Mr. Banerjee; he was very helpful. That's an interesting shop. Very Indian-like."

"That could be because Mr. Banerjee is Indian, Wiggins." Jury was keeping his eye on Morris Two, as the cat had jumped up to the table and was eyeing the mobile pressed to Jury's ear. "Next time, I'll make it a conference call, okay?"

"Conference call? What?"

"Sorry. I wasn't talking to you, Wiggins."

"Is there someone there with you?"

"No. I'll see you in a few minutes." Morris Two was having a wash. A ruse, Jury knew. He was really waiting for Jury to take his eye off his pint and his phone from his ear.

"Right," said Wiggins.

Jury clapped the mobile shut and set it on the table.

Morris Two stopped licking his paw and glared at it. From it to Jury. As the cat seemed to be thinking over the mobile's tune, David Cummins walked in.

Looking, thought Jury, drawn and not very happy.

"David." Jury motioned him over.

"I thought that car might be yours," he said.

"You mean the unmarked Hertz rental with the bullet holes in the windscreen? Yes, I can understand why you'd hit on me straightaway."

David laughed; the laugh made him look a little less ashen.

Jury pushed out a chair. "Sit down. You look like hell. Want a drink? I'm waiting for my sergeant."

He sat down, extracted a cigarette from a pack of Rothmans, and looked at Jury, but Jury's expression was noncommittal. "I can light one for you, too. *Now, Voyager.*" Wanly, he smiled, looked over his shoulder for Sally Hawkins, and, not seeing her, shrugged. "We were wondering if you could stop by the house? Chris wants to talk to you. She has an idea—well, let her tell you it."

That was puzzling. "All right, sure. We'll come round as soon as Sergeant Wiggins gets here. Twenty, thirty minutes?"

David rose. "Good. Thanks." He sketched Jury a small salute and was out the door.

Ten minutes later, Morris Two was back at the window, straining to see the latest arrival.

It was Wiggins, who walked through the door, looked around, sussing out the place as if you couldn't see daylight through the smoke and the people. There were only the three at the other table and a man at the bar, thoroughly juiced.

"There you are, boss." Wiggins pulled out a chair, and Morris Two, who had just claimed it as his own, spat and jumped down.

"That cat's a treat."

"I told you about Morris, didn't I? I think this particular incarnation of him once belonged to the Demon Barber of Fleet Street. Morris hates people. All people."

"Abused as a kitten, it could be."

"He's certainly going to be abused as a cat. Want a beer?" The old Wiggins was more of a lemon squash guy.

"Bit early for me."

"It's after five."

Wiggins made some sort of rocking hand gesture, sending what message Jury couldn't imagine. Then he slid his notebook from an inside pocket, flipped it open. "This shopkeeper, Benjarii, told me he'd given some thought to the photo you'd shown him and remembered Kate Banks had come in a number of times over the course of the last year and that she'd bought staples, you know, bread, milk, butter—staples. Very pleasant, he said, but she wasn't one for chatting people up. But once she'd bought a jar of curried pickle which he'd remarked on as being a favorite of his. Kate Banks said it was also a favorite of her friend's. The implication was, he thought, that this was who she was buying for. It's not much, but it means there is someone around there who knew her well."

"Yes. And someone who might need seven hundred and fifty quid. I know I'm reaching here because the money could have been paid her that night after her escort encounter. But it also could have been cash not earned that night that she was taking to someone. How large an area would that shop encompass for people who shop there regularly? Not very big, I shouldn't think."

"No. There's another shop three streets over and a Europa three streets north. People closer to those would be using them. So I'm guessing a three-block parameter, all four sides. I could narrow that because Mr. Banerjee said she came from that direction, in his case, north. He saw her once or twice cross St. Bride's, coming to his shop, so the area to cover would probably be three blocks each direction."

Jury turned his unfinished pint glass around and around. "It does sound as if Kate were taking care of someone. Some relation?" He turned the glass. "Has anyone ID'd the body yet?"

"They got Una Upshur in. But no one related to Kate Banks. They haven't found any relatives. Sounds as if Kate was pretty much on her own."

"Except for the one she was possibly helping. Maybe that person will go to police. Come on, Wiggins. We're going to see DS Cummins and his wife." Jury, standing, finished off his beer.

As Wiggins got up, Morris Two shot out of his lethal nowhere and streaked between Wiggins's legs, almost tumbling him.

"Bloody cat!" he said as he grabbed the back of the seat for balance.

32

With cups of tea served all round, Chris Cummins fairly beamed at Jury and Wiggins, as if they might be as proud of this collection as she herself.

It certainly could have been said of Sergeant Wiggins, who found her aggregation of shoes even more fascinating than Jimmy Choo's. He appeared to be drawn to these rows of shoes as much as he would have been to a medicine doctor's strange roots, palliative powders, or dried animal parts. At the moment, he had helped himself to a shelf and had pulled down and was studying a sandal with a heel as tall as an Alp and a red sole. The vamp was made up of grass green foil rings twisting up to the ankle. He just stood and stared.

"Sergeant," said Jury mildly, knowing he could not dehypnotize Wiggins, short of shooting him in the back.

Was this what she'd wanted to see him about? To talk about shoes?

But Chris Cummins short-circuited whatever extraneous topic Jury might have been going for by saying, "Christian Louboutin. He's my favorite." Then she reached up and took down one of the high-heeled shoes, this one of blue satin, then its mate, perhaps the better to make her point, turning both over for Wiggins to eye. "Red soles," she said. "Louboutin always does red soles."

"I wonder what it's like to walk on," Wiggins said.

"That," said Chris with perfectly good humor, "I couldn't tell you."

Unmindful of his gaffe, Wiggins plowed on, pulling out one of another pair, the last in the bottom row. They weren't nearly as comely as the others, just unembellished black patent.

"Oh, not those. That's Kate Spade; I never did like her shoes. They're so . . . uninteresting." She turned to look at her husband. "Sorry, dear." Then back to Wiggins, with whom she seemed to have formed a sort of shoe bond. "David brought those back by mistake. He was supposed to get Casadei and he got Kate Spade." She shoved back the uninteresting Kate.

David Cummins didn't seem to appreciate his wife's joking tone. Indeed, Jury thought he went a little pale.

Wiggins, sensing some condition in another he should attend to, changed the subject and said to Cummins, "You were with London police, were you?"

He nodded. "South Ken. I was a DC. Got a promotion when I came here."

Wiggins sighed. "Be careful what you wish for," he said darkly.

Jury raised an eyebrow. "What's that supposed to mean?"

"I'm only thinking of all the extra responsibility. I mean, that's what I found."

Jury rolled his eyes.

"Come on, love," said David. "Let's get to the point." To the other two he said, "Chris is one for the drama."

"You bet I am." She wheeled over to the end of the shelf, reached up, pulled out a chunky-looking dark brown snakeskin shoe.

"Manolo Blahnik!" she said, as if she'd been waiting all her life to cry the name.

Wiggins looked blank.

"Manolo Blahnik, the famous shoe designer."

It was Jury, not Chris, who said this, earning a look from her of admiration and from Wiggins a look that wondered if his boss was daft, knowing stuff like that.

"My upstairs neighbor," said Jury, "has a pair and cited chapter and verse on his shoes." Carole-anne gave him bulletins on her wardrobe changes, too. To Chris Cummins, Jury said, "I'm afraid you've lost me, Mrs. Cummins."

"Chris, please. Lost you?" She looked from one to the other, including her husband in her head shake. "And you call yourselves detectives. All right, give us the photo, love," she said to David.

Jury looked at Cummins.

David opened the same folder that had held the photo of the Jimmy Choo shoes and took out another. He passed it to his wife.

"Now, you see this?" She pointed to the imprint of a shoe, or rather the heel of a shoe. The rest of it was lost in the earth and leaves. "This," she said, tapping the heel, "could have been made by this shoe." Again, she held up the chunky Manolo Blahnik shoe.

David Cummins already had out a magnifying glass, which he handed to Jury wordlessly.

Jury compared the imprint with the heel he held in his hand, then passed glass and photo on to Wiggins. "Has a cast been made of this?"

Cummins nodded. "Yes."

"If it is a shoe, where would the imprint of the rest of it have fallen, do you think?"

"I'd guess the sole was on the hard surface of the patio. The stone is pretty much flush with the ground."

"Forensic thinks it's a heel print?"

"It's certainly possible. They've been rather stumped by it, think it might have been done by the roadworks equipment."

Chris sighed impatiently. "It's a Manolo Blahnik, I'm telling you."

Jury was doubtful, but he smiled at her nonetheless. "Good for you, Chris." Seeing how delighted she was with the results of her detection, he didn't add that there were probably a dozen other things, including shoes, that could have fit the image in the photo. Actually, he *was* impressed; the lady had a very good eye for detail.

"You think the killer was a woman?" said Jury.

She said in a tone heavy with irony, "We do all sorts of things,

Superintendent. Scrub floors, make cookies, kill people. Yes, that's what I'm saying: a woman wearing Manolo Blahniks."

Her husband said, "It's not as tidy as that, Chris."

"Still . . . ," said Jury, picking up the shoe. "Could we borrow this?"

"Yes, of course." She looked over her wall of shoes, smiling. "I knew this lot would come in handy someday."

"London, would you say?" He was rocking the shoe slightly in his hand.

"You couldn't buy them in Amersham. I'd try Sloane Street first. There's his shop there. Besides that, you *might* find shoes in some designer knockoff place or one of those consignment places. I've found several pairs myself at a shop called Design Edge. It's in Kensington High Street. You could try those places."

"You shop in London?"

"Oh, you mean this?" She gave the wheelchair a slap and smiled. "No. But Davey goes to London when he gets days off. Remember, he's the one who brought back the Kate Spade." She laughed.

And David, once again, looked grim. The Kate Spade shoe episode was wearing thin.

Chris wheeled back to the center table and picked up a largish book with a glossy cover sporting a pair of high-heeled emerald green shoes, looking as if they'd been carelessly stepped out of, one lying on its side.

The title was, Jury thought, pretty forced: *Shoe-aholic.* He said, smiling, "I take it you identify with shoe-aholicism?"

She laughed. "You rolled that right out, Superintendent. Yes, I do. Davey brought me this from Waterstone's Friday. It's luscious."

"Not nearly so much as the real thing," said Jury, looking at the wall of shoes. Then he got up. "Thanks so much for the Manolo Blahnik insight. And the tea, of course. We'll look into it."

She sighed. "My theory is being dismissed, I can see that."

"Absolutely not. You ready to go, Wiggins?"

His sergeant was back at the shoes again, looking broody.

★   ★   ★

"What do you think of that heel business? Just her passion for shoes?"

"That's a great deal of money tied up in that collection. Eighty pairs, I counted. Say between five hundred, a thousand a pair, you're looking at around sixty thousand."

Jury smiled. "You counted them. I thought you were just admiring them."

"Don't be daft. This"—he pointed to his head, presumably the brain—"is always ticking over. Where to next?" Wiggins tested the acceleration by gunning the motor and then releasing the pedal.

"The Rexroth house. The people who threw the party. It's not far. It's on this road just a short distance past the pub."

As they pulled away from the curb, Wiggins said, "Speaking of shoes . . ."

Jury rolled his eyes. Were they again?

"I must say, I've a friend who'd look smashing in that sequined number."

Jury wasn't aware Wiggins had a "friend," much less a friend who'd look smashing in sequins.

Wiggins went on: "A DS doesn't make that kind of money."

"No. But his wife's family apparently has that kind."

"Oh." Wiggins frowned and drove on.

33

They found Kit Rexroth on her own, Tip, the husband, absent in the City, performing whatever financial wizardry had made them rich.

Wiggins produced his warrant card, holding it close enough to Kit's face that she could have kissed it.

"Something else, Superintendent? I can't imagine anything we didn't tell you the other night. Will you sit down? Will you take tea?"

The question barely had time to leave her mouth before Wiggins stepped on it, saying, yes, they would.

"Not if it's any trouble," Jury tacked on, loving the accusatory look he got from his sergeant. Traitor.

"Not for me, it isn't. I'm not fixing it." From the table between them, she raised a tinkly little bell.

Jury thought the summoning bell was a fairy story, but apparently not. A maid entered as if she'd been at the door just waiting. Kit asked for tea and some of "those little cakes the cook is hoarding."

A slight bow. An exit.

The myth of the English country house and its workings seemed to be right here in the flesh. But of course it didn't really exist. Staff should hide their dissatisfaction, unlike the maid, who looked as if she were sucking a lemon. Would she spit in the tea?

"What is it, then, Superintendent?"

There was no hostility in the tone, just honest curiosity.

"Your party, Mrs. Rexroth . . ."

She looked off, bemused. "You mean the night of the murder? Whether I saw that young woman? Whether she was here?"

"No. You've answered that. This is about another guest: Harry Johnson."

"Harry Johnson." She again looked bemused. "I don't believe . . . well, there were a lot of people here, as you know, friends of my husband or even friends of friends."

"Still, you claim the dead woman wasn't."

"No. What I claim is I would have known her had she been. A very striking woman. But this Harry Johnson—"

"He was on your guest list. He's tall, about my height, very blond hair, very blue eyes. He said that your husband often lunched in a pub in the City called the Old Wine Shades."

She rubbed the tips of her fingers against her chin, eyes narrowed. "I can ask Tip."

"Johnson said he was here, that he knew you, albeit slightly." Why would he lie about something so easy to check up on? Perhaps because it wasn't really that easy. He'd been here only an hour, Harry had said. Given the large number of guests, it would have been possible that his hosts hadn't seen him. They were an easygoing couple to the point of being vague. Well, if Kit was vague, Harry could always be vaguer.

Tea arrived and was drunk, heartily by Wiggins, despite his earlier three cups. Following this, they left.

"Was he at that party or not?" Jury said, more to himself than to Wiggins. They were sitting in the Black Cat, eating pub food.

"He was invited, that's clear. But Harry Johnson likes to play games."

Jury let out a half-laugh. "You're right there. He certainly likes to tell stories." He called to mind that Gothic tale of Winterhaus, that story within a story within a story. It was Melrose Plant who had pointed out all of those concentric rings moving away from the center each time a fresh stone was skipped in the widening water of Harry's story.

"Plant wonders if Harry Johnson's elaborate story really had anything to do with the murder of Rosa Paston."

Wiggins was having fish and chips. He stopped a limp chip on its way to his mouth. He thought for a moment, said with a shrug, "Maybe he's right."

Jury dropped his knife on his plate. "Don't be daft, Wiggins!" He went back to his bread and cheese and Branston pickle.

"If he wasn't at that party, why would he say he was? Does he want you to suspect him?"

"I wouldn't be surprised. He's winding me up. He wants to see how I'd work it out."

"So much that he'd have you think he had something to do with Mariah Cox's murder?" Wiggins shook his head. "The man must be barmy."

Jury smiled. "Right. That point's already been settled, Wiggins."

34

Mungo trotted out to the kitchen and trotted back to the music room. She's out of the kitchen, so let's eat dinner; we have a lot to do.

Morris was slow to follow him; Morris did not want to do a lot, especially his, as Mungo's "lots" were so complicated.

"Come on, Mrs. Tobias could be back in a minute."

Morris moved quicker.

In the kitchen, across the granite countertop, a profusion of white packages and little white tubs were lined up and open. A stool stood conveniently placed before this cold collation. There were herring, two kinds of cheese, wafer-thin slices of Westphalia ham, smoked salmon, wild Alaskan salmon (or what was left of it), thinly sliced summer sausage.

Morris picked up her paws, one after the other, set them down, again and again. Where had all this food come from?

From that stuck-up deli on Sloane Street, where you drop a week's wages just going through the door. Harry's rich; he doesn't care. Come on, don't just sit there. Get up on the stool. Mungo was earnestly glad for cat-agility. He disliked bounding up to the counter.

But like a fan unfolding, Morris went from floor to counter in a single shake. Amazing how cats could do things—fold their paws in, spring from floor to table.

Go on, toss some food down. I'll have a piece of sausage and some ham and some of that salmon.

Almost on tiptoe, Morris went down the line, here and there stopping to sniff. Umm! Which? Smoked or plain?

Either, I'm not fussy. Don't bother with the white tubs, they're mostly salads.

This one's chopped liver. She slid in her paw and spooned out a bite. Um-um!

Sausage? My sausage?

Oh. Sorry. She slid two summer sausage slices from the paper to the counter's edge.

Mungo caught both pieces, together, in his mouth.

That was brilliant!

He thought so, too. He chewed and thought about his plan for the evening before them. It should work.

This is really good herring. Here— A piece went over the counter and sailed through the air; Mungo swatted it down.

They ate in silence for a minute. Then Mungo's ears perked up. We'd better get out; I think I hear her . . . What're you doing?

Straightening up so she won't suspect—

Never mind, she'll blame it on Schrödinger.

Footsteps sounded on the staircase, and Mungo said, Out!

Morris slid from counter to floor like water spilling. Didn't even bother with the stool, thought Mungo wonderingly.

They sped from the kitchen and through the dining room just before Mrs. Tobias hove into view.

And right on her heels was the cat Schrödinger.

The kitchen door closed behind them.

"Look what you've gone and done!" came shrieking from the other side of the kitchen door.

Mungo, lying under the living room sofa with Morris, enjoyed the sight of a screeching Schrödinger hurled out of the kitchen. It was almost as much fun as watching Jasper land on his arse.

Then he got down to business:

Harry will be back soon. He'll take the car tonight to go to the Old Wine Shades. The idea is to get you into the car—

Why?

You'll see. The window's stuck on the passenger side, stuck about halfway up. Once you're through the window, just climb over into the back and lie down on the floor. When we come to the car, he'll never notice.

You haven't said why we're going there, said Morris.

Because the Spotter might be there.

How am I going to get out of the house without Harry seeing me?

Simple. When he comes in, I'll bark and bounce around as if I'm really glad to see him—that'd make a change—and he'll have all his attention on me. All you need to do is stay close to the wall behind the door, then when he opens it, you slither round the edge and out. Even if he sees you, he'll think you're Schrödinger. She's always running outside.

They had managed to work the blue collar off by pushing at its Velcro tabs so that Mrs. Tobias couldn't tell the difference between the two cats. The only way Harry could tell the difference (and Harry didn't pay much attention, anyway) was when Schrödinger was with her kittens. That meant the extra cat was Morris. Harry put the collar back on, puzzled as to why it didn't stay.

Mungo had pulled it off again. No one around here really took a blind bit of notice; Morris could have been sporting the Union Jack and no one would see. That's what happened when you were too caught up in yourself—Mrs. Tobias with her pies and poached salmon; Harry with, well, Harry.

For another hour they waited side by side on a window seat behind Harry's desk in the living room.

Finally, the Jaguar pulled up at the curb. It was not yet dark, but getting there, the light softer, bluer, diminished.

Come on! Positions! said Mungo.

They bounded off the window seat, ran toward the front door with Mungo squarely in front, Morris against the wall. When the door opened, Mungo barked up a storm and Morris flat-bellied herself around the edge of the door. All she saw was a foot shod in cordovan brown calf leather.

Bark. Bark.

Harry frowned. "What?"

Wouldn't you like to know? Harry couldn't pick up this message, of course, he being human (although Mungo thought that far from settled). Mungo then rushed to the living room and hopped up on the window seat to watch Morris, who was not yet in the car but trying. One try— Whoa! Cat didn't make it. Another— Oops! Almost, but not quite. Then he saw Morris gather herself in that way cats do, every little muscle concentrated, focused . . . There! Morris got her paws hitched over the window and she was in. Mungo wanted to applaud.

Harry was back with the ridiculous lead that Mungo allowed to be snapped onto his collar. Ho-hum. As if he needed one. As if it controlled him. But Mungo tried to "scamper" off the seat, thinking scampering more befitting Harry's idea of dogdom. He stopped short of tail wagging. He wouldn't lower himself.

Off they went out the door, down the white steps to the car. Back door opened, Mungo hopped up to the seat and looked down at Morris lying placidly on the floor, paws tucked in.

All the work. All the work falls to me, thought Mungo. He sent a message to Morris:

When we get there, just repeat what you did in reverse—wait for us to get out of the car, ease yourself out the window, and follow.

No answer came from Morris.

Was the cat asleep?

The Old Wine Shades was in the City, but Harry treated it as his local, despite its being a bit of a drive. It took Harry less than fifteen minutes given the hairsbreadth distance he allowed between his car and the rest of the world: hairsbreadth from other cars, people, curbs, cats, and dogs. Mungo was glad just to get there alive. Harry wound between Embankment and the river as if the car were a zipper, then funneled off into King William Street and then into Arthur.

The Jaguar stopped in a no-parking area right beside the pub, Harry thinking it was his God-given right to park anywhere he chose.

Mungo sent Morris the message to wait, wait until they were out.

You already told me that.

The tone was truculent. Mungo could have done with some appreciation.

Inside, seated at the bar in his favorite place, Harry engaged in one of his winey talks with Trevor.

Mungo stared at the door, wondering where Morris was; Morris must have missed the opening of the door and was stuck outside. For heaven's sakes.

Trevor had gone off somewhere and returned with a bottle, and the two men spent more valuable minutes talking about it.

O Boredom, I salute you!

Where was the Spotter? Mungo knew he was— There! Coming through the door, followed by Morris. The Spotter didn't see her. My God! Couldn't even detectives suss out they were being followed by a cat? Mungo hoped his faith wasn't misplaced.

"Hullo, Harry. Mungo." Jury tossed his coat on a stool and reached down to give Mungo's head a rub. Then he saw Morris. "What the hell's your cat doing here, Harry?" Jury laughed.

Harry looked down. Frowning deeply, he said, "Schrödinger? That's not Schrödinger."

Right! thought Mungo. Right! It's not.

Harry turned and looked down, frowning. "At least I don't think so."

Wrong! Trust Harry not to know his own cat.

"Schrödinger," Jury said with a laugh. "The cat's dead; the cat's alive."

No! thought Mungo. NO no no no no no. Don't go off on that quantum mechanics stuff!

Harry was nonplussed. "How the devil did you get in here, Shoe?"

No oh no oh no!

Morris stuck by Jury's leg, staring up at him. Staring, sending him all sorts of messages, each tumbling over the one before, hoping by sheer volume to penetrate the dense mass of the human brain. I'm not Schrödinger, I'm not Shoe, I'm Morris, Morris, Morris, from the Black Cat in Chesham . . .

"What is this?" asked Jury, drinking the wine Trevor had just poured. "It's good."

Trevor, wine expert, rolled his eyes. "Surprise, surprise, Superintendent."

Mungo sat hard by Morris and joined in: Look, look, this isn't Schrödinger, this isn't Shoe, no no, not Shoe, it's Morris, Mor-risss, MORRIS, M-O-R-R-I-S . . .

Harry, cat completely forgotten, was winding up one of his interminable paeans to the good grape and saying, "So, are you getting anywhere with these two murders?"

Standing on his hind legs, Mungo placed his front paws on the edge of Jury's chair. It's not Shoe— Listen! The Black Cat, the Black Cat, the pub the Black Cat . . .

Morris joined in: Black Cat Black Cat Dora Dora's cat . . .

Jury frowned. "What's with Mungo? He seems distracted." He rubbed the dog's head.

A woman on the other side of Harry bent down to look at the cat and cooed, "What a pretty kitty. What's his name?"

"Schrödinger. It's a she."

Not Schrödinger, she's Morris. Morris. Mungo kept it up.

The woman frowned. "That's a funny name. Whatever does it mean?"

Jury could hear Harry testing the point of each word before he flung them at her like a handful of darts.

"It means 'cat' in quantum physics," he said this without looking at her.

"Well. We're not very friendly, are we?" She sniffed and moved from the stool to a table.

Free of her, Harry went back to the subject. "Be careful, or you'll have another Ripper on your hands. Was she, as they say, 'interfered with'?"

"You think I'm going to give you the details?"

Mungo turned in circles at his feet, while Morris was close to clawing her way up his leg. Mungo thought in a minute he might even bark. Why couldn't the Spotter sort it?

"I don't see why not," said Harry. "The tabloids will dish up details."

Mungo wondered how to spell "Black Cat." Morris was supposed to be staring, staring at the Spotter. It looked as if she were sleeping on her feet. That better hadn't be so.

Jury was looking down at Morris, looking from Morris to Mungo. Mungo watched his face, his expression of real consternation. The dog could almost see the tumblers of the lock clicking: Something about this black cat—and Mungo, Mungo trying to tell me something? . . . Click. Wait. The Black Cat, that pub . . . Click. Dora. Dora's cat . . . Click, click, click. My God! Could this be Dora's—?

Yes yes yes yes. The Spotter was thinking hard, even if Mungo had to make up his thoughts. Mungo waited for the words that would get Morris back to Dora—

Jury said, "Is a dog a lot of trouble?"

Mungo crawled under the bar stool, went down with his paws over his eyes.

Is a dog a lot of trouble?

35

The bloody traffic light had decided its changing days were over. Jury sat behind the wheel, waiting.

I've 'ad enough o' you lot, thinking I'll go red-yellow-green at a moment's notice just t' please you. Well, see 'ow you like sittin' 'ere for several minutes. . . .

Jury hit the steering wheel. Was he going insane? Imagining what was rattling through the head of a traffic light? Next it'd be British Telecom over there in that forlorn-looking telephone box, trying to get a message across to him—

Which made him think of Mungo and Schrödinger . . .

Finally the light changed (reluctantly?), and he turned onto Upper Street. No, there was no doubt in his mind that those two had been trying to tell him something. It didn't surprise him that Mungo had done this, but the black cat?

The black cat.

That cat seemed to be getting along famously with Mungo. They were like conspirators.

Frowning, he pulled up in front of his building, got out and locked the car, and took the steps two at a time. He didn't feel up to a conversation with Mrs. Wassermann tonight and hoped she wasn't looking for him through the window of her basement flat.

* ★ *

He watched the moon through the window of his flat and thought about it.

The black cat wasn't Schrödinger.

Schrödinger and Mungo didn't get along, according to Harry, and that black cat and Mungo were getting along so well, they seemed to be on the same wavelength.

That cat wasn't Harry's cat.

All right, so the cat was a stray. Ridiculous. Harry Johnson taking in a stray cat? And pigs might fly.

Jury knew where he was going with this. Harry had been in Chesham; Harry had been in the Black Cat. And Harry would steal a blind beggar blinder, if it served his purpose.

What *was* his purpose? What in the world would Harry want with Dora's cat?

His first impulse was to drive to Belgravia and make Harry turn over the cat. How could he—or why would he refuse to—let the cat go if it wasn't his cat?

In the middle of this thought there was a knock. He said, "Come in," and Carole-anne appeared in his doorway like a vision, red gold hair glowing as if the moon hung behind her. The light actually came from the wall sconce in the hallway. It was hard enough dealing with Carole-anne when the light was off, much less on.

"Well, come on. We've a date, remember?"

Jury did not, and his expression showed it.

She sighed deeply, still in the lit-up doorway. She checked the small circlet of a watch on her wrist. "It's nearly gone ten. It's not very flattering you forgot."

"I agree. If I had forgotten. But I didn't forget. We don't have a date."

"Yes, we do. Down to the Mucky Duck."

"I didn't forget we had a date to go to the Mucky Duck, either." He bit back a smile. "You've stooped to this, have you? Manufacturing dates. And get out of the doorway, will you? The glow hurts my eyes." He shaded them.

Frowning, she moved into the room.

The view from there was pretty good, too. A sea green or sea blue dress, depending on the way she moved. A mouth of pearly coral lipstick that seemed to have been kissed by that same sea. Long, very thin silver earrings, which darted with shivery little colors as the light hit them.

"Making it up, honestly." She sank down on his sofa and drew a little mirror from her purse, looked in it, saw nothing apparently, snapped it shut, and said, "Friend of yours called." She pointed at Jury's phone as if the friend were trapped inside.

"And . . . ?"

"What?"

"Who was the friend?"

"Well, I don't know, do I?" She had taken a nail file from her bag and sat filing away.

"Actually, yes. As you were the one who took the message."

"Oh. Someone named . . . Fiona? . . . No . . . Felicia? . . ."

"Phyllis?"

"Could've been. You ready?" File back in purse, she was up and dusting off a self that needed no dusting.

"Did Phyllis want me to call her?" Of all the forensic pathologists, medical examiners, or coroners in the British Isles, Dr. Phyllis Nancy was the one Jury would always choose. She was the most able, the most accommodating, the most dependable. If Phyllis said she would have the results of an autopsy back to him at a certain time, it was always there, spot-on. Greenwich could have set the clock by her.

Jury had unhooked his jacket from a chair and was shoving his arms into it, the Mucky Duck clearly his destination one way or the other.

"Not really."

He collected his keys. "Not *really,* but then what aspect of unreality was she interested in?"

"Just something about dinner. Or lunch." Carole-anne yawned. It was all the same to her. "Maybe you were supposed to have a meal with her? Or not. Anyway, she was just reminding you of whatever it is. I couldn't make it out."

They were on their way downstairs now, Carole-anne wearing, he was almost certain, her party pair of Manolo Blahniks. This heel wasn't chunky, as was the heel on the pair in Chris Cummins's collection.

"She sounded," added Carole-anne in her assessment of Phyllis's call, "just as flighty as you do."

The Mucky Duck always lived up to its name (though not the "duck" part), sodden with beer and smoke.

Every man she passed eyeballed Carole-anne, probably hoping Jury was her father. She sat down at a table and asked for a pint of Bass.

"Half-pint is more ladylike," he said, secretly applauding her refusal to participate in the gender issue.

"Half-pint'll get dumped over your head, too."

"You know, you really are crabby tonight," said Jury.

"You'd be too if you had to spend most of it reminding someone they had a date with you." The little mirror came out again and she was inspecting her face for forgotten flaws.

Might as well inspect Rossetti's *Beatrice,* which she greatly resembled. The compact shut. "You still here?"

"I don't want to forget what you look like while I'm gone."

Her eyebrows squiggled. She had a lively frown.

As he left the table, Jury could have sworn six men got up to move on it. When he quickly turned, he could also have sworn they all sat back down again.

Probably just his imagination. But he kept his eye on her off and on while he waited for the barman to take the order.

He returned and set the two pints on the table and then sat himself down.

He folded his arms and leaned toward her. "Now that we're on our date, what shall we talk about?"

Carole-anne took a ladylike sip of her beer and said, "Who's Phyllis?"

36

Wiggins had been here before; he already knew his way around the kitchen and seemed to have made himself invaluable to Myra Brewer. Wiggins had the touch: that's what Jury had been trying to tell him.

It was the next morning, and they were visiting Myra Brewer.

"We're out of biscuits," called Wiggins.

We. Jury loved it.

"Yes, but there's Choc-o-lots fresh. The ones with marshmallow."

"Found them."

Then there was the sound of water running, a kettle being filled. This attention to tea in the midst of death didn't bother Jury, nor did it make Myra Brewer less sympathetic. For it was clear she missed Kate Banks greatly and was very much affected by her death and the manner of it.

So tea, especially with Wiggins on the job, was an antidote as good as any Jury could ever muster. He thought sometimes it was the rituals that got us through.

Jury sat in a heather gray, rough-textured chair in the small flat in St. Bride Street, barely two blocks from Mr. Banerjee's corner store. Myra Brewer, Kate Banks's godmother, lived on the second floor and had trouble, she'd said, with stairs, stairs shamefully inadequate, for the handrail to the first flight had been broken and never mended.

She was in her eighties and not "spry," as she'd told Jury, an understatement if ever he'd heard one.

"There was never any young person good as my Kate. She was a gem, that girl. Come all the way from Crouch End every week, rain or shine—sometimes more than once—and did my bit of shopping for me. Never a cross word, always wanting to help, like 'Myra, let me Hoover that old rug for you.'

"Well, you wouldn't think I'm the luckiest person in the world, but I was lucky in Kate. Sometimes I don't think it's sickness nor being penniless that's hardest; it's being forgot. The worst thing about getting old is people don't look in."

It was one of the saddest testaments to age Jury had ever heard. And a heartfelt epitaph. She was thinking, he supposed, that no one would be looking in now, but she kept that thought to herself. There was little self-pity in her talk.

Wiggins, jacket off, in shirtsleeves, had done himself proud with the tea tray, which he was putting down on a small coffee table. "Here you go, Mrs. B. Done and dusted."

Mrs. B. Jury plucked a Choc-o-lot from a plate.

"Did some bread and butter, too. That's a nice loaf of granary bread." Wiggins separated teacups and saucers and poured a measure of milk into each, then raised the sugar bowl in question. Myra took two spoons, Jury one, Wiggins four.

"Thank you, Mr. Wiggins. Thank you very much," she said, bringing her cup to her mouth and drinking a bit noisily.

Jury set down his cup. "Now, Mrs. Brewer, you said Kate was a friend's daughter?"

"That's right," said Wiggins.

Jury gave him a look, but he knew it failed to temper Wiggins's apparent conviction that he was now one of the Brewers.

"Eugenie," said Myra Brewer, "Eugenie Muldar."

"Kate Muldar, then. What about Kate's husband? Is he in the picture?"

"Oh, my, no, they've been divorced for over a decade. Johnny Banks was his name."

"And with the divorce, was there ill will on his part?"

Myra Brewer shook her head. "No. They'd gotten married so young, they both seemed relieved to be out of it."

"I see." Jury paused, wondering how to ask the question. "Did Kate do any other work you knew of?"

She looked puzzled. "You mean besides her steno job? No. Why?"

"Moonlighting, maybe. You know, lots of women with that sort of job do private work—"

Wiggins carried on: "Like typing up manuscripts, or for business-men who want documents typed, or letters, things like that. A hotel often offers stenographic services to businessmen. Your Kate might have taken on extra work for the extra money. Reason we'd be inter-ested in this is to look at anyone she might have worked for to see if there's anyone who might have wanted to harm her."

"Oh. But you don't think it was someone she knew? I expect I was assuming what happened to Kate was a—what do you call it?—a mugging?"

Jury said, "She wasn't robbed. She had money on her. Tell me, would she have been bringing it to you? Do you need money?"

That was a bit of a twist in the account. Myra gave a short laugh. "I always need money."

"Any particular amount? I mean for a scumbag landlord or Brit-ish Telecom raising its rates? Something generally making your life hell?"

Again, she gave a sharp, joyless laugh. "I should say so. The property manager—that's what they call themselves, these greedy landlords—he'd been trying to get two months' back rent that I don't owe him. I've been to the counsel about it. He says I must pay up or I'll be tossed out with the rubbish. Nice way of putting it, isn't it?"

"That must be extremely worrisome. How much does he claim you owe him?"

"Seven hundred pounds."

Jury nodded. "Had Kate told you she'd bring you the money?"

Genuinely shocked by this, Myra said, "Kate? Kate hadn't that kind of money." She thought for a minute. "Though she was certainly generous with what money she did have. She'd do my shopping for me, like I said, and refuse to take a penny. Kate was a good girl."

"Sounds like it," said Wiggins, pouring himself another cup of tea, adding milk, thoughtfully stirring sugar into it. "We found—"

Jury gave him a kick under the coffee table.

"Found . . . only she appeared to dress quite well."

"Yes, she did. Kate was always nicely turned out. She got those designer clothes at Oxfam."

Wiggins couldn't help himself. "Those shoes? Christian Louboutin? Oh, I shouldn't think Oxfam would have those."

Jury shot Wiggins another warning look. "Maybe they were knockdowns."

This talk of dress bewildered Myra Brewer.

Jury said, "You knew Kate all her life, did you?"

She nodded. "Though I wouldn't see her for long periods. They were here and there. Her mum, Eugenie, never stayed put for long. Restless, poor thing. She'd just go off sometimes, take the kids, sometimes not. She'd leave them with me, usually. We were still best friends even though I thought she didn't do right by the kids. Well, I was Kate's godmother and I should act the part."

"What about Kate's siblings?"

"There was just the one, a brother. They called him Boss, for some reason. He had an unusual name, anyway: Brent. I never did know where that came from. I don't think it was a family name."

Wiggins had his notebook out, which necessitated putting down his cup. "And where might we find them, your friend Eugenie and her son?"

"No joy there, Mr. Wiggins. They're both gone. Eugenie to lung cancer, and the boy, Brent, was in a car crash. Probably joyriding with his friends. His mum had warned him about that."

The voice faded out, as if that had been more than she wanted to say and she was looking through a mist that had collected over tea. She said, "You know, I felt shocking little when they went. It's as if I had just let go?" She was posing the question to the room, not expecting an answer. "Carelessness, I mean. It's like I should've held on to the string tighter. It would be nice to see them again. I expect a lot of us only come to that when it's too late."

There was a silence. Then Jury said, "Probably all of us find the feelings we've misplaced when it's too late. It's not you; it's inevitable; it's the human condition." He was silent for a moment. "That's the whole of her family, then?"

She nodded. "Now there's just me. Maybe that's one of the reasons Kate came round so much." She brought her hand to her forehead. "Well."

Jury gave her a moment, then asked, "What about men? Was there anyone in particular?"

"Not that she ever said. No, she didn't talk about any men friends. I told her, 'Katie, you should be going out, having a bit of fun.' She'd just laugh. She said, 'I haven't yet found a man who could sit alone with a book for half an hour without getting jumpy.' Well, I wasn't sure what she meant by that. I do know Kate was a great reader; she loved books. Her favorite place in London was that big Waterstone's bookshop in Piccadilly."

Myra took the handkerchief from her face and looked anxiously from the one to the other. "But you're suggesting . . . what are you saying? That it was some man she knew? She was all dressed up, you said. Like she was on a date? But then why would she be coming round here?"

"It could be," said Wiggins, "that she'd left someone—her date—and then come round."

"Then it wasn't just some stranger. He must've been here with her. That's shocking, shocking. It's as if it happened right on my doorstep."

"It could have been someone who knew where she was going. That's why we need to know about her friends."

Jury thought they were finished here, at least for now. He took a card from an inside pocket and passed it over to her. "Call me anytime at all if you think of something that might be relevant."

Wiggins put away his notebook and rose, too, lifting his teacup one last time and finishing off the tea. "Thanks for this, Mrs. B." He gestured toward the tray.

"Well, you fixed it, Mr. Wiggins. Come back sometime when you have a minute to spare." She trailed them to the door.

"I might do that. I might just look in sometime." He smiled at her.

The old Wiggins, thought Jury, was back.

37

Mungo wanted to know why Harry had brought out the cat carrier—or dog, he supposed, but forget that; he wasn't going anywhere. The carrier was sitting on the piano bench. He eyed it with suspicion. He realized Harry knew there were two cats in the house; he'd put the blue collar on one of them. And that, Mungo supposed, was to tell the cats apart. All of this puzzled him.

He pulled Elf out of the bottom drawer and carried him around the living room, looking for a drop-off. Maybe he could lift up the top of the window seat bench and drop him in, except Morris was lying on it, like a loaf.

Why are you doing that? said Morris.

It helps me think, Mungo said. It didn't. Mungo was doing it just for the laugh. Elf was hissing and flailing his tiny paws. He'd just started this only in the last week or two.

This isn't getting me back home, Morris said.

Mungo stared at the cat and shook his head (and Elf with it). Nothing but complain, complain since last night at the Old Wine Shades. He gave up trying to find a new place and just dropped Elf in the coal scuttle. The kitten was as black as the lumps around him. That was funny. He said, I don't get it. The Spotter should have sorted it out. He's smart; at least, he once was.

If you think about it, it would take a mind reader to work

out what we were doing. Stare, stare, stare, you said. How could the Spotter tell from that? Morris put her head down on her outstretched paws (a posture she'd picked up from Mungo). I just want to go home.

Whine. Whine. Mungo paced, nails clicking on the hardwood floor, stopping when he heard a scuffle in the kitchen and Mrs. Tobias's raised voice. Probably Schrödinger jumping up on the counter and nicking food. More noise.

Quick! he said to Morris. Hide!

Morris jumped from the window seat and slid slick as a whistle beneath the desk. That's the way with cats, thought Mungo, quicker than time; they made time shrink and clocks run backward.

His bit of philosophizing was broken by Shoe erupting through the kitchen door with a kipper like a knife in her mouth.

Mrs. Tobias was fast on the cat's trail and waving a skillet.

Schrödinger streaked through the living room and then into the great nowhere.

Mungo enjoyed the little chase; it was such a cliché. He'd seen it over and over again in *The Beano*.

"Where's that cat?" came from the hallway. "I'll kill that cat one day." Mrs. Tobias shouted up the stairs: "You'll be out of house and home faster'n you can pinch a kipper, my girl!" She stormed back into the living room, saw Mungo sitting by the kitchen door (to which he'd rushed in order to distance himself and, thus, Mrs. Tobias from the desk). She waved the pan. "Took one of my kippers, Shoe did, stole your master's dinner!"

Master? Who did she think she was kidding?

"And where is he, I'd like to know? It's gone half-seven and him not here yet when he said he wanted to eat then?" Back to the kitchen she marched, muttering.

Mungo knew something was up with that cat carrier, something unpleasant for someone. Oh, not him. Although he wondered sometimes how he'd lasted so long around Harry without getting cuffed or kicked or worse, then told himself not to be modest. But the point was that Harry would no more take a cat to the cat hospital than he'd adopt a disabled orangutan. And much less would he transport Schrödinger himself. So what was going on?

Mungo looked up and saw Shoe coming down the stairs, looking pleased as punch, then giving Mungo an evil look and going into the music room to inspect the kittens. Check. Check. Check. Check. Check. One missing. She dashed into the living room, went from one hiding spot to another, found Elf in the coal scuttle, and dragged him out. She then carried him into the music room, dropped him in the drawer, and swayed over to her favorite spot beneath the little sofa near the bureau, where she promptly went into one of her comas.

Mungo stared from Schrödinger back to the carrier, back and forth, back and forth, working it out. Then he loped back to the desk and told Morris to come out.

Something's going on.

What? said Morris.

I think— He looked at Morris's blue collar, and the penny dropped. Take that off! Morris looked puzzled, so Mungo hit at it, then bit the end and pulled it free from the Velcro tab. Then he rushed into the music room, stealthily made his way to the sofa, stopped to see that Schrödinger was indeed asleep, and dropped the collar near the cat's head. Schrödinger wouldn't wake if it were a hand grenade, pin pulled. Mungo turned and hurried to the bureau, grabbed up Elf again, and trotted across the hall and into the living room just as the door opened.

Mrs. Tobias apparently heard Harry's approach too and came like a little warhorse from the kitchen, talking all the while. "So there you are, Mr. Johnson, just let me tell you what that cat . . ." Her voice dropped to a quieter wrangle out in the hall.

Mungo dropped Elf. Act really mad, he whispered to Morris.

Why?

Just do it, just do it!

As Elf ran off, passing Harry and Mrs. Tobias, Morris hissed and clawed at the air around Mungo's head.

Mungo could hear him telling Mrs. Tobias he'd be having dinner out anyway, so it hardly mattered. Here was Harry saying to Morris,

"So you ate my dinner, did you?" He said to Mungo, "For God's sakes, can't you leave that damned kitten alone?"

But he didn't seem really bothered by it all. He grinned wolfishly.

Oh, how Mungo longed to grin back. Wolfishly.

Mrs. Tobias, in her brown wool coat—too hot for this weather, but she wore it year in and year out—sailed through the living room. She didn't glance at Morris, not minding and not knowing there was another black cat sprawled beneath the sofa in the music room.

"I'll be off, then, Mr. Johnson."

Oh, do be, thought Mungo. All he was waiting for was the next act.

When that act came, it involved a good bit of effing and blinding. Harry was having a hard time of it.

Eventually Harry left, cat carrier in tow. Mungo hopped up to the window seat beside Morris. They watched Harry in the arc of light cast by the sconce beside the door as he descended the stair, and then in the blurry light of the streetlamp. He opened the car door and stowed the carrier before getting in the car himself.

They watched.

Then, pleased, they looked at each other with what would have been smiles had God seen fit to give them to dogs and cats.

Never mind, their minds hummed along as one.

38

The glossy-haired, raven-haired young woman in short skirt and high heels stood outside the Snow Hill police station (almost just around the corner from the spot where Kate Banks was murdered, and didn't that ever give a chill!). She was chewing gum (which she would toss out before she met her client, who hated chewing gum) and wondered why she should volunteer her information to police. What had the Bill ever done for her or her friends, except as good as call them whores? Looking up at the black word "Police" painted on the soft lantern light, she debated the wisdom of going in.

She wouldn't even have thought of coming except it had been Kate, and she'd quite liked Kate. She was a good person, always ready to do you a lunch or a loan or whatever help you needed. Yes, you could count on Kate.

At first it hadn't made sense, and then it had. There was nobody that would've taken a blind bit of notice, except herself. And the sodding cops were of course on the completely wrong end of the stick, barking up the wrong tree, hadn't a clue that just because it was an escort service, that didn't mean it had to be sex and nothing but.

She turned away as two of these police came out of the door and gave her a look. God, she thought, a girl can't even stop a bit before she's accosted.

"Hello, sunshine," said one, cuter than the other.

The other said, "Time to move it along, love."

Fuck you. That's what she wanted to say. *Just fuck you and the horse you came in on. You want to keep running around this murder with your pants down, go ahead, arseholes.*

Standing there, leering, they quite put her off. But not being one to back away immediately from any uncomfortable situation, she reached into a slim shoulder bag made of silvery disks that lapped over each other like fish scales. She removed her compact and opened it. She didn't need to study herself, her eyes or lips or stylish haircut that cost a fortune; she just wanted to assert her right to stand on a city street.

The two uniforms stood there with their big bland smiles and looked at her as if no matter how good she looked, she'd never get invited to the party.

If only they knew. If only they knew that with what she knew, well, she could be a career changer for them, move them right up to captain or inspector or something. If they knew what she knew, she'd be at that party pronto; she'd be ushered in, sat down, and served a glass of Champs straightaway.

She checked her watch—small, platinum, a face circled by some kind of stone she didn't know, except to know they weren't diamonds. A gift from one of her clients.

She couldn't stop here, nor did she want to, with these two buffoons with their truncheons and guns and grins and City of London police insignia on their uniforms, thinking they were special or better than the Met.

Yet there was something—a conscience?—a little brightness in her she couldn't put out that had her taking a step toward the station door before the two seemed to form a wall against her entry. But she thought of Kate, the best among them she knew, who worked days as a stenotypist and was happy doing just that. Kate hadn't liked being with King's Road Companions, but she'd wanted the money to put aside for the future and to take care of an old lady, not even family but a godmother or someone. Whoever paid any attention to godparents, anyway? Well, that was Kate. Kate had loved the very ordinariness of her steno job, liked having to catch the tube every morning, liked being jolted and crushed before erupting into the "antic air" (as she called it) of Piccadilly. Kate had loved almost the dullness of the job. Who could love the dullness of things? she wondered. But if you liked it, did the dullness then shine? She stopped at that thought, thinking she must have a little philosophy in her.

The two coppers still stood there, leering.

So she turned and walked away into the night. The days of the Smoke were long gone, and she wasn't old enough to have seen it anyway, but there was still the heavy mist that slid in from the river, which wasn't far off.

A lot of the girls had stopped temporarily when police said they might be in harm's way, given the two recent murders, that a killer was targeting escorts, and they'd brought up Jack the Ripper—or, more likely, the newspapers had done that.

She stopped in Newgate Street to adjust one of the straps of her sandals. They weren't what you'd choose for walking, but she hadn't far to go, only to St. Paul's. She wondered if her guy'd got religion or something. That was a laugh.

They were to meet round the west side of the cathedral, and he'd said that if she got there before he did, just to wait on a bench in the churchyard, wait by the Becket statue. He was always late, but what did she care? He had to pay for the missed time anyway.

She had started walking again, shoes now under control: beautiful shoes, awful walking. St. Paul's loomed before her. Made her shudder, almost. Someday she would really have to go up to the Whispering Gallery. She'd lived in London all her life, in Camden Town and Cricklewood, and not done a tenth of the things tourists did.

He wasn't there, no surprise. She wandered into the churchyard, found the statue—whoever Becket was, they didn't keep him in very good condition, as he looked to be falling apart in these bushes.

As she looked at the statue, there came the bells. The reverberation shocked her and she clamped her hands over her ears. Nine o'clock. Five more strikes.

Into the din, or rather through it, came a voice: "DeeDee."

Deirdre turned and got another shock.

There was a gun. There was her scream. There were the bells.

39

The unflappable DI Dennis Jenkins from Snow Hill station said to Jury, "We pulled her up straightaway only because she had form—soliciting four years ago in Shepherd Market. Name's Deirdre Small. ID in the bag—" Jenkins gestured toward a clutch of silver scales now with one of the technicians. There were several others scouring the walk on their knees.

Deirdre Small lay in the center of them on the walk, a small ship adrift in her own wake.

"So here's another pro working for an escort service."

"Same agency?"

Jenkins shook his head. "This one's called Smart Set. Has the ring of upmarket sophistication, no? Anyway, I guess it is a leg up—pardon the pun—from the street. Although Shepherd Market . . . well, if you're going to trawl the curb, might as well choose Mayfair, no?"

Jury's smile was slight, almost apologetic, as if Deirdre Small had opened her eyes and caught him at it.

"Same MO, it looks like. Close range, chest. Whether the same weapon, we won't know till later. It must have happened at nine."

Jury frowned. "Then you got here fast. It's only nine-forty." The bell marking the half hour had rung ten minutes ago.

"That's because the person who found her got to us fast. He's over there—tall guy, balding. He was her boyfriend, or client, I should say; he said he was to meet her here at nine and he was seven or eight minutes late. So he found her at nine-oh-seven or -eight. He must have been breathing down the shooter's neck, assuming Deirdre Small was on time. He says she always was. Now, my guess is the killer took advantage of the bells"—Jenkins looked upward toward St. Paul's bell tower—"to muffle the shot."

At this point, one of the SOCO team put something in Jenkins's hand and walked off.

Jury frowned. "But the client could have walked right in on the shooting." He paused. "Unless, of course, he was the one."

"My instinct says . . ." Jenkins squinted at the tall man with the half-bald head. "No. He was pretty quick off the mark calling emergency. He could simply have walked away, left the body to be found by one of these good people." He nodded toward the ring of onlookers being discouraged from coming closer by the crime scene tape and the half-dozen uniforms in front of it. "But, then, on the other hand, he might have thought his name was down on the books and he'd be picked up later and in much hotter water. Still, I think, no, it wasn't him."

"If someone else, whoever it was had to be pretty nervy. That is, unless he knew."

"Knew what?"

"The boyfriend's habitual lateness."

Jenkins turned to look at Jury. "That would mean someone who knew them."

"Friend of hers? Friend of his?"

"He's married. Unsurprisingly."

"Jealous wife?"

Jenkins shrugged. "It's possible. Possible he was followed, too. Or she was."

A metal gurney was being loaded onto an ambulance.

"I think I'll have a word with the boyfriend if you don't mind."

DI Jenkins spread his hands in a don't-mind gesture. "Nicholas Maze is his name."

Jury thanked him and walked over to the bench past the ambulance whose horn was now being brought into play. It wailed out.

"Nicholas Maze? I'm Superintendent Jury, New Scotland Yard CID."

"Look, is there any way to keep this business from getting into the papers?"

Always the first concern. Keep my name out of it. "It's hard to say. But I'm sorry about your friend. How long had you known her?"

Nicholas Maze looked uncomfortable, more uncomfortable than sad. Collar unbuttoned and tie pulled off to one side, but still constricting his neck, he looked like a man who'd just tried to throttle himself. "Over a year," he muttered.

"Then you'd met her often before this?"

A nod that was more a nervous tic came from Maze. "A dozen times, well, more like two dozen times. It was, you know, a convenience."

Maybe for you, thought Jury. "You're married?"

Again, that puppetlike nod, a jerk of the head, as if the movement cost him.

"Does your wife know about the escort service?"

"You mean about DeeDee? Don't be ridiculous. Of course not."

"You're sure of that? That she had no suspicion?"

"Yes. She didn't know—" Quickly, Nicholas Maze looked at Jury. "Ann? You're thinking my wife—?" The man gestured around the courtyard. "Could have done this?" His laugh was short. "She'd be the last woman in London to shoot somebody in a jealous rage."

"What did Deirdre Small tell you about herself?"

"DeeDee? More than I cared to know."

This chilly response made Jury wonder.

"She was a chatterbox, DeeDee was."

Jury waited for more, but it didn't come. "If you could be more specific, Mr. Maze. What did she chatterbox about?"

"Well, she was born in London. Lived all her life here, she was fond of telling me. Cricklewood, I think she said. Not much education; she left school around sixth form."

"Anything about her friends?"

"Look. Dee was a talker. Nonstop sometimes. I didn't listen to most of it, frankly."

"The thing is, you see, information about people she knew could be vital—"

Maze interrupted, surprised. "You're saying you don't think this was just an opportunistic killing? I mean, some crazy just murdered her because she was here?"

"That's what suggests it was planned. Someone knew she'd be here. St. Paul's isn't the most obvious venue for a spontaneous shooting, is it?" Jury said nothing about the other murders in Bidwell Street and Chesham.

Nicholas Maze shook his head. "Can I go now? You're the second one I've told all this to."

"You'll try to think back on what she said, won't you?" Did they ever? Try to forget it as quick as possible, was more likely. "I'll have to check with Detective Inspector Jenkins about your leaving."

"Who's he?"

The man really didn't have the attention span of a flea.

SOCO had gone or was going, and only Jenkins and his young WPC and the uniforms keeping order remained. Most of the onlookers had dispersed. The crime scene tape remained. It would require police presence here tomorrow; St. Paul's was a tourist draw. St. Paul's and a murder even more.

"Cut him loose, Ruthie," said Jenkins to the woman constable. "Tell him we'll probably have to talk to him again and for him to stay close."

"Guv." She nodded and left. Pretty. Jenkins thought so, too, Jury guessed, from the way he watched her go.

He said, "Right now, I know sod-all." He stashed a notebook in his coat pocket. "I'm sending my men round to this Smart Set place tomorrow. You'd say this was done by the same shooter, right?"

"I don't know. The same as Bidwell, yes, but Chesham? If I could only work Chesham into the mix."

"They all worked for escort agencies."

"Yes, but it's location that doesn't make sense. Mariah Cox was in London nearly half the time. Why not kill her in London like the others? Then we'd get the serial killer syndrome."

"I hope the newspapers don't get hold of that angle. I can just see the dailies—" Jenkins drew a banner in the air: " 'Escorted to Death.' That kind of thing. 'Death Has an Escort.' "

Jury smiled. "You're probably right. Did you notice her shoes?"

Jenkins frowned. "Shoes? That again?"

"Strappy sandals." Jury checked his watch, although he didn't need to, as the bells were hammering away at the hour of ten. Jury was thinking of the Old Wine Shades. It wasn't far from here. It wasn't far from Bidwell Street, either. He thought he would stop in for a drink. "You know a pub called the Old Wine Shades?"

"Hm. Yes. Martin's Lane, near King William Street. The river?"

"That's the one. Care to stop for a drink? I'd like you to meet a friend of mine."

"Thanks, but I've got to get home. Take you up on that later, may I?"

"Of course."

"I'd like to meet your friend."

"I think you really would. Good night."

Jenkins gave him a small salute and they parted.

"Supposed to be here around nine. I mean, he usually is on a Monday night, but not tonight." Trevor said this as he poured out a measure of wine into Jury's glass. "On the house, Mr. Jury." Trevor watched carefully to see how Jury's mouth would receive this Haut-Médoc.

Jury definitely responded to "on the house," considering what this glass would cost him if it were on him instead. "That's very generous of you, Trevor." He raised the glass. "Here's to you." He tasted the wine. "Wonderful."

"One of Mr. Johnson's favorites."

"You've known him a long time, have you?"

Trevor had pulled out another bottle and was wiping it down,

giving it a good rub. There were few customers tonight in the Old
Wine Shades, two couples at tables and three men down at the end of
the bar. He took Jury's question to be rhetorical, it seemed. He said,
"Knows his wine, Mr. Johnson does. He once rattled off the names
of every premier cru vineyard in Bordeaux."

The cork was now out of the bottle he'd just rubbed down, and
he was taking it down the bar with two glasses he picked up along
the way.

For the one millionth time, Jury would have given an ear for a
cigarette. He could really understand van Gogh if the man had quit
smoking.

Think. Three women. Three escort agencies. If the paper tried
to make the case for a serial killer, if someone pulled in the Chesham
murder to make three, the police would be faced with panic. The
two women in London looked to have been done by the same person, but he wasn't at all sure that this person had killed Mariah Cox
in Chesham.

Trevor was back, refilling Jury's glass.

"I can't afford this, Trevor."

"Oh, not to worry. Mr. Johnson told me to have this out for him
tonight. Though he should have been in before now—and speak of
the devil," said Trevor, and Jury looked around. "You're quite late,
Mr. Johnson. What've you been up to?"

Harry slid into the tall chair beside Jury, smiling. "Nothing I
wouldn't want to run in the *Times* tomorrow, Trev." He turned the
bottle round. "Good. The St. Seurin. I see he's had half the bottle."

"Two glasses, Harry."

"Set me up a glass, Trevor." To Jury, he said, "God, but you're
looking less than lively."

Jury thought Harry appeared to be the exact opposite. "Death
does that to me. How about yourself?"

Harry had taken out his cigarette case and extracted a cigarette,
which Trevor lit for him with a match from an "Olde Wine Shades"
matchbook. Jury had never noticed the "e" on the end of that fussy
"Olde" before. The pub was, however, very "olde." It dated back to

the Great Fire. Not many buildings standing in London could claim
that antiquity.

Harry blew smoke away from Jury and said, "Yes, I'd say death
puts a damper on things. But it's cheering to know you're on the
case."

"What case is that?"

"Whatever case you're on." Harry lifted his glass, sniffed, and
tasted it.

"I've just come from St. Paul's," Jury said, then asked himself,
annoyed, why he had told him that. Hoping for some reaction. If Jury
had said he'd just come down from the space shuttle or the Pleiades,
it would make no difference. It was impossible to surprise a response
out of Harry Johnson.

Harry looked at his watch. "They still hearing confessions at this
late hour? Maybe I should go." He smiled at Jury. "But I won't. So
what happened at St. Paul's?"

"You'll find out soon enough from the tabloids." Jury twirled his
wineglass, asked, "Where were you an hour ago, Harry?"

Harry shook his head. "Let's see. An hour ago I was just going
through Watford, I think."

"Why were you in Watford?"

Harry said, "No reason, except I was out for a drive. I like to get
beyond the Ring Road. Clears my mind."

"Talk to anybody? Anybody see you?"

Harry signaled to Trevor, who came down the bar with a bottle
wrapped in a napkin. He presented it as if it were a baby in a blanket.
"Very pleasant Chassagne-Montrachet."

That's right, give yourself time.

Harry nodded, and Trevor set about uncorking it. He said to Jury,
"Now. Did I talk to anyone? No. Next question: Do I have an alibi
for the designated time? Alibi for what? There was a murder in the
Lady Chapel? Was this another woman? Another tart—pardon me,
escort?"

Jury didn't answer. He shook his head when Trevor set a clean glass
before him. "No, I've got to be going." Trevor poured Harry's.

Harry said, "So now it's a serial killer. Superintendent Jury: do you honestly think I'd murder three women just like that?"

Jury smiled and slid off his chair. "I wouldn't put it past you, Harry. Night."

He headed for the door.

40

Early the next morning, Jury was in the Snow Hill station talking to Dennis Jenkins.

Jenkins said, "What else do we know about the first victim? Kate Banks? You talked to this woman"—Jenkins flipped open a folder on his desk—"Myra Brewer?"

"Right. But I still don't think Kate Banks is the first; I think she's the second. Stacy Storm—I think she was the first." Jury produced a folder, copies of documents brought from Chesham. "Escort services, all three, and it seems different agencies. We can't find the client who—I'm guessing here—Kate Banks was with. Anyway, according to the record, Kate hadn't an appointment with a client that night. That's what King's Road Companions claimed. What about this Stacy Storm?"

"Also no client booked for the Saturday night. Of course, the usual blather about 'client confidentiality.' You'd think these women were all high-powered attorneys. Like what's-his-name—Cochran? O. J. Simpson's lawyer. He was guilty." Jenkins rocked back in his chair.

"What?"

"O.J. He was guilty."

"Probably, but unless he was Kate's date, I don't much care. The trouble is, I've got nothing when it comes to motive."

Jenkins had come down in his chair and was leafing through the folder, stopping at a page. "You don't think this might have been more than one killer?" Head still bent, he looked up at Jury from under his eyebrows. "No?"

"No. All three were working in the same job, and the killer used the same MO. They were all shot at close range."

"Different guns, though, thirty-eight revolver, twenty-two automatic."

"True. But it's the range that suggests the victims were standing very close to their killer."

Jenkins nodded. "As if the shooter's body were pressed against Deirdre Small's. If it wasn't the boyfriend, or, rather, the client, then who?" Head down, arms folded tight across his chest, he considered. "*Double Indemnity*. Fred MacMurray shoots Barbara Stanwyck in the middle of a kiss. Great scene. But here . . ." He was tapping the folder Jury had just given him. "It wouldn't have been that close." He held up a morgue shot of Stacy Storm. "No, with the first victim there'd have been daylight between them."

Jury liked that. "Not an embrace, then? Not close enough to kiss? But close enough to suggest the victim knew the killer. I mean, that these women would let the killer get that close." He rose, said, "I'm going to have a word with our pathologist. Thanks."

"What do you think? About the proximity of the two?"

The pathologist in this case was Phyllis Nancy; she looked up from the body of Deirdre Small and drew a sheet over her. She seemed puzzled.

"I could demonstrate what Jenkins is talking about if it would help."

Phyllis gave him a look. Grow up.

Ashamed of his glibness in the presence of this girl, Deirdre, who would never stand close to anybody again, Jury said, "Sorry. I don't seem to be on the right track lately."

"I don't see how you could be, what with worrying over Lu Aguilar. As to this . . ." She was looking at the police report. "'You could have seen daylight between them'—what a lovely way of putting it. I think I see what he means, though: one bent over the other. Say the man's already there, sitting at the table, when the woman comes along from the car park. 'Hello. Hello, sweetie—' "

Jury smiled.

"I don't mean you. I can see this Mariah Cox or Stacy Storm coming along to the Black Cat, walking over to him, saying hello, bending over to kiss or embrace him. The gun comes up and at an angle and fires into her chest. It's a hypothesis, of course. But if it happened that way, yes, there would have been daylight between them. I see this Detective Jenkins's point. Except it was nighttime. The shooters of these three women, then, were also their lovers."

"Not necessarily. If the wounds suggest that kind of proximity, there are other people who might do the same thing: friends, relations. The wife of the Chesham detective claims that a heel mark was left by a Manolo Blahnik shoe."

Phyllis was surprised and skeptical. "She thinks a woman did these killings? Well, of course a woman could shoot as well as a man, but somehow the psychology just doesn't seem to fit."

"I agree. And the heel print isn't much evidence. But the embrace, if there was one, could've come from a woman. I've had friends clap me round the shoulders and hug me." Had he really? He was trying to think up somebody—that is, besides Phyllis and Lu—and that thought pinched his eyes shut in a brief spasm.

"Richard? Something wrong?"

Phyllis was regarding him out of concerned and blameless eyes. That was one thing he liked, no, loved, about her. She didn't judge people. He smiled a little and shook his head. "Thanks. I've got to get going."

"All right. 'Bye."

At the door he turned. "Good-bye, sweetie."

41

All the while between the morgue and his office, Jury was trying to think of someone. Carole-anne? No. Mrs. Wassermann? Never. One or two children he knew. Gemma? Abby?

On his way into the office he grunted a hello to Wiggins, who was plugging in the electric kettle. Jury sat down without removing his coat. He picked up a paper clip and started bending it. He was feeling rather ill-used in his hugless universe.

Wiggins was looking at him, eyebrows dancing.

"What?"

"Nothing."

Jury punched in Melrose Plant's number.

Ruthven answered in his most stentorian tones, then greeted Jury as if he'd been lost in a small craft off the coast of Scotland. The call was then overtaken by Melrose.

"You doing anything?" Jury asked.

"Playing with my dog."

Jury crimped his mouth shut.

Melrose went on. "We were about to jettison the naming contest when Dick Scroggs, of all people, chimed in to complain about Lambert Strether: 'Ain't we got enough aggro round 'ere wiffout that Strether nosin' about?' Well, that was it, right there was the name!"

"Strether?"

Melrose blew his impatient curses into the air like smoke. "Of course not! 'Aggro.' It's perfect. Listen: 'Aggrieved.' 'Aghast.' 'Aggro.'"

Aggro. "That's the stupidest name I ever heard for a dog. Besides, his name's Joey."

"That's what the tramp called him, I guess."

"It's on the dog's *collar*." Jury bent another paper clip.

"So what? The tramp went off and left him and hasn't been back."

"We don't call them tramps anymore."

"Beggar? Ticket-of-leave man? Supplicant?"

"Homeless, as you well know." Jury heard barking in the background. "Why isn't Joey outside running around and herding your goat? All that open space to run around in, that's the only reason I—"

"You what?"

"That I can see for having another dog. Where's Mindy, anyway? I haven't seen your dog in ages."

"Hanging out at the Man with a Load of Mischief."

"Well, you should take better care of her. She's old. We're all old. Look, I'm going to Chesham within the hour. Can you leave off playing and drive down to meet me? There's something I'd like you to do."

Melrose was suspicious. "What?"

"I'll tell you when I see you."

Silence. "Well . . ."

Jury was fast losing patience. "Don't give me 'well.' It's hardly more than an hour's drive. You can meet me at the Black Cat."

"All right, then. 'Bye."

Aggro. Jury smashed down the receiver.

Wiggins jumped.

"Sorry. The man ticks me off sometimes." Jury wasn't sure why, exactly. He folded his arms across his chest, hands warming in armpits. "What've you got?"

"About the case, guv?"

"Of *course* about the bloody *case*. Why else would I be here?"
Wiggins pursed his lips.

Jury regarded him narrowly. "The Smart Set escort service. You
went there presumably with one of City police."

"Right." Wiggins pulled out his notebook and the plug of the
electric kettle, which was roaring like a bullet train barreling into
Kyoto. "A Mrs. Rooney. That's the manager's name. Alva Rooney.
She was rightly appalled by Deirdre's murder. As to Deirdre's date the
night before: she didn't want to give me a name, client confidentiality, blah blah blah, sick of hearing that, I am. So I saved myself the
trouble of nicking her and asked if she knew Nicholas Maze. Yes.
That was the man Deirdre was to see. She recognized the name right
away. And seemed genuinely shocked that he'd have shot Deirdre."

"I don't think he did. But she knew Maze well enough for
that?"

"I expect so." Wiggins shrugged.

"How about other men Deirdre Small had been seeing?"

"There were several." Wiggins consulted his notebook and read
off: "William Smythe, Clement Leigh, Jonathon Midges."

Jury smiled slightly. "You mean you didn't have to threaten her
with a warrant?"

"Oh, no. She just reeled them off. Didn't even consult her records.
The woman has a prodigious memory, guv. And she pointed out that
her clients often gave a name other than their own. So she couldn't
say if the names would do us any good."

"Descriptions might, though. Had she any photos?"

"Of her clients? Well, no. The alias wouldn't do you much good
if there were a photo, would it?"

"I worked that out in my own mind, Wiggins. But that doesn't
mean there might not be any. I'm interested that this Mrs. Rooney
is so attuned to her agency she can remember things that fully.
If that's the case, she might be privy to the girls'—women's, I
mean—confidences. Did she talk about Deirdre Small?"

"Not much. Not beyond the fact of her murder. She answered

my questions, but we moved on from the girl to the client, Maze. 'Nice, soft-spoken, polite gentleman, at least on the telephone,' is what she said. Do you think it could've been jealousy on his part that Deirdre was going with other men? Even though that was, after all, her job?"

"I don't think Nicholas Maze could get that worked up over any woman, not enough to kill her. He's too self-serving. Perhaps we should talk to Mrs. Rooney again. When I'm back from Chesham." Jury rose and unhooked his coat from the rack.

Wiggins was frowning. "Don't you find it peculiar that one of these women was murdered in Chesham, while the other two were in London?"

"Of course I do. It's the sticking point."

Wiggins reflected. "Of course, there are serial killers that work over very wide areas. Offhand, though . . . the Yorkshire Ripper, his beat was pretty obvious. Then the Moors Murders, there again . . . No, I wouldn't think he'd turn up in a place like Chesham."

"I wouldn't, either. It makes it appear that these three murders are both connected and not connected. I'll see you later."

Jury left.

In his car, he thought about what he'd just said to Wiggins, that the killings seemed both connected and not connected. The point was important, but he couldn't go anywhere with it. What condition would explain both connection and lack of it? He sat at a red light, thinking about this until the cars behind him honked that the bloody light was green. *Are you color-blind, mate?*

Was that the driver behind him or the light talking?

42

The déjà vu experience was all there for Melrose in the Black Cat: the old man, Johnny Boy, at the small table in the center of the room, muttering, perhaps to his snarly dog, Horace; the stout woman drinking sherry and reading a racing form; and, of course, he himself, stationed at the same table before the same window.

And the girl, Dora, staring at him as he read his *Times*. He rattled the paper open to the inside pages.

"Why haven't you found Morris yet?"

Melrose lowered the paper. "You seem to forget that you told your tale to a CID superintendent. He was supposed to do the finding."

She shook her head. "You were to be one of the finders. Like him."

"I see. Well, my friend is a Scotland Yard detective, whereas I am but a lowly landowner." He wished in earnest the intense eyes would find something else to focus on. He shook his paper, knifed the centerfold with his hand, angry that he hadn't been the brilliant finder himself.

She sighed and shook her head, fielding one more disappointment. "Then why hasn't *he* found Morris? If he works for Scotland Yard, he ought to be able to find a *cat*. How does he keep his job?"

With as much condescension as he could muster, Melrose said, "He has missing people he has to look out for; he can't just—"

"But if he can't find a cat, how can he ever find a person? Finding people's a lot harder."

"I beg your pardon. It is much harder to find a cat than a person. A cat is much smaller and can get into places a person can't."

"A cat can't read street signs, so it's harder for her to know where she is."

"Don't be silly, cats find things by instinct; they don't have to read." What point was being made? He'd forgotten. He rustled his paper and gave it a snap.

Then, to his consternation *another* black cat emerged from behind the bar. Was this the one that had been there before? Was this black cat #2? It sat watchfully. Then black cat #1 sprinted by again, going for the gold.

"Wait a minute," he said, clutching Dora's shoulder. "Wait. One. Minute." He pointed. "There are *two* black cats now; one of them's new." He thought this was the case; they looked alike, except for small differences one could pick out when they got close to each other, which they didn't want to do. The new one (if he was right) was overzealous to the point of frenzy. He hurried here and hurried there as if he were looking for something.

She turned and regarded the new black cat. "That's not Morris either."

Tossing down his paper, Melrose thought, This is where I came in.

The Cat
Came Back

43

He would have left, too, had Richard Jury not that moment walked into the pub.

Sally Hawkins chose the same moment to appear behind the bar. She waved, then called to Dora, who ignored her.

"I have the strange feeling that everything's happening all over again," he said as Jury put his hand on Dora's shoulder, smiled, and sat down.

"Meaning?" said Jury.

"There's yet another black cat, and Dora here says it's not Morris, either. I can't stand it. The black cat cosmos is made up of a zillion cats who aren't any of them Morris. It's *got* to be Morris."

"Don't you think Dora"—she by now having shoved in next to Jury—"knows her own cat?"

"No," said Melrose, in a tone that didn't leave it open to question.

Dora said, "He told me you couldn't find Morris because cats are too hard to find."

"Really? It's always been my experience they were pretty easy. Could you go over and ask Sally to do me a pint of something?"

Immediately, Dora ran over to the bar and was conveying the message. Sally nodded, raised a circled thumb and forefinger, as if having a pint of something were a victory for them both.

"So where's this new cat?"

"He just dashed by; didn't you see him? Now he's gone into that niche by the fireplace."

Jury looked round. It was just about the size of a drawer. He turned that over.

Dora was returning slowly with Jury's beer.

"They really shouldn't let you do that," said Melrose. "A seven-year-old purveyor of beer."

Dora, sitting down again, took up the cat cudgel. "Well, *he* said"— she darted a look at Melrose—"Scotland Yard policemen weren't any good at finding cats."

"A misquote! I didn't say—"

"You did too!" Dora stood up in her seat, hands mashed on hips.

"Never mind," said Jury. "I found Morris."

Both of them stared, mouths open in equal astonishment.

Dora's closed first. "But—" She looked around the room. "Where is she?"

"In London. Don't worry. She's okay."

Melrose's tone was icy, suggesting no congratulations were in order, "Then why didn't you bring her?"

"Because I need her in London for a little while."

"What?"

"What?"

Their "whats" bumped into each other. At their twinned expressions, Jury wanted to laugh. They seemed to have changed selves, Melrose looking seven and Dora forty-seven, with her little creased forehead and startled eyes. "Now, this new cat: just when did it turn up?" asked Jury, who already knew.

"Today . . . no, last night. It's always rushing around except when it goes over and sits in that hollow place. We don't know why it's kind of crazy. And it has a mean temper. Sally thinks it must belong to someone because it was wearing a collar. But it came off."

"I'd like to see it."

"Why?" said Melrose.

"Evidence."

"Oh, please." Melrose rolled his eyes as Dora slid out again and ran to the bar.

Jury raised his voice and turned toward the fireplace. "Schrö-dinger!" The others, the old man and racing lady, looked at him as if he'd gone mad. So did Schrödinger, who left her cubbyhole and rushed over to the table, sniffed at his shoe, and rushed off again.

Dora was back with the collar.

The blue collar was the same one the other black cat had been wearing when she'd appeared with Mungo in the Old Wine Shades. Smiling, Jury stared out the window. How in hell had they done it? How? They just had.

"Schrödinger?" said Melrose. "Now, I could be crazy—"

Jury nodded. "You're getting warm."

"Funny. But the last I heard, Schrödinger was Harry Johnson's cat."

Dora said, "That's a funny name."

"The owner is a funny guy."

"But I want Morris," Dora said before Sally Hawkins called her away.

If not Morris, then Joey. Or someone. Jury looked down, studied his pint.

"Are you saying this is Harry Johnson's cat?"

Jury nodded and drank his beer.

"What is it doing here?"

"I expect Harry brought her here."

Melrose dropped his head in his hands. "Why? Why? Why? Do I want to hear the answer?"

"Probably not. 'The cat came back.' It's Harry having his little joke. Don't you remember he sucked me into his story about the Gaults with that enigmatic comment 'The dog came back'?"

"This was a joke?"

"Um-hm. There's a murder in Chesham and I'm stuck with it. Harry knows it. So he's just getting his mite of revenge because I'm still on his case."

"He's crazy. Why would he bring his cat here?"

"Well, he didn't know it was his, did he? He thought he was bringing Morris back."

"So he couldn't tell his own cat?"

"Not him. Not without the collar. He put a collar on Morris in order to tell them apart. Now, the real mystery is how Morris got the collar off and onto Schrödinger. I suspect Mungo managed that little trick. Easy enough to get it off; it's just a Velcro closure. Well, we'll never know."

"You're just leaving Schrödinger here and Morris with Harry?"

"No, of course not. *You're* going to get Morris back."

Melrose stared, not at Jury but at some impossible image in his head. Then he collected his cigarettes and lighter, stuffed them into his pockets, drank off his beer, and said, "That's it."

When he got up, Jury pulled him down by his sleeve. "It's perfectly simple. You'll go to Harry's. I have a dog, I mean cat, carrier in the car—"

"Why? What would you have a carrier for?" Melrose had sat down again.

"It's . . . Wiggins's. He got a hamster. We'll put the carrier in your car. You'll be staying at Boring's." Pleased, Jury drank his beer.

"Is there any part of my life you don't have plans for? Why will I be staying at Boring's?"

"Because you're going to London."

"I have no plans to go to London."

"You do now. That's the second thing: Have you ever used an escort service?"

Melrose sat back and regarded Jury through narrowed and suspicious eyes. "No, and I don't plan to in the future."

"Here's a change in your future plans: Smart Set, Valentine's, King's Road Companions. You choose."

"Oh, thanks very much. None of the above. I don't fancy sex I have to pay for."

"Who said you had to?"

"Pay for it?"

"No, have it."

"Well, that's what those escort places are for."

"Not necessarily. You can have an escort for a lot of things. Just take her to dinner or a show or for a walk in Green Park or to the Royal Albert Hall or to the Vic—"

"Can you see me taking a woman of that sort to the Victoria and Albert?"

"Christ, but you're a snob. I never knew you were a snob."

"Yes, you did."

"Well, but you're not. Look at all your canoodling with the Crippses. Anyone who can hang around White Ellie and Ash the Flash by definition is not a snob. Not to mention Piddlin' Pete." Jury gave a brief but beery laugh. "And what about Bea? Yes, Bea. You didn't waste any time taking her to the National Gallery. She's a lot more EC3 than SW1."

"Bea's an artist."

"I know. But her accent's Brixton. So go ahead, choose: Smart Set, Valentine's, King's Road."

Melrose continued to stare at Jury.

"Oh, for God's sakes. I'll go first." Jury was certain that Rosie Moss knew more than she'd told him; now was as good a time as any to ring her. He did. "Rosie, hello. Richard Jury . . . yes, that one. Look, if you've nothing on, how about a drink tomorrow night . . . No? . . . Thursday night, then?" He danced his eyebrows at a leery-eyed Melrose Plant. "Okay, I will. Thanks." Jury rang off. "See? Simple as that? Rosie's with Valentine's. So you take one of the others."

"If you were actually talking to someone just now. You could have been faking the whole thing."

Jury just gave him a look.

"Oh, very well. Smart Set. I like the name better."

"Right." Jury got out his mobile phone. "We'll call that first."

Melrose threw up his hands. "Wait a minute: you think I'm going to do this right now?"

"Why not? I did it right now."

"You don't trust me to do it?"

"No."

"Hell." Melrose reached over and grabbed the mobile. "What's the number?"

Jury slid a page from his small notebook across to Melrose. "Don't forget the London code's just changed."

Melrose glared. "I'm not a child." He tapped in the number and waited for the ring. "Yes . . . hello . . . I was just wondering . . . I'm going to be in London—"

Jury held up a page on which he'd been writing.

"—tomorrow and I'm interested in your, uh, service."

Jury went on writing.

"And I was just wondering about the procedure . . . Yes . . . Yes."

Jury held up his note: *"They'll want to know what kind of girl."*

"Oh, I'm not particular—no, wait, I'd say a blonde, tallish, good-looking, of course, but then you wouldn't have one that's bad-looking, would you, a-ha?"

A twitter came out of the mobile.

"That sounds all right . . . Where will I be staying? At my club. Boring's. It's in Mayfair . . . Oh, cocktails and dinner, I think . . . At my club? Well . . . look, I'll get in touch after I get to London to pick a place to meet . . . Yes." He gave her his particulars, including a credit card number. He had to wrestle the card out of his leather billfold. "Yes. Good-bye." Melrose gave the mobile and a dirty look to Jury, who smiled and stowed it in his pocket.

Dora was back again, sitting down beside Jury, ignoring Sally Hawkins. "When you go to London," she said to Melrose, "will you go to this person's house and get Morris?"

"No," he said to her. Ignoring Dora's crestfallen look, he turned to Jury. "Now, what are your instructions? I mean, about how to behave on a first date?"

"I don't care what you do as long as you get the information." Jury thought of the cabdriver who'd whisked him to the animal hospital, and smiled. The Knowledge."

Jury looked at his watch. "Got to go. I want to make a few stops before I head back to London."

"What about this infernal kidnapping of Morris? When am I supposed to do that?"

"After your hot date tomorrow night. So the day after. And *don't* use the Rolls; take one of your other wrecks. The Bentley. It's pretty old as I remember.'

"There's the Jag."

"You don't own a Jaguar."

"I could always buy one. I mean, we want to do this right."

"Why are you sodden with money, whilst I just have to squeak along?"

Melrose shrugged. "Justice? You can have my Bentley."

"Thanks. And remember, this isn't a kidnapping. Kidnapping is what Harry did. You'll be going to London anyway for your date." Jury smiled. "I'll let you know the exact time to appear at Harry's house. He lives in Belgravia. You know where that is."

"'You know where that is,'" Melrose mimicked. "Yes, sport, I know. What's his address?"

Jury told him.

"So when Harry comes to the door—incidentally, I'm sure Harry will remember me after that drama in the Old Wine Shades."

"Harry won't be coming to the door." Jury's smile was even broader. "Harry will be elsewhere."

44

"They're calling them 'the Escort Murders,' subhead 'Serial Killer on the Loose?' At least they made it a question." DS Cummins had turned the paper around so that Jury could see for himself the headline and the photos beneath it. There were two of the Valentine's and Smart Set agencies, together with what looked like agency photographs, one of Deirdre Small and one of Mariah Cox using the name "Stacy Storm." Kate Banks was missing, as was the King's Road Companions agency. Beneath these photos was a smaller one of Rose Moss, who was "helping police with their inquiries."

Jury and Cummins were sitting in the Chesham station.

Cummins went on: "I guess they're all related, only . . ."

"Only what? I'm open to intuition."

Cummins scratched his ear. He looked awfully young. Jury envied him the boyishness so close to the surface. He thought of Rosie Moss. He worried about her, to tell the truth. He hoped he wasn't leading her on, making that date with her.

"Well, it doesn't feel right, that it's a serial killer."

"Why?"

"I think it's because . . . Mariah being murdered in Chesham, not London."

"Exactly. Mariah Cox was murdered because she was Mariah Cox, or Stacy Storm, not because she was an escort. That it would be the same for the other two would follow, wouldn't it? They're connected, but not by escort services, by something else. We have to find out the something else."

David Cummins smiled. "Chris thinks so, too, the escort business doesn't have anything to do with the murders. Chris thinks it's all about shoes."

Jury really laughed for the first time in days. "Tell her I can send someone round to talk to Jimmy Choo."

"And Louboutin, the red sole guy. Those shoes look like they stepped in blood."

Edna Cox came to the door looking a little less worn out, but not much. She seemed, oddly, glad to see Jury, maybe because he was one of the few left who connected her with Mariah. He hoped he wasn't the only one.

He was seated with a cup of tea, not speaking of her niece and the other victims until she'd stopped bustling around and was herself sitting down.

"These other two women, Mrs. Cox—Deirdre Small and Kate Banks—do those names mean anything to you?"

She shook her head. The paper, the same one Cummins had shown to Jury, was lying on a rust-colored ottoman. Edna Cox picked it up. "No. But I've seen her somewhere." As Cummins had done, she turned the paper so Jury could see. Her finger was tapping the picture of Rosie Moss. "Adele Astaire, it says her name is." A little *hmpf!* of disbelief followed.

Jury was surprised. "You've seen her where? I thought all you knew of her was the name."

"That's right. I'd never seen these girls. I mean, their pictures. No, Adele Astaire is a made-up name just like Stacy Storm is. You'd think"—pause for a sip of tea—"they could come up with better names than those, wouldn't you?"

Jury thought he'd better not prompt her with Adele's real name just now. "This Adele Astaire—do you recall where you saw her?"

She set down the cup and was prepared to really exercise her brain. "I've been trying to bring it to mind ever since I saw that picture." She shook her head. "But I can't."

"Could she have come here at all, I mean, to Chesham, with Mariah?"

Edna Cox's eyes shut tightly, as if squeezing the last drop from memory. "No. No, I'm sure not. At least that's not where I saw her."

Jury waited, but when she added nothing, he said, "Her real name is Rose Moss. Does that mean anything to you?"

Edna frowned down to study either the hands in her lap or the carpet of cabbage roses at her feet. Then she tilted her head a bit, as in the way of one trying to hear an indistinct or distant sound. Her eyes widened. "A film! There was a film long ago that I remember seeing with my sister, Mariah's mum, when they lived in London. Mariah must've heard us talking about it, and laughed and said something like its being funny, the way the film had got the name the wrong way round. It was called *Moss Rose*. She thought it very funny."

"You think Rose Moss was someone she knew?"

"Well, it must've been a school chum, maybe. Mariah wouldn't have been more than eight or nine, I shouldn't think. But you've talked to the girl; what did this Moss girl say? Did she recognize Mariah?"

"She knew her by Stacy Storm, you see. And when I told her the real name, she didn't say she knew your niece."

Edna Cox leaned her head on her hand, fisted round a handkerchief. A tear tracked slowly down her face. "My Mariah making up such a name. It's a sad name, isn't it? It's so false. It's so falsely like a film star, isn't it? My Mariah."

Understandable that she'd settled on the name instead of the whole charade. Denial, he supposed, our last refuge. "Why do you think Mariah went to such trouble to appear, well, plain, when she was clearly so striking?"

Or was the striking one, the escort, the real Mariah?

Was either identity real? Neither?

Edna Cox shook her head. "She was prettier as a child; she seemed to grow into plainness somehow. Even then, she was fairly quiet and uncomplaining, not a lot of energy. This other self of hers—I don't know where that came from."

"You'd have had no reason to think it, but is it possible she was suffering a mental illness, what's thought of as a personality dissociation? You know—where the sick person splits into one or more other selves?"

The aunt frowned. "Oh, no. At least there's no history at all of that kind of thing in the family."

Jury nodded. If it were some sort of personality split, what would it mean to this case? It was certainly not one of Mariah's selves that had killed the other two women. Mariah had been the first one to die.

Jury rose, thanked Edna Cox, and offered to do for her anything he could, which, they both knew, was nothing. Still, the offer. "I'll be going back to London. You have my card? You know where to reach me. Please do, if you need me."

She took some comfort in this and said good-bye.

45

D
r. Phyllis Nancy peeled off the skin-thin green gloves and dropped them into the gutter of the table where Deirdre Small lay, shrunken in death, hollowed out, deflated.

"I wanted another look at the bullet wounds, the trajectory of the bullet. Your suspect, the client she was meeting—if he is a suspect . . ." Phyllis looked at her notes.

Jury nodded. "Nicholas Maze. DI Jenkins doesn't think he did it."

"Then Jenkins is probably right. Maze, I believe, is very tall; the victim was quite short. The trajectory would have been different—"

"Even at close range?"

She nodded. "It would still make a difference."

Jury looked at the face of Deirdre Small, wiped clean of all expression, and knew the expressions that had once played over it: it would have been a game face, a face put on to meet the demands of her world. Because of her background, her job, her small structure, she must have conceded a lot. More, he bet, than the intelligent and beautiful Kate Banks or the ambiguous Mariah Cox.

Three of you, he thought. Dead for no reason, died for nothing, killed because you were an inconvenience in some way, murdered because of someone's greed, or rage, or fear, or guilt. How do you connect? How were you alike?

He looked up, nodded back to the body of Deirdre Small. "What did she tell you, Phyllis?"

"Not nearly as much," said Dr. Nancy with a little smile, "as she told you. Dinner?"

He nodded. She took off her apron, went to collect her things, and they left the morgue.

"The neurologists," said Phyllis, "aren't very hopeful. But I expect that comes as no surprise."

Jury studied his crispy fish, something Wiggins liked to order, but not he. It looked like a puzzle.

Phyllis was studying him. Did he himself look like a puzzle? He was stalling for a reply to the neurologists' prognoses. He could think of nothing.

"You're at a loss." She tilted her head. "There was never anything you could do, Richard. There's nothing now."

He shook his head. "I know. It's not so much what I could do as what I could feel. Should feel." He looked up from his fish, then back again. He wasn't very hungry.

"Ambivalence is—"

"It's more than that. Or less than." Jury leaned back and took in the room, crowded as always. Here the crowding didn't bother him; the customers, perfect strangers, seemed familiar. In the familiar din and chatter, there was privacy. He caught sight of Danny Wu, bending over a table, being solicitous of the couple there. Danny could work a room as well as any politician. He smiled. "This place is comforting."

"It is, yes. It's one of those home places, a place that's a stand-in for home, whatever that might mean. For me, there's a chemist's near my flat. It's a little sort of run-down place, but I like to go in it. There's even an armchair. I sit in it and read labels."

"Phyllis—" He laughed, more delighted than surprised. This woman was so accomplished. Also beautiful, also rich. The source of her money was a mystery to him.

"For some people it's a certain kind of shop, for some, bookstores—it doesn't have to be a place, anyway—what we think of as home. For an artist it might be paint; for a writer, words." She sighed and cut off a bite of fish.

"I was at the hospital this morning," she continued. "One of her doctors is a good friend and he told me. It's still possible she'll come out of it, Richard. This makes it difficult to decide—well, Lu's uncle was there."

Jury waited.

"He's the closest relation she has or, at least, according to him."

"You saw him?"

She nodded. "Yes, he was there with Dr. McEvoy. My friend."

"Lu told me a little about him, the uncle. She was very fond of him. Other than that, she never talked about her life." He picked up the chopsticks, moved them awkwardly. "Now, what's left of it?"

"I'm really sorry, Richard."

She was, too.

It wasn't, thought Jury, one of Phyllis's "home places," the hospital, but he thought the nursing staff made an effort to keep it from being absolutely foreign.

A grandmotherly looking nurse, small and rotund, whose uniform badge gave her name as Mae Whittey, came round from behind the nurses' station to tell him Ms. Aguilar had been moved earlier that day and that she would take him to her room. He did not want to know to what section, for he was afraid of the answer. It might be the Hopeless Ward.

Nurse Mae Whittey's crepe-soled shoes made gasping little sucks at the floor as she walked. She told him that one of the rooms they passed was being "refurbished," hence the thick plastic across the doorless doorway. The heavy plastic put Jury in mind of one of those temporary tents thrown up at an archaeological dig.

"Mind those tools," she said, indicating a bucket and equipment left lying against the wall. Her role seemed less nurse and more guide through an excavation, seeing to it that Jury didn't put a foot wrong.

Their steps echoed in the soundless corridor. He didn't understand the silence, given many of the doors to the rooms were halfway open.

"Here you are," she said, but it was apparently "Here *we* are," for she went in with him.

And as if she were a member of their tiny family, she stood beside him to look down at the still form of Lu Aguilar, as composed as an effigy in a church. Yet Nurse Whittey's presence was oddly unobtrusive. Jury had to admit to himself he was even grateful for it. He remembered the heavy weight of aloneness he had felt two months ago, back in March, when his cousin Sarah had died up in Newcastle. He had walked around London for several hours, unable to settle on a park bench or a coffee bar or in his thoughts. There was an orphaned quality to loneliness.

This room looked just like the other room, except for the addition of fresh flowers, sprays of the most gorgeous orchids he had ever seen, sitting in a vase on the bedside table. They reminded him he had always come empty-handed. "Someone's been to see her. Was it her uncle?"

"Oh, no, it was Dr. Nancy brought those. Aren't they gorgeous? So many shades of red. Brazilian orchids, she said. Ms. Aguilar's from Brazil, apparently. Dr. Nancy said something from her own country to keep her company." Nurse Whittey smiled. "That's just like her. Doctor Nancy, I mean." She turned to him. "You know Doctor Nancy, don't you? I believe she mentioned you. I thought myself that perhaps she must be a friend of the patient, but she said, no, just the good friend of a good friend."

"Yes." Jury didn't know what to say.

"Well, I'm just terribly sorry," Mae Whittey said. She looked down at Lu. "She's so terribly young."

Of course, all rules of protocol should have had the nurse leaving, and leaving him alone. Yet they stood there together for some moments in a companionable silence for which Jury was grateful, but which he didn't understand. Perhaps Nurse Whittey always had that effect on people.

While she made microscopic adjustments to the bedclothes, Jury went to the window and looked out. A view different yet the same. He looked around to see the nurse rearranging the orchids that blazed in the colorless room. Prometheus returning fire to benighted mortals.

He said, "You know, there was a great actress named Dame May Whitty. Same name, spelled differently." He smiled at her.

"Oh, my, yes. I remember her well. There was that one where she was on a train—yes, and just disappeared, didn't she?"

"Hitchcock," said Jury. He looked off through the window that gave out on the same square of land as the one Lu had been in before. *"The Lady Vanishes."*

46

Alice Dalyrimple.

How could one take seriously as an escort a woman with such a Victorian name as Alice Dalyrimple?

"Miss Dalyrimple will be your escort." *Alice Dalyrimple,* so snobbily intoned by a Miss Crick of the Smart Set escort service. Miss Crick had been entrusted with the appointment book. Melrose felt he had landed in the middle of a Jane Austen novel.

"Now, Mr. Plant, a bit more information. What is your given name?"

Why, wondered Melrose, had he used his last name? Men seeking the services of escort agencies gave out fictional names, surely. At least he could make up a first name: "Algernon. That's my first name." From Jane Austen to Oscar Wilde.

"Algernon. Very good."

Did the name have to meet with her approval?

"Now, we were to decide upon a meeting place."

His mind ranged over venues, from the Hole in the Wall underneath Waterloo Bridge to Buckingham Palace, where he fantasized presenting Miss Dalyrimple to the queen. In the midst of these unfruitful thoughts, Melrose looked round at the several sluggish old gents in various stages of slumber and said to her, "Boring's. My club in Mayfair."

"Oh. And this is permitted by the club, is it?"

Miss Crick's question was the first indication that they knew Smart Set wasn't turning up in *Burke's Peerage*. It encouraged him to be fulsome: "Oh, my, yes. Yes, we're quite an open and wide-awake group here." He decided this after one of the old men snuffled himself out of a coma. The only thing less awake would be the burial vaults in Westminster.

"Yes," he began, "all she—"

"Miss Dalyrimple?"

Ah! Had he shown bad escort manners in his overly familiar use of "she"? "Miss Dalyrimple need only present herself at the reception desk and they will inform me."

"I see. You will not be at the door yourself?"

Only if I'm the doorman. "I'll be in the Members' Room."

"And now, could I just verify your credit card number?"

"I believe I gave that to someone already."

"But not to me."

Good God, isn't that what police said when one objected to being asked the same questions over and over? The woman should work for the Met.

"You know, I'd always thought the payment would be made at the end of things."

"That's true. But this is just in case, you know."

In case of what? A heart event in the middle of things? Miss Dalyrimple's discovering she had walked not into an exclusive club but into a tattoo parlor? London's being overrun by rivers of rats? He pulled out his wallet and thumbed through his little stash of cards and recited the number. He and Miss Crick then parted.

Now here he sat in the sleepy environs of Boring's with a book he was trying to force himself to read, waiting for Miss Alice Dalyrimple. They would have dinner here, drinks and then dinner. There was no quieter place to have a conversation about the murders. Surely it would be on her mind, escorts being murdered. How did she know he wasn't the one? Here these women were, going out with and having sex with potential serial killers, and seemingly careless of it. Had the snarky Miss Crick shown any concern? No. But then, she wasn't the one going out.

Well, Jury didn't think the danger was in the escort business itself.

If the women in this kind of work weren't being murdered because of that work, and if it wasn't coincidence they happened to be in it— then what did that leave? It meant, didn't it, they had something else in common—

"My God! If it isn't Lord Ardry!"

"Colonel Neame." Melrose got up to shake the hand of the elderly, pink-cheeked former RAF pilot. "I was just wondering if you were around."

"Always am, dear boy, except for my brief walks to the Ritz and Fortnum's."

Ritz for tea, Fortnum & Mason for silk-worsted suits and caviar counter. "Your itinerary must be the envy of London. And this," Melrose went on, his arm out flung to take in the Members' Room, "is the only way to live."

"Well, it's restful, of course. But I think a bit more animation wouldn't go unappreciated. My, my!" He was looking toward the entrance to the Members' Room.

A buxom blonde in a flimsy dress that looked to be made up of chiffon scarves stood at the entrance. The slowly turning fan of bamboo and palm fronds above her set the multiscarved garment in motion. The rest of the motion of bouncy breasts and churning hips was taken care of by the woman herself.

"Who, in God's name, is this?" The tone was not unappreciative.

This could only be Miss Dalyrimple.

Melrose answered Colonel Neame, "This would be my guest, if I'm not mistaken."

"Oh ho, my boy! Well done, well done!"

Melrose wanted to tell him he could do it himself, if he'd just yank out a phone directory. If anything could awaken the Rip van Winkles in the room, it was surely Alice Dalyrimple maneuvering herself toward him in her silver sandals.

"Miss Dalyrimple? I'm Algernon Plant." He caught the colonel's raised eyebrows.

"How j'ya do?"

Given Miss Crick's rather hesitant description of her escort, Melrose had formed a cloudy image of a passable imitation of gentility. But Miss Dalyrimple, in her gait and her guise, did nothing to present a picture of good breeding. (The last horse to win the Gold Cup had done far better there.) And any hope of even passable credentials was blown to smithereens when she opened her mouth. Melrose wondered if even Marilyn Monroe, before her voice coach got to her, had sounded something like this. Alice's voice was a breathless squeak.

He introduced her to Colonel Neame, who was staring so hard that his eyeballs looked as if they were on stems. Gruffly, he said, "Yes, yes, so nice."

"Pleased, I'm sher," answered Alice.

They all sat, Alice in a flounce and a flutter of the scarf dress. Melrose hoped she wouldn't start in immediately stripping and settling the scarves round Colonel Neame.

"Miss Dalyrimple—"

"Oh, for heaven's sikes, call me Alice." Seated beside him on the sofa, Alice tucked her hand through his elbow and gave the arm a pat. "We're going to 'ave some fun, sweetie, ain't we?"

Her eyelids were so heavy with dustings of gold and green, they came down like little shutters. She was wearing a multitude of perfumes, scents that were fighting for prominence.

"Care for a drink?" Melrose asked.

"Wouldn't say no, would I? I'll 'ave a tequila and lime."

Colonel Neame thought this laughable. "Doubt you'll get anything quite that involved here, Miss Dalyrimple."

"Involved?" Her eyebrows danced.

"Oh, we only mean that Boring's runs more to the straight offerings of whiskey and gin."

"I'll be a monkey's. Gin, then."

Melrose wasn't surprised as he ordered up drinks for all of them. He and Colonel Neame had been drinking that old standby, eighteen-year-old Macallan's. The little redheaded porter took their order and whisked himself off.

Opening his mouth to express a thought that hadn't yet formed, Melrose shut it when he saw Polly Praed standing in the entryway, not looking at all like Alice Dalyrimple. Polly was wearing her old standby mustard-colored suit, a color that Melrose had tried to get her to jettison long ago. It hardly did justice to her eyes, the most beautiful eyes he had ever seen. They were a limitless, bottomless purple blue, staring at him—he was sure—accusingly, though too far off to really tell.

Polly was here not by accident, but by design. Melrose had called her and enlisted her help. A mystery writer, he had said, might be expected to grill someone associated with an escort agency as the three murdered women had been.

Yesterday, he had said, "You'd be doing me a great favor, Polly."

"Good. Then you'll owe me."

He hadn't counted on that. Being in Polly's debt could result in having to read a new manuscript, a chore she'd asked him to perform in the past. This was a chore he'd always managed to get out of; it was bad enough reading the published books. Or not-reading them. The new book he was not-reading was the one on the cushion beside him. Not-reading required an inventive mind: how to convey to the author he'd read a book when he hadn't. That usually involved reading the beginning and making it up from there.

He quickly stuffed the book between the cushion and the arm of the sofa. The title alone was enough to kill off brain cells: *Within a Budding Grave*. The last one he had not-read was *The Gourmandise Way*. In her personal Search for Lost Time (and he hoped she didn't find enough of it to write another dozen books), Polly had gone on this Proustian rant. The dust jacket of the latest had disclosed that the plot turned on a mistaken burial—they'd buried the wrong man. God only knew what would follow from that. He wondered why she was squandering her talent, for she was genuinely talented. Why was she messing it about? Letting it drift like a baby Moses into the bulrushes?

"Polly! Over here!" as if they were on the loading deck of the *Queen Elizabeth*.

Polly made her way over—suspicious, he now could see.

Before Melrose could try to lighten the atmosphere, Colonel Neame was on his feet, pumping her hand, saying, "Miss Praed! We met last time you were here, and I just want to tell you how very much I enjoyed *The Gourmandise Way*."

Melrose shuddered. The book about a chef's deadly dinner, with that nod to Proust.

Polly thanked Colonel Neame and tucked herself into the wing chair beside him. She was staring from Melrose to Alice, who had now received her gin and was downing it. The porter handed over the other two drinks and waited for this new guest's order.

"Nothing . . . Oh, no, wait, I'll have a sherry. Whatever kind you have."

"Wonderful to see you, Polly. You'll have dinner?" Turning to Alice, Melrose said, "You won't mind, will you, if Miss Praed joins us?"

Both women looked at him uncertainly. He gave them both a fool's grin. *What did you expect? I'm an idiot.* Polly, he knew, would be happy to subscribe to this, but Alice might feel it a bit insulting.

Alice Dalyrimple, who certainly would mind, shrugged and said, "Suit yerself." She rearranged her décolletage—would that neckline sink any farther? Could that cleavage be yet more pronounced? Yes to both. Sitting forward with her small hands on her knees, she looked grimly at this mustard-suited woman who was now taking her sherry from the porter. But suddenly and impishly, she returned to her original cuteness level and gave Polly (who jumped) a swat on the knee. "Oh, I get it! Ain't you two a riot?"

Melrose and Polly, dumb to her meaning, only looked at each other.

Then Alice leaned toward Colonel Neame, laughed as if bubbles were coming out of her nose, and said, "Come on now, sweetie, make it a foursome!" Then, "O' course, it'll cost ya!" The laugh was almost silvery, for there was money in it.

The three managed to get into the dining room without further incident (or making it a foursome). Dinner had an impromptu feel: a patched-together quality, insofar as Boring's could ever seem patched together.

Young Higgins, Boring's oldest waiter, would never permit it. If Miss Dalyrimple had floated scarves about him, Young Higgins would remain as resolutely unflinching as any of the Palace Guards.

"We have escargots tonight, my lord." At Alice's wrinkled nose, he put in, "Snails."

It was a relief to find Young Higgins was as much of a class artist as he himself. Melrose smiled. "I'll have them." Remembering his manners, he said, "Oh, sorry, Polly. What'll you have?"

"Soup," she said curtly.

"Me, I don't think I want a starter," said Alice. "Watching my weight." She twinkled. "So just bring me another one of these, love!" She held out her gin glass, which Higgins took with a sniff.

"Madam."

They all ordered the roast beef.

Enough of this, thought Melrose; let's get down to it. "Polly, here, is a mystery writer," he said, leaning over the table toward Alice.

Alice was impressed. "That book the Colonel was talkin' about, you wrote it? I never!"

Melrose said, leaning even closer into Alice's disturbing neckline, "Polly's really good at murders."

"Oh, Jesus Christmas! Are you going to write about us?"

Young Higgins was slipping soup and escargots before Polly and Melrose and a fresh gin before Alice, then going soundlessly off. It gave Polly a few seconds to take in the "us."

Alice said, "You know, us escorts."

"I might," she said, sotto voce. "That's what I'm thinking of doing; that's why I'm in London: research. How lucky to meet you."

Spearing a radish from the small plate of complimentary crudités that looked hard as enamel, Alice said, also sotto voce, "Well, if you ask me, this crazy person's nothing but a sex maniac."

An interesting conclusion, thought Melrose. "Why do you say that? It would appear sex mania is what he's against. Although, to think it's sex at all is making an assumption."

"That's so true," Alice said, leaning toward Polly. "People think the wrong ideas about escort services. They think they're just about sex."

They are, thought Melrose. For a few minutes, they ate in silence.

"But aren't they about sex?" asked a braver Polly as Young Higgins appeared with their entrées.

Alice said in a sharpish way, "They most as-sur-ed-ly are not. Just look at the three of us, we're 'aving a meal, ain't we? Whatever comes later, that's up to you two. Oh, what nice-looking beef! D'ya 'ave any tomato sauce, dear?"

Young Higgins was not used to being called "dear," nor did the icy look he gave Miss Dalyrimple suggest he was inclined to get used to it. Or perhaps what called forth that stony expression was, rather, the request for tomato sauce. He set down the other two plates and turned to the wine cooler.

Melrose and Polly paid no attention to the Pinot Noir being poured because they were back there a beat, with the "whatever comes later" remark. To keep from laughing, Melrose snatched up his glass and gulped. The wine came out his nose. He coughed.

Polly recovered. "Why do you call this killer a sex maniac?"

"Prob'ly he can't—you know—perform. Wouldn't surprise me if he's one of Valentine's, or one of the others. DeeDee—Deirdre Small, the one got herself murdered—didn't agree, though. Said he'd probably turn out to be her steady." Alice giggled and quickly stopped, probably recalling what had happened to Deirdre Small.

Pay dirt! Pay dirt! He could have kissed Alice Dalyrimple, except she'd have him under the table in two seconds flat. "You knew this Deirdre Small?"

"O' course I knew her. She was with Smart Set, too, don't forget.

Nice girl was DeeDee. It's such a shame." She carried on carving up more beef, sans tomato ketchup.

"You knew her well?" said Melrose.

"Oh, yeah. Pretty well. We went to the cinema sometimes, stuff like that."

"Had you seen her recently?" Polly asked.

"A week ago, maybe." Alice picked up her empty glass. "Just before she got murdered." She set down the glass. "She was worried about something. . . ."

"About what?" said Melrose.

"Well, she never said, did she?" Alice looked blankly over the dining room.

Polly asked, "Do you think it could have been one of her . . . clients, then, that did this? Maybe somebody got jealous of her other men?"

Alice frowned. "You mean you think it coulda been personal?"

"Couldn't it have? I mean, it doesn't have to be some maniac just killing off escorts."

"It'd be hard to think DeeDee'd get on the wrong side of any-body, she's so nice. I don't know all the ones she dated. . . . Didn't police arrest her date for that night?"

Melrose said, "From what I read, they only questioned him."

"If it was Nick, police can forget about it. DeeDee always said he was dull as dishwater. A whiner, too. Whined about his wife, whined about his work. Not much get-up-and-go, you know? 'My Nick's not exactly got a steel spine; more like spaghetti,' she used to say." She paused. "When I said DeeDee was worried about some-thing . . . well, it was something she thought maybe she should see police about. . . ." Again her voice trailed away.

Melrose was all ears. "And she didn't give you any hint at all as to what it was?"

Alice shook her head, played with her fork, looked disquieted. To Melrose she said, "You seem awful interested in the murders."

"Not him," said Polly quickly. "Me. Did you ever talk to police? I mean, did you tell them about DeeDee?"

"No. I don't much like police."

Then Alice said, "I knew that other one, too, that got her picture in the paper. Calls herself Adele Astaire? Escorts are kinda, I guess you'd say, clubby. I guess we feel we've got to stick together. People make it sound like we're working the curb in Shepherd Market or under London Bridge." She giggled up some wine. "But it ain't like that, that's chalk and cheese, those two jobs."

Melrose was even more dumbfounded. "You know Adele Astaire?"

Alice's nod was tentative, as if she weren't sure she wanted to get into this.

Polly said, "So you didn't tell police you knew either of these women?"

She screwed up her face. "Why would I? I say let them sort it. Besides, I don't know anything, really."

"But tell us," Polly went on. "What you do know about this Adele?"

"Not much to tell, is there? We was in school together. Adele—what was her real name?—was a cheeky kid. Still was, I bet. Always wanted to be a dancer, she did. I think maybe that's why she went on the job, thinking she'd get herself the money she'd need to study. I doubt she did, but I dunno. Haven't seen her in years." Alice pushed her plate back and now blew out her cheeks as if she'd just run the mile. "What's the pud?"

Dessert—sticky toffee pudding—came and went, and at about that rate of speed.

Polly put down her napkin and announced she was off to the ladies' room. This, Melrose knew, was to give him an opportunity to take care of Alice. Melrose did. But not without difficulty. His best excuse was that, really, he and Alice could hardly get together with Polly here. To which Alice acted surprised the arrangement hadn't been made already and that they could still . . . No, no, we couldn't, said Melrose, slipping Alice the money for the evening's encounter, feeling he had got off lightly; feeling, indeed, twice that sum wouldn't have paid for the information.

So he paid her twice that sum.

★   ★   ★

"Polly, you were marvelous."

"It's a curse."

They were finishing up brandies in the Members' Room. Polly had to make the last train back to Littlebourne.

"You've been checking your watch about every thirty seconds, so you obviously want to check in with Superintendent Jury."

They both got up. Melrose recalled just then that he'd stuffed Polly's book in between the cushion and arm of the chair and now dug it out. Naturally, he hadn't read enough of it to say anything halfway intelligent. He held it out. "Will you autograph this for me?"

She looked at the book, then up at him. "When you've read it." Smiling, Polly walked out.

47

Jury put down the phone and sat staring at Wiggins. He was not really seeing Wiggins, only the images in his own mind, his response to Melrose Plant's telephone call.

"What?" said Wiggins, indisposed because he couldn't sort out what was wrong with the plug on the flex to the electric teakettle. "What?" he said again.

Jury flinched a little, Wiggins being as far from his mind as the electric kettle. "Sorry. That was Plant on the line. He said the woman he had a meal with last night knows Rose Moss, aka Adele Astaire."

Wiggins stopped fiddling with the plug. "What did he find out?"

"They'd been school chums years ago. The woman—the one Melrose Plant was with—is one of Smart Set's escorts."

"Mr. Plant . . ." Wiggins snorted. "Can't picture Mr. Plant—him who was Lord Ardry—in company with a slag." But apparently he could picture it, for something was putting him in a better humor. He snickered.

"Don't enjoy it too much, Wiggins. He did it because I told him to. Her name's Alice Dalyrimple." Jury smiled at the name.

"But then if she's with Smart Set . . . so was Deirdre Small."

"Yes. And DeeDee, as she called Deirdre, was worried about something, was even thinking of going to police."

"Is this Alice involved, then?"

"I don't think so. She was just the one supplied by the agency."

"Then if she knows the Moss woman, does she—or did she—know Stacy Storm . . . Mariah Cox?"

"No."

"Well, then, it doesn't sound very significant, boss." He had finally fitted the plug into an outlet. The kettle had water in it.

"But it is. It's the connection. Look: we assume because three women working for these different escort outfits are murdered, the connection is the work itself—all three on the game. As the newspapers have made bloody sure people would think that's the connection. But the connection between the three victims could have nothing at all to do with the sex angle, the escort service. It's the women themselves. Here, at least, are two who know each other. It was reasonable to assume that the women working for these agencies were going with some psychopath who hated girls on the game. That's what people think.

"We dug around in the past of the three victims and found nothing. Maybe that's because we didn't know what to look for. Now, I want you to look in on Myra Brewer. She knew Kate Banks all her life. I bet she has photos, albums of them, maybe stuff from her school days. I want to know if Kate knew either of the others."

Jury was up and wrestling his arms into his coat. "Me, I'm off to have lunch with Harry Johnson."

"You don't mind my saying so, you seem a little obsessed with Harry Johnson, guv." The blessed kettle whistled. Wiggins immediately popped a Typhoo bag in his mug and poured water over it.

Self-satisfaction steeped along with the tea.

Coat on, Jury went to Wiggins's desk and leaned on it. "Harry Johnson was in Chesham the night Mariah Cox was murdered; he was at home, he says—his only witness being Mungo—the night Kate Banks was shot; he was supposed to be in the Old Wine Shades, which is but a few minutes from St. Paul's, around eight or nine the night Deirdre Small was murdered at nine o'clock. He showed up at the Shades nearer to ten. I was there."

"But, sir—what's his motive?"

Jury turned at the door with a wicked smile. "Because he could."

The spot of lunch, more a spot of Château Latour, was overseen by Mungo, who unwedged himself from between the legs of Harry's bar stool to stand at attention when Jury walked in.

"Mungo, how's it going?" Jury scratched him between the ears.

Mungo sat with his tail threshing the floor.

"And how's your case going?" asked Harry. Not waiting for an answer, since he knew he wouldn't get one, Harry went on. "Remember the Poe story? 'The Black Cat'? Do you believe in evil spirits?"

"Only you, Harry." Jury nodded to Trevor, who then set a glass before him and poured the Burgundy.

"I'll just get your lunches."

"Ploughman's okay?" asked Harry. "That's what I ordered."

"Excellent."

Harry nodded to Trevor, who went off for the food.

"As I was saying, the cat may have more to do with the whole thing than you credit it with."

Jury raised his glass and looked at the shifting grape red colors against the light. "Really?" He smiled.

"The cat disappears the night after what's-her-name . . . ?" Harry snapped thumb and finger together, frowned as if making a real effort.

"Stacy Storm."

"What a ridiculous name. Anyway, after that night . . ."

Jury knocked back nearly half of the wine. "That night you were in Chesham. The Rexroth party. Ms. Storm was also meaning to attend but was, you could say, detained."

Trevor returned with two white oval plates of cheese (cheddar, Stilton, Derbyshire), bread, Branston pickle, and pickled onion and set the plates before them.

Harry's eyebrows rose. "Is that a fact?"

"But her gentleman friend attended, the one she was supposed to meet."

"And you pulled him in and roughed him up and now you can leave me alone."

Jury shrugged. "For all we know, her friend might've been you."

"Don't be ridiculous." Harry was arranging a pickled onion on top of cheese on top of the thick bread.

Trevor had come with fresh glasses and a fresh bottle of another Bordeaux Jury had never heard of, but then he'd never heard of most of them.

Harry nodded at the label, and Trevor uncorked the bottle and poured.

They had four glasses now on the counter. Fine with Jury, who was having a swell time. They ate and drank in a silence that might almost have been called companionable, when Harry said, "Let's go back to 'The Black Cat.'"

"The pub?"

"The story. What's fascinating is the pure randomness of the crime."

"By random, you mean lacking motive? Any crime that looks as if the perpetrator simply picked off the subject arbitrarily could be said to be motiveless, right?"

"I suppose that's so. But there's a sense of power in doing something just because you can." He smiled and drank off the rest of his wine, then crumpled his napkin on his plate. "Ah, that was good. But now I really have to run. Sorry."

Then Jury said, "Police want to talk to you, Harry."

"You are."

Jury hoped he could ruffle him, but apparently not.

"Will you be in later this afternoon? There's a City policeman, Detective Inspector Jenkins, who might want to drop by. With me."

"Fine with me," said Harry.

"Oh," said Jury, as if he'd only now thought of it. "I was in Chesham yesterday. At the Black Cat."

Harry looked at him. "Oh, really?"

"There was a black cat there."

Having finished his lunch, Harry was pulling keys out of his pocket. How did he make it appear like a rabbit out of a hat? He was off his stool and working his arms into the black cashmere coat that Jury coveted. He smiled. "It's called the Black Cat. Would the presence of one be surprising?"

"No. But this was a second black cat. Actually a third, but we won't go into that. No, this was a different one than was there before. Rather, they're both there."

"My God! The cat came back! That sounds familiar." Twirling the keys on his finger, Harry smiled. He took a step nearer Jury. "You didn't fuck it up again, did you?" Laughing, he was across the room and, laughing, out through the door.

Jury smiled at the remains of his lunch. No, you murdering sociopath, I didn't fuck it up again.

In the Snow Hill station of the City police, some five minutes from St. Paul's and some ten from the Old Wine Shades, DI Jenkins was considering what Jury had said and biting the corner of his mouth. "God knows I'm catching enough flak on this that any suspect, including the prime minister, would help."

"What about Nicholas Maze?"

"I'm getting bugger-all from him. I mean, according to the journalists we've got a serial killer loose. You can imagine." Jenkins folded his arms across his chest. "Is this enough to bring this guy in? Sounds a little"—he rocked his hand back and forth—"squishy. You think it's enough he was in Chesham at the time of the Cox woman's murder?"

"That's not all. He was at the Rexroth party; she was supposedly on her way there. I don't think Harry Johnson goes to many parties."

Jenkins brought the chair in which he'd been leaning back down to the floor. "But if he intends to murder Mariah-Stacy, why in bloody hell would he show himself, especially at something as public as a party?"

Jury shook his head. "I don't know."

Jenkins scratched his ear. "The other two victims. He didn't have an alibi either time. But just because he hadn't an alibi . . . ?" Jenkins shrugged.

Jury scraped his chair closer to Jenkins's desk and leaned on the desk, arms folded. "Look: if Harry Johnson weren't Harry Johnson, I'd agree, it's too flimsy. But Harry Johnson murdered one of his lady friends in a place in Surrey. I couldn't prove it. He also kidnapped two kids out there and put them in the basement of his Belgravia house—"

Jury paused. He didn't want to tell Jenkins a dog had actually saved the kids. Here it was again: the absolute ludicrousness of the story. But he plowed on nonetheless. "He told me this involved story about his best friend's wife, son, and dog—'The dog came back.'" He heard Harry saying it right now in his head.

"The dog?" said Jenkins.

"The dog."

The cat came back. Harry, you swine. Jury knew what had happened. He wasn't going to tell Jenkins. That was the whole point: he wanted Jenkins to hear it from Harry himself. Now it was the cat; the cat was the alibi. Jury smiled.

"What's funny?" Jenkins smiled, too.

Jury wiped the smile off his face. "Nothing. Look, it's surely enough to bring him in for questioning, even if not enough to hold him."

Jenkins nodded. "I expect so." He rose. "But what was so funny?"

"Relentless bastard, aren't you?"

"Yes."

48

DS Alfred Wiggins gave the impression of a man who would always tip his hat to a lady, had he been wearing a hat; indeed, he seemed to feel the lack of a hat because he couldn't raise it.

"Why, Mr. Wiggins, how very nice!" said Myra Brewer. "How very nice of you to look in."

"My pleasure, Mrs. B." He walked in the door, which she had opened wider.

"Now, what can I get you? I just made tea and was about to pour myself a cup."

"Tea would be welcome." He was shaking free of his coat. "A bit nippy out there, all of a sudden."

She had his coat folded over her arm and was smoothing it. "And it's been so warm. But that's weather for you. Well, you can't count on weather, but you can on tea." After putting the weather in its place and hanging his coat in the hall cupboard, she made for the kitchen. "You just make yourself comfortable; I'll get down another cup and be back in a tick."

If there was one thing Wiggins knew how to do, it was to make himself comfortable. He sat in the same armchair he'd occupied before. He sighed, shut his eyes briefly, enjoying the quiet of the parlor set off by the homey clatter coming from the kitchen. Yes, this was definitely his milieu, and he was happy to be in it.

He scooted down in the chair and crossed an ankle over a knee and looked around, not with his detective's eye, but with the eye of a homebody. A little clock ticked on the mantel; a group of fairings sat on the inset bookshelves to the right of the electric fireplace. Above it hung a bucolic scene of cows in a field and sheep lounging beneath a big oak tree. The picture listed slightly. It probably needed two hooks, not just one. Put a hammer in his hand and he could fix it.

A rattle of crockery announced Myra Brewer's return. He rose smartly to take the tray from her hands and to place it on the table between the easy chairs.

"Thank you. And I brought some of those Choc-o-lots you like."

"Is that a seed cake there?"

"Fresh baked."

That must have been what was scenting the air when he walked in.

There was more conversation that might have been considered desultory by anyone who couldn't appreciate a cup of Taylor's Fancy Ceylon or a cake as fine as lawn.

The reason why he had come, he said, "not to bring up the painful subject of your goddaughter, but—you remember Superintendent Jury?" But why should she, as Wiggins, sitting here, had nearly forgotten him? "He was interested in anything you might have that would help with her background. What I mean is . . ." Wiggins helped himself to a slice of seed cake and considered how to raise the subject of Kate Banks's night work. "I expect you know, I mean, from reading the papers, as it's been all over them, what sort of other work Kate was doing. . . ."

But Myra Brewer was made of sturdier stuff than Wiggins supposed. Crisply, she nodded and said, "Yes. She was working for one of those escort places. Well, who am I to judge her? No, not Kate. It doesn't take away from Kate one bit that she was doing that."

Wiggins admired her attitude. "The point is, we've discovered that one woman at one of these agencies knew the third victim. Superintendent Jury thinks there might be other links amongst these women. This is the best seed cake I've ever eaten."

She smiled. Her cup and saucer rested on her lap. She stopped smiling and studied it. "You mean, did Kate know the others?" Myra shook her head. "She might have done, but I don't think so. There's no way of telling now." Her eyes returned to her cup.

"No, of course not. But we thought you might have some old pictures, photographs, snapshots of Kate with friends."

"Well, now, I do have an album or two."

"Is it possible she went to school with either Mariah Cox—she who called herself Stacy Storm as a professional name—or Deirdre Small? They were all pretty close to each other in years."

"Kate attended several schools. I remember Roedean was one. If you'll just wait a moment . . ."

"*Roedean?*" Wiggins was surprised. "But that's one of our best schools."

Myra had risen and now looked down at him, still sitting with his slice of cake. "You think a girl working at what she did, being an escort, do you think she couldn't have the brains for a school like Roedean?"

"No, I wouldn't have thought so." It was always a source of delight to Jury that Wiggins was completely literal.

Myra shook her head at such intransigence. "I don't care what's said, Kate Muldar was a smart girl, a first-rate student. I told you she liked that big bookshop in Piccadilly, Waterstone's. She loved to go in there and get books and sit in their café and read. That was what she loved—not pubs, not going dancing or anything like that—just stopping in that bookshop." Myra sighed. "I'll get the photograph album."

49

The mobile was charged, but Jury had just shut it off, not wanting any disturbance while talking to Harry Johnson.

At the same time Wiggins was enjoying Myra Brewer's seed cake, Jury was enjoying the view of Belgravia from the top of Harry's steps, flanked by the two stone lions.

The door was opened by little Mrs. Tobias, Mungo by her side (or under her feet). Of course she remembered Superintendent Jury, then took a moment to study Detective Inspector Jenkins's warrant card.

"I think he's expecting us," said Jury.

"Oh, yes, sir. Come in, please."

She showed them into the living room, or, rather, Mungo did. He was in the lead.

Harry rose from a settee on the other side of a silver coffee service and welcomed them heartily.

Jury marveled that the scene in which he now found himself was an exact replica of the one in which he and DI Tom Dryer had turned up a month or so before to slap the cuffs on Harry. Metaphorically speaking, because the cuffs were never slapped on. It was uncanny, really, the similarity: the settee, the coffee, the *Times*, that silver cigarette box. In a moment, he would offer them coffee. And cigarettes.

"Coffee, gentlemen?"

They declined. Harry took a cigarette from the box and offered the box to DI Jenkins. He knew better than to offer it to Jury. "Please sit down." He waved them into a couple of dark leather chairs. Jenkins took one; Jury didn't. Jury remained in the doorway, leaning against the doorjamb.

Jenkins spoke: "Mr. Johnson, I'm investigating the case of a young woman who was murdered two nights ago in St. Paul's churchyard."

"Ah, yes. I read about it." Harry rattled the paper to indicate where.

"Superintendent Jury here is under the impression you knew her. Deirdre Small, her name was."

Harry smiled one of his blinding smiles. "Superintendent Jury is under the impression I've known everyone murdered in London."

"And have you?" asked Jenkins in a wonderfully affable way before he sat back and crossed his legs.

Jury would recommend him for a citation.

Harry laughed. "No, not all."

"Including Miss Small? You didn't know Deirdre Small?"

Harry shook his head. "No. Sorry."

Mungo, who had left the room, now returned with Morris (sans blue collar, of course, which was in Chesham). Both were sitting at Jury's feet, both staring upward, hard, in a breath-holding manner.

Jenkins said, "You didn't know her, then?"

"Of course not. I've just said that."

"And the other two murdered women—Stacy Storm and Kate Banks?"

"No, I didn't know them, either. Look, am I a suspect in this triple murder?"

But he said it with a smile, and not a nervous one, either. It was the smile of one who's played an enormous joke on his pals.

Which was, at least, how Jury took it. And just how it was, he was pretty sure.

"Because if I am—I'm remarkably short on alibis."

"Why do you say that, sir?"

"At the time of these murders, I was alone. No witnesses. I live alone, you see. I'm assuming the news"—he picked up the *Times* beside him—"was accurate in its reporting of the time of death? I was here by myself. That is, except in the case of the Small woman. That night, I was in Chesham."

"In Chesham?" said Jenkins.

"That's right."

There was a pause. Then Jenkins said, "If you stopped anyplace in or around Chesham, someone probably saw you and would remember."

"I don't think so." He smiled. Harry was eating it up, his exposure to guilt, enjoying being a suspect as most people would enjoy not being one.

"Why did you go to Chesham, Mr. Johnson?"

"Because of the cat."

Jenkins turned halfway round to regard the cat sitting like a statue at Jury's feet.

"No," said Harry. "Not that one. That's my cat. I'm talking about another black cat." His glance shifted to Jury. "You can ask Superintendent Jury." Harry's smile was all over the place. "I'm sure he's worked it out that I went to Chesham because of the cat."

Jenkins turned to Jury, eyebrows raised, looking for some sort of corroboration.

"What cat?" said Jury.

50

It was the first time Jury had ever seen Harry Johnson flummoxed.

Harry said to Jenkins, "It was a joke, Inspector. And Superintendent Jury's in on it."

Jury had mastered many looks in his time, but the one of puzzlement he now pasted on his face he knew might be the best. "Joke? I've been a little busy with three murders; there's hardly been time for jokes." God, how he'd love a cigarette. To light up while he went on holding up this door frame, that would be the image of unbeaten, unbeatable cop. If Trevor had appeared at his elbow with a bottle of Montrachet, Jury'd have drained it dry.

Mungo and Morris looked almost as if they were joining in this celebration, their paws dancing. At least, that's how Jury preferred to see them.

"Very funny indeed, Superintendent," said Harry. To Jenkins, he said, "It's a long story, Inspector."

"I'm good with long stories, Mr. Johnson. If you'd accompany us to the station, I'd appreciate being told it."

Harry got to his feet, uttering imprecations under his breath. "Am I under arrest?"

"No, sir, not at all. You'd just be helping us with our inquiries."

Harry sighed. "You know this is ridiculous. All because of the damned cat."

Outside, Jury remembered to switch on his mobile and saw he had a half-dozen missed messages. They were all from Wiggins. He told Jenkins he had to make a call.

"I've a photo here to show you, boss. It's important."

Wiggins didn't tell him why, refusing to give up that information in the interest of suspense, apparently. No, Jury had got to look at it because Wiggins wasn't sure.

"As soon as I get through with Harry Johnson, Wiggins." He looked around for Plant's car. There was one sitting across the street, an old model Bentley. A hand ventured out of the driver's side window, and two fingers formed a V. Jury rolled his eyes. Was he supposed to do that back? At least he didn't have to cross the street and give a secret handshake.

Jury got in the car beside Jenkins.

Melrose waited until the car with the three men pulled away from the curb before reaching into the backseat for the cat carrier and the True Friends cap.

He tilted the rearview mirror to check how he looked. He looked idiotic. The cap looked like a little boat sailing on the pale waves of— Oh, for God's sake! It was ridiculous enough without waxing poetic about it!

Melrose pushed back the visor. Yes, he had to wear it. There were many things he didn't look like, and an animal rescuer was right up there at the head of the list, right after Niels Bohr. That impersonation had also been done so that Jury could get into Harry's house. Were they to spend their lives trying to get into Harry's house? Harry had gotten a big kick out of the Niels Bohr act.

His silk wool suit was a bit upmarket for the pittance of a salary he must've been getting from an animal shelter. He exchanged the suit jacket for an ancient canvas one that looked starched enough to stand up to several attack dogs. With that on, and the hat, he got out of the car, pulling the carrier after him.

Had Jury said that Wiggins just got himself a hamster? That sounded unlikely.

Melrose walked up the stone steps. It was a handsome brick edifice with white steps that looked just scrubbed, and stone lions that managed to complement the house without being pretentious.

He rang the bell, waited, hoped no one was there—wrong, here was someone opening the door: a very small woman, looking puzzled, who he assumed was the housekeeper.

"Mrs. Tobias? My name is Melrose Pierce." He must have been thinking of Mildred. "I've come for Mr. Johnson's cat?"

Mrs. Tobias went from puzzled to suspicious. "F'r his cat? What? Come for Schrödinger? What on earth for? Don't tell me—" She flapped her hand at him. "Take her and good riddance. There she sits. I've got my pies in the oven."

Melrose stared after her. That was it? That was all? Pies in the oven? And he'd been prepared to be extremely clever. Well, he hadn't needed his hat after all. He could have forced his way in with a mask and a gun and she'd still have said, "Take the silver; I've got my pies in the oven."

There she sat: Morris, looking black and blameless.

And beside her a dog that surely must be the incomparable Mungo. "It's an honor," said Melrose, bowing.

Do I know you? thought Mungo. This one did look a little familiar. He was wearing a funny hat with a bill, like a duckbill. And why was he putting Morris in that carrier? Why didn't Mrs. Tobias object? But then Mrs. Tobias thought the cat was Schrödinger. Now he was closing the flaps and all Mungo could see was Morris's eye. And now this Daffy Duck was carrying Morris to the door.

Bad. Bad. Bad. *Bad*. The Duckbill opened the door and went out, with Mungo right behind him before the door closed. Mungo was right on the Duck's heels. Down the steps, stealthily. How stealthy could you be in bright sunlight on marble steps? But the Duck didn't notice.

The driver's side of the car was against the curb. The Duck opened the door, started to slide in the box, changed his mind, opened the rear door, and leaned in with the box—

Mungo was in the front seat in a split second.

—back out the rear door, into the front door.

Mungo was over the front seat into the back just as the Duck slid himself into the driver's seat, shut the door, and started the car.

Were they all completely blind, these people? A whole animal sanctuary, a whole Noah's Ark of animals, could have followed the Duck down those steps and he'd never have seen them. Are humans all so self-entranced they just don't see what's going on around them?

Although this diatribe was not aimed at Morris, Morris answered: Yes.

Mungo was up now on the backseat beside the box, looking at Morris's eye. Even though he couldn't see the rest of her through the holes, he knew Morris was sitting with her paws clapped to her chest.

Am I being kidnapped again? Wasn't once enough? asked Morris.

You'd think so.

But maybe we're going home.

Home. Mungo mused. If Hansel and Gretel had been forced to depend on humans to get them home, they'd have had to drop ordnance maps all over the woods.

Mungo raised up and looked out the window. He thought he saw Westminster. They were still in London.

He lay down. Morris's eye wasn't there anymore at the hole. Morris was asleep.

Mungo sighed. All of these people, all over the place. Why's it always down to me?

51

Languidly, Harry smoked. No, he didn't want his solicitor. He hadn't done anything except borrow a cat for a few days.

"To be precise," said Jenkins, sitting across the table from him, "the word is 'kidnapped.' Or 'stolen.' That's pretty much the way we look at it, and it's illegal, sir. That dog of yours, Ringo? How would you like it—"

Ringo. Jury laughed silently.

"Mun-go," said Harry. "How would I like it if somebody kidnapped Mungo? Nobody could. Mungo's too smart. I wouldn't have a dog around who wasn't."

Jury raised his eyes heavenward. He was leaning against the wall, letting Jenkins take care of Harry.

"If we could go back to the Monday night, Mr. Johnson. You were in Chesham? But you've no one to substantiate that story?"

"That's right. And this is repetitious. That certainly isn't enough to charge me. You have no evidence that I even knew this woman, Debra whatever—"

"Deirdre Small."

"—so you'd hardly have any evidence to show I killed her."

"Let's go back to the first victim, Mariah Cox, or Stacy Storm, as she called herself. She was also on her way to that party at the Rexroths'. The one you attended."

Harry raised his eyebrows. "And?"

"A coincidence, is that?"

"Well, it must be, since I never met this Storm woman. Never even saw her."

Jury shoved himself away from the wall and moved over to the table. He sat down on one corner. "You know what bothers me about this, Harry?"

Harry checked the lit end of his cigar, blew on it softly. "What?"

"You don't go to parties."

Harry looked completely surprised.

Jury smiled.

"Are you trying to say that I wasn't there?"

"Oh, you were there all right. What I'm wondering is why you were there. Do you know a man named Simon Santos?"

"Never heard of him."

"He was Stacy's date for that evening."

Harry looked from Jury to Jenkins and back again. "Then why in hell have you dragged me in for questioning? It would seem he's the one you want."

"Unless, of course, you thought Stacy was your personal property and you didn't much like her meeting Mr. Santos."

"Oh, bloody hell," said Harry. "You know me better than that."

"I do?" said Jury, looking genuinely puzzled.

Jenkins said, "You didn't know either one of these women?"

"Of course not."

"You went to Chesham to return a cat—the one you'd taken. Why would you do that? Why not just keep it or get rid of it some way? Take it to a shelter."

Jury thought Jenkins didn't realize he was using reason to try to explain completely unreasonable behavior.

"Because I wanted the cat to reappear, to come back. I've told you, it was a joke. A joke on Superintendent Jury."

"Yet Superintendent Jury doesn't get it."

"Oh, he gets it all right. He seems to be returning the favor." Harry turned partway in his chair, not far enough that he could actually see Jury, just enough to let Jury know he was aware he was there.

Jury smiled, saying nothing.

"All right," said Jenkins in a tone that suggested it was not "all right," that it was indeed idiotic. "Perhaps someone did see you. A man with a cat carrier might be noticed."

"No one saw me, Inspector. I took pains that no one would."

Mention of the carrier reminded Jury to check his watch. It was by now nearly five, almost an hour since they'd left Harry's house. Plant would be well away by now. Halfway to Chesham.

"Let's talk about the second victim. Kate Banks. On the night she was murdered, you were at home?"

"Yes, again."

"You were alone."

Harry nodded. "Yes, as I said."

"Are you familiar with the King's Road Companions escort service? Or Smart Set or Valentine's?"

Harry's expression was contemptuous. "Inspector, I've never used an escort service in my life. Highly paid and well-organized prostitution."

"Perhaps not all of them. King's Road Companions claims to work just that way. Companionship, either alone or at social functions. No sex."

"You believe that, do you?"

"I'm inclined to after talking with several of the women who work for it. It's different from the escort services."

Jury wondered if the difference was significant. Poor Kate. Her death moved him in a way the others' hadn't. Perhaps because she seemed such a good person.

Fifteen minutes later, he left Snow Hill after Jenkins said to him, "You know we can't hold him much longer."

"Try." Jury thanked him and left.

Jury didn't take off his coat so much as cast it off, aiming it in the general direction of the office coatrack. "Is it getting cold or am I getting old? You don't really have to think about it, Wiggins. So where's this photo?"

Holding the picture, Wiggins slapped it down on Jury's desk. "It's from Myra Brewer's album. Taken on Brighton pier. Prepare to be surprised, boss. The girls are friends of Kate Banks."

Jury glanced at the line of girls. "I don't see Deirdre Small or Mariah Cox here."

"I didn't say they were. Look again."

Jury did so. His glance stopped on the face of the unsmiling girl—aggressively unsmiling, if there were such an expression. As if she hated the person holding the camera.

"Bloody hell. Christine Cummins."

"Her name's not Christine, sir. It's Crystal, Crystal North back then. Which is probably why we missed any connection to Mrs. Cummins when we were checking these women's backgrounds. Not that we'd've come up with every single friend or acquaintance. . . . But what do you think, guv?"

Jury sat staring at the photo. "I don't. I don't have one bloody idea, Wiggins."

"Maybe this time it is coincidence. I know you hate that word, only . . ."

Jury leaned back. "The trouble with coincidence in this case is that Chris Cummins didn't say anything about knowing Kate Banks. Not a word."

"Maybe she just saw the write-up in the papers or heard the news and didn't put the murdered Kate together with her old Roedean chum Kate. Of course, we don't know she went there. And these girls in the photo didn't necessarily go there. Although Myra Brewer seemed to think they were all school chums."

"'A pricey public school on the coast,' that's what David Cummins said. That could certainly have meant Roedean. It's near Brighton."

"There're a lot of pricey schools. That could just be coincidence, too."

Jury shook his head. "Could be, but . . ." He checked his watch, got up. "I've got to get back to my place and change my clothes. I've got a date with our girl from Valentine's. Stacy Storm's flatmate."

"You mean Adele Astaire?"

"Right. Aka Rose Moss." He retrieved his coat, which had fallen to the floor. "Come on, it's nearly six. Good job, Wiggins."

Walking down the corridor, Wiggins said, "What about Harry Johnson?"

"Jenkins took him in for questioning. 'Helping us with our inquiries.'" Jury snickered.

"Do you honestly think he killed these women?"

"No." Jury smiled.

52

After a scanty half an hour's presence in the Black Cat, Mungo had already divested a tubby man sitting at the bar of half a banger; been offered a hard-boiled egg, which he'd turned down, not knowing what to do with it; got a large portion of beans on toast (eaten the beans and left the toast) belonging to a couple who'd been having a quiet meal at a table by the fireplace.

Sally Hawkins, who was having no success at all in shooing Mungo away from the tables, complained bitterly to Melrose. "Who's that dog that's been all over the room begging food off my customers?"

Melrose put down his book and looked puzzled. "What dog?"

"That dog!" The finger she pointed had a cutting edge. "That mutt that's begging his dinner." It was a table where a lone man sat. Melrose stood up, hoping the "mutt" attribution hadn't reached Mungo's ears. Mungo had now drifted from the beans-on-toast couple to a man by himself with a paper and a ploughman's. The man was handing Mungo down a bit of cheese.

Melrose adjusted his glasses, as if the fractional realignment of glasses with eyes would reacquaint him with the dog. "I have no idea."

She stood with hands on hips. "Well, he came in with you!"

Melrose leaned back from her. "With me? I believe you're

mistaken. I brought Dora's cat back." His injured tone suggested that this act of mercy and heroism was being unkindly repaid. "Dora is certainly happy."

"Well, the dog was with Morris, is what I'm saying."

Melrose laughed. "With Morris? I don't think so. Morris—" Here he ran his hand over Morris, who was in her favorite spot by a window, where light was fast deepening into dusk. "Morris strikes me as a cat who would hardly strike up a friendship with a gypsy dog." He picked up his book. It was called *A Dog's Life*. Not the best choice for a man who had no interest in dogs.

"You're telling me the dog's a stray?"

Melrose shut his eyes as if his patience were wearing thin. "I'm not telling you anything, other than I don't feel I should be held responsible for knowing the dog's provenance. He appears to be well-mannered—that is, he's not fighting your customers for food— so I'd assume he belongs to someone in Chesham here."

"He's been round all the tables."

"Just as long as he's not eating with a runcible spoon."

"A what?"

Melrose was saved from reciting "The Owl and the Pussycat" by the return of Dora, who veritably bounced into the chair beside Morris (never mind Melrose).

Mungo chose this moment to turn up, too, at their table. Great.

He hauled himself up beside Morris, lay down, and tried to fold in his paws.

Sally Hawkins nodded toward the two. "There's something awful matey about those two. The dog acts like it knows Morris. Like they're mates."

Just as she said that, Schrödinger (if it was Schrödinger) raced by with the other black cat (unless that was Schrödinger instead) on her heels. They pulled up under the table of the elderly lady with the racing form. The two cats nearly brought her down as all of their ten legs got caught up together.

"Bloody beasts," the elderly lady muttered, and went for them with the racing form. "You know, Mrs. Hawkins, you've got three cats in here. You might think more about that problem than about the one dog."

Melrose checked his watch. Why in hell didn't Jury call? What was he supposed to do now?

53

On his way to Islington, Jury got out his mobile, found Plant's number, and punched it in.

"Where are you? . . . You're still in Chesham? Why haven't you started back with Schröd . . . What do you mean you can't tell the difference? . . . Well, look at their eyes, what color are they? . . . Yellowish . . . what does that mean? . . . Oh, for God's sake . . . we can't keep Harry at the station for bloody ever. . . ."

On Melrose's end, he asked, "How was I to know there'd be three black cats to deal with? They all look alike. . . . Dora? Well, of course I asked Dora. She knows Morris; Morris is all she's sure of. She could tell Morris on a moonless night in an alley of black cats. But she can't tell Schrödinger, she's never seen him before, and the other one Sally Hawkins dragged in—"

"Listen," said Jury, "just stuff one or the other into that carrier, shove it in the car, and get back to Belgravia. You've a fifty percent chance of being right, which is what you usually have, and Harry himself might not even know the difference. At least it'll do for a bit."

"All right all right all right. What do you mean, 'what I usually have'?"

Melrose found himself talking to a dead phone. He shook it, as if Jury might fall out.

He tossed his mobile on the table and turned to Dora, who'd been listening to the call with great interest. Adults saying dumb things. "What'd he say? What're you going to do?"

"What are *we* going to do, you mean. You are going to help me get those cats into the carrier and the car."

They both checked to see that Morris was still here and not over there. Yes.

Schrödinger (whichever one she was) and Morris Two were behind the bar. They were at opposite ends of a piece of something—rope, meat, fishbone, who knew?—pulling it in opposite directions.

"You go for one cat; I go for the other. That's the only way I can think to do it."

Dora said, "I don't want to get scratched."

Melrose ignored that and pulled out the carrier from under the table in the window. "I'm going to put it right on this side of the bar so they don't see it." They moved to the bar, and he opened the top of the box. "We'll go about this slowly."

Dora looked dubious.

Stealthily, they approached.

Melrose grabbed one cat, which rewarded him by slicing the air at his ear with its claws.

"I've got her, I've got her!" yelled Dora, wrestling the other one to the ground.

"Okay, we'll take both." He pulled over the carrier and together he and Dora shoved in the cat she was holding; Melrose then shoved in the other one with great effort and a good deal of yowling. He shut it, then grabbed it up and headed, once again, for his car and London.

54

The phone rang as Jury was tying his tie. He picked it up and eyed the tie, wondering if it was sending the right message. It had bunnies on it; they were minute ones, but you could tell they were bunnies if you looked closely. Where in hell had he got it?

"Jury."

It was DI Jenkins, calling from the Snow Hill station. "I really have nothing I can hold him on."

"Then just cut him loose. He didn't do it."

During the brief silence on the other end of the line, Jury wondered where he had got this tie. And was that a speck of egg or just another bunny?

"You know he didn't?" said Jenkins.

"No, but I'm pretty certain." He was more than "pretty" certain.

"Well. The reason nobody saw him in Chesham was because he went to pains that nobody would see him. He didn't want to be associated, he said, with the bloody swine of a cat—"

"'Swine of a cat': I like it. Go on." The phone's flex was long enough to get him to the bottle of Macallan on the little table beneath the window, which was what mattered, he had pointed out to Carole-anne. He poured out a measure.

"He's still saying it was a joke. On you. And you knew it."

Jury knew all right, but it annoyed him that Jenkins seemed on the verge of believing Harry Johnson, pathological liar. No, wait, this story actually wasn't a lie. "I don't know what he's talking about." Jury observed that his glass was too tall for a whiskey glass, and he told himself to get some proper ones.

"It's to do with a dog," Jenkins labored on. "The one at the house that took a fancy to you."

"Mungo."

"He says he told you a very convoluted story about his friend disappearing with that dog and, well, frankly, the man sounded a little mad."

"He is. He's a nutter. He told me the story and later denied ever telling it. It was a series of stories, actually. Don't let him con you, Dennis. He's a great con artist."

"But I'm not going to get any more out of him."

"Thanks for doing this. Sorry you had to waste your time on him."

As Jury said this, Carole-anne walked into his living room so he could waste his time on her.

"Think nothing of it," Jenkins said. "I rather enjoyed listening to him. He reminds me of Bruno. You know, the calculating, manipulating bastard in *Strangers on a Train*."

Jury said, "You know, you're right. I never thought of that. Good night, Dennis." He put down the phone and said to Carole-anne, "Make yourself at home."

Carole-anne had sat herself on the sofa and started flicking through the magazine she'd found there. One of hers, not Jury's. He didn't read *BeautyPLUS*. "Why're you wearing your best suit?" Her tone was thick with suspicion.

"Because I'm going out."

Apparently puzzled, she said, "Out?" as if there were no such place, at least not for him.

Was he really supposed to expand upon out-ness?

"With somebody?" she said.

"Yes. You don't know her."

She shut her eyes against the news. Not just a woman, but a new one, as if he kept a stable of women to which he was always adding.

"Who is she?"

"You don't know her." He said it again.

Carole-anne slapped over another page of *BeautyPLUS*.

If there was one thing Carole-anne didn't need, it was PLUS. The building would be in meltdown.

Jury leaned over to tie his shoe, getting eye level with Carole-anne's silver-and-gold sandal, straps intertwined. Strappy. "What kind of shoes are those?"

She shut the magazine and looked at her feet as if she needed reminding. "Manolo Blahnik."

"Another pair? You have that kind of money?"

"That consignment shop on Upper Street."

He wondered what reversal of fortune could make a woman sell off her Manolo Blahniks. "Tell me: why would a woman spend hundreds on Manolo Blahnik when she could get a perfectly good sandal like that at the Army-Navy?"

"Are you daft?" She actually put by the magazine to assess his daftness.

Jury waited for shoe guidance and got none. "Well? Why? It's a reasonable question."

Apparently not. She retrieved *BeautyPLUS* and continued sorting through it for nuggets.

"You think the answer is that obvious."

"Of course." She stretched out one leg and let the silver sandal dangle from her toes.

Definitely designer legs, he thought.

She said, "Did you ever see a shoe like this at the Army-Navy?"

"No, but then I've never looked for one."

"Believe me." Thinking this an adequate response, she drew back her foot.

"All right, then listen to this, Miss Shoe-savvy: I've got three women murdered and the only connection between them is they were all escorts and all wearing designer shoes."

"You mean those 'Escort Murders' they keep talking about?" When he nodded she said, "Well? Tell me about it."

"No. It's an ongoing investigation."

Aggrieved, Carole-anne said, "What about the shoes? What designer?"

"Jimmy Choo."

"Sweet!"

"Not so much for the victim; she's dead."

"Well, Jimmy Choo didn't do it. Were they all his shoes?"

"No. There was the French designer . . . Christian Lou-something."

Carole-anne consulted her shoe memory bank and her eyes widened. "Christian Louboutin? Red soles?"

"That's the lad, yes."

"Those shoes cost a fortune. How does your average working girl afford them?"

"Sales or shoplifting. Anyway, would these escorts be considered 'average working girls'? They've probably got rich clients. You're beautifully silvered up tonight. Where are you going?"

"Clubbing." She lay on the couch, ankles crossed. She must be the only woman in London who would get herself up, looking perfect, and then toss herself down any old way.

"Anyone I know?" said Jury.

"No. We don't know each other's anyones." Head on the sofa arm, she held the magazine up to the light of the lamp. Her red gold hair burned in the light.

"Does yours have a name?"

"Monty."

"And what does Monty do?"

"Sells pricey cars. You're awful nosy tonight. I never asked you a lot of questions."

"No, but my date isn't pleasure. It's work. It's part of the investigation."

Carole-anne brightened considerably, which was hard to do considering her hair was already on fire and her silver dress and strappy shoes were soon to follow.

"Get out from under that light before you blow us all to hell and gone."

"Huh?" She swung herself around, but not at his insistence, plunked her Manolo Blahniks on the floor, and leaned toward him, her elbows on her knees.

It was a view not without merit. It was a good thing she was young enough to be his daughter! *Excuse me, mate, but why's that a good thing?*

"Are you going undercover, then?"

"No, I'm going above cover."

Her brow tightened in a kind of frown. "You mean this person knows who you are?"

"She does indeed. She just doesn't know why I asked her out. She thinks I fancy her."

"Well, you don't."

It wasn't a question. "She's a bit young for me."

"So's the queen. What's she look like?"

"Like a schoolgirl. Apparently, her clients go for that kind of look."

"Pervs." The buzzer rang downstairs. "That'll be Monty. You can tell me the rest later." She rose and pulled up the back strap of her silver shoe, then wriggled a little in her dress, which she pulled down.

"Be careful," he said.

"Careful?"

"Well, I've got these women on my mind, I guess. Some man did for them."

She brushed back her hair. "Well, it wasn't Monty. Anyway, what makes you so sure it was a man? I know girls that'd kill for a pair of Christian Louboutins. 'Night."

And she was out of his flat and clicking those four-inch heels down the steps while he was still pondering that last statement.

55

By the time Melrose got to Belgravia, day was night, or nearly. He sat—they sat, Melrose and the two cats—in his car, watching Harry Johnson's house on the other side of the square. He had let one out of the carrier so they wouldn't kill each other. What he wanted to do was simply take the one in the carrier around in back and shove her through a doggie door, if there was one.

Well, he could do the animal shelter bit again, but not if Harry Johnson was in the house.

Melrose pulled out his mobile and, fingering the scrap of paper from his wallet on which he'd scribbled it, punched in the number.

When the housekeeper answered—it must be she, for it sounded like the woman who'd opened the door before—he asked for Mr. Johnson. Oh, too bad, he wasn't at home.

"No," said Melrose, "no message. I'll just ring him again. Thank you." He flipped the mobile shut and turned around to have a look at Schrödinger, if it was. The second cat, looking equally annoyed, had stuffed herself under the seat. Mean eyes peered out.

The first cat, on whom he was betting his 50 percent chance of success, was not at all happy to see him. Every time he looked at her, she hissed. She despised him, which irritated Melrose to death, considering he was making this effort on her behalf.

He got out and opened the rear door and reached across the

backseat for the carrier. This was done to the tune of numerous hisses. He put on his True Friends cap and dragged out the carrier. The cat hissed mightily.

"Put a sock in it," he said, and slammed the door.

"Mrs. . . . Toby, isn't it?" Melrose raised his cap.

"Tobias, sir." She looked down at the carrier. "Well, I'm happy to see Schrödinger's not come to grief."

No she wasn't. She was frowning all over her face. Melrose said, "I feel rather awful about this mix-up."

"Mix-up? I don't understand." Her arms crossed over her bosom, she was scratching at her elbows.

"I got the wrong address, the wrong Johnson. It was not Mr. Harry Johnson's animal I was to collect, but a Mr. *Howard* Johnson's. And he lives in Cadogan Square, not Belgravia. It's so stupid; I was given the wrong information. At any rate, here's your cat back. Now, can you assure me it is your cat?" If not, I've got another one in the car.

Mrs. Tobias bent down and got a hiss for her trouble. "Oh, that's Schrödinger"—it came out "Shunger"—"nasty-tempered thing."

"Yes, I'd have to agree with you there." Melrose opened the carrier and the cat made straight for the bureau in the room across the hall.

"I guess she did miss them kittens." Mrs. Tobias sighed.

Relieved of the one cat, he said, "I do apologize again."

"Oh, never mind, sir. 'Long as the cat's back before Mr. Johnson." She opened the door for him and, after he passed through it, looked out and around. "But I do wonder . . . you didn't happen to see a little dog about, did you?"

"Dog?"

This would come to tears, he just knew it.

56

Cigar was a West End club so cool and laid-back, you could walk right past it and never know it was there.

Which was what Jury did. He wondered if that wasn't a great metaphor for most of what passed for life. Most of the time you could walk right past it.

Its brick facade, its small brass plaque (that no one would be able to see from more than three feet away), its little wrought-iron fence, and its un-uniformed doorman—unless the black turtleneck sweater, black wool jacket, black jeans, all of the black pretensions, were to be taken as a uniform—all of this made the place look helplessly hip.

The black-garbed gatekeeper didn't do anything except smile slightly and nod. He wasn't there to check credentials; he was only there to assure customers that this was Mayfair, W1, and Cigar was exclusive.

Inside, he thought about checking his coat with the blonde in the small gated enclosure but decided to keep it in case of the need for a quick getaway. He was a few minutes late, so unless Rosie Moss decided to keep him waiting, she'd be here.

The room put him in mind of last century's London before the coal fires were damped down and the city was called "the Smoke." The club meant its name. Through vistas of smoke, he looked the wide room over: the gorgeous brunette sitting at the bar, eyeing him; a tawny-haired woman at one of the roulette tables, where a villainous-looking croupier whipped the wheel around; two blondes, like paper cutouts, sitting close together, dripping a lot of jewelry.

His eye traveled back; he had missed her just as he had missed the club itself—but why wouldn't he? She turned out to be the gorgeous brunette at the bar, smiling at him. The hair was all curls, no bunches; the candy stripes exchanged for a long black skirt, slit to the knee; black halter top; black fringed shawl; and jade green Christian Louboutin shoes on her feet, one of which she was swinging so that the shoe hung precariously from her toe. So this was Rosie Moss: Dark hair. Black dress. Red soles.

Killer looks.

"You didn't recognize me."

"You could say that."

"I don't always look twelve years old."

"I can see that."

Red-soled shoe now firmly on her foot, she pushed out the stool next door. "Here. Saved it for you. I had to turn a few guys away."

"Half the male population of London, more likely."

The barman was there in a blood red suede waistcoat. Jury looked at Rosie's glass, questioning. She raised a fairly fresh martini. He ordered whiskey, then when the fellow waited, he realized he'd have to name it. This wasn't Trevor, after all.

"Macallan?"

The barman nodded and drifted off to whatever crypt they aged the whiskey in.

Jury said, "Do you transform yourself this easily and often?"

She was plucking a cigarette from an ebony case and offering him the case. He refused for the thousandth heartbreaking time in three years.

"Who says it's easy?"

"All right. I was merely observing your chameleonlike qualities."

"I have other, even better qualities."

Oh, hell, it was to be a night of double entendres. He wasn't up to it. "Do you mind if I call you Rosie, instead of Adele?"

She shrugged, obviously disappointed that he couldn't come up with a better question.

"How did you get into this work?"

"Took my clothes off."

The barman was back with his whiskey. This, he could use. He drank off half of it. "And saw your future."

"Pretty much." Her smile was unpleasant, as if she had a bad taste in her mouth. She sipped her martini. It was a strange color, probably one of those boutique martini mutants that were popular among drinkers who didn't like martinis.

Jury took a chance. "You didn't like her, did you?"

An artfully arched eyebrow went up. "You mean Stacy? I didn't mind her; I hardly knew her. Why? I should be unconsolable now she's dead? I should wrap myself in sackcloth and ashes? Throw myself into the Thames? Jump from the top of Nelson's Column?"

Jury laughed. "No, but you seem to have given some thought to it."

The pale look, the whiteness that had suddenly touched her cheekbones, now was swept away as if it were snow in the wind. It was a rather dramatic turn. Her next move was another.

Rose leaned into him, her hand on his wrist, the hand then traveling slowly up his arm. "This is supposed to be a bit of time together, a few drinks, a few laughs, a meal, and then who knows?"

He did, for one. Strange he felt no desire for her, no ardor. He felt himself to be almost clinically cold. It was, of course, as he'd told Carole-anne, not a date for pleasure but for work. Still, that wouldn't have been reason for feeling he was made of ice. Was it because of the terrible condition of Lu Aguilar? Guilt? No, because it certainly hadn't stopped him getting into bed with Phyllis (the very thought of whom started the ice melting). No, there was something missing, something not coming across.

Then he thought, She's acting. That was part of it. Of course, he imagined she often did. The thing was, there was no real ardor on her part, either. All of her actions were rote, which wouldn't be surprising except that she wasn't here in the role of escort; he hadn't hired her. It was a plain old date. Why did she need the act? He said, "This chap in Chesham Stacy was engaged to . . ."

Abruptly, Rose polished off the rest of her drink and held out the glass for another, held it out not to Jury but to the barman, who nodded. "Engaged? Don't be daft. That what he told you?" Her tone was strangely spiteful. She stubbed out her cigarette. "Bobby never meant anything to her. He was just for laughs."

The serious, sympathetic Bobby Devlin was hardly a fellow a girl would keep by her "for laughs." He thought Rose had it exactly the wrong way round. It was the men Mariah-Stacy was having casual sex with who were there for laughs.

"Anyway," Rosie went on, "he wasn't her type at all. That bewildered-little-boy act? Oh no, that wasn't—" She stopped midsentence. She had said too much.

Jury watched her try to backtrack.

"I mean, that's the impression she gave me."

" 'Bewildered-little-boy' act'? That's more of a thing you'd see, rather than something you'd be told, and certainly not told you by Mariah herself. So when did you meet him?"

She looked off, round the room. "Oh, I just ran into him once, you know, by accident."

"Bobby Devlin told me he rarely went to London; he hates it. So I'm assuming you ran into him in Chesham. You didn't mention that. Indeed, it's strange, especially since you know so little about Mariah's life. But you did know about her, didn't you? You knew her intimately. She pretty much kept Bobby under wraps."

Rose ignored the martini placed before her and slid the cigarette case back into her bag. She snapped the bag shut and reached for the pashmina shawl that she'd draped across the back of her chair. "This is getting boring, you know that? I don't know why I've got to spend the evening talking about Stacy Storm."

"You don't have to. But it's either here or later at the station."

Her eyes hardened. "This wasn't a date at all, was it, not a proper date? This was just to get something out of me, find out things." She pulled the black shawl around her and leaned toward him. "Next you'll be saying I had something to do with her murder, won't you?"

"No. You were in London. Don't worry; we checked out your alibi."

She looked so stunningly self-satisfied at that, Jury wanted to laugh.

"You mean you don't think I ran over to Chesham in my Manolo Blahniks and shot her? Well, good for you. Ta very much for the drinks." She slid from the stool and walked across a room that was growing ever more crowded.

But Jury hardly registered her departure.

Manolo Blahniks?

While he was walking toward the Green Park tube station, his mobile ding-ding-dinged and he considered throwing it down in front of the Mayfair Hotel and stomping it to death.

How childish. "Jury."

"It's me," said Wiggins. "I did find somebody connected with Roedean. Taught there twenty years ago and remembers 'her girls,' as she called them. Specifically, Kate Banks. Name's Shirley Husselby. You want the Brighton address?"

"Yes."

Wiggins gave it to him. "You going there, then?"

"First thing tomorrow. Thanks, Wiggins."

Jury didn't stomp the mobile to death. Reprieve.

57

How did these places seem never to change? It was pleasant, he thought, looking across this shingle beach toward the sea. Time seemed to have stopped here and, without meaning to, stayed.

He turned and walked along King's Road, facing the sea. Years ago he had been here on a case, one of the saddest cases of his career. But they were all sad, weren't they?

Walking on, Jury had no trouble finding the house. It was on a narrow street just off Madeira Drive with a long view of the sea. It was one of a line of terraced houses, the numbers uniform and easy to see on the white posts to which they were attached. He used the dolphin door knocker, wondering what it was about dolphins that made them so popular as door knockers. He heard an approach and then what seemed to be a mild argument on the other side of the door until finally it opened with a yank.

The woman who yanked it was elderly and fragile-looking and, he assumed, must be Shirley Husselby. She was the one Wiggins had found. He took out his ID, saying, "I'm Superintendent Richard Jury. My sergeant called?" He didn't know why he made a question of it, unless it was to give this small woman the opportunity to say, "I don't think so."

"Oh, yes. I'm sorry for the delay opening the door. This door will be troublesome." She gave it a little kick. "You don't look like a super-intendent. I expected someone short, stout, gray, and squinting."

Jury thought of Racer and smiled.

"Do come in." She threw out her arm, ushering him in. Then she explained further. "It's the 'superintendent' part. That's a very high rank of policeman for one so young."

"Me? I'm not young at all, I'm—"

Her finger to her lips, she stopped him. "Superintendent, don't tell people your age. It's none of their business. I never do. Any-way, you look young and quite handsome. Please"—she held out her arm again, toward the front room—"just go on through, but watch that runner! The fringe wants to catch at your heel and send you sprawling."

Jury thanked her for the warning. The fringe said nothing.

In the living room, he was warned not to sit on the armchair to the left of the fireplace unless he wanted a good pinching. "The springs in that chair are so temperamental I never know what they'll do. Just sit beside me on the sofa; I think it's on its good behavior."

Jury looked around at this quite ordinary, very comfortable-looking room: a crisp fire burning, old but good chairs and tables, pretty cream linen, and tulip-patterned slipcovers—all of them look-ing welcoming but apparently full of traps for the unwary.

"Now, I've just made fresh coffee." The silver tray and coffee ser-vice sat on a coffee table before the sofa, steam rising from the spout. There were cream, sugar, and small biscuits. All of it looked quite nonthreatening.

"Be careful of the coffee. It's hotter than you might think. Cream? Sugar?"

Jury declined cream and sugar but took the china cup and saucer carefully. "Thank you." The coffee was no hotter than coffee ought to be. He thought she had a watchful air, as if she were prepared to call Emergency if the first sip had him on his back on the floor. Then he said, "I expect you've heard about this series of murders in London?"

"Yes. You want to talk to me about Kate Banks, is that right?"

He thought her cup rattled against the saucer as she set it down. "She was one of the best students I ever had. I felt absolutely terrible when I read about her. I just couldn't believe it. Why, of all people . . ." She shook her head. Her mouth shut tightly, as if holding back emotions that threatened to overflow.

"You think it so unlikely something such as that would happen to her?"

"Of course. She was universally liked at school. Roedean, that is. Really, she was a remarkable person." Miss Husselby rose and went to the fireplace, saying, "Oh, this fire is unbelievably lazy, and then sometimes it will just shoot out!" She poked at the recalcitrant logs, burning by whim. Nothing in Miss Husselby's world cooperated.

When she'd reseated herself, Jury said, "Please go on about Kate."

"She was very smart, intelligent, and just a very good person, liked, as I said, by everyone. She was the sort who could settle disputes—you know, who could act as go-between. The girls trusted her, and deservedly so." Miss Husselby sipped her coffee, then sat back. "It was too bad her mother was so flighty. Undependable. The very opposite of her daughter. Kate was simply a rock. One could lean on Kate, young as she was."

Jury said, "There was another girl, I believe a friend of hers. Crystal North."

"Oh, Crystal." The tone changed, suggesting that Crystal North was an entirely different kettle of fish. "I don't know that I'd call her a 'friend' of Kate's, though she certainly wanted to be. She wanted to be best friends—in fact, I think she wanted to *be* Kate, if you know what I mean. Kate didn't like her very much. But Crystal generally got what she wanted; unfortunately she had no tolerance for frustration. And she would play with other people's lives."

"How?"

"I remember once she cheated on a test; she copied answers from the paper of a girl beside her. The girl came to me about it. It came down to one of them, one of them had to have copied, but which one? The tutor favored Crystal; Crystal was a great manipulator, see.

The tutor gave them an ultimatum: if one of them didn't admit to cheating, he'd have to fail both of them. And Crystal let that happen. She was going to fail in any event, so telling the truth gained her nothing. It's one thing to act stupidly when the only victim is you yourself; it's quite another thing to make someone else, some innocent person, pay."

Jury thought of the zebra crossing. The hand stretched out to stop traffic. The car unable to stop. The miscarriage.

Miss Husselby continued: "There was a boy here in Brighton. Crystal had been going out with him. He was only the son of a greengrocer and had no money at all, whereas the Norths, Crystal's family—well, they had plenty. I was surprised Crystal took to him, but she did. He was charming. I used to buy my vegetables at their shop. Charming and handsome." She looked at Jury as if to include him in the little circle of charm and looks. "A number of the girls were mad about him. Which probably was the reason Crystal wanted him. No one else could gain a toehold—

"Until he saw Kate. And that was the end of Crystal. Kate didn't do anything; she wouldn't have. But even though she wouldn't go out with him, he was still a goner. She was like a field of lavender. One whiff and you were out cold." Miss Husselby laughed, rather liking her analogy.

"When he broke it off with Crystal, she was beside herself. But there was nothing she could do." Miss Husselby sighed and sat looking at the mantelpiece. Or, rather, the painting over the mantel. "There it goes again." She rose and walked to the painting and adjusted its slight imbalance with the tip of her finger. She walked back. The minute her back was turned, it resumed its uneven keel. "Forgive me," she said. "What was I saying?"

"About Kate and this young fellow." He didn't reintroduce the lavender field.

She sighed and poured them both some more coffee. He knew it would be tepid but didn't mind. "Thank you."

"I did keep up with Kate until a few years ago. But I lost all trace of Crystal."

Jury took out the photo, the snapshot of the girls on the pier. "Is Crystal among these girls?"

She took the picture, looked, nodded. "Right there. Frowning. These are Kate's friends. But I don't see . . . Oh, of course, Kate would have been the photographer, wouldn't she? That explains the frown on Crystal's face." She handed the snapshot back to Jury.

"Then you don't know about the accident."

"What accident?"

"Crystal's." Jury told her.

Her eyes widened. "That's terrible. But what foolishness, to cross when traffic's coming. Just because the pedestrian has the right of way doesn't mean a car's going to stop. Those crossings can be treacherous. There, you see." She spread her hands wide. "There you have it. Playing with her unborn child's life. Just to make a point. What happened to Crystal? I assume she must have been hurt."

"Yes, rather badly. Almost completely paralyzed from the waist down. She pretty much lives in a wheelchair."

"I should feel sorry, you know. I wish I did." She leaned toward Jury, imparting a confidence. "She'd have done anything, beg, borrow, or steal, to hold on to Davey—"

"Davey?"

"The greengrocer's son."

For a long moment, Jury just stared at her. Then he asked, "His name wasn't Cummins, by any chance?"

"Why, yes. Do you know him?"

"I do." Jury sat silent, thinking. Then he rose. "You have no idea how much this has helped, Miss Husselby. I can't thank you enough."

She reclaimed his coat from the small closet, saying, "I'm glad I could be of help. I've so little to do these days. I do hope you can untangle things." She made to open the door, but it was stuck. "Oh, blast this door. It'll get me in the end."

Jury opened it, smiling. He doubted much would get Shirley Husselby down.

58

It was the anonymity of train rides that Jury liked. The presence of other people who didn't know you and didn't want to. No one felt obligated to speak. A train ride was a small-talk vacuum.

There were only ten or a dozen other passengers traveling to London, all engaged in reading or gazing out of windows at the Sussex countryside, or else plugged into earphones or mobiles.

Across the aisle sat a pretty woman in her late thirties or early forties. It was hard to guess ages anymore, especially of children, who these days seemed to peak at thirteen or fourteen and go downhill from there. Children looked older than they were, adults younger.

It wasn't the woman's face that had caught his attention, but her shoes. Strappy. What a great word. He wished there were some quality in a person that word would fit.

Strappy sandals. Jimmy Choo? Tod's? Prada? No, he didn't think so. She was nicely but not richly dressed, not enough to be wearing Jimmy Choo. The shoes were sea green, very graceful. He had never noticed women's shoes before, unless he'd a reason to look; the ones he'd seen of late, the shoes, he had to admit were quite beautiful. More works of art than shoes—which was, of course, what the designer meant them to be. He shut his eyes and pictured Carole-anne's shoes.

What he was doing here was deliberately distracting his attention

from the case. He was trying not to go over the conversation with
Shirley Husselby because he thought he should leave it for a while; if
he could let it settle, maybe something would surface. It had certainly
been worth the trip to Brighton: that Chris, or Crystal, Cummins
had gone to school with Kate Banks yet hadn't admitted how well
she had known her.

There was a point in a case when Jury felt it was all there and finding it was rather like shooting a pinball machine; like a series of steel
balls in the channel of a pinball machine, all waiting for someone's
hand to shoot them onto a field of possibilities, targets, numbered
holes, rubber bumpers, and the players needing to exert just the right
amount of pressure to send the balls into the holes.

Chris, or Crystal, had, in the end, married Davey.

Jury's question was, why hadn't David Cummins been more
forthcoming about their having known Kate Banks, and known her
well? David was a policeman; he knew that kind of information could
be vital.

He must not have wanted it to be.

At Jury's signal, the porter stopped and Jury asked for tea and a
jam roll that he eyed but did not eat.

He rested his head on the headrest and sipped his tea while the
train throbbed into Redhill station. A few people rose to get off, looking bleary-eyed, as if they'd just been hauled by the Trans-Siberian
express instead of the Southern Railway from Brighton. A few got
off, a few got on. He tried not to notice, trying to hold on to the
pleasure of anonymity.

Soon to be breached. Through half-closed eyes, he watched a
small, stout man settle himself opposite with a rustling and crackling
noise that turned out to be a sandwich and a bag of crisps placed on
the table between them. Then a slurp and smack that turned out to
be coffee. His fellow passenger did not take closed eyes as a barrier
to conversation or companionship. The train clung stubbornly to
Redhill; he wished it would move. It did.

"Care for one?" He was holding the bag of crisps across the
table.

Some people didn't appreciate the finer points of train travel. Jury opened his eyes, smiled, shook his head. "No, thanks."

"That looks good."

Jury realized he meant the jam roll. "Got it from the tea trolley."

The man looked over his shoulder but didn't see the trolley. "Think I might have one myself when it comes by."

"Might not be by again before London. We're not far out. Have this one."

"Oh, now—"

"Really. Go ahead. I'm not hungry. I don't know why I got it." He smiled. "Throwback to childhood, I guess. Jammies."

The man pulled the jam roll toward him, smiling, too. "Thanks. Name's Mattingly, incidentally." Mr. Mattingly held out his hand.

Jury shook it. "Richard Jury."

"Speaking of childhood. I've just been with my sister for two days. We had great times, we did, as kids. She's in a bad way now. Real bad." Looking away from the jam roll to the scenery sliding past, he sounded sad.

"I'm sorry."

Mr. Mattingly nodded and went on. "It's a trial, no doubt about it. She's holding on. I don't see how, and neither does she. Nothing but skin and bones now." He wrestled the plastic off the jam roll.

Skin and bones. Which was probably why Mattingly was intent on stuffing down whatever he could. Not so much for himself, but in aid of his sister. He bit off half the roll. "Quite nice, this."

Jury could think of nothing to say. He looked out at the building up of urban scenery, the gray, uneven edges of London's outlying landscape.

Mattingly went on about his sick sister, dying sister, apparently. He finished his jam roll, drank his coffee, still talking ten minutes later when the train whined and screeched into Victoria.

Where had all the rest of these people got on? he wondered. Over twice as many as there'd been leaving Brighton. They stood in the aisle and managed to stumble forward as if they were being prodded with guns and bayonets. Jury didn't know what brought this violent image to mind.

Behind him, Mr. Mattingly was still discoursing about life and death. "Sometimes I wonder if it's not more merciful, the people that help you out of it. . . . That's what she said herself and asked me if I knew anyone. 'Cora, where'd I ever meet up with anyone like that, my dear?' Still," Mattingly went on, "I could hardly blame the woman. God."

They were down the "Mind the Gap" step and onto the platform now. "Sorry," said Mattingly, switching his small bag to his other hand so that he could shake hands with Jury again. "Not much more boring than to have to listen to some stranger on a train talking at you."

It went through Jury's mind then: Bruno.

Reminds me of Bruno, Jenkins had said. The steel ball was rolling across the surface of the pinball machine in Jury's mind. He watched it fall into the hole and said, "No, I'm very glad you did talk to me, Mr. Mattingly." It was the truth. "I'm terribly sorry about your sister."

"Yes. Thanks. Well, I'll be off. Thanks again for the cake."

Mr. Mattingly swung on down the platform, while Jury stood in place and watched him go. No, he wasn't really seeing anything except his own mental images.

That was what Jury had been trying to remember. Bruno. Hitchcock.

Strangers on a Train.

59

Instead of fighting his way through the underground rush hour, Jury stood in the queue for a taxi. It was long but manageable. While he waited, his mobile sounded and he grabbed it to hit the talk button, but not before he'd picked up a few smug smiles from those who'd recognized the ring. A grown man, imagine. He thought he'd done well by simply remembering to charge it.

It was Jenkins.

"We've got something here, Richard. I can't say if there's any significance. It's a receipt for a book. From Waterstone's. Date is the day Kate Banks was murdered. It was found by a uniform when he was helping to take down crime scene tape."

Jury was next in line. He said, "Hold on, Dennis," as the next cab pulled up. "I'm getting into a cab." He gave the driver his address, climbed in, shut the door. "Right. Receipt found where?"

"Wedged down between pavement stones. Why didn't forensic find it that night? Beats me."

But not Jury. "Your SOCO people would have found it; they didn't because it wasn't there."

Jenkins pondered this. "You mean it was planted?"

"Yes. What's the book? Is it on the receipt?"

"It's been rained on, wait a minute . . . *Shoe-aholic,* whatever that might be."

Jury looked out the window; they were just passing through Clerkenwell. "I know about Jimmy Choo and Manolo Blahnik because I know a 'shoe-aholic.' I'll save you some legwork, Dennis. The person this is going to lead to is a detective with Thames Valley police. Detective Sergeant David Cummins. He bought the book when he was in London. You'll want to talk to him."

Jenkins sounded disbelieving. "Thames Valley police? A detective? You're way ahead of me."

"Not at all. I just happened to know about the book because I saw it in Cummins's house."

"This is pure gold, isn't it."

Jury smiled. "That, or at least plate. Worth the trip, I assure you. I'll be going to High Wycombe headquarters tomorrow. Want to come?"

"Yes, but I can't. I've got some bureaucratic nonsense to take care of."

"I'll fill you in later."

Jenkins said he'd be waiting and rang off.

The cab pulled up to Jury's house. Lights everywhere. Were they having a rave? Why were the lights on in his flat? Carole-anne could be in there teaching the salsa to a roomful of Mexicans. He paid the driver, gave him a big tip.

As the cab pulled away, Jury thought about the receipt left at the crime scene. He shook his head.

On the part of the shooter, that had been a huge mistake. That person should have let well enough alone.

He was right about Carole-anne. He was wrong about the Mexicans. She was talking to Dr. Phyllis Nancy, both of them standing in his living room.

Oh, Christ, he'd done it again—forgotten.

Yet she smiled at him. That was Phyllis. "Who," she said, "would want to eat at the Ivy when they could dine here? Its charming ambience, its mood lighting, its early-detective decor."

Said Carole-anne, "She's being funny."

"Phyllis, I'm so sorry." He turned to Carole-anne. "I'm glad to see you've met Doctor Nancy. Which of you got here first?"

"Had to let her in, didn't I?" Carole-anne's tone was querulous. It would be. Jury would be hearing about this for weeks. She turned on her heel and went into the kitchen. "She brought food: sausages and eggs, cheese, bread, some red wine. Good. I can do a nice fry-up." She reappeared at the kitchen door. "Okay with you, Super?"

"Shouldn't you be asking if it's okay with Phyllis?"

"It is. She brought the food, after all."

Phyllis said, "It's certainly okay with me if you're doing the cooking."

"Good," said Jury. "Phyllis and I will sit here and drink wine. Sounds like a winning scheme to me."

Carole-anne was reevaluating her KP duty. "I'll have some wine too between turning the sausages."

Jury pulled glasses from an old armoire he'd picked up from a sale of Second World War stuff held at the Imperial War Museum. They were used to hold guns, originally. This fascinated him. He set the glasses on the coffee table and looked at Phyllis. "This was really sweet of you, Phyllis."

"Yes, it really was thoughtful," Carole-anne called from the kitchen. "I've had it in mind all day to get eggs and sausages, and hash browns too. Only you didn't get any hash browns." She pointed out this weak spot in their menu when she carried in the bottle of wine.

"You're right," said Phyllis. "I should have thought of that."

"Probably just as well. I'm watching my weight." She appraised Phyllis, who was sitting not on the sofa but in a chair, making her hold on Jury speculative.

Carole-anne noticed this. She smiled.

Jury knew this small act of generosity on the part of Phyllis was beyond Carole-anne to work out. She wouldn't understand it, much less perform it. Jury poured wine into three glasses.

Carole-anne said, "That's a nice one, that. Had a glass at the Mucky Duck the other evening."

As the wine was in a gallon jug—Phyllis had a keen sense of

humor—Jury wasn't surprised that the Mucky Duck featured it. "Maybe I should have Trevor taste it."

"Who's Trevor?" asked Carole-anne, taking a drink of her wine.

"The wine guy at the Shades. Knows everything."

"Quite nice, this. Of course, I don't purport to be an expert. Like Trevor."

Jury laughed. Conversation could be a minefield for Carole-anne. It was so easy to put a foot wrong.

"How was Brighton?" asked Phyllis. "Worth it?"

Carole-anne, who, to her chagrin, hadn't known about Brighton, went back to the kitchen as if she couldn't care less.

"It was, definitely," said Jury. "Except I missed our date," he added sotto voce.

And sotto voce, Phyllis answered, "But we're having it."

An awful clatter came from the kitchen, as if a half-dozen pot tops were being bowled across the floor.

"Sorr-ee!" yelled Carole-anne, sticking her head round the kitchen door. "Dropped the skillet!" The head disappeared.

Jury leaned across the table, his hand stretched toward Phyllis. "Sit over here."

Phyllis smiled but shook her head and was about to say something when another series of rattles came from the kitchen.

"Oh, God, but I'm clumsy tonight!" The ginger hair poked round the doorway. "A plate. Hope it wasn't the good china!"

"It better not be the stuff I bought at Christie's."

Carole-anne shrugged as she studied their relative positions: a coffee table apart, good. She moved back into the kitchen. There came a bright sizzle from (Jury supposed) the reclaimed frying pan.

"I forgot, I forgot," said Jury, putting his hands through his hair, "the uncle, Lu's uncle. You said—"

"No, not yet," said Phyllis quickly, reaching across the table. "He hasn't done anything yet. There's still a chance, you know, I think more of one than—"

"Here we are!" fluted Carole-anne, ushering in two plates filled with fried eggs, buttered bread, and sausages.

Jury frowned, taking the plate she held out. "That was awfully quick." He inspected the sausages. "You sure these are done, Carole-anne? It's only been a few minutes."

"Of course it is. I'll just get mine." She hurried off, hurried back, carrying a nonmatching blue plate, and sat down beside Jury.

The phone rang. Jury rose to answer it, his plate in hand.

It was Wiggins. "Guv, Harry Johnson called several times today."

"Out of jail, is he?" Jury sniggered and forked up a bite of sausage. He had the phone wedged on his shoulder.

"What he wants is, he wants to know what you did with his dog. You know—Mungo."

60

"DI Jenkins sent it over. Said you'd want to see it," said
Wiggins.

Jury had just come into the office carrying a plastic bag and now looked at the receipt from Waterstone's. He heard the voice of Kate's godmother, talking about her love of books: *that big Waterstone's bookshop in Piccadilly.* The date was the day of Kate's murder. The time registered was 11:00 a.m. Chris Cummins had mentioned David bought it in London Friday.

"I was thinking about it, you know, being found at the crime scene." Wiggins was stirring his tea slowly, as if the spoon were a divining rod. "It doesn't have to be Cummins's receipt. Other people bought that book."

"Two other people, Wiggins. I was just over in Piccadilly. Waterstone's sold three copies that day. Not many people would be that interested in a glamour book about shoes on any one day. It's coffee table, a lot of photographs, pricey. On top of that, do you think one of the other two buyers, he or she, just happened to drop the receipt at the spot Kate Banks was murdered? I might be able to stretch coincidence that far if the book had been a best seller—but not this book." He took out and held up the glossily jacketed book he'd just bought at Waterstone's. He'd been standing since he'd come in; now he sat down.

"What does it mean?"

"It means the killer did a stupid thing—went back and planted the receipt."

"You mean to make it look like Cummins—"

"Yes."

"So what you're saying is, Cummins didn't kill Kate Banks."

"No, he didn't kill her; he loved her. According to Shirley Husselby, he was besotted with her." Jury paused to look at Wiggins's cup. "You must have added eye of newt to that tea instead of sugar the way you're stirring. Get your skates on." Jury opened the door and was through it before Wiggins could ask where they were going.

He didn't drink his tea; he frowned at it. Eye of newt rather put him off.

Not much over an hour later, they pulled into the car park beside High Wycombe police headquarters. Jury had called David Cummins from the car and asked to see him there.

Cummins was in the muster room with a dozen other detectives and uniforms when Jury and Wiggins walked in. He looked pleased to see them, which wrenched Jury's heart, really. He liked Cummins; he was sorry about what was going to happen.

"What's all this about?" Cummins's smile went from Jury to Wiggins. He pulled a couple of chairs around to the desk for them.

In proximity were three or four other detectives at their desks. Jury said, "Can we find someplace a little less public?"

The smile dimmed, but Cummins said, "Come on."

They walked down a hall to an interview room, went in, and sat down, Wiggins off to one side, notebook out.

Jury said, "Have a look at this, will you, David?" He'd pulled out the copy of the receipt and placed it before Cummins.

"Yeah. For that book I bought Chris the other day. About shoes—but why . . . ?"

"Police found this yesterday at the crime scene, on the pavement where Kate's body was found."

The head that had been lowered to look at the bit of paper didn't rise. Jury left it for several seconds. He knew it was the mention of Kate. Cummins wasn't a controlled-enough actor to put on a blank face at that.

Finally, Cummins picked up the receipt again, as if it would change by alchemy into a thing that would explain all of this. He just shook his head. "You lost me; you've completely lost me. But the receipt, I didn't lose that. It's at home. There's a box Chris keeps receipts in."

"No, I don't think it's there, David."

There was a silence except for Wiggins's pen scratching on paper.

David looked up at Jury. "You think I was there—where Kate was . . ." But he didn't seem able to say "murdered."

"How could this receipt have got there?"

David made the same point that Wiggins had earlier. "It belonged to somebody else who bought the book. That's obvious. At least to me."

"You were in Waterstone's, weren't you, on the Friday? You went to London on Fridays."

He nodded. He was too much a detective not to see where this was going. Where, he knew, it had already gone.

"Two other copies of the book were sold that day, later in the afternoon. Of the three of you, how many would happen to be at the spot where Kate Banks was murdered?"

Cummins shook his head. "No matter how improbable, it must have been one of the others because I know I wasn't there." He became agitated, running his hands through his hair, down his tie, fiddling with a pencil.

Jury leaned across the table and put his hand around David's arm. "David, you knew Kate Banks when she was Kate Muldar; you knew her much better than you've led us to believe. And Chris knew her, too." He leaned back. "Why don't you tell me about back then?"

David nodded. "The truth—"

That would be nice, thought Jury. But he didn't say it. Cummins was having a bad time, and it was soon to get worse.

"It was in Brighton. Chris and I were going together, more or less. But when I saw Kate"—his smile said he was seeing her again—"I forgot everything else. I forgot I was just a grocer's son; I forgot I had no career and no prospects. I forgot I had no money. I forgot Chris. That sounds impossibly exaggerated, I know, but it's literally true. Nothing I did could set Kate aside. It wasn't her looks, though God knows they were grand. Kate was the nicest person I ever knew."

"That's what I've heard from her godmother. She was a very good person."

David nodded. "I can't explain except to say I was dazzled, if you know what I mean."

Jury knew about dazzle. The first time he'd seen Phyllis Nancy, that night of the Odeon shooting, coming toward him holding a black case, wearing a long green gown and diamond earrings that hung beneath her dark red hair. That was dazzle.

"Yes. Go on."

"I was working for my dad, filling bags with onions, lettuces, potatoes. I can't imagine a job less . . . sexy. I can still remember wishing I were a copper, a CID man." He laughed. "God. Has anybody got a cigarette?" He looked at Jury, then around at Wiggins.

Jury said, "Wiggins, go out there and see if you can scare up some smokes. And matches." As Wiggins left, Jury said, "How did Chris react to this? To Kate and you in Brighton?"

"You can imagine. We broke up. They—Kate and Chris—were in school; it was their last year at Roedean. I didn't see Kate after that. I think Chris got rid of her. I think she told her something that really put her off. I don't know. Kate just seemed to dissolve into the past."

"And then she was back in the present. Maybe sitting in that coffee bar in Waterstone's."

"How did you know that?"

"You liked books. She liked books and the coffee bar there. Her godmother, Myra Brewer, told us."

"I thought I was seeing things. Nearly twenty years and Kate Muldar hadn't changed, not by . . ." He looked round as if searching for some measuring device to explain to Jury how much she had not changed by.

There was gut-wrenching pathos in it.

"Not by a hairsbreadth." He settled on a cliché. Sometimes starved language was all you had.

The door opened then, and Wiggins came through with the smokes, a half-pack of Rothmans. He set this on the table, a book of matches on top.

David thanked him, shook out a cigarette, and sat smoking.

"Not all of these London trips were undertaken to visit the shoe emporiums of Upper Sloane Street, were they?"

David was silent, flicking ash from his cigarette into a dented metal tray with "Bass" written across it. He looked at Jury. The look was the answer.

"How many times did you meet with Kate Banks?"

"I can't say exactly, a dozen, maybe."

Jury smiled. "You can say exactly, David. You could recite it as surely as a prisoner of war giving name, rank, serial number."

Weakly, David smiled. "I expect so. We met a dozen times in the last four months."

"And before that? In London? Three years ago?"

His head went down again, as if dodging a blow. "What makes you think I was seeing her then?"

"Because of the way you're acting right now. I was merely guessing before. But I wouldn't be surprised if that's the reason you left London."

He said hastily, "Chris didn't know. . . ."

Jury just looked at him. "Yet Chris insisted you leave, didn't she?"

The nod was the barest movement of his head.

"Did Kate know you were married?"

The nod was more emphatic. "But not to Chris. I didn't tell Kate that."

"Why not?"

David blew out his cheeks. "Kate would think it was happening all over again, and she wouldn't've let it."

"It *was* happening all over again." Jury leaned closer to him across the table, so close they might have breathed each other's breath. "And Chris knew it."

His alarm all too evident, Cummins looked at Jury and then past him, as if his wife might be waiting there in the shadows. Then he was consumed with panic-anger: "That's ridiculous! Where do you get that idea, for God's sake?"

"For one thing, to state what's a cliché, wives seem to sense these things; they know if their husbands are straying. But more than that: you were careless. Which isn't surprising, given your feelings for Kate. You said it earlier: she shut everything else out. Nothing else mattered. If she could do that to you at age eighteen, how much more could she at age thirty-seven?"

"But what do you mean by 'careless'?"

"You'd have to have been; you were besotted. You'd have come home with perfume on your coat, lipstick on your shirt—"

"Of course I didn't—"

"Not that precisely, maybe, but you were so preoccupied, you couldn't have taken great care in rubbing out all of the signs of another woman. Kate Banks was lovely. And other things. I saw her. Dead, there was still something ineffable. I wished when I saw her I'd known her."

David Cummins sat looking at his hands, fingers laced on the table.

"How did you feel when you found out she was working for an escort service?"

"It wouldn't've made any difference; nothing made any difference except being with her. This one service wasn't really a sex thing. There are men who really do want companionship. But, still, it wouldn't have made any difference."

"You were going to leave Chris, weren't you?"

He nodded, wiping the wetness from his face with the heel of his hand. He sniffed. "But I didn't know what to do. I mean, with Chris in that wheelchair."

Wiggins heard the tears even though he didn't see them. He was on his feet in an instant with a fresh handkerchief, which he laid on the table before Cummins, who picked it up, shook it open, and held it like a flag of truce.

Wiggins sat down again, tilted his chair against the wall, and reclaimed his notebook and pen.

Cummins picked up the copy of the receipt, tossed it down.

Jury scraped back his chair. Wiggins rose, too, but David still sat. "Next you're going to tell me Chris killed her."

"No, I'm not going to tell you that. She could hardly have managed to get herself to the city, could she? Though God only knows she'd have wanted to."

"She didn't know it was Kate."

Poor sod, thought Jury. "Yes."

"I don't think—"

"And you're wrong. Bring the crime scene photos of that shoe impression." Jury got up. "Come on."

"What?"

Jury knew Cummins had heard him, but probably any answer he gave at this point would be "What?"

"I want to talk to your wife. Bring the photos. Chris might recognize something."

David nodded. "The photos are in the incident room." He went off.

Wiggins watched Jury. "It really looks as if you think—"

Jury cut him off. "I do."

In another moment, David was back. He held up the photos. "I still say she didn't know."

"The moment you made the mistake of bringing home the despised shoes by Kate Spade, I'll bet she knew. My guess is she hated Kate Spade just because of the name. You must have been out of your bloody mind, David."

61

hris Cummins wheeled herself to the door in what Jury thought was record time. Her husband had called her in that moment he'd gone for the photos. Jury knew he would; he wanted to see what his wife would betray if she thought her husband was in big trouble.

His guess was, nothing.

"Three more somber faces I've never seen. Be sure you leave your shoes at the door." Chris Cummins's laugh was just this side of combative.

Wiggins smiled. Neither of the other men did.

"Come on, I'm making tea. The kettle's about to go."

They followed her, even David, as if this were no longer his house, his wife. As if he were merely stopping by like the others.

In the kitchen, the tray was ready with cups and saucers, milk and sugar. So she'd been expecting company. Jury didn't comment.

The kettle screamed and she reached for it, but Wiggins got there first. Wiggins would always get there first, thought Jury. And he was always undervaluing Wiggins. He felt ashamed about that, about a lot of things. Perhaps he was sharing in the general shame.

"Thank you, Sergeant Wiggins," said Chris.

"My pleasure, ma'am."

They moved into the room she called the old parlor, the "shoe room." Glinting like jewelry, the shoes in their miraculous flashes of turquoise, rose, amber, red, made him see why women were seduced by them. One couldn't have found a more alluring arrangement of jewels in all of Hatton Garden.

And Chris Cummins couldn't walk in any of them.

They sat around the table in the comfortable floral armchairs. Chris poured the tea, Wiggins helped. David waded right in: "Police found the receipt for your book, the one I bought in Waterstone's. It was found at the scene where Kate Banks was murdered."

About to pick up her teacup, she frowned, looking from her husband to Jury to Wiggins. "What are you talking about? The receipt—"

Jury knew she would use the same argument her husband had, and she did.

"—must be someone else's."

And Jury made the same objection to this theory.

She stared at him. "This is ridiculous. It was in the book and I put it in the box where I keep receipts. That inlaid box, David. Go look."

David got up and went to the heavy piece of furniture, pulled out a wooden box, inlaid, fancy for a receipt receptacle. He was riffling through the bits of paper. "It's not here."

"Here, give me it." Impatiently, she had her hand out for the box.

Jury said, "He's right. It's not there."

"How do you know that?" At Jury, she leveled a disdainful expression. It wasn't very convincing. "Look. Look. If you're . . . Look. David scarcely knew her, and nor did I. I'd—we'd forgotten all about her. The name really didn't register."

Wiggins spoke: "It registered a bit more than that, didn't it?"

Chris looked again at Wiggins, Jury, and came to rest on her husband. "David? What's going on?"

The alarm, thought Jury, was pretty convincing.

"Kate and I met again. We met a number of times." David had turned to gaze out the window.

From Chris came the standard proofs of surprise, thought Jury. He said, "But you already knew that, didn't you?"

"What are you talking about? Of course I didn't." Her voice caught on the tightness in her throat, the unshed tears.

"That's why you wanted her dead. It had already happened once before, when the three of you were young. In Brighton. To have it happen again would be unbearable."

"Are you trying to say I killed her? I got myself to London, to that street she died on, and then back? In case you haven't noticed, I'm in a wheelchair." She slapped the arm of it, almost as if to show it was solid and she was in it.

"I'm not saying you murdered her. You had her murdered."

Chris's face was set in a convincing semblance of shock. "*What?* I paid someone—?"

"No. You're too smart not to realize that if you hire a shooter, blackmail might soon follow; you'd be forever in the grip of a hired killer."

"Well, then, I obviously didn't do it myself, and I didn't pay anyone to do it. How did I manage it? A curse?" She laughed.

It was the most unpleasant laugh Jury had ever heard. "You did the only thing that would secure the killer's silence: you traded murders."

David, if it was possible, went even paler, more drawn. His skin looked stretched. "What?"

Jury did not look at him; he kept his eyes on Chris, who lost, with this last statement, her careless laughter. "Your victim pretty much came to you; I mean, you didn't have to go all the way to London. She was your half of the bargain: Mariah Cox. Stacy Storm."

Her mouth worked, but she said nothing for a moment. Then, "What earthly reason . . . ? I had no reason to murder Mariah Cox. The librarian?"

"I know you didn't have a reason. That's the point. There would be no motive. But the irony is, you thought you'd be killing a complete stranger. You didn't know Stacy Storm would wind up being someone from Chesham whom you knew. You didn't recognize her at first. But she recognized you. But at that point, facing her there in the Black Cat's patio, you couldn't think quick enough to rationalize the meeting. You didn't have much choice, so you shot her anyway.

"Neither did Rose Moss have a motive for killing Kate Banks. But you did. Just as Rose Moss *did* have a motive for murdering Mariah Cox. For what I imagine was a very brief time, they were lovers, until Mariah called it off. Yes, it was all about to change, and not in Rose's favor. And that, she couldn't stand."

The silence in the room was so dense, it was like a heavy material, weighted as the velvet curtains in Simon Santos's living room. He stopped. No one spoke. Chris's look of deep concentration told him her mind was working furiously to counter what he'd said.

So he said more. "That Waterstone's receipt. You managed to get it to Rose Moss. What you were thinking was that David was the only person who could possibly have dropped it. You worked out the same thing I did: that probably no more copies of that book would be sold at that time on that day. But what you seemed to forget was that you were the only other person who possessed that receipt. You overcorrected, Chris. You tried to frame David, forgetting that you could also be pointing to yourself—"

"Chris." David still stood, his head against the cold glass of the windowpane. He was not really speaking to her; the name came out as a breath, a sigh.

Jury went on. "But that was an easy mistake to make, since who would suspect you of murdering Kate Banks?"

Chris said, "This is all highly imaginative, but I don't see any evidence at all." As if to mock him, she made an elaborate survey of the room. She smiled.

Jury ignored the comment. "The Manolo Blahnik heel print was especially inventive."

Her smile widened. She seemed to be enjoying herself now. "Then whose, if not his?"

"Well, it wasn't a heel print, was it." Jury walked over to the corner of the wall of shoes. "It was this." He pulled out one of the crutches. "You could hardly ride your wheelchair to the spot where you killed Mariah Cox. So you had to use crutches—"

"What do you mean? I can't manage on crutches!"

"Of course you can. Given your well-muscled arms, I'd say you'd gotten in a lot of practice. At first I assumed that came from getting the wheelchair about; stupid of me, as it's electric, isn't it? It was the one detail you didn't think through. Strange the way the mind works: in solving one problem, we create another. You solved the problem of going to Lycrome Road in a wheelchair. If you used crutches, under that long black coat"—here Jury turned to the coatrack—"probably no one driving in a car would notice. And of course you had the advantage of the roadworks, didn't you? Hardly anyone in the pub and no cars in the car park. But the crutches created a problem. You did a pretty good job of staying on the hard surface—the car park, the patio—but there was that one deep little print left in the earth." Jury paused. "I've got to hand it to you, Chris. If anyone did think that print wasn't the heel of a shoe, you'd be sunk, wouldn't you? You think fast. Manolo Blahnik!

"That was the very thing that put me onto Rose Moss as the other party in this whole thing. It's funny, or vain, but I thought Rose Moss rather fancied me. Wrong. She went out with me to find out how much I knew. She wasn't turned on to me at all. Rose isn't interested in men; she's a lesbian. She thought Mariah was, too. And she isn't like you, Chris. She hasn't your nerve; she hasn't your acting ability; she'll cave in an eyeblink; she'll give you up in a second if it means saving herself.

"Before she left me in that club, she said, 'You mean you don't think I ran over to Chesham in my Manolo Blahniks and shot her?' Very careless of her. That supposed Manolo Blahnik heel print was never mentioned in the media. The only way she could have heard that was from you or police. And she certainly didn't hear it from David or me. So it was down to you, Chris. It's pretty much all down to you."

In the only out-of-control moment she'd ever had around Jury, Chris Cummins picked up the teapot and threw it at the cubbyholes full of shoes, where it shattered.

62

Not terribly refreshed by his night at Boring's, Melrose pulled up (yet again) in the Black Cat's car park. He felt his life to be pretty much circumscribed by Chesham-London, London-Chesham, Chesham-London, et cetera, et cetera. He might as well buy some hovel here in Chesham and settle down.

Melrose got out of the car and trudged wearily round the corner of the pub, when he heard the cat yowling. He stopped and trudged back and opened the rear door. The cat, Morris Two, electrified by its stint in the car and its overnight stay at Boring's, streaked out and around back to who knew where. Melrose's life seemed to be nothing but waiting on animals. Instead of settling down in Chesham, why didn't he get a job at the London Zoo? He pulled the cat carrier out of the backseat and plodded back.

At the side entrance he looked through the window, where Mungo and Morris stared out at him, as if he were the troublemaker here and not them. Wearily, he opened the door, wondering how in hell he was going to get Mungo in the car and back to London.

Oh, well. He went up to the bar, greeted Sally Hawkins, and asked for a double Balmenach.

"Oh, now," she said cheekily, "a bit early in the day for a double, isn't it, love?"

"You're right, so give me two singles."

She laughed and slid the glass under the optics.

Whiskey in hand, he walked over to the table by the window, peering as he did so at elderly Johnny Boy and, under the table, his dog, Horace. He sat down at the table and glared at Mungo, who wasn't interested.

Here came Dora to slide in beside him and ask, "Did you get the cat back all right?" He could tell from her tone that the prospect of failure excited her more than that of success.

Melrose nodded. "Now, all I have to do is get you-know-who to London."

He wasn't fooling Mungo, who slid off the chair and trotted to the bar.

Melrose looked after him. "Maybe I could fob off Horace on Mungo's owner."

"Horace and Mungo don't look a bit alike."

"They're both dogs, aren't they?"

"Listen," whispered Dora. "Mungo's behind the bar—"

"Knifing the foam from those glasses of Guinness, is he?"

Two fresh pints sat beneath the beer pulls, settling.

"I think Sally's put down food for him," whispered Dora as if Mungo might hear her. "We can get him if we're careful. His back's turned. I'll go over and you come with the carrier. But you keep out of sight."

Dora started over, and after slugging back his whiskey, Melrose picked up the carrier and went toward the bar, skirting the tables. Dora must have grabbed Mungo, for he heard an uncustomary "yip!" and he quickly opened the top of the carrier so that Dora could shovel Mungo in. "Good work, Dora!"

But Dora was looking toward the front of the pub and in a raging whisper said, "Your friend's just come in!"

Melrose turned and saw Jury. "Sit on it!" he whispered back.

Dora flopped down on the carrier and nearly squashed Mungo. It wasn't substantial enough to sit. Quickly, she rose and stood in front of it.

Melrose picked up the two pints of unclaimed Guinness, cried out, "Richard!" and walked toward him.

Johnny Boy tried to stop him, saying, "'Ere now, that's my beer."

Melrose ignored him. "Have a drink!" he said to Jury. "Let's sit. There's Morris! Told you I did it."

But Morris was more interested in Mungo's fate than in Jury. She was sitting staunchly before the carrier.

Jury drank some beer and watched this.

Dora slewed around and was petting Morris, making it appear that this was the reason for Morris's move. It wasn't. Morris wanted to talk to Mungo.

Can't you get out?

Probably. I haven't really put my mind to it.

The Spotter just came in.

Mungo was alert and sat up and tried to look back at the table, but of course he couldn't turn around in the carrier to see out in that direction.

If you wanted to, you could get him over here. Just bark.

I only bark as a last resort.

Oh. Isn't this?

I don't know yet.

"What's in the carrier?" asked Jury. He gave Melrose a level look. "It's not Schrödinger, is it?"

"What? What? Of course not. I told you I took Schrödinger back to Belgravia. It was rather slick, if I do say—"

"You could be lying." Jury started up.

Melrose yanked him down. "Well, ta very much. All the trouble I went to. It's just Karl."

"Karl? Who's Karl?"

"The other black cat. If you remember, there were three."

"Karl. My Lord, don't people name their animals Boots or Princess or Spot anymore?"

"Guess not." Change the subject. "How's the investigation going?"

"It's close to the end, I think." Jury started up again. "Right now—"

Melrose pulled him down again.

"What's the matter with you? I've got to get back to London. This is still an ongoing investigation and I've got to interview someone."

"Oh, London! Yes, by all means. Remember, you're coming to Ardry End after."

"When I get done with this, yes." He took another swallow of beer. "Thanks for the drink."

Dora waved from the carrier, and Jury sketched her a salute just as his mobile went into its performance of "Three Blind Mice." He was out the door.

Melrose rushed to the carrier, picked it up, and moved to the door that led to the car park.

"He's back!" cried Dora.

Melrose dumped the carrier and turned. There was Jury again.

"Guess who that was on the phone? Harry Johnson, if you can believe it. He wants to know what in hell happened to his dog."

Melrose squinted. "What dog?"

63

Mungo was having none of it.

Well, some of it, perhaps. There's not much you can do against four hands stuffing you into a box and then sitting on you. It's always a battle between cleverness and brute force, isn't it? Then into the car, heave-ho, and the Duck into the driver's seat, and they were off.

He wished he could have got free of the carrier before the car left the Black Cat car park so that he could have pressed his face against the rear window and waved good-bye, good-bye, as was always done in films.

But he could still send the message to Morris: Good-bye, I'll see you soon. Morris had very nearly jumped in the car but had been torn between leaving and staying and had made the wrong choice, of course, and stayed.

Cats. How much fun could a cat have sitting on a table in the sun for endless hours without going stark raving mad with boredom? Never mind, he would see Morris again.

But at the moment, he was intent upon working his way out of this carrier. It wouldn't be too difficult as long as someone wasn't sitting on it. It was closed only by a couple of stuck-together flaps, and the Duck hadn't even done them up properly. He'd been all in a hurry to get Mungo out the door of the pub. What Mungo couldn't understand was why the Spotter hadn't twigged it.

Come on, is it that difficult to sort out? Cat carrier. Cat *outside* it. Something inside. *Dog missing.* What conclusion would one draw from that? What might the something inside the carrier *be*? If the Spotter couldn't work out that equation, how could he sort a murder case?

Mungo had worked his paw up against the flap, wedged it into the flap, and worked it back and forth patiently. He got it open. He climbed out, stealth being his middle name. The Duck was driving, humming away. . . .

Mungo pulled up to a window. He wanted to see just where they were, for instinct told him the Duck was going the wrong way—

Slough? What in God's name were they doing in *Slough*? He watched as the car plowed round the roundabout twice. The Duck didn't even know where—oh, there he went, missed it again!

LONDON RING ROAD
M4   M25   M40

Missed it *again*! What was it with humans? Had they no instinct for direction? Had they no maps in their minds? Good grief, even eels could swim from Europe to Bermuda; monarch butterflies could fly from Canada to Mexico; cows in a field could all point true north— but the Duck couldn't manage to get out of Slough?

Mungo slid down to the seat and went back to the carrier. Might as well have a kip. It's all going to come to tears anyway.

He crawled back into the carrier and didn't bother pulling the flaps or this shambles of the human race in with him.

And the Duck drove on.

64

Rose Moss came to the door, looking as she had the first time Jury had seen her: cotton dress, hair in bunches, feet this time in a different pair of furry slippers, white with floppy ears. It made Jury wonder for a moment if he must be wrong, if this was the woman who had sat with him in Cigar; if this was the woman who had killed one person and probably two.

"Hello, Rose."

It looked as if she might shut the door in his face but thought better of it and opened it wider instead. "Come to give me a hard time, have you?" she said as he entered.

He smiled. "Yes."

"Me, I'm having a drink. If you want one."

"I don't mind. Whiskey's fine."

"Ha! Listen to him. It better be, as it's all I have."

Jury tossed his coat onto a chair and watched her walk toward the small tray table of faded flowers where the bottles were. How could the woman in Cigar, her feet encased in Christian Louboutin heels, be here now wearing bunny slippers?

"Rose . . ."

"Pardon? Adele to you, love."

"Oh, we're no longer friends?"

She handed him a glass with barely enough whiskey to copper-line the bottom. "Let the good times roll."

Jury held it up.

Rose took a seat not by him on the sofa but in a small armchair opposite with her half-finger of whiskey.

"Tell me about Stacy, will you?"

She stopped the progress of the glass to her mouth and recrossed her legs. The slippers were outsized, as big as Ping-Pong paddles.

"What's to tell, may I ask?"

"Well, she lived here for upwards of six months with you, off and on. Both of you worked for Valentine's. You must have known her a little better than you seemed to last time I was here? You knew she wanted to marry Bobby Devlin."

This made her look at anything else in the room but Jury. Her gaze drifted.

Jury's silence made her look at him. Finally, he said, "I've met him, talked to him, of course, as police are always suspicious of family and lovers. He's a nice guy, was really in love with Stacy, only he knew her as Mariah Cox, village librarian."

Her eyes glittered, metallic. "She didn't love him."

"Why do you say that? She was going to marry him; at least that's what she told her aunt."

She shook her head in a wide arc, side to side, eyes tightly shut, as Jury had seen children do, denying whatever they wanted to shut out. "She didn't love him. She loved me." Her hands clapped against her chest.

The point, its awful implications thrown to the winds, had to be made. It had to be known, whatever betrayal Stacy Storm was intent on committing, that she, Rosie, had the final claim on Stacy and that Mariah Cox was a masquerade, a persona Stacy had invented to throw everybody off the scent.

"Who cooked the idea up, Rose? Was it you or Chris Cummins?"

Rose sat back, turning her glass in her hands. For a long time, she was silent.

She was not stupid. Jury knew she was assessing the situation, wondering. How much had Chris told Jury? Would it be a better tack to deny knowing her? Or to blame it on her?

Her legs were thrust straight out, toes slanting inward. He wished it weren't Rosie; he tried to form some scenario in his mind that would let it not be her.

"Chris Cummins," she said, blaming it on her. "She's clever. I'm not. She wanted her husband to keep away from this woman."

"How did Chris know about her?"

Rose shrugged and lit a cigarette. "I don't know. But she said they'd been seeing each other—him and this Kate Banks—for a long time. This woman was someone both of them had known before, when they all were young. She told me her plan."

"How did you two come to know each other?"

"Chance. I was in Amersham several weeks ago. I stopped off for a drink at the White Harts bar. She was sitting at a table by herself, reading a paper. One of the rags, you know, and I just sat down on the other side of the table, and the newspaper stretched out with its juicy sideshow murders. Not that I'd've taken a blind bit of notice, not of the paper or her or much else, because I was in a right sweat over Stacy. Stacy'd started talking about this fellow and that she might be leaving me. I couldn't believe it. Her talking about getting married. To a man. Talking about it like we'd never meant a thing to each other. I just grabbed my keys and got out and ran to my car and drove. Drove around London, then out of it."

"That was taking a chance, wasn't it, that someone would remember? Chris Cummins was in a wheelchair."

"Crutches. She got around pretty good on crutches. Only she didn't use them, she said, in Chesham. She didn't want people to know."

"How did she get to Amersham?"

"Bloke she knew, someone that could keep his mouth shut. It was like a game with her, you know. What she could get away with. Even murder."

"Still, crutches would have called attention to her, to both of you."

But it hadn't called attention to them because no one had inquired at the White Hart in Amersham if anyone there had seen . . . what?

Rose said, "We thought it was worth the chance. You don't know what it's like to be so—to want somebody dead before you'd see her with someone else."

"No, I suppose I don't. How did you know Kate Banks would be where she was that night?"

"I followed her, didn't I? All Chris knew was Kate used to live in Crouch End, so I called up the King's Road place and told 'em I was a messenger service and I was given the wrong street address in Crouch End. I just chose a street there at random to make it sound more believable, and this stupid cow gave me the right address. She shouldn't've done." Her expression told him she wished he'd comment on the artfulness of her plan.

And he did. "Couldn't have done it better myself, Rosie." He waited a moment so that she could be pleased with herself, then asked, "What did Deirdre Small have to do with all this?"

Rose was biting the skin around her thumbnail. "Nothing, really, except she knew about it."

Jury tried not to look shocked. She had said it so casually, as if it were hardly worth spending time on. "How? How did Deirdre know?"

"I told her." She stopped chewing on her thumb. "It was her gun. I didn't know how to get hold of one, and I remembered Deirdre'd told me about this gun she'd got at a pawnshop somewhere. North London, I think it was. She carried it for protection, even though it was illegal. Deirdre"—Rose picked up her warm drink—"was a friend of mine."

A friend of mine. And look what the friendship bought her.

"And she wondered what you wanted the gun for—"

"I said to take care of somebody. That was stupid; I should've made up something. Chris wasn't happy about that. It was Chris told me what to do. See, Deirdre had told me about her date with this creepy guy, at least I thought he was, and meeting him at St. Paul's. So I went along there a little before nine. And she was there. I waited for the bells and then shot. That was smart, wasn't it?" Again, her self-satisfied smile seemed to want him to note her artfulness.

"It was," said Jury, feeling forlorn.

"And I left the gun. I thought it would be traced back to Dee, and since it was the same gun that killed Kate, well, police would think DeeDee Small had done it. Killed Kate and then shot herself. That wasn't bad thinking, was it?"

"No. Very clever. Except the site of the bullet wound made it difficult for her to have turned the gun on herself." The plan had backfired, he didn't say, in more ways than one.

"Oh." She sighed. "I wanted to go to Chesham, you know, make up some excuse to see the boyfriend, just to see what sort of person Stacy preferred to me. But, of course, I had to stay right away from Chesham and Chris." She frowned and asked, as if it were strange, as if she'd only just thought of it, "How'd you know it was me?"

"Shoes."

Her frown deepened as she looked down at her big slippers, as if they might be the ones that shopped her.

All of them, really, he thought. All of that fascination with Jimmy Choo and Louboutin and Manolo Blahnik. "Red soles."

Rosie seemed amazed that this copper would know Louboutin. "You mean the ones I was wearing on our date?"

Our date. Rosie seemed to retreat further and further from the world of a grown-up here and now into a past of dates and furry slippers. It must be difficult for her to integrate the persona of the sultry woman in Cigar. She was, he thought sadly, crumbling right before his eyes.

"It was your comment about Manolo Blahnik, remember? Did I think you rushed out in your Manolos and shot Kate Banks? The only person who could have told you about that supposed heel mark is Chris Cummins. She's the only person besides the police who knew."

"That wasn't very smart of me." Again, she was studying her feet.

"How did you two communicate?"

"With those toss-away mobile things." She looked up at him then, as if he might not know. "You can't trace calls on them."

He nodded. "Rosie . . ." Her face looked small and pinched. "You're going to have to come along with me." Jury felt even more forlorn. He shouldn't feel this way. She had shot two people in cold blood.

And yet it hadn't been cold, had it? For her, probably even more than for Chris Cummins, it was all a parlor game, and his being here was the last move in it. What she said next confirmed this notion.

"I guess so. I guess I lost." She got up. "I have to change my clothes."

He knew he shouldn't let her out of his sight, but he did. It was a terraced house, a second-floor flat, with no means of egress except for the door, unless she meant to throw herself out a bedroom window. He doubted she would do that.

While she was gone, Jury looked around the room, whose details now he better understood: the row of Beatrix Potter figures on the shelf of the arched bookcase, the Paddington Bear lamp, the display of shells—the accoutrements of childhood. With its high ceiling, long windows, arched shelves, the room had the bones of sophistication, but she had drawn over it the skin of naïveté.

When she walked back in, she was once again the woman who'd surprised him in Cigar. Her outfit, a blue shawl-necked sweater and straight black skirt, was not as clingy as the dress she'd worn, but it was still potent. She had applied makeup, not too much, and had traded the slippers for dark-brown-and-black-ribboned shoes with skyscraper heels.

She swung the strap of a small handbag up to her shoulder. It matched the shoes. "Whose shoes, Rosie?"

"Valentino. You like them?" She held out a foot as if he were about to fit it with a glass slipper.

"I certainly do."

"Okay, let's go," she said to him.

Once through the door, she locked it. She preceded him along the narrow hall that led to the top of the stairs. At one point she stumbled, the skyscraper heels proving too much even for her, but she righted herself and went on, a girl dying to be grown up, stumbling in her mother's high-heeled shoes.

65

J ury found him, not surprisingly, in the garden on the narrow path
screened by masses of tulips and foxglove. He heard the snip of the
shears and saw the floppy hat. The sun was hot on Jury's head. The
willow and Japanese maple spilled sunlight across the path.

"Hello, Bobby."

Bobby was standing near a canvas of creeping phlox so variously
tinted in watercolors that it might have been painted by one of the
Impressionists. He was immersing an armful of purple tulips in a
bucket of water. He rose from his kneeling position. "Mr. Jury." He
took off his hat and wiped his arm across his forehead and smiled
bleakly. "I'm just cutting some flowers for the church." He paused. "A
funeral." Again, he paused. "Will police ever release Mariah's body
for burial?"

Jury could tell from the look—a drowned look, as if Bobby
himself had been plunged into water like the stems of the cut
flowers—that any news would be bad news. Jury hoped this wasn't.
"Very soon, I expect. Look, we're fairly certain we've got the person
who murdered Mariah, Bobby. Not much of a consolation for you,
but at least something."

Absently, Bobby clicked the garden shears. "Who?"

"It'll be public soon enough." He went on to tell him about the
double murder, Chris Cummins and Rose Moss.

Bobby sat down hard on the white iron bench. "Good God." He looked up at Jury as if trying to assess his presence. Real or not?

Jury sat beside him. "Not that it makes it easier to understand, but Rose Moss was obsessed with Mariah. Well, that pretty much goes without saying."

"Are you saying Mariah was gay?" He frowned in disbelief. "That's not—"

Jury shook his head. "Gay? No. The affair—if it can even be called that—was probably very brief and for Mariah, probably an experiment, or just something she was curious about. And there's only Rose Moss's account, so how much is true, how much wishful thinking, I don't know. Anyway, Mariah knew in a short while, sex with another woman just didn't appeal to her. I know you thought Mariah was very retiring, but—"

Bobby was shaking his head. "Not that way. She was good at sex, she was very good, a lot better than me. It was as if she had some old knowledge of it. I don't know how to say it." He scratched his head. "As if it came naturally. Not from a lot of experience of it, but as if she were discovering it as she went along, almost as if I inspired her or something." He laughed abruptly. "Talk about wishful thinking."

"I don't think it is, Bobby, not where you were concerned. She was giving up that life. She wanted to be with you."

Bobby smiled ruefully, pinched a dry leaf from the stem of a daisy near the bench. "You're saying that to make me feel better."

"I'm not. She really loved you. It's what got her killed." Jury was sorry he'd said that, for it sounded brutal when he'd meant to be consoling. "I'm sorry. That sounded as if you were at fault."

"No it doesn't. I'm glad you told me. I really didn't know if Mariah loved me, because there was always something held back. I knew there was more to her than what she was letting me see. I knew all of those weekend absences had to do with something other than visiting some old school chum or working an extra job. I knew there was more than that."

They sat for a few moments in the generous light and silence of the garden where Bobby Devlin seemed completely at home. Jury thought there was solace here, his gaze traveling up the path with its deep borders of dianthus and lavender and roses, the soft air pungent with their perfume; at the drifts of snowdrops, cornflowers, and poppies, at life illimitable.

"It bloody sucks, doesn't it, life?" Bobby eventually said, his voice verging on tears.

Jury wasn't about to tell his companion beside him on the bench that he was a fortunate man. "It bloody does," he said. Then, as if to appease some god of the garden, added, "Sometimes."

66

"So what," asked Jury, "were you doing in Slough?"

"Trying to get out of it," said Melrose.

They were tromping along the old road that led to the Man with a Load of Mischief, which sat atop a gentle hill that overlooked the village of Long Piddleton. They were looking for Melrose's dog, Mindy, who often came up here to sleep in the courtyard. Joey was walking beside Jury, occasionally rushing at some small rustling in the undergrowth.

Melrose went on: "Haven't you noticed the motorways all mass together there? There's the M4, the M40, the M25—"

"M25's the Ring Road."

Melrose stopped. "Thank you. I *know* it's the Ring Road."

"Why were you going back to London, anyway? You'd done all that. And I will say done a fair job, too."

"A 'fair' job, is that all I get?"

"A fairly good one, then."

Melrose stopped again. "Don't knock yourself out with the approval. Has it occurred to you that I get all the rum jobs? The fools' errands? You, on the other hand, get the glamour stuff. You get to shoot up half of London—"

"I don't carry a gun, as you know. I can't imagine what you might have forgotten that was worth a trip all the way back to Boring's."

Melrose sighed. "What difference does it make?" He turned to clap at the dog.

"Aggro," said Jury, then repeated it, in case Melrose was missing the annoyance in his voice. "Aggro. What a bloody awful name."

Melrose shook his head. "No it isn't. It fits with the names of my horse and my goat."

How could he say that without strangling?

Melrose continued: "Listen, just be glad Theo Wrenn-Browne didn't get to name him. He was all for Aardvark."

Jury winced.

"I pointed out the word 'Aardvark" didn't have the 'g' sound, so that was out."

"Really? The only reason you stood against Aardvark was because it lacks a 'g'?"

"Aggrieved, Aghast, Aggro. Horse, goat, dog. It's brilliant."

Jury rolled his eyes at the empty air. A waste of time rolling them at Melrose Plant. "His name's Joey," he said for the umpteenth time.

For the umpteenth time, Melrose ignored it.

Jury sighed. "Anything decided in the Jack and Hammer will end in tears."

Joey (aka Aggro) was trotting along beside Jury, who stopped every once in a while to rub the dog's head. Every time he did this, Joey would make a sound in his throat and bounce up toward Jury's hand.

Melrose picked up a long stick and was brandishing it at nothing in particular. It was the time of day in which everything—trees, road, hedgerows—looked burnished. "The idea was that neither of these women had any connection with their victims." They'd been discussing the case. "But Chris Cummins did know Stacy Storm; she knew her as the librarian."

"True," said Jury. Only she didn't know before she appeared that night at the pub that Stacy Storm *was* Mariah Cox. If she had, she might not have gone through with it. It gave her a bad scare to find out who the woman she'd murdered really was."

"Good Lord, it must be hard on her husband. Hard in any circumstances, but for a policeman . . . ? Is she in the nick right now?"

"Yes. But not for long, I expect. She'll be arraigned, and then who knows? What's worse for David Cummins is that the woman Chris Cummins arranged to have shot was the love of his life. He'd lost her a long time ago. Now, he lost her again."

"That's terrible." Melrose tossed out a stick for Joey to chase, but the dog didn't. He walked amiably along by Jury's side.

"I don't know why he likes you more than me," Melrose said.

"Because I don't call him Aggro." Jury wondered if Joey remembered the dark doorway where he had found him and the mince he'd bought and tried to feed him, and Dr. Kavitz, and Joely at the animal hospital.

It had been on that night after Jury had left St. Bart's Hospital, after he'd seen Lu. The night he'd actually talked to her. There had been no talking yesterday.

After his lunch with Phyllis, he'd gone to the hospital, walked down the same white corridor with the same feelings of inadequacy—worse, the fear of feeling the wrong thing again.

Either the room was cold or he had brought the cold with him. He shivered inside his lightweight raincoat.

She lay as she had the last time, as if she hadn't moved a finger since he'd last seen her. She looked frozen; that had caused his shivering. The tangle of wires and tubes led to what was keeping her alive or recording her body's functions.

He pulled over the straight-backed chair and sat down. He watched over her for a long time, he was not sure how long. The light had changed by the time he left.

The way he'd been with her before the accident tumbled through his mind. Her skin, her lips, her hands on him. Her black hair.

He reached out and took her hand. "Wake up, Lu."

Mindy was asleep in the courtyard and opened her eyes only when Melrose and Jury came along. But she did show an interest in Joey, who was walking about, sniffing.

Neither of them could understand why the dog Mindy felt this connection to the past. She had belonged to the owner of the Man with a

Load of Mischief. That person had, of course, abandoned the dog, just as he abandoned everything else. Pub, people, honor, decency.

They stood looking at the half-timbered facade of the meandering building, its white paint chipped and faded, its rear door sinking into the ground. The small leaded-glass windows were strangled by the vines that grew around them. The place hadn't been tenanted in years.

"It's a handsome old pub, charming, too, despite its unfortunate last days," said Melrose.

"What I think is that all of you should chip in and buy it. Then you can sit around and talk uselessly anytime you want."

Melrose was appalled, but not at their uselessness. "You can't just up and change things that way. You can't change the mise-en-scène. No, we've got to sit at the same table, in the same chairs, with the same longcase clock ticking in the background—"

"What clock? I don't remember a clock."

"All right. I just tossed that in. There's always a longcase clock in stories. My point being if you start changing anything, then the whole cloth unravels. Come on, Mindy."

Mindy struggled up but didn't come on.

"Don't be silly; it wouldn't unravel if the Jack and Hammer got blown to smithereens. That's assuming you and your gang weren't idling along inside. You'd all get back together around some rock. Yes, you'd manage to meet at Stonehenge if no other venue were possible."

They had left the pub and were proceeding along the road back to Ardry End, with Mindy behind and Joey keeping a slow pace with the old dog.

Melrose said, "That's one of the dumbest things I've ever heard."

Jury didn't think so; he was enjoying the image. Weren't there a few big rocks lying on the Stonehenge site that could serve as a table? He turned and looked back at the Man with a Load of Mischief and was glad somehow that it had remained tenantless. As if it were waiting for them all to come again.

Melrose threw another stick and ran after it, as if to fetch it himself, as if teaching the dog how to do it. "Come on, Aggro! Fetch!"

Jury didn't even bother raising his voice. "His name's Joey."